Edgar Huntly

or
Memoirs of a Sleepwalker

by CHARLES BROCKDEN BROWN

Edited for the Modern Reader by
David Stineback
UNION COLLEGE

COLLEGE & UNIVERSITY PRESS · *Publishers*

NEW HAVEN, CONN.

New Material, Introduction and Notes
by DAVID STINEBACK

MANUFACTURED IN THE UNITED STATES OF AMERICA BY
UNITED PRINTING SERVICES, INC.
NEW HAVEN, CONNECTICUT

The Masterworks of Literature Series

WILLIAM S. OSBORNE, *Editor*
Southern Connecticut State College

Edgar Huntly; or
Memoirs of a Sleepwalker

Contents

Introduction

This edition of Charles Brockden Brown's *Edgar Huntly*, the first in four decades, is intended to correct an imbalance for the student of American literature. Brown is increasingly receiving the critical attention he deserves, not only as the first noteworthy novelist in America but also as the first writer of fiction who attempted to support himself by his pen. But the availability of criticism on Brown's contribution to American literature has, in some respects, tended to outrun the availability of the contribution itself. The first of his four major novels, *Wieland,* continues to appear in more and more editions, along with editions of *Ormond* and *Arthur Mervyn.* The fate of *Edgar Huntly; or, Memoirs of a Sleepwalker,* however, has been a different story. Whether or not one considers this Brown's best novel, and some critics do, it is at least his most challenging novel, the work in which he takes the greatest risks with his imagination. Moreover, in its preoccupation with the "prodigious or the singular" in human affairs, *Edgar Huntly* reflects more closely the dominant concerns of later American fiction than any of Brown's other novels. What Richard Chase has called the "romance" quality of the classic American novel, in which "the field of action is conceived not so much as a place as a state of mind—the borderland of the human mind where the actual and the imaginary intermingle,"[1] is central to *Edgar Huntly.* One only has to think for a moment to find direct descendants in Poe's *Narrative of A. Gordon Pym,* Hawthorne's "Ethan Brand" and "Young Goodman Brown," Melville's *Pierre,* "Benito Cereno," and "Bartleby," Twain's *Connecticut Yankee,* James's *The Turn of the Screw,* and Faulkner's *Absalom, Absalom!,* to name

[1] Richard Chase, *The American Novel and Its Tradition* (Garden City, N.Y.: Doubleday, 1957), p. 19.

7

just a few. The horror of a rational mind and active conscience encountering its own radical limitations has been a predominantly American counterpart of the classic Gothic novel with its "castles and chimeras." As the first American novelist to explore the nature and consequences of that encounter, Charles Brockden Brown deserves close attention.

I

No United States existed when Charles Brockden Brown was born in Philadelphia, in 1771, to Quaker parents. Withdrawn and precocious from an early age, he revealed an intense interest in writing and drawing; but he spent only five years in the Friends' Latin School, which he left at the age of sixteen. Instead of college, he turned immediately to the study of law and apprenticed himself to a prominent Philadelphia firm in 1787, while maintaining at the same time an irrepressible interest in European literature and philosophy. He helped to form a literary club in Philadelphia, read the works of Enlightenment thinkers, and was drawn for a time to their radical critique of social institutions (later modified for him in the 1790's by the additional gothicism of William Godwin's thought). Eventually the combination of these ideas with Brown's natural love of solitude, verging at times on misanthropy, led to his abandonment of the legal profession before he ever practiced it in favor of a writing career, in 1792 or 1793. This was no easy decision for Brown to make, since it meant disappointing a great number of relatives and friends. In the decade following, he was to feel a deep and continuing guilt over his decision; yet he held to the conviction that in fiction, not law, he could come closer to "making the world something better than I find it."[2]

Through the patronage of influential friends like Elihu Hubbard Smith, a Connecticut physician, and William Dunlap, a New Jersey dramatist and theater manager, Brown widened his circle of literary acquaintances in the East; and he sat down to devote himself completely to the "self-indulgence" of making his imagination pay in a new country preoccupied with survival. These efforts led to the beginning of a "Philadelphia novel" in 1795 (perhaps the germ of the later *Arthur Mervyn*); an unpublished novel called *Sky-Walk* in 1797; and *Alcuin*, a tract on women's rights, in 1798. But

---

[2] Quoted in Harry R. Warfel, *Charles Brockden Brown: American Gothic Novelist* (Gainesville: University of Florida Press, 1949), p. 11.

it was with the publication of *Wieland; or, The Transformation* in 1798 that one of the truly prolific periods of creativity in American fiction began. By the end of the following summer, in addition to editing a literary magazine, Brown had published three more full-length novels: *Ormond; or, The Secret Witness* and *Arthur Mervyn; or, Memoirs of the Year 1793* (Part I) and *Edgar Huntly*. This feat could only have been accomplished by writing several novels at the same time, none of them with sufficient care and precision. But the student of these strenuous efforts must continually remind himself that Brown was driven not only by a desperate need for money but also by a desire to prove to himself the worth of his chosen calling in a young, active country that was hardly congenial to that choice. This cultural predicament was aptly described by William Prescott, one of Brown's early biographers:

> We had none of the buoyant, stirring associations of a romantic age,
> . . . none of the picturesque varieties of situation or costume; everything lay on the same dull, prosaic level; in short, we had none of the
> most obvious elements of poetry, at least so it appeared to the vulgar
> eye.[3]

America's "spick-and-span" aspect, Prescott concluded, tended to turn any writer away from the serious aspects of his trade and toward "the broad, garish sunshine of everyday life."[4]

This is indeed the direction Charles Brockden Brown chose after the "doleful tones" of *Edgar Huntly*, when he published Part II of *Arthur Mervyn* (1800) and his two sentimental novels, *Clara Howard* (1800) and *Jane Talbot* (1801), with their emphasis, in Brown's words, on "moral causes and daily incidents."[5] From this point on in his brief literary career, he virtually abandoned fiction for the greater popular security of pamphleteering and editing, a marriage in 1804, and a six-year partnership with his two brothers in a Philadelphia mercantile business. Certainly Brown's death from tuberculosis in 1810, at the age of thirty-nine, ended a life of limited satisfaction by his own standards.

---

[3] William H. Prescott, "Life of Charles Brockden Brown," *The Library of American Biography*, ed. Jared Sparks (New York: Harper and Brothers, 1839), I, 174.

[4] *Ibid.*

[5] Quoted in David Lee Clark, *Charles Brockden Brown: Pioneer Voice in America* (Durham, N.C.: Duke University Press, 1952), p. 181.

But of course it is present-day standards that are of concern here. And one must begin by acknowledging the fact that Brown's four major novels, despite their carelessness and confusion and the incredible concentration they sometimes require to follow their story lines, are impressive works of art for their day and age. Furthermore, at least two of them—*Wieland* and *Edgar Huntly*—can stand on their own merits apart from their historical context. Generally speaking, all of these works are initiation stories: of innocence into evil, of reason into insanity, of pride into humility. In the case of *Ormond*, the heroine of the novel is threatened, and finally educated in the dangers of life, by the attempt of a cunning member of a secret revolutionary organization to seduce her. *Arthur Mervyn* is Brown's most naturalistic novel and recounts the picaresque journey of an ambitious young man through a Dickensian maze of problems, including a plague-ridden city. Clara Wieland's journey, in contrast to the wordly initiation of Arthur Mervyn, moves her to the boundaries of her own mind in a desperate attempt to grasp the fact that her brother is the confessed murderer of his wife and children and the would-be murderer of Clara herself. But it is finally *Edgar Huntly*, which is set in a far less civilized environment than the other novels, that represents Charles Brockden Brown's closest approach to the prototypical initiation story in which the protagonist's physical journey is inseparable from his psychological journey.

II

Thirteen years ago, in *Love and Death in the American Novel*, Leslie Fiedler did his best to identify Charles Brockden Brown as America's first "mythopoeic" writer. Contrary to Vernon Parrington's emphasis on Brown's "political romanticism"[6] (as opposed to the "literary romanticism" of his gothic art), Fiedler insisted that Brown was "an anti-realist in almost all respects, moving his irresolute and inconsistent protagonists through a time and space carelessly defined and bearing only a fitful, largely accidental resemblance to the facts of history and geography."[7] Fiedler's general interpretation of Brown's work, as well as his specific re-

---

[6] Vernon L. Parrington, *Main Currents in American Thought* (New York: Harcourt, Brace and Company, 1930), II, 190.

[7] Leslie Fiedler, *Love and Death in the American Novel*, rev. ed, New York: Dell, 1966), pp. 154-55.

vival of *Edgar Huntly*—"the most successful and characteristic of his gothic romances"[8]—was long overdue; but his conclusions had been anticipated by Prescott over a century before:

> Brown does not direct himself, like [Washington Irving and James Fenimore Cooper], to the illustration of social life and character. He is little occupied with the exterior forms of society. He works in the depths of the heart, dwelling less on human life than the sources of it.[9]

This is especially true of *Wieland* and *Edgar Huntly*, where Brown's use of a first-person narrator throughout has a special thematic function. Though one continually encounters the first-person narrative in all of Brown's major works, only in *Wieland* and *Edgar Huntly* does it directly serve his artistic purpose: the confrontation of a single personality with its "sources" and "depths." Thus it is obvious, as *Edgar Huntly* progresses, that Huntly himself (like Jack Burden in *All the King's Men*, for example) is ultimately recounting his own perilous journey and not simply the journey of Clithero Edny, the suspected murderer and insane alter-ego whom Huntly pursues into the Pennsylvania wilderness. Even Fiedler's conclusion that *Edgar Huntly* is "the account of a young man who begins by looking for guilt in others and ends by finding it in himself; who starts out in search of answers but is finally satisfied with having defined a deeper riddle than those he attempted to solve" is too generous.[10] It would be more accurate to say that Huntly merely "discovers" rather than "defines" a deeper riddle, and only begins to find the guilt that is within himself.

Certainly at first glance, Edgar Huntly seems an ordinary enough narrator, a young man whose intentions and conduct appear, on the surface, to be normal, even admirable. As he describes himself, he is distinguished by "sleek locks, neat apparel, pacific guise, sobriety and gentleness of aspect," and a "limited and uniform" life. Most important, he places a high value on the pursuit of knowledge for its own sake and on the purity of his benevolence in attempting to satisfy his "curiosity" about certain mysterious

[8] *Ibid.*, p. 156.
[9] Prescott, p. 176.
[10] Fiedler, p. 157.

events.[11] He is, in short, the sort of narrator that a reader would be likely to trust, or at least suspend judgment toward. This is a crucial point, for the imaginative success of the novel depends on the degree to which Brown's reader is drawn into sharing Huntly's curiosity.

In a sense, this was the standard by which some early reviewers criticized *Wieland*: it was either not mysterious enough, because what appeared to be supernatural—the "Gothic" devices of spontaneous combustion and ventriloquism—turned out to be natural; or it was not natural enough, since the actual phenomena of spontaneous combustion and ventriloquism were too obscure to mean much to Brown's readers. In *Edgar Huntly*, on the other hand, somnambulism was at least as mysterious as ventriloquism and certainly more familiar to the public, as Brown himself pointed out in his preface to the novel. This sort of interpretation, of course, has its obvious limitations: what seems mysterious in a particular time and place may seem innocuous in another. But it is also true that Sigmund Freud has come and gone since the publication of *Edgar Huntly*, and the mystery of sleep and the power of the human mind have, if anything, been heightened and made more compelling for the public. To a much greater extent than *Wieland*, *Edgar Huntly* has benefited and will continue to benefit from the passage of time, as we privately struggle to gain control over what seems increasingly uncontrollable in our lives.

III

Begun at the conclusion of the events he recounts, Huntly's narrative is put in the form of a letter to Mary Waldegrave, his fiancée and the sister of his best friend who has recently been murdered by an unknown assailant. The events of the narrative cover a period in 1787 of about twenty-five days, followed, the reader is told, by the "weeks" Huntly has spent describing them. Then Huntly's long letter is followed in the novel and "months" later in time by three very short letters—two from Huntly to his patron, Sarsefield, and one in return—which serve as a ironic commentary on the declaration with which Huntly begins his own

---

[11] In this, he is akin to Carwin, the ventriloquist in *Wieland*, and to Arthur Mervyn, who persistently see themselves as neutral agents in the often tragic lives of those around them.

account to Mary Waldegrave: "What light has burst upon my ignorance of myself and of mankind! How sudden and enormous the
transition from uncertainty to knowledge!" The final letters re-
veal, incontrovertibly, that, whatever the ambitious narrator has
learned from the remarkable incidents he describes, he hasn't
learned enough. As a direct consequence of his inquisitiveness
and supposed benevolence, both before and after his letter to
Mary, a total of seven persons have died (not including a miscarriage), another has been seriously injured, and three more have
barely avoided being killed, including Huntly himself.

In the opening chapter of the novel, as he is brooding over
Waldegrave's death, Huntly discovers Clithero Edny asleep and
sobbing beneath the tree where Waldegrave was murdered. Convinced that this is more than a coincidence ("What but the murder
of Waldegrave could direct his steps hither?"), he presumes Edny's
guilt and resolves to make him the "subject of my scrutiny." But
Huntly dutifully, and rather prophetically, questions his own motives before proceeding:

> For what purpose shall I prosecute the search? What benefit am I
> to reap from this discovery? . . . I was not insensible, at that moment,
> of the impulses of vengeance, but they were transient. . . . Yet I was
> fearful of the effects of my hasty rage, and dreaded an encounter in
> consequence of which I might rush into evils which no time could
> repair, nor penitence expiate.

"Curiosity is vicious," he decides, "if undisciplined by reason, and
inconducive to benefit."

Yet, like the rationalist he is in matters of morality and religion,
Huntly finally concludes that "curiosity, like virtue, is its own
reward":

> Knowledge is of value for its own sake, and pleasure is annexed to
> the acquisition, without regard to anything beyond. It is precious
> even when disconnected with moral inducements and heartfelt
> sympathies; but the knowledge which I sought by its union with
> these was calculated to excite the most complex and fiery sentiments
> in my bosom.

At this point in the novel, the reader has no way of measuring the
significance of this final declaration from Huntly. Only with his
subsequent actions does it become clear that Huntly's motiva-

tion transcends vengeance, benevolence, and duty and moves him, obsessively, toward the uncharted depths of his own personality, represented by the rugged and mazelike wilderness into which he pursues Clithero.

Like the captain in Joseph Conrad's *The Secret Sharer*, Huntly identifies in some mysterious way with the "murderer" he discovers. So, when Clithero, still sleepwalking, leads Huntly to the "verge of a considerable precipice," from which "a dreary vale was discoverable, embarrassed with the leafless stocks of bushes and encumbered with rugged and pointed rocks," Huntly remarks that "this scene reminded me of my situation":

> It was in the highest degree rugged, picturesque, and wild. The vale, though I had never before viewed it by the glimpses of the moon, suggested the belief that I had visited it before.

Hints like this one in the novel, along with the narrator's passing references to the "wanderings of my reason and my freaks of passion" in the past, prepare the reader for Huntly's own conversion to a sleepwalker, lost in the wilderness of his mind.

When Huntly finally confronts Clithero, four days after first discovering him beneath the tree, and expresses his suspicions of murder, he also asserts, rather dubiously, that "a transient passenger would probably have acted as I have done" even if he didn't know about Waldegrave's death. ("Would not anyone, from similar appearances," he asks later, "have drawn similar conclusions?") Then, true to his pursuit of knowledge for its own sake and the preservation of his own "equanimity," Huntly insists on being Clithero's comforter, as well as his accuser: "Were futurity laid open to my view, and events, with their consequences, unfolded, I might see reason to embrace the assassin as my best friend." With this, Clithero promises a "confession of crimes" and bolts into Inglefield's house, where he had been working as a hired hand. Huntly's reaction to this exchange, on the following day, is important, again for the light it throws on his motivation and character:

> My condition was not destitute of enjoyment. My stormy passions had subsided into a calm, portentous and awful. My soul was big with expectation. I seemed as if I were on the eve of being ushered into a world whose scenes were tremendous and sublime. The suggestions of sorrow and malice had, for a time, taken their flight, and yielded place to a generous sympathy, which filled my eyes with tears, but had more in it of pleasure than of pain. That Clithero was instrumen-

tal to the death of Waldegrave, that he could furnish the clue explanatory of every bloody and mysterious event that had hitherto occurred, there was no longer the possibility of doubting. "He,
indeed," said I, "is the murderer of excellence; and yet it shall be
my province to emulate a father's clemency, and restore this unhappy man to purity and peace."

Huntly's self-righteous faith in his own healing powers is crucial
here; but, more than this, his tempting conviction that he can be
"ushered into a world whose scenes were tremendous and sublime," without endangering his own composure and equanimity,
is a touchstone for the success of the entire novel. The reader, too,
wants to believe this is possible; he shares Huntly's supposedly
harmless curiosity.

Chapters four through eight are Clithero's overlong account of
his "crimes," which have nothing to do with the death of Waldegrave: and he begins with an appropriate charge against Huntly:

> You are unacquainted with the man before you. The inferences which
> you have drawn, with regard to my designs and my conduct, are a
> tissue of destructive errors. You, like others, are blind to the most
> momentous consequences of your own actions. You talk of imparting
> consolation. You boast the beneficence of your intentions.
> You set yourself to do me a benefit. What are the effects of your
> misguided zeal and random efforts? They have brought my life
> to a miserable close. They have shrouded the last scene of it in
> blood. They have put the seal to my perdition.

Until Huntly's interposition, Clithero had been increasingly able to
relegate his memories of the past to those hours when he was
asleep; but Huntly has brought them to light and forced Clithero to
vindicate himself by admitting "imputations still more atrocious."
So Clithero recounts his service in Ireland to a virtuous and aris-
tocratic lady, Mrs. Lorimer; his eventual mother-son relationship
with her; his engagement to the abandoned daughter of Arthur
Wiatte, Mrs. Lorimer's twin brother, presumed dead; Mrs.
Lorimer's strange and abiding love for her evil brother; Wiatte's
return and Clithero's killing of him in self-defense; Clithero's belief
that Mrs. Lorimer would not forgive him, would in fact wish to die
herself, and therefore his own attempt to kill her, nearly
killing his fiancée in the process; Mrs. Lorimer's collapse and supposed death; and Clithero's subsequent flight to America. He also
mentions a man named Sarsefield, whose marriage to Mrs. Lorimer

had been prevented by Wiatte and who returned to Dublin, coincidentally, at the same time as Wiatte himself. Sarsefield, of course, turns out to be Edgar Huntly's own teacher and friend in America prior to his return to Ireland. With this revelation, the common ground between Clithero and Huntly begins to grow.

Following Clithero's account of his "sin" and guilt, he flees again into the wilderness. Yet even though he has convincingly removed himself from any connection with Waldegrave's murder, Clithero's torment increasingly fascinates Huntly:

> Could I not restore a mind thus vigorous, to tranquil and wholesome existence? Could I not subdue his perverse disdain and immeasurable abhorrence of himself? His upbraiding and his scorn were unmerited and misplaced. Perhaps they argued frenzy rather than prejudice; but frenzy, like prejudice, was curable. Reason was no less an antidote to to the illusions of insanity like this, than to the illusions of error.

From motives still unclear, Huntly has urgently assumed the role of Clithero's savior and, after several days' wait, sets out to find him among the "craggy eminences and deep dells" of Norwalk which he had investigated in the past with Sarsefield.

What once seemed mere curiosity is obviously, by this point in the novel, an obsession with Huntly: determined to pursue Clithero beyond the "customary paths of men" and thus gain a "thorough knowledge of his actions," past and present, he penetrates caves, crosses chasms, avoids the attack of a leaping panther, leaves food for Clithero when he finds him, breaks into Clithero's private trunk, and digs around the tree where he first discovered him, unearthing in the process a copy of Mrs. Lorimer's personal vindication of her harsher actions toward her brother.

These events bring Huntly to his delayed account in Chapter Thirteen of his relationship with the dead Waldegrave, whom he insists was "pure from all offense." This is a particularly important chapter, since it provides the reader with his first insight into the personal history of Brown's narrator and immediately precedes the radical shift in the novel to Huntly's own sleepwalking, his "rebirth" in the mysterious cave, and his encounter with the grotesque and malevolent band of Indians. First, however, he has a fitful sleep in which the "incongruous and half-seen . . . image of Waldegrave flitted before me," out of anger, Huntly presumes, over some duty he has neglected to perform for his dead friend. He recalls a promise to Waldegrave's sister to transcribe for her Waldegrave's letters to him, thus recording the "intellectual existence and moral pre-eminence of my friend." So Huntly determines to postpone his involvement with Clithero for a day, in order to carry out this agreement. The reader learns immediately, however, that the "half-indignant apparition" of Waldegrave had appeared, Huntly believes, to deter him from transcribing the letters. He is further told that Waldegrave had flirted for a time with a form of atheism, which he later repudiated, but that Huntly himself had been persuaded to some extent by those creeds which attempted "to deify necessity and universalize matter; to destroy the popular distinction between soul and body, and to dissolve the supposed connection between the moral condition of man anterior and subsequent to death." When Huntly eventually goes to his locked cabinet and finds the letters missing, he is "lost in horror and amazement." Yet even though his uncle insists that he has heard him walking upstairs during the night, it never occurs to Huntly that he might have been sleepwalking and have hidden the letters himself for some reason. By the following evening his thoughts have gradually returned again to Clithero.

This brief chapter, coming where it does in the novel, is far more suggestive than it might seem on the surface. What Charles Brockden Brown appears to be giving his reader (how consciously will never be known) is a personal history for Huntly that is similar, in some ways, to Clithero's. Edny retains under lock and key, and then hides while sleepwalking, a copy of Mrs. Lorimer's defense of her actions toward her brother, and Huntly does the same with Waldegrave's letters; both manuscripts express the misguided beliefs, as well as the virtues, of their authors; and neither writer wants the manuscripts made public. But, while Clithero shows no desire to vindicate his past conduct by revealing the character of his patroness, Huntly is urged by Mary Waldegrave, in effect, to contravene her brother's wishes and disclose the negative religious influence, by her standards, that he had and continues to have on Huntly. Thus, Huntly's own sleepwalking and concealing of the letters seem to reflect not merely his unconscious loyalty to Waldegrave's wishes or his fear of the effect that Waldegrave's earlier beliefs will have on his sister, but also, Brown suggests, his fear of self-revelation and its consequent effect on his relationship with Mary Waldegrave.

This episode, combined with the appearance of Weymouth in Chapter Fourteen, who claims Mary's inheritance from Waldegrave

as his own, heightens Huntly's fears. Though Weymouth's claim
is just, Waldegrave has left no record of it; and Huntly is forced
to defend the claim to Mary. The impossibility of their marriage
(since without the inheritance they are both poor) becomes apparent, as does the impossibility of Huntly's providing for his sisters
once his uncle in Solesbury dies and leaves his estate to his own son,
"who is a stranger and an enemy to us." Brown's reader now real-
izes that all of Edgar Huntly's future plans had been prompted by
Waldegrave's death—"the most disastrous and propitious [event]
which could have happened"—and have been destroyed by Weymouth's reappearance. As in the case of Clithero, Huntly's hopes
have suddenly disintegrated through the arrival of an unexpected
agent. But unlike Clithero. whose troubles resulted directly from
Wiatte's death, Huntly is plunged into the darkness of his own
mind by the revival of Waldegrave—through the suspicious presence of Clithero at the tree, the request from Mary for a copy of
Waldegrave's letters, and the return of Weymouth.

With Chapter Sixteen, the pace of *Edgar Huntly* decidedly
quickens. Huntly awakens in the pit of a cave thirty miles from his
uncle's house (which he incorrectly assumes is the same cave he had
passed through in pursuit of Clithero) and embarks on his alarming
trail of bloodshed and suffering. (This is the section of the novel,
incidentally, which Brown excerpted for publication in the first
volume of his monthly magazine.) Weeks later, as he is relating his
adventures in a "languishing and feeble state," Huntly's sleep,
like Clithero's, is still disturbed by his memories:

> Solitude and sleep are now no more than the signals to summon up
> a tribe of ugly phantoms. Famine, and blindness, and death, and
> savage enemies, never fail to be conjured up by the silence and dark-
> ness of the night. I cannot dissipate them by any efforts of reason.
> My cowardice requires the perpetual consolation of light. My heart
> droops when I mark the decline of the sun, and I never sleep but with
> a candle burning at my pillow. If, by any chance, I should awake and
> find myself immersed in darkness, I know not what act of desperation I
> might suddenly be impelled to commit.

The same wilderness that had once seemed sublime to Huntly
when he traversed it in the past with Sarsefield as his guide has become demonic, survived only through his own savagery and in-
stincts: by drinking the blood of the panther he kills, by destroying a band of hostile Indians (whom he mistakenly believes have

murdered his uncle and sisters),[12] by traversing cliffs and rivers, and by begging for food. In recounting his attack on the Indians at Queen Mab's hut, Huntly puts his change of character into words:

> All my education and the habits of my life tended to unfit me for a contest and a scene like this. But I was not governed by the soul which usually regulates my conduct. I had imbibed, from the unparalleled events which had lately happened, a spirit vengeful, unrelenting, and ferocious.

"Such are the deeds," he laments at one point, "which perverse nature compels thousands of rational beings to perform and to witness." And later, in his amazement over rediscovering Waldegrave's letters in a neighboring house, he sums up the nature of his experiences:

> Passage into new forms, overleaping the bars of time and space, reversal of the laws of inanimate and intelligent existence, had been mine to perform and to witness.

The further fact that Sarsefield has returned to America, passed the sleepwalking Huntly on the road to Solesbury, pursued him into the wilderness after the death of Huntly's uncle in a clash with Indians, and then exchanged shots with him on the ledge when they mistake each other for savages only complicates the consequences of Huntly's initial transformation. For it is Huntly's own "rationality" that has largely precipitated the perversity of nature and the "reversal of inanimate and intelligent existence." If he had not indulged his "curiosity" in the pursuit of Clithero's private history; if he had not stubbornly resisted, in the name of knowledge, Waldegrave's desire to destroy his own letters; if he had not simply relied on a lack of explanation from Waldegrave to justify the mysterious inheritance; and if he had not assumed that the presence of his own

---

[12] It should be mentioned that *Edgar Huntly* is the first American novel of any quality to deal with Indians. As in so many early American novels, the Indians are little more than grotesque forms and are described here, for example, in the same terms as the "savage" and "detested race" of panthers, Huntly is also given a common excuse for his ferocity: his parents were murdered in their sleep by Indians. But, these things considered, it is also well to remember that it is Huntly who is narrating his adventures, not Brown, and that the distinction is important.

gun in the hands of the Indians meant the certain death of his uncle and sisters; if he were not, in other words, a preeminently rational man, then much of the suffering he encounters and causes might have been averted. As Brown's more astute critics have pointed out, the perversity of nature and the chilling speechlessness of its "dusky" inhabitants are fearful projections of Huntly's own mind, however rugged and hostile they may be in actuality.

Sarsefield's reappearance with Mrs. Lorimer as his wife does serve to reestablish a life of comfort for Huntly and his sisters. Like Clithero in the past, he is given the opportunity to be embraced "as a son" by Sarsefield's wife and perhaps even to marry Clithero's former fiancèe. By pursuing Clithero, therefore, he has arrived at Clithero's point of greatest happiness. But to have done so, Huntly has had to insist throughout on Clithero's innocence and potential rehabilitation; and this assumption leads him to the ironic climax of the novel.

Astounded by Clithero's own reappearance in America, Sarsefield has no interest whatever in Huntly's benevolence toward him, or even, once Clithero is found again, in healing the wounds given him by the Indians. After hearing Clithero's story, through Huntly, Sarsefield still asserts that "he can never be regarded with complacency by my wife. . . . Common ills are not without a cure less than death, but here all remedies are vain." He only reluctantly agrees to tell Clithero that Mrs. Lorimer did not die after all, and then leaves on a trip to Virginia (where he remains as Huntly is recounting his adventures to Mary Waldegrave). The narrative ends at this point with the anticlimactic revelation that Waldegrave was killed by one of the marauding Indians. Nothing more is said about the fate of Weymouth and the money that Mary has inherited.

The three letters that follow, however, provide a further insight into the urgency of Huntly's "infatuation" with Clithero and his inability to "admit the belief that his misery is without a cure." "Months" have passed and Sarsefield has returned to New York when Huntly hastily informs him that he has told Clithero of Mrs. Lorimer's existence there, after Clithero had fled again to the wilderness and Huntly had found him living in Queen Mab's hut. The evidence that Clithero was working for a nearby farmer apparently was enough to convince Huntly that Clithero's "fatal and gloomy thoughts. . . have somewhat yielded to tranquillity." Yet Huntly still pitied Clithero for his "disastrous and humiliating" existence, "compared with his youthful hopes and actual merits," and decided that to tell him of Mrs. Lorimer's presence

> would dissipate the sanguinary apparition that haunted him, cure his diseased intellects, and restore him to those vocations for which his talents, and that rank in society for which his education, had qualified him.

Even after Clithero, in his madness, has rushed out of the hut to find and kill his former patroness, Huntly pleads his own innocence to Sarsefield:

> I cannot forget that my unfortunate temerity has created this evil. Yet who could foresee this consequence of my intelligence? . . . I shall not escape your censure, but I shall, likewise, gain you compassion. I have erred, not through sinister or malignant intentions, but from the impulse of misguided, indeed, but powerful, benevolence.

The obvious issue, of course, is whether it really matters that Huntly's intentions have not been "sinister or malignant." Like other characters before him in Brown's novels—Carwin in *Wieland*, Ormond, and Arthur Mervyn—Huntly insists upon his benevolent intentions despite their self-serving and often destructive consequences. To a much greater extent, however, than in any of his previous works Brown is questioning in *Edgar Huntly* whether good intentions can ever be reliably measured apart from their consequences, whether knowledge for its own sake is ever justified.

Appropriately, Sarsefield has the final word in the novel; and the reader discovers from his letter that, in disregarding Sarsefield's concern for his wife, Huntly also knew that his letters to New York might be opened by her if he sent them, as he did, to Sarsefield's home. When she reads Huntly's second letter, she collapses and has a miscarriage. As for Clithero, he is captured before he can reach her and then commits suicide.

IV

Perhaps the most fitting literary analogy to the error of Edgar Huntly's intentions is Lord Jim's leniency toward Gentleman Brown in Conrad's novel. Though Huntly is not precisely looking for a second chance in life, his pity, like Jim's, is directly related to the superior image of himself that he wishes to retain: the image of the ultimate accuser and the ultimate comforter. Furthermore, like A. Gordon Pym, Captain Ahab, Ethan Brand, Hank Morgan, and the governess in *The Turn of the Screw*, among others, Edgar Huntly begins as a pursuer of knowledge beyond himself and ends in being pursued by the truth within himself. Though he can declare to his fiancée, "How total is our blindness with regard to our own performances," he can never fully accept the implications and consequences of his "unfortunate" rashness toward Clithero.

As "the first American novel," in the words of one critic, "to use the wild American landscape as a gothic symbol of the unconscious psyche,"[13] *Edgar Huntly* reveals both the remarkable experiences of Brown's narrator and his remarkable inability to learn from those experiences. It suggests, quite simply, that we largely create the terrors of our lives—the "precipices" of our minds— by attempting to deny their existence. We are animals, Brown seems to be saying, to the extent that we reject our animality; and we risk insanity to the extent that we reject its potential in ourselves. This is the moral of *Edgar Huntly* for the twentieth-century reader.

---

[13] Paul Levine, "The American Novel Begins," *American Scholar*, XXXV (1965-66), 146.

Selected Bibliography

No single secondary source is particularly reliable for an understanding of both Brown's life and work. Donald Ringe's *Charles Brockden Brown* (New York: Twayne, 1966) contains the best discussions of the novels in general and *Edgar Huntly* in particular, while David Lee Clark's *Charles Brockden Brown: Pioneer Voice in America* (Durham, N.C.: Duke University Press, 1952) is the most thorough treatment of Brown's life and the philosophical influences on his work (though it is brief and weak on the novels themselves). Harry R. Warfel's *Charles Brockden Brown: American Gothic Novelist* (Gainesville: University of Florida Press, 1949) is concise and readable, but is less than a full discussion of the influences upon Brown or of his own novels and influence. Of the early biographies, William Dunlap's *The Life of Charles Brockden Brown* (Philadelphia: James P. Parke, 1815) has been the basic source of first-hand information on Brown's career, despite its diffuseness, and reprints some of Brown's letters and fragments. William Prescott's "Life of Charles Brockden Brown," first published in 1834 in Volume I of *The Library of American Biography*, edited by Jared Sparks, still does the best job of placing Brown in the intellectual and cultural context of his time. In addition to these sources, Richard Chase, Leslie Fiedler, and R. W. B. Lewis, in particular, have perceptively discussed individual novels in their wide-ranging studies of American literature.

Among the many articles on Brown in recent years, two deserve special mention. For a general estimate of his contribution to the persistent image of "flight" in the form and content of the American novel, see Paul Levine, "The American Novel Begins," *American Scholar*, 35 (1965-66), 134-48; and for a specific discussion of his fictional techniques, see W. B. Berthoff, " 'A Lesson on Concealment': Brockden Brown's Method in Fiction, "*Philological Quarterly*, 27 (1958), 45-57, which accurately identifies Brown's dramatization of particular principles and ideas through the conflict of personalities. Before one can have a full and just understanding of Brown's talents, Berthoff's thesis needs to be applied, in some form or another, to Brown's major works. The remarkable thing about Brown's fiction is not that he sought to be a "moral painter," as he called himself, but that he managed to divorce himself so thoroughly from his art, out of a rigorous and honest fascination with life.

A Note on the Text

I have followed closely the edition of *Edgar Huntly* printed by David McKay Publishers in 1887; this edition has been collated with the first edition of 1799. By present-day standards, Brown's novels are tiresomely overpunctuated, largely due to his fondness for multiple phrases and clauses in the same sentence and his habitual use of commas to separate phrases with a single subject or verb. But I have altered none of these conventions (except to make them more consistent). To have done so would have effectually destroyed the rhythm of Brown's prose (however tedious it may be at times) and violated the intentions of Brown's narrator, who places the highest premium on deliberation and precision. Most of the changes that have been made simply modernize spelling and, in some cases, streamline sentences that were badly fragmented and confused by punctuation in earlier editions. No editions of *Edgar Huntly* prior to 1900 corrected the first-edition error of numbering two consecutive chapters "XIV"; the change has been made here.

D.S.

Edgar Huntly; or
Memoirs of a Sleepwalker

TO THE PUBLIC.

The flattering reception that has been given, by the public, to Arthur Mervyn, has prompted the writer to solicit a continuance of the same favor, and to offer to the world a new performance.

America has opened new views to the naturalist and politician, but has seldom furnished themes to the moral painter. That new springs of action and new motives to curiosity should operate,—that the field of investigation, opened to us by our own country, should differ essentially from those which exist in Europe,—may be readily conceived. The sources of amusement to the fancy and instruction to the heart, that are peculiar to ourselves, are equally numerous and inexhaustible. It is the purpose of this work to profit by some of these sources; to exhibit a series of adventures, growing out of the condition of our country and connected with one of the most common and most wonderful diseases or affections of the human frame.

One merit the writer may at least claim: that of calling forth the passions and engaging the sympathy of the reader by means hitherto unemployed by preceding authors. Puerile superstition and exploded manners, Gothic castles and chimeras, are the materials usually employed for this end. The incidents of Indian hostility and the perils of the Western wilderness are far more suitable; and for a native of America to overlook these would admit of no apology. These, therefore, are, in part, the ingredients of this tale, and these he has been ambitious of depicting in vivid and faithful colors. The success of his efforts must be estimated by the liberal and candid reader.

C.B.B.

I

I sit down, my friend, to comply with thy request. At length does the impetuosity of my fears, the transports of my wonder, permit me to recollect my promise and perform it. At length am I somewhat delivered from suspense and from tremors. At length the drama is brought to an imperfect close, and the series of events that absorbed my faculties, that hurried away my attention, has terminated in repose.

Till now, to hold a steadfast pen was impossible; to disengage my senses from the scene that was passing or approaching, to forbear to grasp at futurity, to suffer so much thought to wander from the purpose which engrossed my fears and my hopes, could not be.

Yet am I sure that even now my perturbations are sufficiently stilled for an employment like this? That the incidents I am going to relate can be recalled and arranged without indistinctness and confusion? That emotions will not be reawakened by my narrative, incompatible with order and coherence? Yet when I shall be better qualified for this task I know not. Time may take away these headlong energies, and give me back my ancient sobriety; but this change will only be effected by weakening my remembrance of these events. In proportion as I gain power over words, shall I lose dominion over sentiments. In proportion as my tale is deliberate and slow, the incidents and motives which it is designed to exhibit will be imperfectly revived and obscurely portrayed.

Oh, why art thou away at a time like this. Wert thou present, the office to which my pen is so inadequate would easily be executed by my tongue. Accents can scarcely be too rapid; or that which words should fail to convey, my looks and gestures would suffice to communicate. But I know thy coming is impossible. To leave this spot is equally beyond my power. To keep thee in ignorance of what has happened would justly offend thee. There is no method of informing thee except by letter, and this method must I, therefore, adopt.

How short is the period that has elapsed since thou and I parted, and yet how full of tumult and dismay has been my soul during that period! What light has burst upon my ignorance of myself and

31

of mankind! How sudden and enormous the transition from uncertainty to knowledge!

But let me recall my thoughts; let me struggle for so much composure as will permit my pen to trace intelligible characters. Let
me place in order the incidents that are to compose my tale. I
need not call on thee to listen. The fate of Waldegrave was as fertile of torment to thee as to me. His bloody and mysterious catastrophe equally awakened thy grief, thy revenge, and thy curiosity.
Thou wilt catch from my story every horror and every sympathy
which it paints. Thou wilt shudder with my foreboding and dissolve with my tears. As the sister of my friend, and as one who honors me with her affection, thou wilt share in all my tasks and all
my dangers.

You need not be reminded with what reluctance I left you. To
reach this place by evening was impossible, unless I had set out
early in the morning; but your society was too precious not to be
enjoyed to the last moment. It was indispensable to be here on Tuesday, but my duty required no more than that I should arrive by
sunrise on that day. To travel during the night was productive of
no formidable inconvenience. The air was likely to be frosty and
sharp, but these would not incommode one who walked with speed.
A nocturnal journey in districts so romantic and wild as these,
through which lay my road, was more congenial to my temper than
a noonday ramble.

By nightfall I was within ten miles of my uncle's house. As the
darkness increased, and I advanced on my way, my sensations sunk
into melancholy. The scene and the time reminded me of the friend
whom I had lost. I recalled his features, and accents, and gestures,
and mused with unutterable feelings on the circumstances of his
death.

My recollections once more plunged me into anguish and per-
pexity. Once more I asked, Who was his assassin? By what motives could he be impelled to a deed like this? Waldegrave was pure
from all offense. His piety was rapturous. His benevolence was a
stranger to remissness or torpor. All who came within the sphere
of his influence experienced and acknowledged his benign activity.
His friends were few, because his habits were timid and reserved;
but the existence of an enemy was impossible.

I recalled the incidents of our last interview, my importunities
that he should postpone his ill-omened journey till the morning,
his inexplicable obstinacy, his resolution to set out on foot during

a dark and tempestuous night, and the horrible disaster that befell him.

The first intimation I received of this misfortune, the insanity
of vengeance and grief into which I was hurried, my fruitless
searches for the author of this guilt, my midnight wanderings and
reveries beneath the shade of that fatal elm, were revived and re-
acted. I heard the discharge of the pistol, I witnessed the alarm of
Inglefield, I heard his calls to his servants, and saw them issue forth
with lights and hasten to the spot whence the sound had seemed
to proceed. I beheld my friend stretched upon the earth, ghastly
with a mortal wound, alone, with no traces of the slayer visible,
no tokens by which his place of refuge might be sought, the motives of his enmity or his instruments of mischief might be detected.

I hung over the dying youth, whose insensibility forbade him to
recognize his friend, or unfold the cause of his destruction. I accompanied his remains to the grave; I tended the sacred spot where
he lay; I once more exercised my penetration and my zeal in pursuit of his assassin. Once more my meditations and exertions were
doomed to be disappointed.

I need not remind thee of what is past. Time and reason seemed
to have dissolved the spell which made me deaf to the dictates of
duty and discretion. Remembrances had ceased to agonize, to urge
me to headlong acts, and foster sanguinary purposes. The gloom
was half dispersed, and a radiance had succeeded sweeter than
my former joys.

Now, by some unseen concurrence of reflections, my thoughts
reverted into some degree of bitterness. Methought that to ascertain the hand who killed my friend was not impossible, and to
punish the crime was just. That to forbear inquiry or withhold punishment was to violate my duty to my God and to mankind. The
impulse was gradually awakened that bade me once more to seek
the elm; once more to explore the ground; to scrutinize its trunk.
What could I expect to find? Had it not been a hundred times examined? Had I not extended my search to the neighboring groves
and precipices? Had I not pored upon the brooks, and pried into
the pits and hollows, that were adjacent to the scene of blood?

Lately I had viewed this conduct with shame and regret; but in
the present state of my mind it assumed the appearance of conform-
ity with prudence, and I felt myself irresistibly prompted to repeat my search. Some time had elapsed since my departure from
this district,—time enough for momentous changes to occur. Expe-

dients that formerly were useless might now lead instantaneously to the end which I sought. The tree which had formerly been shunned by the criminal might, in the absence of the avenger of blood, be incautiously approached. Thoughtless or fearless of my return, it was possible that he might, at this moment, be detected hovering near the scene of his offenses.

Nothing can be pleaded in extenuation of this relapse into folly. My return, after an absence of some duration, into the scene of these transactions and sufferings, the time of night, the glimmering of the stars, the obscurity in which external objects were wrapped, and which, consequently, did not draw my attention from the images of fancy, may in some degree account for the revival of those sentiments and resolutions which immediately succeeded the death of Waldegrave, and which, during my visit to you, had been suspended.

You know the situation of the elm, in the midst of a private road, on the verge of Norwalk, near the habitation of Inglefield, but three miles from my uncle's house. It was now my intention to visit it. The road in which I was travelling led a different way. It was requisite to leave it, therefore, and make a circuit through meadows and over steeps. My journey would, by these means, be considerably prolonged; but on that head I was indifferent, or rather, considering how far the night had already advanced, it was desirable not to reach home till the dawn.

I proceeded in this new direction with speed. Time, however, was allowed for my impetuosities to subside and for sober thoughts to take place. Still I persisted in this path. To linger a few moments in this shade, to ponder on objects connected with events so momentous to my happiness, promised me a mournful satisfaction. I was familiar with the way, though trackless and intricate, and I climbed the steeps, crept through the brambles, leaped the rivulets and fences with undeviating aim, till at length I reached the craggy and obscure path which led to Inglefield's house.

In a short time, I descried through the dusk the widespread branches of the elm. This tree, however faintly seen, cannot be mistaken for another. The remarkable bulk and shape of its trunk, its position in the midst of the way, its branches spreading into an ample circumference, made it conspicuous from afar. My pulse throbbed as I approached it.

My eyes were eagerly bent to discover the trunk and the area beneath the shade. These, as I approached, gradually became visible. The trunk was not the only thing which appeared in view. Somewhat else, which made itself distinguishable by its motions, was likewise noted. I faltered and stopped.

To a casual observer this appearance would have been unnoticed. To me, it could not but possess a powerful significance. All my surmises and suspicions instantly returned. This apparition was human, it was connected with the fate of Waldegrave, it led to a disclosure of the author of that fate. What was I to do? To approach unwarily would alarm the person. Instant flight would set him beyond discovery and reach.

I walked softly to the roadside. The ground was covered with rocky masses, scattered among shrub-oaks and dwarf-cedars, emblems of its sterile and uncultivated state. Among these it was possible to elude observation and yet approach near enough to gain an accurate view of this being.

At this time, the atmosphere was somewhat illuminated by the moon, which, though it had already set, was yet so near the horizon as to benefit me by its light. The shape of a man, tall and robust, was now distinguished. Repeated and closer scrutiny enabled me to perceive that he was employed in digging the earth. Something like flannel was wrapped round his waist and covered his lower limbs. The rest of his frame was naked. I did not recognize in him anyone whom I knew.

A figure, robust and strange, and half naked, to be thus employed at this hour and place, was calculated to rouse up my whole soul. His occupation was mysterious and obscure. Was it a grave that he was digging? Was his purpose to explore or to hide? Was it proper to watch him at a distance, unobserved and in silence, or to rush upon him and extort from him, by violence or menaces, an explanation of the scene?

Before my resolution was formed, he ceased to dig. He cast aside his spade and sat down in the pit that he had dug. He seemed wrapped in meditation; but the pause was short and succeeded by sobs, at first low and at wide intervals, but presently louder and more vehement. Sorely charged was indeed that heart whence flowed these tokens of sorrow. Never did I witness a scene of such mighty anguish, such heart-bursting grief.

What should I think? I was suspended in astonishment. Every sentiment, at length, yielded to my sympathy. Every new accent of the mourner struck upon my heart with additional force, and tears found their way spontaneously to my eyes. I left the spot where

I stood, and advanced within the verge of the shade. My caution had forsaken me, and, instead of one whom it was duty to persecute, I beheld, in this man, nothing but an object of compassion.

My pace was checked by his suddenly ceasing to lament. He snatched the spade, and, rising on his feet, began to cover up the pit with the utmost diligence. He seemed aware of my presence and desirous of hiding something from my inspection. I was prompted to advance nearer and hold his hand, but my uncertainty as to his character and views, the abruptness with which I had been ushered into this scene, made me still hesitate; but, though I hesitated to advance, there was nothing to hinder me from calling.

"What, ho!" said I. "Who is there? What are you doing?"

He stopped; the spade fell from his hand; he looked up and bent forward his face towards the spot where I stood. An interview and explanation were now, methought, unavoidable. I mustered up my courage to confront and interrogate this being.

He continued for a minute in his gazing and listening attitude. Where I stood I could not fail of being seen, and yet he acted as if he saw nothing. Again he betook himself to his spade, and proceeded with new diligence to fill up the pit. This demeanor confounded and bewildered me. I had no power but to stand and silently gaze upon his motions.

The pit being filled, he once more sat upon the ground, and resigned himself to weeping and sighs with more vehemence than before. In a short time the fit seemed to have passed. He rose, seized the spade, and advanced to the spot where I stood.

Again I made preparation as for an interview which could not but take place. He passed me, however, without appearing to notice my existence. He came so near as almost to brush my arm, yet turned not his head to either side. My nearer view of him made his brawny arms and lofty stature more conspicuous; but his imperfect dress, the dimness of the light, and the confusion of my own thoughts, hindered me from discerning his features. He proceeded with a few quick steps along the road, but presently darted to one side and disappeared among the rocks and bushes.

My eye followed him as long as he was visible, but my feet were rooted to the spot. My musing was rapid and incongruous. It could not fail to terminate in one conjecture, that this person was *asleep*. Such instances were not unknown to me, through the medium of conversation and books. Never, indeed, had it fallen under my own observation till now, and now it was conspicuous, and environed with all that could give edge to suspicion and vigor to inquiry. To stand here was no longer of use, and I turned my steps towards my uncle's habitation.

II

I had food enough for the longest contemplation. My steps partook, as usual, of the vehemence of my thoughts, and I reached my uncle's gate before I believed myself to have lost sight of the elm. I looked up and discovered the well-known habitation. I could not endure that my reflections should so speedily be interrupted. I therefore passed the gate, and stopped not till I had reached a neighboring summit, crowned with chestnut-oaks and poplars.

Here I more deliberately reviewed the incidents that had just occurred. The inference was just, that the man, half clothed and digging, was a sleeper; but what was the cause of the morbid activity? What was the mournful vision that dissolved him in tears, and extorted from him tokens of inconsolable distress? What did he seek, or what endeavor to conceal, in this fatal spot? The incapacity of sound sleep denotes a mind sorely wounded. It is thus that atrocious criminals denote the possession of some dreadful secret. The thoughts, which considerations of safety enable them to suppress or disguise during wakefulness, operate without impediment and exhibit their genuine effects, when the notices of sense are partly excluded and they are shut out from a knowledge of their entire condition.

This is the perpetrator of some nefarious deed. What but the murder of Waldegrave could direct his steps hither? His employment was part of some fantastic drama in which his mind was busy. To comprehend it demands penetration into the recesses of his soul. But one thing is sure: an incoherent conception of his concern in that transaction bewitches him hither. This it is that deluges his heart with bitterness and supplies him with ever-flowing tears.

But whence comes he? He does not start from the bosom of the earth, or hide himself in airy distance. He must have a name and a terrestrial habitation. It cannot be at an immeasurable distance from the haunted elm. Inglefield's house is the nearest. This may be one of its inhabitants. I did not recognize his features, but this was owing to the dusky atmosphere and to the singularity of his garb. Inglefield has two servants, one of whom was a native of this district, simple, guileless, and incapable of any act of violence.

He was, moreover, devoutly attached to his sect. He could not be the criminal.

The other was a person of a very different cast. He was an emigrant from Ireland, and had been six months in the family of my friend. He was a pattern of sobriety and gentleness. His mind was superior to his situation. His natural endowments were strong, and had enjoyed all the advantage of cultivation. His demeanor was grave, and thoughtful, and compassionate. He appeared not untinctured with religion; but his devotion, though unostentatious, was of a melancholy tenor.

There was nothing in the first view of his character calculated to engender suspicion. The neighborhood was populous. But, as I conned over the catalogue, I perceived that the only foreigner among us was Clithero. Our scheme was, for the most part, a patriarchal one. Each farmer was surrounded by his sons and kinsmen. This was an exception to the rule. Clithero was a stranger, whose adventures and character, previously to his coming hither, were unknown to us. The elm was surrounded by his master's domains. An actor there must be, and no one was equally questionable.

The more I revolved the pensive and reserved deportment of this man, the ignorance in which we were placed respecting his former situation, his possible motives for abandoning his country and choosing a station so much below the standard of his intellectual attainments, the stronger my suspicions became. Formerly, when occupied with conjectures relative to the same topic, the image of this man did not fail to occur; but the seeming harmlessness of his ordinary conduct had raised him to a level with others, and placed him equally beyond the reach of suspicion. I did not, till now, advert to the recentness of his appearance among us, and to the obscurity that hung over his origin and past life. But now these considerations appeared so highly momentous as almost to decide the question of his guilt.

But how were these doubts to be changed into absolute certainty? Henceforth this man was to become the subject of my scrutiny. I was to gain all the knowledge, respecting him, which those with whom he lived, and were the perpetual witnesses of his actions, could impart. For this end I was to make minute inquiries, and to put seasonable interrogatories. From this conduct I promised myself an ultimate solution of my doubts.

I acquiesced in this view of things with considerable satisfaction.

It seemed as if the maze was no longer inscrutable. It would be quickly discovered who were the agents and instigators of the murder of my friend.

But it suddenly occurred to me, for what purpose shall I prosecute this search? What benefit am I to reap from this discovery? How shall I demean myself when the criminal is detected? I was not insensible, at that moment, of the impulses of vengeance, but they were transient. I detested the sanguinary resolutions that I had once formed. Yet I was fearful of the effects of my hasty rage, and dreaded an encounter in consequence of which I might rush into evils which no time could repair, nor penitence expiate.

"But why," said I, "should it be impossible to arm myself with firmness? If forbearance be the dictate of wisdom, cannot it be so deeply engraven on my mind as to defy all temptation, and be proof against the most abrupt surprise? My late experience has been of use to me. It has shown me my weakness and my strength. Having found my ancient fortifications insufficient to withstand the enemy, what should I learn from thence but that it becomes to strenghten and enlarge them?

"No caution, indeed, can hinder the experiment from being hazardous. Is it wise to undertake experiments by which nothing can be gained, and much may be lost? Curiosity is vicious, if undisciplined by reason, and inconducive to benefit."

I was not, however, to be diverted from my purpose. Curiosity, like virtue, is its own reward. Knowledge is of value for its own sake, and pleasure is annexed to the acquisition, without regard to anything beyond. It is precious even when disconnected with moral inducements and heartfelt sympathies; but the knowledge which I sought by its union with these was calculated to excite the most complex and fiery sentiments in my bosom.

Hours were employed in revolving these thoughts. At length I began to be sensible of fatigue, and, returning home, explored the way to my chamber without molesting the repose of the family. You know that our doors are always unfastened, and are accessible at all hours of the night.

My slumbers were imperfect, and I rejoiced when the morning light permitted me to resume my meditations. The day glided away, I scarcely know how, and, as I had rejoiced at the return of morning, I now hailed, with pleasure, the approach of night.

My uncle and sisters having retired, I betook myself, instead of following their example, to the *Chestnut-hill*. Concealed among its rocks, or gazing at the prospect which stretched so far and so wide around it, my fancy has always been accustomed to derive its highest enjoyment from this spot. I found myself again at leisure to recall the scene which I had witnessed during the last ngiht, to imagine its connection with the fate of Waldegrave, and to plan the means of discovering the secret that was hidden under these appearances.

Shortly, I began to feel insupportable disquiet at the thoughts of postponing this discovery. Wiles and stratagems were practicable, but they were tedious, and of dubious success. Why should I proceed like a plotter? Do I intend the injury of this person? A generous purpose will surely excuse me from descending to artifices. There are two modes of drawing forth the secrets of another: by open and direct means and by circuitous and indirect. Why scruple to adopt the former mode? Why not demand a conference, and state my doubts, and demand a solution of them, in a manner worthy of a beneficent purpose? Why not hasten to the spot? He may be, at this moment, mysteriously occupied under this shade. I may note his behavior; I may ascertain his person, if not by the features that belong to him, yet by tracing his footsteps when he departs, and pursuing him to his retreats.

I embraced this scheme, which was thus suggested, with eagerness. I threw myself with headlong speed down the hill and pursued my way to the elm. As I approached the tree, my palpitations increased, though my pace slackened. I looked forward with an anxious glance. The trunk of the tree was hidden in the deepest shade. I advanced close up to it. No one was visible, but I was not discouraged. The hour of his coming was, perhaps, not arrived. I took my station at a small distance, beside a fence, on the right hand.

An hour elapsed before my eyes lighted on the object of which they were in search. My previous observation had been roving from one quarter to another. At last, it dwelt upon the tree. The person whom I before described was seated on the ground. I had not perceived him before, and the means by which he placed himself in this situation had escaped my notice. He seemed like one whom an effort of will, without the exercise of locomotion, had transported hither, or made visible. His state of disarray, and the darkness that shrouded him, prevented me, as before, from distinguishing any peculiarities in his figure or countenance.

I continued watchful and mute. The appearances already de-

scribed took place on this occasion, except the circumstance of digging in the earth. He sat musing for a while, then burst into
sighs and lamentations.

These being exhausted, he rose to depart. He stalked away with a
solemn and deliberate pace. I resolved to tread, as closely as possible, in his footsteps, and not to lose sight of him till the termination of his career.

Contrary to my expectation, he went in a direction opposite to
that which led to Inglefield's. Presently, he stopped at bars, which
he cautiously removed, and, when he had passed through them,
as deliberately replaced. He then proceeded along an obscure path,
which led across stubble-fields, to a wood. The path continued
through the wood, but he quickly struck out of it, and made his
way, seemingly at random, through a most perplexing undergrowth
of bushes and briers.

I was, at first, fearful that the noise which I made behind him,
in trampling down the thicket, would alarm him; but he regarded
it not. The way that he had selected was always difficult: sometimes considerable force was requisite to beat down obstacles; sometimes it led into a deep glen, the sides of which were so steep as
scarcely to afford a footing; sometimes into fens, from which some
exertions were necessary to extricate the feet; and sometimes
through rivulets, of which the water rose to the middle.

For some time I felt no abatement of my speed or my resolution.
I thought I might proceed, without fear, through brakes and dells
which my guide was able to penetrate. He was perpetually changing
his direction. I could form no just opinion as to my situation or distance from the place at which we had set out.

I began at length to be weary. A suspicion. likewise, suggested
itself to my mind, whether my guide did not perceive that he was
followed, and thus prolonged his journey in order to fatigue or elude
his pursuer. I was determined, however, to baffle his design.
Though the air was frosty, my limbs were bedewed with sweat and
my joints were relaxed with toil, but I was obstinately bent upon
proceeding.

At length a new idea occurred to me. On finding me indefatigable
in pursuit, this person might resort to more atrocious methods of
concealment. But what had I to fear? It was sufficient to be upon
my guard. Man to man, I needed not to dread his encounter.

We at last arrived at the verge of a considerable precipice. He
kept along the edge. From this height, a dreary vale was discover-

able, embarrassed with the leafless stocks of bushes and encumbered with rugged and pointed rocks. This scene reminded me of my situation. The desert tract called Norwalk, which I have often mentioned to you, my curiosity had formerly induced me to traverse in various directions. It was in the highest degree rugged, picturesque, and wild. This vale, though I had never before viewed it by the glimpses of the moon, suggested the belief that I had visited it before. Such a one I knew belonged to this uncultivated region. If the opinion were true, we were at no inconsiderable distance from Inglefield's habitation. "Where," said I, "is this singular career to terminate?"

Though occupied with these reflections, I did not slacken my pursuit. The stranger kept along the verge of the clifff, which gradually declined till it terminated in the valley. He then plunged into its deepest thickets. In a quarter of an hour he stopped under a projecture of the rock which formed the opposite side of the vale. He then proceeded to remove the stalks, which, as I immediately perceived, concealed the mouth of a cavern. He plunged into the darkness, and in a few moments his steps were heard no more.

Hitherto my courage had supported me, but here it failed. Was this person an assassin, who was acquainted with the windings of the grotto, and who would take advantage of the dark to execute his vengeance upon me, who had dared to pursue him to these forlorn retreats; or was he maniac, or walker in his sleep? Whichever supposition were true, it would be rash in me to follow him. Besides, he could not long remain in these darksome recesses, unless some fatal accident should overtake him.

I seated myself at the mouth of the cave, determined patiently to wait till he should think proper to emerge. This opportunity of rest was exceedingly acceptable after so toilsome a pilgrimage. My pulse began to beat more slowly, and the moisture that incommoded me ceased to flow. The coolness, which for a little time was delicious, presently increased to shivering, and I found it necessary to change my posture, in order to preserve my blood from congealing.

After I had formed a path before the cavern's mouth, by the removal of obstructions, I employed myself in walking to and fro. In this situation I saw the moon gradually decline to the horizon, and, at length, disappear. I marked the deepenings of the shade and the mutations which every object successively underwent. The vale was narrow, and hemmed in on all sides by lofty and precipitous cliffs. The gloom deepened as the moon declined, and the faintness of starlight was all that preserved my senses from being useless to my own guidance.

I drew nearer the cleft at which this mysterious personage had entered. I stretched my hands before it, determined that he should not emerge from his den without my notice. His steps would, necessarily, communicate the tidings of his approach. He could not move without a noise which would be echoed to, on all sides, by the abruptness by which this valley was surrounded. Here, then, I continued till the day began to dawn, in momentary expectation of the stranger's reappearance.

My attention was at length excited by a sound that seemed to issue from the cave. I imagined that the sleeper was returning, and prepared therefore to seize him. I blamed myself for neglecting the opportunities that had already been afforded, and was determined that another should not escape. My eyes were fixed upon the entrance. The rustling increased, and presently an animal leaped forth, of what kind I was unable to discover. Heart-struck by this disappointment, but not discouraged, I continued to watch, but in vain. The day was advancing apace. At length the sun arose, and its beams glistened on the edges of the cliffs above, whose sapless stalks and rugged masses were covered with hoarfrost. I began to despair of success, but was unwilling to depart until it was no longer possible to hope for the return of this extraordinary personage. Whether he had been swallowed up by some of the abysses of this grotto, or lurked near the entrance, waiting my departure, or had made his exit at another and distant aperture, was unknown to me.

Exhausted and discouraged, I prepared, at length, to return. It was easy to find my way out of this wilderness by going forward in one direction, regardless of impediments and cross-paths. My absence I believed to have occasioned no alarm to my family, since they knew not of my intention to spend the night abroad. Thus unsatisfactorily terminated this night's adventures.

III

The ensuing day was spent partly in sleep, and partly in languor and disquietude. I incessantly ruminated on the incidents of the last night. The scheme that I had formed was defeated. Was it likely that this unknown person would repeat his midnight visits to the elm? If he did, and could again be discovered, should I resolve to undertake a new pursuit, which might terminate abortively, or in some signal disaster? But what proof had I that the same route would be taken, and that he would again inter himself alive in the same spot? Or, if he did, since his reappearance would sufficiently prove that the cavern was not dangerous, and that he who should adventure in might hope to come out again in safety, why not enter it after him? What could be the inducements of this person to betake himself to subterranean retreats? The basis of all this region is *limestone*, a substance that eminently abounds in rifts and cavities. These, by the gradual decay of their cementing parts, frequently make their appearance in spots where they might have been least expected. My attention has often been excited by the hollow sound which was produced by my casual footsteps, and which showed me that I trod upon the roof of caverns. A mountain cave and the rumbling of an unseen torrent are appendages of this scene, dear to my youthful imagination. Many of romantic structure were found within the precincts of Norwalk.

These I had industriously sought out; but this had hitherto escaped my observation, and I formed the resolution of some time exploring it. At present I determined to revisit the elm, and dig in the spot where this person had been employed in a similar way. It might be that something was here deposited which might exhibit this transaction in a new light. At the suitable hour, on the ensuing night, I took my former stand. The person again appeared. My intention to dig was to be carried into effect on condition of his absence, and was, consequently, frustrated.

Instead of rushing on him, and breaking at once the spell by which his senses were bound, I concluded, contrary to my first design, to wait his departure, and allow myself to be conducted whithersoever he pleased. The track into which he now led me

45

was different from the former one. It was a maze, oblique, circuitous, upward and downward, in a degree which only could take
place in a region so remarkably irregular in surface, so abounding
with hillocks and steeps and pits and brooks, as *Solesbury*. It
seemed to be the sole end of his labors to bewilder or fatigue his
pursuer, to pierce into the deepest thickets, to plunge into the
darkest cavities, to ascend the most difficult heights, and approach
the slippery and tremulous verge of the dizziest precipices.

I disdained to be outstripped in this career. All dangers were
overlooked, and all difficulties defied. I plunged into obscurities,
and clambered over obstacles, from which, in a different state of
mind, and with a different object of pursuit, I should have recoiled
with invincible timidity. When the scene had passed, I could not
review the perils I had undergone without shuddering.

At length my conductor struck into a path which, compared with
the ruggedness of that which we had lately trodden, was easy and
smooth. This track led us to the skirt of the wilderness, and at no
long time we reached an open field, when a dwelling appeared,
at a small distance, which I speedily recognized to be that belonging to Inglefield. I now anticipated the fulfillment of my predictions. My conductor directed his steps towards the barn, into which
he entered by a small door.

How were my doubts removed! This was no other than Clithero
Edny. There was nothing in his appearance incompatible with
this conclusion. He and his fellow servant occupied an apartment
in the barn as a lodging-room. This arduous purpose was accomplished, and I retired to the shelter of a neighboring shed, not so
much to repose myself after the fatigues of my extraordinary journey, as to devise further expedients.

Nothing now remained but to take Clithero to task; to repeat
to him the observations of the two last nights; to unfold to him my
conjectures and suspicions; to convince him of the rectitude of my
intentions; and to extort from him a disclosure of all the circumstances connected with the death of Waldegrave which it was in
his power to communicate.

In order to obtain a conference, I resolved to invite him to my
uncle's to perform a certain piece of work for me under my own
eyes. He would, of course, spend the night with us, and in the
evening I would take an opportunity of entering into conversation
with him.

A period of the deepest deliberation was necessary to qualify

myself for performing suitably my part in this projected interview.
I attended to the feelings that were suggested in this new state of
my knowledge. I found reason to confide in my newly-acquired
equanimity. "Remorse," said I, "is an ample and proper expiation
for all offenses. What does vengeance desire but to inflict misery?
If misery come, its desires are accomplished. It is only the obdurate
and exulting criminal that is worthy of our indignation. It is common
for pity to succeed the bitterest suggestions of resentment. If the
vengeful mind be delighted with the spectacle of woes of its own
contriving, at least its canine hunger is appeased, and thenceforth
its hands are inactive."

On the evening of the next day, I paid a visit to Inglefield. I
wished to impart to him the discoveries that I had made, and to
listen to his reflections on the subject. I likewise desired to obtain
all possible information from the family respecting the conduct
of Clithero.

My friend received me with his usual kindness. Thou art no
stranger to his character; thou knowest with what paternal affection I have ever been regarded by this old man; with what solicitude the wanderings of my reason and my freaks of passion have
been noted and corrected by him. Thou knowest his activity to
save the life of thy brother, and the hours that have been spent by
him in aiding my conjectures as to the cause of his death, and in-
culcating the lessons of penitence and duty.

The topics which could not but occur at such a meeting were
quickly discussed, and I hastily proceeded to that subject which
was nearest my heart. I related the adventures of the two preceding
nights, and mentioned the inference to which they irresistibly led.

He said that this inference coincided with suspicions he had
formed, since our last interview, in consequence of certain communications from his housekeeper. It seems the character of
Clithero had, from the first, exercised the inquisitiveness of this
old lady. She had carefully marked his musing and melancholy
deportment. She had tried innumerable expedients for obtaining
a knowledge of his past life, and particularly of his motives for
coming to America. These expedients, however profound and ad-
dressful, had failed. He took no pains to elude them. He contented himself with turning a deaf ear to all indirect allusions and
hints, and, when more explicitly questioned, with simply declaring
that he had nothing to communicate worthy of her notice.

During the day he was a sober and diligent workman. His evenings he spent in incommunicative silence. On Sundays, he always rambled away, no one knew whither, and without a companion. I have already observed that he and his follow servant occupied the same apartment in the barn. This circumstance was not unattended to by Miss Inglefield. The name of Clithero's companion was Ambrose. This man was copiously interrogated by his mistress, and she found him by no means so refractory as the other.

Ambrose, in his tedious and confused way, related that, soon after Clithero and he had become bedfellows, the former was considerably disturbed by restlessness and talking in his sleep. His discourse was incoherent. It was generally in the tone of expostulation, and appeared to be entreating to be saved from some great injury. Such phrases as these: "have pity," "have mercy," were frequently intermingled with groans, and accompanied with weeping. Sometimes he seemed to be holding conferences with someone who was making him considerable offers on condition of his performing some dangerous service. What he said in his own person, and in answer to his imaginary tempter, testified the utmost reluctance.

Ambrose had no curiosity on the subject. As this interruption prevented him at first from sleeping, it was his custom to put an end to the dialogue, by awakening his companion, who betrayed tokens of great alarm and dejection on discovering how he had been employed. He would solicitously inquire what were the words that he had uttered; but Ambrose's report was seldom satisfactory, because he had attended to them but little, and because he grudged every moment in which he was deprived of his accustomed repose.

Whether Clithero had ceased from this practice, or habit had reconciled his companion to the sounds, they no longer occasioned any interruption to his slumber.

No one appeared more shocked than he at the death of Waldegrave. After this event his dejection suddenly increased. This symptom was observed by the family, but none but the housekeeper took the trouble to notice it to him, or build conjectures on the incident. During nights, however, Ambrose experienced a renewal of his ancient disturbances. He remarked that Clithero, one night, had disappeared from his side. Ambrose's range of reflection was extremely narrow. Quickly falling asleep, and finding his companion beside him when he awoke, he dismissed it from his mind.

On several ensuing nights he awakened in like manner, and always found his companion's place empty. The repetition of so strange an incident at length incited him to mention it to Clithero. The latter was confounded at this intelligence. He questioned Ambrose with great anxiety as to the particulars of this event, but he could gain no satisfaction from the stupid inattention of the other. From this time there was a visible augmentation of his sadness. His fits of taciturnity became more obstinate, and a deeper gloom sat upon his brow.

There was one other circumstance, of particular importance, mentioned by the housekeeper. One evening someone on horseback stopped at this gate. He rattled at the gate, with an air of authority, in token of his desire that someone would come from the house. Miss Inglefield was employed in the kitchen, from a window of which she perceived who it was that made the signal. Clithero happened, at the same moment, to be employed near her. She, therefore, desired him to go and see whom the stranger wanted. He laid aside his work and went. The conference lasted above five minutes. The length of it excited in her a faint degree of surprise, inducing her to leave her employment and pay an unintermitted attention to the scene. There was nothing, however, but its duration that rendered it remarkable.

Clithero at length entered, and the traveller proceeded. The countenance of the former betrayed a degree of perturbation which she had never witnessed before. The muscles of his face were distorted and tremulous. He immediately sat down to his work, but he seemed, for some time, to have lost all power over his limbs. He struggled to avoid the sight of the lady, and his gestures, irresolute or misdirected, betokened the deepest dismay. After some time, he recovered, in some degree, his self-possession; but, while the object was viewed through a new medium, and the change existed only in the imagination of the observer, a change was cercertainly discovered.

These circumstances were related to me by Inglefield and corroborated by his housekeeper. One consequence inevitable flowed from them. The sleepwalker, he who had led me through so devious a tract, was no other than Clithero. There was, likewise, a strong relation between this person and him who stopped at the gate. What was the subject of discourse between them? In answer to Miss Inglefield's interrogatories, he merely said that the traveller inquired whither the road led which, at a small distance forward, struck out of the principal one. Considering the length of the interview, it was not likely that this was the only topic.

My determination to confer with him in private acquired new force from these reflections. Inglefield assented to my proposal. His own affairs would permit the absence of his servant for one day. I saw no necessity for delay, and immediately made my request to Clithero. I was fashioning an implement, I told him, with respect to which I could not wholly depend upon my own skill. I was acquainted with the dexterity of his contrivances and the neatness of his workmanship. He readily consented to assist me on this occasion. Next day he came. Contrary to my expectation, he prepared to return home in the evening. I urged him to spend the night with us; but no: it was equally convenient, and more agreeable to him, to return.

I was not aware of this resolution. I might, indeed, have foreseen that, being conscious of his infirmity, he would desire to avoid the scrutiny of strangers. I was painfully disconcerted; but it occurred to me that the best that could be done was to bear him company, and seize some opportunity, during this interval, of effecting my purpose. I told him that, since he would not remain, I cared not if, for the sake of recreation, and of a much more momentous purpose, I went along with him. He tacitly, and without apparent reluctance, consented to my scheme, and, accordingly, we set off together. This was an awful crisis. The time had now come that was to dissipate my uncertainty. By what means should I introduce a topic so momentous and singular? I had been qualified by no experience for rightly conducting myself on so critical an emergency. My companion preserved a mournful and inviolable silence. He afforded me no opening by which I might reach the point in view. His demeanor was sedate, while I was almost disabled, by the confusion of my thoughts, to utter a word.

It was a dreadful charge that I was about to insinuate. I was to accuse my companion of nothing less than murder. I was to call upon him for an avowal of his guilt. I was to state the ground of my suspicions, and desire him to confute or confirm them. In doing this, I was principally stimulated by an ungovernable curiosity; yet, if I intended not the conferring of a benefit, I did not, at least, purpose the infliction of evil. I persuaded myself that I was able to exclude from my bosom all sanguinary or vengeful impulses; and that, whatever should be the issue of this conversation, my equanimity would be unsubdued.

I revolved various modes of introducing the topic by which my mind was engaged. I passed rapidly from one to another. None of

them were sufficiently free from objection to allow me to adopt
it. My perplexity became, every moment, more painful, and my
ability to extricate myself, less.

In this state of uncertainty, so much time elapsed that the elm
at length appeared in sight. This object had somewhat of a mechanical influence upon me. I stopped short, and seized the arm of my
companion. Till this moment, he appeared to have been engrossed
by his own reflections, and not to have heeded those emotions
which must have been sufficiently conspicuous in my looks.

This action recalled him from his reverie. The first idea that occurred to him, when he had noticed my behavior, was that I was
assailed by some sudden indisposition.

"What is the matter?" said he, in a tone of anxiety: "are you not
well?"

"Yes," replied I,—"perfectly well. But stop a moment; I have
something to say to you."

"To me?" answered he, with surprise.

"Yes," said I. "Let us turn down this path" (pointing, at the same
time, to that along which I had followed him the preceding night).

He now partook, in some degree, of my embarrassment.

"Is there anything particular?" said he, in a doubting accent.
There he stopped.

"Something," I answered, "of the highest moment. Go with me
down this path. We shall be in less danger of interruption."

He was irresolute and silent, but, seeing me remove the bars
and pass through them, he followed me. Nothing more was said
till we entered the wood. I trusted to the suggestions of the moment. I had now gone too far to recede, and the necessity that
pressed upon me supplied me with words. I continued:

"This is a remarkable spot. You may wonder why I have led you
to it. I ought not to keep you in suspense. There is a tale connected
with it, which I am desirous of telling you. For this purpose I have
brought you hither. Listen to me."

I then recapitulated the adventures of the two preceding nights.
I added nothing, nor retrenched anything. He listened in the deepest silence. From every incident, he gathered new cause of alarm.
Repeatedly he wiped his face with his handkerchief, and sighed
deeply. I took no verbal notice of these symptoms. I deemed it
incumbent on me to repress nothing. When I came to the con-
cluding circumstance, by which his person was identified, he heard
me without any new surprise. To this narrative I subjoined the in-

quiries that I had made at Inglefield's, and the result of those inquiries. I then continued in these words:

"You may ask why I subjected myself to all this trouble. The mys-
teriousness of these transactions would have naturally suggested
curiosity in anyone. A transient passenger would probably have
acted as I have done. But I had motives peculiar to myself. Need
I remind you of a late disaster? That it happened beneath the shade
of this tree? Am I not justified in drawing certain inferences from
your behavior? What they are, I leave you to judge. Be it your task
to confute or confirm them. For this end I have conducted you
hither.

"My suspicions are vehement. How can they be otherwise? I call
upon you to say whether they be just."

The spot where we stood was illuminated by the moon, that had
now risen, though all around was dark. Hence his features and person were easily distinguished. His hands hung at his side. His eyes
were downcast, and he was motionless as a statue. My last words
seemed scarcely to have made any impression on his sense. I had
no need to provide against the possible suggestions of revenge. I
felt nothing but the tenderness of compassion. I continued, for some
time, to observe him in silence, and could discover no tokens of a
change of mood. I could not forbear, at last, to express my uneasiness at the fixedness of his features and attitude.

"Recollect yourself. I mean not to urge you too closely. This topic
is solemn, but it need not divest you of the fortitude becoming a
man."

The sound of my voice startled him. He broke from me, looked
up, and fixed his eyes upon me with an expression of affright. He
shuddered and recoiled as from a spectre. I began to repent of my
experiment. I could say nothing suitable to this occasion. I was obliged to stand a silent and powerless spectator, and to suffer this
paroxysm to subside of itself. When its violence appeared to be
somewhat abated, I resumed:

"I can feel for you. I act not thus in compliance with a temper
that delights in the misery of others. The explanation that I have
solicited is no less necessary for your sake than for mine. You are no
stranger to the light in which I viewed this man. You have witnessed the grief which his fate occasioned, and the efforts that I
made to discover and drag to punishment his murderer. You heard
the execrations that I heaped upon him, and my vows of eternal revenge. You expect that, having detected the offender, I will hunt

him to infamy and death. You are mistaken. I consider the deed as sufficiently expiated.

"I am no stranger to your gnawing cares; to the deep and incurable despair that haunts you, to which your waking thoughts are prey, and from which sleep cannot secure you. I know the enormity of your crime, but I know not your inducements. Whatever they were, I see the consequences with regard to yourself. I see proofs of that remorse which must ever be attendant on guilt.

"This is enough. Why should the effects of our misdeeds be inexhaustible? Why should we be debarred from a comforter? An opportunity of repairing our errors may, at least, be demanded from the rulers of our destiny.

"I once imagined that he who killed Waldegrave inflicted the greatest possible injury on me. That was an error, which reflection has cured. Were futurity laid open to my view, and events, with their consequences, unfolded, I might see reason to embrace the assassin as my best friend. Be comforted."

He was still incapable of speaking; but tears came to his relief. Without attending to my remonstrances, he betrayed a disposition to return. I had, hitherto, hoped for some disclosure, but now feared that it was designed to be withheld. He stopped not till we reached Inglefield's piazza. He then spoke, for the first time, but in a hollow and tremulous voice:

"You demand of me a confession of crimes. You shall have it. Sometime you shall have it. When it will be, I cannot tell. Something must be done, and shortly."

He hurried from me into the house, and, after a pause, I turned my steps homewards. My reflections, as I proceeded, perpetually revolved round a single point. These were scarcely more than a repetition, with slight variations, of a single idea.

When I awoke in the morning, I hied, in fancy, to the wilderness. I saw nothing but the figure of the wanderer before me. I traced his footsteps anew, retold my narrative, and pondered on his gestures and words. My condition was not destitute of enjoyment. My stormy passions had subsided into a calm, portentous and awful. My soul was big with expectation. I seemed as if I were on the eve of being ushered into a world whose scenes were tremendous but sublime. The suggestions of sorrow and malice had, for a time, taken their flight, and yielded place to a generous sympathy, which filled my eyes with tears, but had more in it of pleasure than of pain. That Clithero was instrumental to the death of

Waldegrave, that he could furnish the clue explanatory of every
bloody and mysterious event that had hitherto occurred, there was
no longer the possibility of doubting. "He, indeed," said I, "is the
murderer of excellence; and yet it shall be my province to emulate
a father's clemency, and restore this unhappy man to purity and
to peace."

Day after day passed, without hearing anything of Clithero. I
began to grow uneasy and impatient. I had gained so much, and
by means so unexpected, that I could more easily endure uncertainty with respect to what remained to be known. But my patience
had its limits. I should, doubtless, have made use of new means
to accelerate this discovery, had not his timely appearance made
them superfluous.

Sunday being at length arrived, I resolved to go to Inglefield's,
seek an interview with his servant, and urge him, by new importunities, to confide to me the secret. On my way thither, Clithero
appeared in sight. His visage was pale and wan, and his form emaciated and shrunk. I was astonished at the alteration which the
lapse of a week had made in his appearance. At a small distance
I mistook him for a stranger. As soon as I percieved who it was, I
greeted him with the utmost friendliness. My civilities made little
impression on him, and he hastened to inform me that he was
coming to my uncle's, for the purpose of meeting and talking with
me. If I thought proper, we would go into the wood together, and
find some spot where we might discourse at our leisure and be
exempt from interruption.

You will easily conceive with what alacrity I accepted his invi-
tation. We returned from the road into the first path, and proceeded in silence, till the wildness of the surrounding scenery informed us that we were in the heart of Norwalk. We lighted on a
recess, to which my companion appeared to be familiar, and which
had all the advantages of solitude, and was suitable to rest. Here
we stopped. Hitherto my companion had displayed a certain degree
of composure. Now his countenance betokened a violent internal
struggle. It was a considerable time before he could command his
speech. When he had so far effected the conquest of his feelings, he
began.

IV

You call upon me for a confession of my offenses. What a strange fortune is mine! That a human being, in the present circumstances, should make this demand, and that I should be driven, by an irresistible necessity, to comply with it! That here should terminate my calamitous series! That my destiny should call upon me to lie down and die, in a region so remote from the scene of my crime; at a distance so great from all that witnessed and endured their consequences!

You believe me to be an assassin. You require me to explain the motives that induced me to murder the innocent. While this is your belief, and this the scope of your expectations, you may be sure of my compliance. I could resist every demand but this.

For what purpose have I come hither? Is it to relate my story? Shall I calmly sit here, and rehearse the incidents of my life? Will my strength be adequate to this rehearsal? Let me recollect the motives that governed me, when I formed this design. Perhaps a strenuousness may be imparted by them which, otherwise, I cannot hope to obtain. For the sake of those, I consent to conjure up the ghost of the past, and to begin a tale that, with a fortitude like mine, I am not sure that I shall live to finish.

You are unacquainted with the man before you. The inferences which you have drawn, with regard to my designs and my conduct, are a tissue of destructive errors. You, like others, are blind to the most momentous consequences of your own actions. You talk of imparting consolation. You boast the beneficence of your intentions. You set yourself to do me a benefit. What are the effects of your misguided zeal and random efforts? They have brought my life to a miserable close. They have shrouded the last scene of it in blood. They have put the seal to my perdition.

My misery has been greater than has fallen to the lot of mortals. Yet it is but beginning. My present path, full as it is of asperities, is better than that into which I must enter when this is abandoned. Perhaps, if my pilgrimage had been longer, I might, at some future day, have lighted upon hope. In consequence of your interference, I am forever debarred from it. My existence is henceforward to be invariable. The woes that are reserved for me are incapable alike of alleviation or intermission.

But I came not hither to recriminate. I came not hither to accuse others, but myself. I know the retribution that is appointed for guilt like mine. It is just. I may shudder at the foresight of my punishment and shrink in the endurance of it; but I shall be indebted for part of my torment to the vigor of my understanding, which teaches me that my punishment is just. Why should I procrastinate my doom and strive to render my burden more light? It is but just that it should crush me. Its procrastination is impossible. The stroke is already felt. Even now I drink of the cup of retribution. A change of being cannot aggravate my woe. Till consciousness itself be extinct, the worm that gnaws me will never perish.

Fain would I be relieved from this task. Gladly would I bury in oblivion the transactions of my life. But no! My fate is uniform. The demon that controlled me at first is still in the fruition of power. I am entangled in his fold, and every effort that I make to escape only involves me in deeper ruin. I need not conceal, for all the consequences of disclosure are already experienced. I cannot endure a groundless imputation, though to free me from it I must create and justify imputations still more atrocious. My story may at least be brief. If the agonies of remembrance must be awakened afresh, let me do all that in me lies to shorten them.

I was born in the county of Armagh. My parents were of the better sort of peasants, and were able to provide me with the rudiments of knowledge. I should doubtless have trodden in their footsteps, and have spent my life in the cultivation of their scanty fields, if an event had not happened, which, for a long time, I regarded as the most fortunate of my life, but which I now regard as the scheme of some infernal agent, and as the primary source of all my calamities.

My father's farm was a portion of the demesne of one who resided wholly in the metropolis and consigned the management of his estates to his stewards and retainers. This person married a lady who brought him great accession of fortune. Her wealth was her only recommendation in the eyes of her husband (whose understanding was depraved by the prejudices of luxury and rank), but was the least of her attractions in the estimate of reasonable beings.

They passed some years together. If their union were not a source of misery to the lady, she was indebted for her tranquillity to the force of her mind. She was, indeed, governed, in every action of her life, by the precepts of duty, while her husband listened to no calls but those of pernicious dissipation. He was immersed in all the vices that grow out of opulence and a mistaken education.

Happily for his wife, his career was short. He was enraged at the infidelity of his mistress, to purchase whose attachment he had lavished two-thirds of his fortune. He called the paramour, by whom he had been supplanted, to the field. The contest was obstinate, and terminated in the death of the challenger.

This event freed the lady from many distressful and humiliating obligations. She determined to profit by her newly-acquired independence, to live thenceforward conformably to her notions of right, to preserve and improve, by schemes of economy, the remains of her fortune, and to employ it in the diffusion of good. Her plans made it necessary to visit her estates in the distant provinces.

During her abode in the manor of which my father was a vassal, she visited his cottage. I was at that time a child. She was pleased with my vivacity and promptitude, and determined to take me under her own protection. My parents joyfully acceded to her proposal, and I returned with her to the capital.

She had an only son of my own age. Her design, in relation to me, was that I should be educated with her child, and that an affection, in this way, might be excited in me towards my young master, which might render me, when we should attain to manhood, one of his most faithful and intelligent dependents. I enjoyed, equally with him, all the essential benefits of education. There were certain accomplishments, from which I was excluded, from the belief that they were unsuitable to my rank and station. I was permitted to acquire others, which, had she been actuated by true discernment, she would, perhaps, have discovered to be far more incompatible with a servile station. In proportion as my views were refined and enlarged by history and science, I was likely to contract a thirst of independence, and an impatience of subjection and poverty.

When the period of childhood and youth was past, it was thought proper to send her son to improve his knowledge and manners by a residence on the continent. This young man was endowed with splendid abilities. His errors were the growth of his condition. All the expedients that maternal solicitude and wisdom could suggest were employed to render him a useful citizen. Perhaps this wisdom was attested by the large share of excellence which he really possessed; and that his character was not unblemished proved only that no exertions could preserve him from the vices that are inherent in wealth and rank, and which flow from the spectacle of universal depravity.

As to me, it would be folly to deny that I had benefited by my opportunities of improvement. I fulfilled the expectation of my mistress, in one respect. I was deeply imbued with affection for her son and reverence for herself. Perhaps the force of education was evinced in those particulars, without reflecting any credit on the directors of it. Those might merit the name of defects, which were regarded by them as accomplishments. My unfavorable qualities, like those of my master, were imputed to my condition, though, perhaps, the difference was advantageous to me, since the vices of servitude are less hateful than those of tyranny.

It was resolved that I should accompany my master in his travels, in quality of favorite domestic. My principles, whatever might be their rectitude, were harmonious and flexible. I had devoted my life to the service of my patron. I had formed conceptions of what was really conducive to his interest, and was not to be misled by specious appearances. If my affection had not stimulated my diligence, I should have found sufficient motives in the behavior of his mother. She condescended to express her reliance on my integrity and judgment. She was not ashamed to manifest, at parting, the tenderness of a mother, and to acknowledge that all her tears were not shed on her son's account. I had my part in the regrets that called them forth.

During our absence, I was my master's constant attendant. I corresponded with his mother, and made the conduct of her son the principal theme of my letters. I deemed it my privilege, as well as duty, to sit in judgment on his actions, to form my opinions without regard to selfish considerations, and to avow them whenever the avowal tended to benefit. Every letter which I wrote, particularly those in which his behavior was freely criticized, I allowed him to peruse. I would, on no account, connive at or participate in the slightest irregularity. I knew the duty of my station, and assumed no other control than that which resulted from the avoiding of deceit, and the open expression of my sentiments. The youth was of a noble spirit, but his firmness was wavering. He yielded to temptations which a censor less rigorous than I would have regarded as venial, or, perhaps, laudable. My duty required me to set before him the consequences of his actions, and to give impartial and timely information to his mother.

He could not brook a monitor. The more he needed reproof the less supportable it became. My company became every day less agreeable, till at length there appeared a necessity of parting. A separation took place, but not as enemies. I never lost his respect. In his representations to his mother, he was just to my character and services. My dismission was not allowed to injure my fortune, and his mother considered this event merely as a new proof of the inflexible consistency of my principles.

On this change in my situation, she proposed to me to become a member of her own family. No proposal could be more acceptable. I was fully acquainted with the character of this lady, and had nothing to fear from injustice and caprice. I did not regard her with filial familiarity, but my attachment and reverence would have done honor to that relation. I performed for her the functions of a steward. Her estates in the city were put under my direction. She placed boundless confidence in my discretion and integrity, and consigned to me the payment, and, in some degree, the selection and goverment, of her servants. My station was a servile one, yet most of the evils of servitude were unknown to me. My personal ease and independence were less infringed than that of those who are accounted the freest members of society. I derived a sort of authority and dignity from the receipt and disbursement of money. The tenants and debtors of the lady were, in some respects, mine. It was, for the most part, on my justice and lenity that they depended for their treatment. My lady's household-establishment was large and opulent. Her servants were my inferiors and menials. My leisure was considerable, and my emoluments large enough to supply me with every valuable instrument of improvement or pleasure.

These were reasons why I should be contented with my lot. These circumstances alone would have rendered it more eligible than any other, but it had additional and far more powerful recommendations, arising from the character of Mrs. Lorimer, and from the relation in which she allowed me to stand to her.

How shall I enter upon this theme? How shall I expatiate upon excellencies which it was my fate to view in their genuine colors, to adore with an immeasurable and inextinguishable ardor, and which, nevertheless, it was my hateful task to blast and destroy?

Yet I will not be spared. I shall find, in the rehearsal, new incitements to sorrow. I deserve to be supreme in misery, and will not be denied the full measure of a bitter retribution.

No one was better qualified to judge of her excellencies. A casual spectator might admire her beauty, and the dignity of her demeanor. From the contemplation of those, he might gather motives for loving or revering her. Age was far from having withered her complexion, or destroyed the evenness of her skin; but no time could rob her of the sweetness and intelligence which animated her features. Her habitual beneficence was bespoken in every look. Always in search of occasions for doing good, always meditating scenes of happiness, of which she was the author, or of distress, for which she was preparing relief, the most torpid insensibility was, for a time, subdued, and the most depraved smitten by charms of which, in another person, they would not perhaps have been sensible.

A casual visitant might enjoy her conversation, might applaud the rectitude of her sentiments, the richness of her elocution, and her skill in all the offices of politeness. But it was only for him who dwelt constantly under the same roof to mark the inviolable consistency of her actions and opinions, the ceaseless flow of her candor, her cheerfulness, and her benevolence. It was only for one who witnessed her behavior at all hours, in sickness and in health, her management of that great instrument of evil and good, money, her treatment of her son, her menials, and her kindred, rightly to estimate her merits.

The intercourse between us was frequent, but of a peculiar kind. My office in her family required me often to see her, to submit schemes to her consideration, and receive her directions. At these times she treated me in a manner in some degree adapted to the difference of rank and the inferiority of my station, and yet widely dissimilar from that which a different person would have adopted in the same circumstances. The treatment was not that of an equal and a friend, but still more remote was it from that of a mistress. It was merely characterized by affability and condescension, but as such it had no limits.

She made no scruple to ask my counsel in every pecuniary affair, to listen to my arguments, and decide conformably to what, after sufficient canvassings and discussions, should appear to be right. When the direct occasions of our interview were dismissed, I did not of course withdraw. To detain or dismiss me was indeed at her option; but, if no engagement interfered, she would enter into general conversation. There was none who could with more safety to herself have made the world her confessor; but the state of society in which she lived imposed certain limitations on her candor. In her intercourse with me there were fewer restraints than on any other occasion. My situation had made me more intimately acquainted with domestic transactions, with her views respecting her son, and with the terms on which she thought proper to stand with those whom old acquaintance or kindred gave some title to her good offices. In addition to all those motives to a candid treatment of me, there were others which owed their efficacy to her maternal regard for me, and to the artless and unsuspecting generosity of her character.

Her hours were distributed with the utmost regularity, and appropriated to the best purposes. She selected her society without regard to any qualities but probity and talents. Her associates were numerous, and her evening conversations embellished with all that could charm the senses or instruct the understanding. This was a chosen field for the display of her magnificence; but her grandeur was unostentatious, and her gravity unmingled with haughtiness. From these my station excluded me; but I was compensated by the freedom of her communications in the intervals. She found pleasure in detailing to me the incidents that passed on those occasions, in rehearsing conversations and depicting characters. There was an uncommon portion of dramatic merit in her recitals, besides valuable and curious information. One uniform effect was produced in me by this behavior. Each day I thought it impossible for my attachment to receive any new accessions, yet the morrow was sure to produce some new emotion of respect or of gratitude, and to set the unrivalled accomplishments of this lady in a new and more favorable point of view. I contemplated no change in my condition. The necessity of change, whatever were the alternative, would have been a subject of piercing regret. I deemed my life a cheap sacrifice in her cause. No time would suffice to discharge the debt of gratitude that was due to her. Yet it was continually accumulating. If an anxious thought ever invaded my bosom, it arose from this source.

It was no difficult task faithfully to execute the functions assigned to me. No merit could accrue to me from this source. I was exposed to no temptation. I had passed the feverish period of youth. No contagious example had contaminated my principles. I had resisted the allurements of sensuality and dissipation incident to my age. My dwelling was in pomp and splendor. I had amassed sufficient to secure me, in case of unforeseen accidents, in the enjoyment of competence. My mental resources were not despicable, and the external means of intellectual gratification were boundless. I enjoyed an unsullied reputation. My character was well known in that sphere which my lady occupied, not only by means of her favorable report, but in numberless ways in which it was my fortune to perform personal services to others.

V

Mrs. Lorimer had a twin brother. Nature had impressed the same image upon them, and had modelled them after the same pattern. The resemblance between them was exact to a degree almost incredible. In infancy and childhood they were perpetually liable to be mistaken for each other. As they grew up, nothing, to a superficial examination, appeared to distinguish them, but the sexual characteristics. A sagacious observer would, doubtless, have noted the most essential differences. In all those modifications of the features which are produced by habits and sentiments, no two persons were less alike. Nature seemed to have intended them as examples of the futility of those theories which ascribe everything to conformation and instinct and nothing to external circumstances; in what different modes the same materials may be fashioned, and to what different purposes the same materials may be applied. Perhaps the rudiments of their intellectual character, as well as of their form, were the same; but the powers that in one case were exerted in the cause of virtue were, in the other, misapplied to sordid and flagitious purposes.

Arthur Wiatte (that was his name) had ever been the object of his sister's affection. As long as he existed, she never ceased to labor in the promotion of his happiness. All her kindness was repaid by a stern and inexorable hatred. This man was an exception to all the rules which govern us in our judgments of human nature. He exceeded in depravity all that has been imputed to the arch-foe of mankind. His wickedness was without any of those remorseful intermissions from which it has been supposed that the deepest guilt is not entirely exempt. He seemed to relish no food but pure unadulterated evil. He rejoiced in proportion to the depth of that distress of which he was the author.

His sister, by being placed most within the reach of his enmity, experienced its worst effects. She was the subject on which, by being acquainted with the means of influencing her happiness, he could try his malignant experiments with most hope of success. Her parents being high in rank and wealth, the marriage of their daughter was, of course, an object of anxious attention. There is no event on which our felicity and usefulness more materially depends, and with regard to which, therefore, the freedom of choice and the exercise of our own understanding ought to be less infringed; but this maxim is commonly disregarded in proportion to the elevation of our rank and extent of our property.

The lady made her own election; but she was one of those who acted on a comprehensive plan, and would not admit her private inclination to dictate her decision. The happiness of others, though founded on mistaken views, she did not consider as unworthy of her regard. The choice was such as was not likely to obtain the parental sanction, to whom the moral qualities of their son-in-law, though not absolutely weightless in the balance, were greatly inferior to the considerations of wealth and dignity.

The brother set no value on anything but the means of luxury and power. He was astonished at that perverseness which entertained a different conception of happiness from himself. Love and friendship he considered as groundless and chimerical, and believed that those delusions would, in people of sense, be rectified by experience; but he knew the obstinacy of his sister's attachment to these phantoms, and that to bereave her of the good they promised was the most effectual means of rendering her miserable. For this end he set himself to thwart her wishes. In the imbecility and false indulgence of his parents he found the most powerful auxiliaries. He prevailed upon them to forbid that union which wanted nothing but their concurrence, and their consent to endow her with a small portion of their patrimony, to render completely eligible. The cause was that of her happiness and the happiness of him on whom she had bestowed her heart. It behooved her, therefore, to call forth all her energies in defense of it, to weaken her brother's influence on the minds of her parents, or to win him to be her advocate. When I reflect upon her mental powers, and the advantages which should seem to flow from the circumstance of pleading in the character of daughter and sister, I can scarcely believe that her attempts miscarried. I should have imagined that all obstacles would yield before her, and particularly in a case like this, in which she must have summoned all her forces, and never have believed that she had struggled sufficiently.

Certain it is that her lot was fixed. She was not only denied the husband of her choice, but another was imposed upon her, whose recommendations were irresistible in everyone's apprehension but her own. The discarded lover was treated with every sort of contumely. Deceit and violence were employed by her brother to bring his honor, his liberty, and even his life, into hazard. All these iniquities produced no inconsiderable effect on the mind of the lady. The machinations to which her love was exposed would have exasperated him into madness, had not her most strenuous exertions been directed to appease him.

She prevailed on him at length to abandon his country, though she thereby merely turned her brother's depravity into a new channel. Her parents died without consciousness of the evils they inflicted, but they experienced a bitter retribution in the conduct of their son. He was the darling and stay of an ancient and illustrious house, but his actions reflected nothing but disgrace upon his ancestry, and threatened to bring the honors of their line to a period in his person. At their death the bulk of their patrimony devolved upon him. This he speedily consumed in gaming and riot. From splendid he descended to meaner vices. The efforts of his sister to recall him to virtue were unintermitted and fruitless. Her affection for him he converted into a means of prolonging his selfish gratifications. She decided for the best. It was no argument of weakness that she was so frequently deceived. If she had judged truly of her brother, she would have judged not only without example, but in opposition to the general experience of mankind. But she was not to be forever deceived. Her tenderness was subservient to justice. And when his vices had led him from the gaming-table to the highway, when seized at length by the ministers of law, when convicted and sentenced to transportation, her intercession was solicited when all the world knew that pardon would readily be granted to a suppliant of her rank, fortune, and character, when the criminal himself, his kindred, his friends, and even indifferent persons, implored her interference, her justice was inflexible. She knew well the incurableness of his depravity; that banishment was the mildest destiny that would befall him; that estrangement from ancient haunts and associates was the condition from which his true friends had least to fear. Finding entreaties unavailing, the wretch delivered himself to the suggestions of his malice, and he vowed to be bloodily revenged on her inflexibility. The sentence was executed. That character must indeed be monstrous from which the execution of such threats was to be dreaded. The event sufficiently showed that our fears on this head were well grounded. This event, however, was at a great distance. It was reported that the felons, of whom he was one, mutinied on board the ship in which they had been embarked. In the affray that succeeded, it was said that he was killed.

Among the nefarious deeds which he perpetrated was to be numbered the seduction of a young lady, whose heart was broken by the detection of her perfidy. The fruit of this unhappy union was a daughter. Her mother died shortly after her birth. Her father was careless of her destiny. She was consigned to the care of a hireling, who, happily for the innocent victim, performed the maternal offices for her own sake, and did not allow the want of a stipulated recompense to render her cruel or neglectful.

This orphan was sought out by the benevolence of Mrs. Lorimer and placed under her own protection. She received from her the treatment of a mother. The ties of kindred, corroborated by habit, was not the only thing that united them. That resemblance to herself which had been so deplorably defective in her brother was completely realized in his offspring. Nature seemed to have precluded every difference between them but that of age. This darling object excited in her bosom more than maternal sympathies. Her soul clung to the happiness of her *Clarice* with more ardor than to that of her own son. The latter was not only less worthy of affection, but their separation necessarily diminished their mutual confidence.

It was natural for her to look forward to the future destiny of *Clarice*. On these occasions she could not help contemplating the possibility of a union between her son and niece. Considerable advantages belonged to this scheme, yet it was the subject of hope rather than the scope of a project. The contingencies were numerous and delicate on which the ultimate desirableness of this union depended. She was far from certain that her son would be worthy of this benefit, or that, if he were worthy, his propensities would not select for themselves a different object. It was equally dubious whether the young lady would not think proper otherwise to dispose of her affections. These uncertainties could be dissipated only by time. Meanwhile she was chiefly solicitous to render them virtuous and wise.

As they advanced in years, the hopes that she had formed were annihilated. The youth was not exempt from egregious errors. In addition to this, it was manifest that the young people were disposed to regard each other in no other light than that of brother and sister. I was not unapprised of her views. I saw that their union was impossible. I was near enough to judge of the character of Clarice. My youth and intellecutal constitution made me peculiarly susceptible to female charms. I was her playfellow in childhood, and her associate in studies and amusements at a maturer age. This situation might have been suspected of a dangerous tendency. This tendency, however, was obviated by motives of which I was, for a long time, scarcely conscious.

I was habituated to consider the distinctions of rank as indelible. The obstructions that existed, to any wish that I might form, were like those of time and space, and, in their own nature, as insuperable.

Such was the state of things previous to our setting out upon our travels. Clarice was indirectly included in our correspondence. My letters were open to her inspection, and I was sometimes honored with a few complimentary lines under her own hand. On returning to my ancient abode, I was once more exposed to those sinister influences which absence had at least suspended. Various suitors had, meanwhile, been rejected. Their character, for the most part, had been such as to account for her refusal, without resorting to the supposition of a lurking or unavowed attachment.

On our meeting she greeted me in a respectful but dignified manner. Observers could discover in it nothing not corresponding to that difference of fortune which subsisted between us. If her joy, on that occasion, had in it some portion of tenderness, the softness of her temper and the peculiar circumstances in which we had been placed being considered, the most rigid censor could find no occasion for blame or suspicion.

A year passed away, but not without my attention being solicited by something new and inexplicable in my own sensations. At first I was not aware of their true cause; but the gradual progress of my feelings left me not long in doubt as to their origin. I was alarmed at the discovery, but my courage did not suddenly desert me. My hopes seemed to be extinguished the moment that I distinctly perceived the point to which they led. My mind had undergone a change. The ideas with which it was fraught were varied. The sight or recollection of Clarice was sure to occasion my mind to advert to the recent discovery, and to revolve the considerations naturally connected with it. Some latent glows and secret trepidations were likewise experienced, when, by some accident, our meetings were abrupt or our interviews unwitnessed; yet my usual tranquillity was not as yet sensibly diminished. I could bear to think of her marriage with another without painful emotions, and was anxious only that her choice should be judicious and fortunate.

My thoughts could not long continue in this state. They gradually became more ardent and museful. The image of Clarice occurred with unseasonable frequency. Its charms were enhanced by some nameless and indefinable additions. When it met me in the way I was irresistibly disposed to stop and survey it with particular attention. The pathetic cast of her features, the deep glow of her cheek, and some catch of melting music she had lately breathed, stole incessantly upon my fancy. On recovering from my thoughtful moods, I sometimes found my cheeks wet with tears that had fallen unperceived, and my bosom heaved with involuntary sighs.

These images did not content themselves with invading my wakeful hours, but, likewise, encroached upon my sleep. I could no longer resign myself to slumber with the same ease as before. When I slept, my visions were of the same impassioned tenor.

There was no difficulty in judging rightly of my situation. I knew what it was that duty exacted from me. To remain in my present situation was a chimerical project. That time and reflection would suffice to restore me to myself was a notion equally fallacious. Yet I felt an insupportable reluctance to change it. This reluctance was owing not wholly or chiefly to my growing passion, but to the attachment which bound me to the service of my lady. All my contemplations had hitherto been modelled on the belief of my remaining in my present situation during my life. My mildest anticipations had never fashioned an event like this. Any misfortune was light in comparison with that which tore me from her presence and service. But, should I ultimately resolve to separate, how should I communicate my purpose? The pain of parting would scarcely be less on her side than on mine. Could I consent to be the author of disquietude to her? I had consecrated all my faculties to her service. This was the recompense which it was in my power to make for the benefits that I had received. Would not this procedure bear the appearance of the basest ingratitude? The shadow of an imputation like this was more excruciating than the rack.

What motive could I assign for my conduct? The truth must not be told. This would be equivalent to supplicating for a new benefit. It would more become me to lessen than increase my obligations. Among all my imaginations on this subject, the possibility of a mutual passion never occurred to me. I could not be blind to the essential distinctions that subsist among men. I could expatiate, like others, on the futility of ribbons and titles, and on the dignity that was annexed to skill and virtue; but these, for the most part, were the incoherences of speculation, and in no degree influenced the stream of my actions and practical sentiments. The barrier that existed in the present case I deemed insurmountable. This was not even the subject of doubt. In disclosing the truth, I should be conceived to be soliciting my lady's mercy and intercession; but this would be the madness of presumption. Let me impress her with any other opinion than that I go in search of the happiness that I have lost under her roof. Let me save her generous heart from the pangs which this persuasion would infallibly produce.

I could form no stable resolutions. I seemed unalterably convinced of the necessity of separation, and yet could not execute my design. When I had wrought up my mind to the intention of explaining myself on the next interview, when the next interview took place my tongue was powerless. I admitted any excuse for postponing my design, and gladly admitted any topic, however foreign to my purpose.

It must not be imagined that my health sustained no injury from this conflict of my passions. My patroness perceived this alteration. She inquired with the most affectionate solicitude into the cause. It could not be explained. I could safely make light of it, and represented it as something which would probably disappear of itself, as it originated without any adequate cause. She was obliged to acquiesce in my imperfect account.

Day after day passed in this state of fluctuation. I was conscious of the dangers of delay, and that procrastination, without rendering the task less necessary, augmented its difficulties. At length, summoning my resolution, I demanded an audience. She received me with her usual affability. Common topics were started; but she saw the confusion and trepidation of my thoughts, and quickly relinquished them. She then noticed to me what she had observed, and mentioned the anxiety which these appearances had given her. She reminded me of the maternal regard which she had always manifested towards me, and appealed to my own heart

whether anything could be said in vindication of that reserve with
which I had lately treated her, and urged me, as I valued her good
opinion, to explain the cause of a dejection *that was too visible.*

To all this I could make but one answer: "Think me not, madam,
perverse or ungrateful. I came just now to apprise you of a resolution that I had formed. I cannot explain the motives that induce
me. In this case, to lie to you would be unpardonable, and, since
I cannot assign my true motives, I will not mislead you by false
representations. I came to inform you of my intention to leave your
service, and to retire, with the fruits of your bounty, to my native
village, where I shall spend my life, I hope, in peace."

Her surprise at this declaration was beyond measure. She could
not believe her ears. She had not heard me rightly. She compelled
me to repeat it. Still I was jesting. I could not possibly mean what
my words imported.

I assured her, in terms still more explicit, that my resolution
was taken and was unalterable, and again entreated her to spare
me the task of assigning my motives.

This was a strange determination. What could be the grounds
of this new scheme? What could be the necessity of hiding them
from her? This mystery was not to be endured. She could by no
means away with it. She thought it hard that I should abandon her
at this time, when she stood in particular need of my assistance
and advice. She would refuse nothing to make my situation eligible. I had only to point out where she was deficient in her treatment of me, and she would endeavor to supply it. She was willing
to augment my emoluments in any degree that I desired. She could
not think of parting with me; but, at any rate, she must be informed
of my motives.

"It is a hard task," answered I, "that I have imposed upon myself. I foresaw its difficulties, and this foresight has hitherto prevented me from undertaking it; but the necessity by which I am
impelled will no longer be withstood. I am determined to go; but
to say why is impossible. I hope I shall not bring upon myself the
imputation of ingratitude; but this imputation, more intolerable
than any other, must be borne, if it cannot be avoided but by this
disclosure.

"Keep your motives to yourself," said she. "I have too good an
opinion of you to suppose that you would practice concealment
without good reason. I merely desire you to remain where you
are. Since you will not tell me why you take up this new scheme,

I can only say that it is impossible there should be any advantage in this scheme. I will not hear of it, I tell you. Therefore, submit to my decree with a good grace."

Notwithstanding this prohibition, I persisted in declaring that my determination was fixed, and that the motives that governed me would allow of no alternative.

"So, you will go, will you, whether I will or no? I have no power to detain you? You will regard nothing that I can say?"

"Believe me, madam, no resolution ever was formed after a more vehement struggle. If my motives were known, you would not only cease to oppose, but would hasten, my departure. Honor me so far with your good opinion as to believe that, in saying this, I say nothing but the truth, and render my duty less burdensome by cheerfully acquiescing in its dictates."

"I would," replied the lady, "I could find somebody that has more power over you than I have. Whom shall I call in to aid me in this arduous task?"

"Nay, dear madam, if I can resist your entreaties, surely no other can hope to succeed."

"I am not sure of that," said my friend, archly; "there is one person in the world whose supplications, I greatly suspect, you would not withstand."

"Whom do you mean?" said I, in some trepidation.

"You will know presently. Unless I can prevail upon you, I shall be obliged to call for assistance."

"Spare me the pain of repeating that no power on earth can change my resolution."

"That's a fib," she rejoined, with increased archness. "You know it is. If a certain person entreat you to stay, you will easily comply. I see I cannot hope to prevail by my own strength. That is a mortifying consideration, but we must not part; that is a point settled. If nothing else will do, I must go and fetch my advocate. Stay here a moment."

I had scarcely time to breathe, before she returned, leading in Clarice. I did not yet comprehend the meaning of this ceremony. The lady was overwhelmed with sweet confusion. Averted eyes and reluctant steps might have explained to me the purpose of this meeting, if I had believed that purpose to be possible. I felt the necessity of new fortitude, and struggled to recollect the motives that had hitherto sustained me.

"There!" said my patroness; "I have been endeavoring to per-

suade this young man to live with us a little longer. He is determined, it seems, to change his abode. He will not tell why, and
I do not care to know, unless I could show his reasons to be groundless. I have merely remonstrated with him on the folly of his
scheme, but he has proved refractory to all I can say. Perhaps your
efforts may meet with better success."

Clarice said not a word. My own embarrassment equally disabled me from speaking. Regarding us both, for some time, with
a benign aspect, Mrs. Lorimer resumed, taking a hand of each
and joining them together:

"I very well know what it was that suggested this scheme. It is
strange that you should suppose me so careless an observer as not
to note, or not to understand, your situation. I am as well acquainted with what is passing in your heart as you yourself are, but why
are you so anxious to conceal it? You know less of the adventurous-
ness of love than I should have suspected. But I will not trifle with
your feelings.

"You, Clithero, know the wishes that I once cherished. I had
hoped that my son would have found, in this darling child, an object worthy of his choice, and that my girl would have preferred
him to all others. But I have long since discovered that this could
not be. They are nowise suited to each other. There is one thing
in the next place desirable, and now my wishes are accomplished.
I see that you love each other; and never, in my opinion, was a
passion more rational and just. I should think myself the worst of
beings if I did not contribute all in my power to your happiness.
There is not the shadow of objection to your union. I know your
scruples, Clithero, and am sorry to see that you harbor them for
a moment. Nothing is more unworthy of your good sense.

"I found out this girl long ago. Take my word for it, young man,
she does not fall short of you in the purity and tenderness of her
attachment. What need is there of tedious preliminaries? I will
leave you together, and hope you will not be long in coming to a
mutual understanding. Your union cannot be completed too soon
for my wishes. Clarice is my only and darling daughter. As to you,
Clithero, expect henceforth that treatment from me, not only to
which your own merit entitles you, but which is due the husband
of my daughter." With these words she retired, and left us
together.

Great God! deliver me from the torments of this remembrance.
That a being by whom I was snatched from penury and brutal ig-

norance, exalted to some rank in the intelligent creation, reared to affluence and honor, and thus, at last, spontaneously endowed with all that remained to complete the sum of my felicity, that a being like this—but such thoughts must not yet be. I must shut them out, or I shall never arrive at the end of my tale. My efforts have been thus far successful. I have hitherto been able to deliver a coherent narrative. Let the last words that I shall speak afford some glimmering of my better days. Let me execute without faltering the only task that remains for me.

VI

How propitious, how incredible, was this event! I could scarcely confide in the testimony of my senses. Was it true that Clarice was before me, that she was prepared to countenance my presumption, that she had slighted obstacles which I had deemed insurmountable, that I was fondly beloved by her, and should shortly be admitted to the possession of so inestimable a good? I will not repeat the terms in which I poured forth, at her feet, the raptures of my gratitude. My impetuosity soon extorted from Clarice a confirmation of her mother's declaration. An unrestrained intercourse was thenceforth established between us. Dejection and languor gave place, in my bosom, to the irradiations of joy and hope. My flowing fortunes seemed to have attained their utmost and immutable height.

Alas! They were destined to ebb with unspeakably greater rapidity, and to leave me, in a moment, stranded and wrecked.

Our nuptials would have been solemnized without delay, had not a melancholy duty interfered. Clarice had a friend in a distant part of the kingdom. Her health had long been the prey of a consumption. She was now evidently tending to dissolution. In this extremity she entreated her friend to afford her the consolation of her presence. The only wish that remained was to die in her arms.

This request could not but be willingly complied with. It became me patiently to endure the delay that would thence arise to the completion of my wishes. Considering the urgency and mournfulness of the occasion, it was impossible for me to murmur, and the affectionate Clarice would suffer nothing to interfere with the duty which she owed to her dying friend. I accompanied her on this journey, remained with her a few days, and then parted from her to return to the metropolis. It was not imagined that it would be necessary to prolong her absence beyond a month. When I bade her farewell, and informed her on what day I proposed to return for her, I felt no decay of my satisfaction. My thoughts were bright and full of exultation. Why was not some intimation afforded me of the snares that lay in my path? In the train laid for my de-

74

struction, the agent had so skillfully contrived that my security was not molested by the faintest omen.

I hasten to the crisis of my tale. I am almost dubious of my strength. The nearer I approach to it, the stronger is my aversion. My courage, instead of gathering force as I proceed, decays. I am willing to dwell still longer on preliminary circumstances. There are other incidents without which my story would be lame. I retail them because they afford me a kind of respite from horrors at the thought of which every joint in my frame trembles. They must be endured, but that infirmity may be forgiven which makes me inclined to procrastinate my suffering.

I mentioned the lover whom my patroness was compelled, by the machinations of her brother, to discard. More than twenty years had passed since their separation. His birth was mean and he was without fortune. His profession was that of a surgeon. My lady not only prevailed upon him to abandon his country, but enabled him to do this by supplying his necessities from her own purse. His excellent understanding was, for a time, obscured by passion; but it was not difficult for my lady ultimately to obtain his concurrence to all her schemes. He saw and adored the rectitude of her motives, did not disdain to accept her gifts, and projected means for maintaining an epistolary intercourse during their separation.

Her interest procured him a post in the service of the East India Company. She was, from time to time, informed of his motions. A war broke out between the Company and some of the native powers. He was present at a great battle in which the English were defeated. She could trace him by his letters and by other circumstances thus far, but here the thread was discontinued, and no means which she employed could procure any tidings of him. Whether he was captive, or dead, continued, for several years, to be merely matter of conjecture.

On my return to Dublin, I found my patroness engaged in conversation with a stranger. She introduced us to each other in a manner that indicated the respect which she entertained for us both. I surveyed and listened to him with considerable attention. His aspect was noble and ingenuous, but his sunburnt and rugged features bespoke a various and boisterous pilgrimage. The furrows of his brow were the products of vicissitude and hardship, rather than of age. His accents were fiery and energetic, and the impassioned boldness of his address, as well as the tenor of his discourse, full of allusions to the past, and regrets that the course of events had not been different, made me suspect something extraordinary in his character.

As soon as he left us, my lady explained who he was. He was no other than the object of her youthful attachment, who had, a few days before, dropped among us as from the skies. He had a long and various story to tell. He had accounted for his silence by enumerating the incidents of his life. He had escaped from the prisons of Hyder, had wandered on foot, and under various disguises, through the northern district of Hindostan. He was sometimes a scholar of Benares, and sometimes a disciple of the Mosque. According to the exigencies of the times, he was a pilgrim to Mecca or to Juggernaut. By a long, circuitous, and perilous route, he at length arrived at the Turkish capital. Here he resided for several years, deriving a precarious subsistence from the profession of a surgeon. He was obliged to desert this post, in consequence of a duel between two Scotsmen. One of them had embraced the Greek religion, and was betrothed to the daughter of a wealthy trader of that nation. He perished in the conflict, and the family of the lady not only procured the execution of his antagonist, but threatened to involve all those who were known to be connected with him in the same ruin.

His life being thus endangered, it became necessary for him to seek a new residence. He fled from Constantinople with such precipitation as reduced him to the lowest poverty. He had traversed the Indian conquests of Alexander, as a mendicant. In the same character, he now wandered over the native country of Philip and Philopoemen. He passed safely through multiplied perils, and finally, embarking at Salonica, he reached Venice. He descended through the passes of the Apennines into Tuscany. In this journey he suffered a long detention from banditti, by whom he was waylaid. In consequence of his harmless deportment, and a seasonable display of his chirurgical skill, they granted him his liberty, and compelled him to endure their society. The time was not misemployed which he spent immured in caverns and carousing with robbers. His details were eminently singular and curious, and evinced the acuteness of his penetration, as well as the steadfastness of his courage.

After emerging from these wilds, he found his way along the banks of the Arno to Leghorn. Thence he procured a passage to America, whence he had just returned, with many additions to his experience, but none to his fortune.

This was a remarkable event. It did not at first appear how far its consequences would extend. The lady was, at present, disengaged and independent. Though the passion which clouded her early prosperity was extinct, time had not diminished the worth of her friend, and they were far from having reached that age when love becomes chimerical and marriage folly. A confidential intercourse was immediately established between them. The bounty of Mrs. Lorimer soon divested her friend of all fear of poverty. "At any rate," said she, "he shall wander no farther, but shall be comfortably situated for the rest of his life." All his scruples were vanquished by the reasonableness of her remonstrances and the vehemence of her solicitations.

A cordial intimacy grew between me and the newly-arrived. Our interviews were frequent, and our communications without reserve. He detailed to me the result of his experience, and expatiated without end on the history of his actions and opinions. He related the adventures of his youth, and dwelt upon all the circumstances of his attachment to my patroness. On this subject I had heard only general details. I continually found cause, in the course of his narrative, to revere the illustrious qualitites of my lady, and to weep at the calamities to which the infernal malice of her brother had subjected her.

The tale of that man's misdeeds, amplified and dramatized by the indignant eloquence of this historian, oppressed me with astonishment. If a poet had drawn such a portrait, I should have been prone to suspect the soundness of his judgment. Till now I had imagined that no character was uniform and unmixed, and my theory of the passions did not enable me to account for a propensity gratified merely by evil, and delighting in shrieks and agony for their own sake.

It was natural to suggest to my friend, when expatiating on this theme, an inquiry as to how far subsequent events had obliterated the impressions that were then made, and as to the plausibility of reviving, at this more auspicious period, his claims on the heart of his friend. When he thought proper to notice these hints, he gave me to understand that time had made no essential alteration in his sentiments in this respect; that he still fostered a hope, to which every day added new vigor; that, whatever was the ultimate event, he trusted in his fortitude to sustain it, if adverse, and in his wisdom to extract from it the most valuable consequences, if it should prove properous.

The progress of things was not unfavorable to his hopes. She treated his insinuations and professions with levity; but her arguments seemed to be urged with no other view than to afford an opportunity of confutation; and, since there was no abatement of familiarity and kindness, there was room to hope that the affair would terminate agreeably to his wishes.

VII

Clarice, meanwhile, was absent. Her friend seemed, at the end of a month, to be little less distant from the grave than at first. My impatience would not allow me to wait till her death. I visited her, but was once more obliged to return alone. I arrived late in the city, and, being greatly fatigued, I retired almost immediately to my chamber.

On hearing of my arrival, Sarsefield hastened to see me. He came to my bedside, and such, in his opinion, was the importance of the tidings which he had to communicate, that he did not scruple to rouse me from a deep sleep——

At this period of his narrative, Clithero stopped. His complexion varied from one degree of paleness to another. His brain appeared to suffer some severe constriction. He desired to be excused, for a few minutes, from proceeding. In a short time he was relieved from this paroxysm, and resumed his tale with an accent tremulous at first, but acquiring stability and force as he went on:

On waking, as I have said, I found my friend seated at my bedside. His countenance exhibited various tokens of alarm. As soon as I perceived who it was, I started, exclaiming, "What is the matter?"

He sighed. "Pardon," said he, "this unseasonable intrusion. A light matter would not have occasioned it. I have waited for two days past, in an agony of impatience, for your return. Happily you are, at last, come. I stand in the utmost need of your counsel and aid."

"Heaven defend!" cried I. "This is a terrible prelude. You may, of course, rely upon my assistance and advice. What is it that you have to propose?"

"Tuesday evening," he answered, "I spent here. It was late before I returned to my lodgings. I was in he act of lifting my hand to the bell, when my eye was caught by a person standing close to the wall, at the distance of ten paces. His attitude was that of

79

one employed in watching my motions. His face was turned towards me, and happened, at that moment, to be fully illuminated by the rays of a globe-lamp that hung over the door. I instantly recognized his features. I was petrified. I had no power to execute my design, or even to move, but stood, for some seconds, gazing upon him. He was in no degree disconcerted by the eagerness of my scrutiny. He seemed perfectly indifferent to the consequences of being known. At length he slowly turned his eyes to another quarter, but without changing his posture, or the sternness of his looks. I cannot describe to you the shock which this encounter produced in me. At last I went into the house, and have ever since been excessively uneasy."

"I do not see any ground for uneasiness."

"You do not then suspect who this person is?"

"No."

"It is Arthur Wiatte."

"Good heaven! It is impossible. What! my lady's brother?"

"The same."

"It cannot be. Were we not assured of his death? That he perished in a mutiny on board the vessel in which he was embarked for transportation?'

"Such was rumor, which is easily mistaken. My eyes cannot be deceived in this case. I should as easily fail to recognize his sister, when I first met her, as him. This is the man; whether once dead or not, he is at present alive, and in this city."

"But has anything since happened to confirm you in this opinion?"

"Yes, there has. As soon as I had recovered from my first surprise, I began to reflect upon the measures proper to be taken. This was the identical Arthur Wiatte. You know his character. No time was likely to change the principles of such a man, but his appearance sufficiently betrayed the incurableness of his habits. The same sullen and atrocious passions were written in his visage. You recollect the vengeance which Wiatte denounced against his sister. There is everything to dread from his malignity. How to obviate the danger, I know not. I thought, however, of one expedient. It might serve a present purpose, and something better might suggest itself on your return.

"I came hither early the next day. Old Gowan, the porter, is well acquainted with Wiatte's story. I mentioned to him that I had reason to think that he had returned. I charged him to have a watch-

ful eye upon everyone that knocked at the gate, and that, if this
person should come, by no means to admit him. The old man
promised faithfully to abide by my directions. His terrors, indeed,
were greater than mine, and he knew the importance of excluding
Wiatte from these walls."

"Did you not inform my lady of this?"

"No. In what way could I tell it to her? What end could it answer?
Why should I make her miserable? But I have not done. Yesterday morning Gowan took me aside, and informed me that Wiatte
had made his appearance, the day before, at the gate. He knew him,
he said, in a moment. He demanded to see the lady, but the old
man told him she was engaged, and could not be seen. He assumed
peremptory and haughty airs, and asserted that his business was
of such importance as not to endure a moment's delay. Gowan persisted in his first refusal. He retired with great reluctance, but said
he should return tomorrow, when he should insist upon admission
to the presence of the lady. I have inquired, and find that he has
not repeated his visit. What is to be done?"

I was equally at a loss with my friend. This incident was so un-
looked for. What might not be dreaded from the monstrous depravity of Wiatte? His menaces of vengeance against his sister still
rung in my ears. Some means of eluding them were indispensable.
Could law be resorted to? Against an evil like this, no legal provision had been made. Nine years had elapsed since his transportation. Seven years was the period of his exile. In returning, therefore, he had committed no crime. His person could not be law-
fully molested. We were justified merely in repelling an attack.
But suppose we should appeal to law: could this be done without
the knowledge and concurrence of the lady? She would never permit it. Her heart was incapable of fear from this quarter. She would
spurn at the mention of precautions against the hatred of her brother. Her inquietude would merely be awakened on his own account.

I was overwhelmed with perplexity. Perhaps if he were sought
out, and some judgment formed of the kind of danger to be dreaded
from him, by a knowledge of his situation and views, some expedient might be thence suggested.

But how should his haunts be discovered? This was easy. He had
intimated the design of applying again for admission to his sister.
Let a person be stationed near at hand, who, being furnished with
an adequate description of his person and dress, shall mark him
when he comes, and follow him when he retires, and shall forth-

with impart to us the information on that head which he shall be able to collect.

My friend concurred in this scheme. No better could, for the present, be suggested. Here ended our conference.

I was thus supplied with a new subject of reflection. It was calculated to fill my mind with dreary forebodings. The future was no longer a scene of security and pleasure. It would be hard for those to partake of our fears who did not partake of our experience. The existence of Wiatte was the canker that had blasted the felicity of my patroness. In his reappearance on the stage there was something portentous. It seemed to include in it consequences of the utmost moment, without my being able to discover what these consequences were.

That Sarsefield should be so quickly followed by his arch-foe; that they started anew into existence, without any previous intimation, in a manner wholly unexpected, and at the same period—it seemed as if there lurked, under those appearances, a tremendous significance, which human sagacity could not uncover. My heart sunk within me when I reflected that this was the father of my Clarice. He by whose cruelty her mother was torn from the enjoyment of untarnished honor, and consigned to infamy and an untimely grave. He by whom herself was abandoned in the helplessness of infancy, and left to be the prey of obdurate avarice, and the victim of wretches who traffic in virgin innocence. Who had done all that in him lay to devote her youth to guilt and misery. What were the limits of his power? How may he exert the parental prerogatives?

To sleep, while these images were haunting me, was impossible. I passed the night in continual motion. I strode, without ceasing, across the floor of my apartment. My mind was wrought to a higher pitch than I had ever before experienced. The occasion, accurately considered, was far from justifying the ominous inquietudes which I then felt. How, then, should I account for them?

Sarsefield probably enjoyed his usual slumber. His repose might not be perfectly serene, but when he ruminated on impending or possible calamities his tongue did not cleave to his mouth, his throat was not parched with unquenchable thirst, he was not incessantly stimulated to employ his superfluous fertility of thought in motion. If I trembled for the safety of her whom I loved, and whose safety was endangered by being the daughter of this miscreant, had he not equal reason to fear for her whom he also loved, and who, as the sister of this ruffian, was encompassed by the most alarming perils? Yet he probably was calm while I was harassed by anxieties.

Alas! The difference was easily explained. Such was the beginning of a series ordained to hurry me to swift destruction. Such were the primary tokens of the presence of that power by whose accursed machinations I was destined to fall. You are startled at this declaration. It is one to which you have been little accustomed. Perhaps you regard it merely as an effusion of frenzy. I know what I am saying. I do not build upon conjectures and surmises. I care not, indeed, for your doubts. Your conclusion may be fashioned at your pleasure. Would to Heaven that my belief were groundless, and that I had no reason to believe my intellects to have been perverted by diabolical instigations!

I could procure no sleep that night. After Sarsefield's departure I did not even lie down. It seemed to me that I could not obtain the benefits of repose otherwise than by placing my lady beyond the possibility of danger.

I met Sarsefield the next day. In pursuance of the scheme which had been adopted by us on the preceding evening, a person was selected and commissioned to watch the appearance of Wiatte. The day passed as usual with respect to the lady. In the evening she was surrounded by a few friends. Into this number I was now admitted. Sarsefield and myself made a part of this company. Various topics were discussed with ease and sprightliness. Her societies were composed of both sexes, and seemed to have monopolized all the ingenuity and wit that existed in the metropolis.

After a slight repast the company dispersed. This separation took place earlier than usual, on account of a slight indisposition in *Mrs. Lorimer*. Sarsefield and I went out together. We took that opportunity of examining our agent, and, receiving no satisfaction from him, we dismissed him for that night, enjoining him to hold himself in readiness for repeating the experiment tomorrow. My friend directed his steps homeward, and I proceeded to execute a commission with which I had charged myself.

A few days before, a large sum had been deposited in the hands of a banker, for the use of my lady. It was the amount of a debt which had lately been recovered. It was lodged here for the purpose of being paid on demand of her or her agents. It was my present business to receive this money. I had deferred the performance of this engagement to this late hour, on account of certain preliminaries which were necessary to be adjusted.

Having received this money, I prepared to return home. The inquietude which had been occasioned by Sarsefield's intelligence had not incapacitated me from performing my usual daily occupaions. It was a theme to which, at every interval of leisure from business or discourse, I did not fail to return. At those times I employed myself in examining the subject on all sides; in supposing particular emergencies, and delineating the conduct that was proper to be observed on each. My daily thoughts were, by no means so fear-inspiring as the meditations of the night had been.

As soon as I left the banker's door, my meditations fell into this channel. I again reviewed the recent occurrences, and imagined the consequences likely to flow from them. My deductions were not, on this occasion, peculiarly distressful. The return of darkness had added nothing to my apprehensions. I regarded Wiatte merely as one against whose malice it was wise to employ the most vigilant precautions. In revolving these precautions nothing occurred that was new. The danger appeared without unusual aggravations, and the expedients that offered themselves to my choice were viewed with a temper not more sanguine or despondent than before.

In this state of mind I began and continued my walk. The distance was considerable between my own habitation and that which I had left. My way lay chiefly through populous and well-frequented streets. In one part of the way, however, it was at the option of the passenger either to keep along the large streets, or considerably to shorten the journey by turning into a dark, crooked, and narrow lane. Being familiar with every part of this metropolis, and deeming it advisable to take the shortest and obscurest road, I turned into the alley. I proceeded without interruption to the next turning. One night-officer, distinguished by his usual ensigns, was the only person who passed me. I had gone three steps beyond when I perceived a man by my side. I had scarcely time to notice this circumstance, when a hoarse voice exclaimed, "Damn ye, villain, ye're a dead man!"

At the same moment a pistol flashed at my ear, and a report followed. This, however, produced no other effect than, for a short space, to overpower my senses. I staggered back, but did not fall.

The ball, as I afterwards discovered, had grazed my forehead, but without making any dangerous impression. The assassin, perceiving that his pistol had been ineffectual, muttered, in an enraged tone, "This shall do your business!" At the same time, he drew a knife forth from his bosom.

I was able to distinguish this action by the rays of a distant lamp, which glistened on the blade. All this passed in an instant. The attack was so abrupt that my thoughts could not be suddenly recalled from the confusion into which they were thrown. My exertions were mechanical. My will might be said to be passive, and it was only by retrospect and a contemplation of consequences that I became fully informed of the nature of the scene.

If my assailant had disappeared as soon as he had discharged the pistol, my state of extreme surprise might have slowly given place to resolution and activity. As it was, my sense was no sooner struck by the reflection from the blade, than my hand, as if by spontaneous energy, was thrust into my pocket. I drew forth a pistol.

He lifted up his weapon to strike, but it dropped from his powerless fingers. He fell, and his groans informed me that I had managed my arms with more skill than my adversary. The noise of this encounter soon attracted spectators. Lights were brought, and my antagonist discovered bleeding at my feet. I explained, as briefly as I was able, the scene which they witnessed. The prostrate person was raised by two men, and carried into a public house nigh at hand. I had not lost my presence of mind. I at once perceived the propriety of administering assistance to the wounded man. I dispatched, therefore, one of the bystanders for a surgeon of considerable eminence, who lived at a small distance, and to whom I was well known. The man was carried into an inner apartment and laid upon the floor. It was not till now that I had a suitable opportunity of ascertaining who it was with whom I had been engaged. I now looked upon his face. The paleness of death could not conceal his well-known features. It was Wiatte himself who was breathing his last groans at my feet!

The surgeon, whom I had summoned, attended, but immediately perceived the condition of his patient to be hopeless. In a quarter of an hour he expired. During this interval, he was insensible to all around him. I was known to the surgeon, the landlord, and some of the witnesses. The case needed little explanation. The accident reflected no guilt upon me. The landlord was charged with the care of the corpse till the morning, and I was allowed to return home, without further impediment.

VIII

Till now my mind had been swayed by the urgencies of this occasion. These reflections were excluded, which rushed tumultuously upon me the moment I was at leisure to receive them. Without foresight of a previous moment, an entire change had been wrought in my condition.

I had been oppressed with a sense of the danger that flowed from the existence of this man. By what means the peril could be annihilated, and we be placed in security from his attempts, no efforts of mind could suggest. To devise these means, and employ them with success, demanded, as I conceived, the most powerful sagacity and the firmest courage. Now the danger was no more. The intelligence in which plans of mischief might be generated was extinguished or flown. Lifeless were the hands ready to execute the dictates of that intelligence. The contriver of enormous evil was, in one moment, bereft of the power and the will to injure. Our past tranquillity had been owing to the belief of his death. Fear and dismay had resumed their dominion when the mistake was discovered. But now we might regain possession of our wonted confidence. I had beheld with my own eyes the lifeless corpse of our implacable adversary. Thus, in a moment, had terminated his long and flagitious career. His restless indignation, his malignant projects, that had so long occupied the stage and been so fertile of calamity, were now at an end!

In the course of my meditations, the idea of the death of this man had occurred, and it bore the appearance of a desirable event. Yet it was little qualified to tranquillize my fears. In the long catalogue of contingencies, this, indeed, was to be found; but it was as little likely to happen as any other. It could not happen without a series of anterior events paving the way for it. If his death came from us, it must be the theme of design. It must spring from laborious circumvention and deep-laid stratagems.

No. He was dead. I had killed him. What had I done? I had meditated nothing. I was impelled by an unconscious necessity. Had the assailant been my father, the consequence would have been the same. My understanding had been neutral. Could it be? In a space so short, was it possible that so tremendous a deed had been executed? Was I not deceived by some portentous vision? I had witnessed the convulsions and last agonies of Wiatte. He was no more, and I was his destroyer!

Such was the state of my mind for some time after this dreadful event. Previously to it I was calm, considerate, and self-collected. I marked the way that I was going. Passing objects were observed. If I adverted to the series of my own reflections, my attention was not seized and fastened by them. I could disengage myself at pleasure, and could pass, without difficulty, from attention to the world within, to the contemplation of that without.

Now my liberty, in this respect, was at an end. I was fettered, confounded, smitten with excess of thought, and laid prostrate with wonder! I no longer attended to my steps. When I emerged from my stupor, I found that I had trodden back the way which I had lately come, and had arrived within sight of the banker's door. I checked myself, and once more turned my steps homeward.

This seemed to be a hint for entering into new reflections. "The deed," said I, "is irretrievable. I have killed the brother of my patroness, the father of my love."

This suggestion was new. It instantly involved me in terror and perplexity. How shall I communicate the tidings? What effect will they produce? My lady's sagacity is obscured by the benevolence of her temper. Her brother was sordidly wicked—a hoary ruffian, to whom the language of pity was as unintelligible as the gabble of monkeys. His heart was fortified against compunction, by the atrocious habits of forty years; he lived only to interrupt her peace, to confute the promises of virtue, and convert to rancor and reproach the fair fame of fidelity.

He was her brother still. As a human being, his depravity was never beyond the health-restoring power of repentance. His heart, so long as it beat, was accessible to remorse. The singularity of his birth had made her regard this being as more intimately her brother than would have happened in different circumstances. It was her obstinate persuasion that their fates were blended. The rumor of his death she had never credited. It was a topic of congratulation to her friends, but of mourning and distress to her. That he would one day reappear upon the stage, and assume the dignity of virtue, was a source of consolation with which she would never consent to part.

Her character was now known. When the doom of exile was

pronounced upon him, she deemed it incumbent on her to vindicate herself from aspersions founded on misconceptions of her
motives in refusing her interference. The manuscript, though unpublished, was widely circulated. None could resist her simple
and touching eloquence, nor rise from the perusal without resign-
ing his heart to the most impetuous impulses of admiration, and
enlisting himself among the eulogists of her justice and her fortitude. This was the only monument, in a written form, of her genius.
As such it was engraven on my memory. The picture that it described was the constant companion of my thoughts.

Alas! It had, perhaps, been well for me if it had been buried in
eternal oblivion. I read in it the condemnation of my deed, the
agonies she was preparing to suffer, and the indignation that would
overflow upon the author of so signal a calamity.

I had rescued my life by the sacrifice of his. Whereas I should
have died. Wretched and precipitate coward! What had become
of my boasted gratitude? Such was the zeal that I had vowed to
her. Such the services which it was the business of my life to perform. I had snatched her brother from existence. I had torn from
her the hope which she so ardently and indefatigably cherished.
From a contemptible and dastardly regard to my own safety I had
failed in the moment of trial, and when called upon by Heaven
to evince sincerity of my professions.

She had treated my professions lightly. My vows of eternal devotion she had rejected with lofty disinterestedness. She had ar-
raigned my impatience of obligation as criminal, and condemned
every scheme I had projected for freeing myself from the burden
which her beneficence had laid upon me. The impassioned and
vehement anxiety with which, in former days, she had deprecated
the vengeance of her lover against Wiatte, rung in my ears. My
senses were shocked anew by the dreadful sounds, "Touch not
my brother. Wherever you meet with him, of whatever outrage
he be guilty, suffer him to pass in safety. Despise me; abandon
me; kill me. All this I can bear even from you; but spare, I implore
you, my unhappy brother. The stroke that deprives him of life will
not only have the same effect upon me, but will set my portion
in everlasting misery."

To these supplications I had been deaf. It is true I had not rushed
upon him unarmed, intending no injury nor expecting any. Of that
degree of wickedness I was, perhaps, incapable. Alas! I have immersed myself sufficiently deep in crimes. I have trampled under

foot every motive dear to the heart of honor. I have shown myself unworthy the society of men.

Such were the turbulent suggestions of that moment. My pace slackened. I stopped, and was obliged to support myself against a wall. The sickness that had seized my heart penetrated every part of my frame. There was but one thing wanting to complete my distraction. "My lady," said I, "believed her fate to be blended with that of Wiatte. Who shall affirm that the persuasion is a groundless one? She had lived and prospered, notwithstanding the general belief that her brother was dead. She would not hearken to the rumor. Why? Because nothing less than indubitable evidence would suffice to convince her? Because the counter-intimation flowed from an infallible source? How can the latter supposition be confuted? Has she not predicted the event?

"The period of terrible fulfillment has arrived. The same blow that bereaved *him* of life has likewise ratified her doom.

"She has been deceived. It is nothing more, perhaps, than a fond imagination. It matters not. Who knows not the cogency of faith? That the pulses of life are at the command of the will? The bearer of these tidings will be the messenger of death. A fatal sympathy will seize her. She will shrink, and swoon, and perish, at the news!

"Fond and short-sighted wretch! This is the price thou hast given for security. In the rashness of thy thought, thou saidst, 'Nothing is wanting but his death to restore us to confidence and safety.' Lo! the purchase is made. Havoc and despair, that were restrained during his life, were let loose by his last sigh. Now only is destruction made sure. Thy lady, thy Clarice, thy friend, and thyself are, by this act, involved in irretrievable and common ruin!"

I started from my attitude. I was scarcely conscious of any transition. The interval was fraught with stupor and amazement. It seemed as if my senses had been hushed in sleep, while the powers of locomotion were unconsciously exerted to bear me to my chamber. By whatever means the change was effected, there I was.

I have been able to proceed thus far. I can scarcely believe the testimony of my memory that assures me of this. My task is almost executed; but whence shall I obtain strength enough to finish it? What I have told is light as gossamer, compared with the insupportable and crushing horrors of that which is to come. Heaven, in token of its vengeance, will enable me to proceed. It is fitting that my scene should thus close.

My fancy began to be infected with the errors of my understanding. The mood into which my mind was plunged was incapable of any propitious intermission. All within me was tempestuous and dark. My ears were accessible to no sounds but those of shrieks and lamentations. It was deepest midnight, and all the noises of a great metropolis were hushed. Yet I listened as if to catch some strain of the dirge that was begun. Sable robes, sobs, and a dreary solemnity encompassed me on all sides. I was haunted to despair by images of death, imaginary clamors, and the train of funeral pageantry. I seemed to have passed forward to a distant era of my life. The effects which were to come were already realized. The foresight of misery created it, and set me in the midst of that hell which I feared.

From a paroxysm like this the worst might reasonably be dreaded, yet the next step to destruction was not suddenly taken. I paused on the brink of the precipice, as if to survey the depth of that frenzy that invaded me; was able to ponder on the scene, and deliberate, in a state that partook of calm, on the circumstances of my situation. My mind was harassed by the repetition of one idea. Conjecture deepened into certainty. I could place the object in no light which did not corroborate the persuasion that, in the act committed, I had insured the destruction of my lady. At length my mind, somewhat relieved from the tempest of my fears, began to trace and analyze the consequences which I dreaded.

The fate of Wiatte would inevitably draw along with it that of his sister. In what way would this effect be produced? Were they linked together by a sympathy whose influence was independent of sensible communication? Could she arrive at a knowledge of his miserable end by other than verbal means? I had heard of such extraordinary copartnerships in being and modes of instantaneous intercourse among beings locally distant. Was this a new instance of the subtlety of mind? Had she already endured his agonies, and like him already ceased to breathe?

Every hair bristled at this horrible suggestion. But the force of sympathy might be chimerical. Buried in sleep, or engaged in careless meditation, the instrument by which her destiny might be accomplished was the steel of an assassin. A series of events, equally beyond the reach of foresight with those which had just happened, might introduce, with equal abruptness, a similar disaster. What, at that moment, was her condition? Reposing in safety in her chamber, as her family imagined? But were they not deceived? Was she not a mangled corpse? Whatever were her situation, it could not be ascertained, except by extraordinary means, till the morning. Was it wise to defer the scrutiny till then? Why not instantly investigate the truth?

These ideas passed rapidly through my mind. A considerable portion of time and amplification of phrase are necessary to exhibit, verbally, ideas contemplated in a space of incalculable brevity. With the same rapidity I conceived the resolution of determining the truth of my suspicions. All the family, but myself, were at rest. Winding passages would conduct me, without danger of disturbing them, to the hall, from which double staircases ascended. One of these led to a saloon above, on the east side of which was a door that communicated with a suite of rooms occupied by the lady of the mansion. The first was an antechamber, in which a female servant usually lay. The second was the lady's own bedchamber. This was a sacred recess, with whose situation, relative to the other apartments of the building, I was well acquainted, but of which I knew nothing from my own examination, having never been admitted into it.

Thither I was now resolved to repair. I was not deterred by the sanctity of the place and hour. I was insensible to all consequences but the removal of my doubts. Not that my hopes were balanced by my fears. That the same tragedy had been performed in her chamber and in the street, nothing hindered me from believing with as much cogency as if my own eyes had witnessed it, but the reluctance with which we admit a detestable truth.

To terminate a state of intolerable suspense, I resolved to proceed forthwith to her chamber. I took the light and paced, with no interruption, along the galleries. I used no precaution. If I had met a servant or robber, I am not sure that I should have noticed him. My attention was too perfectly engrossed to allow me to spare any to a casual object. I cannot affirm that no one observed me. This, however, was probable from the distribution of the dwelling. It consisted of a central edifice and two wings, one of which was appropriated to domestics, and the other, at the extremity of which my apartment was placed, comprehended a library, and rooms for formal and social and literary conferences. These, therefore, were deserted at night, and my way lay along these. Hence it was not likely that my steps would be observed.

I proceeded to the hall. The principal parlor was beneath her chamber. In the confusion of my thoughts, I mistook one for the other. I rectified, as soon as I detected, my mistake. I ascended, with a beating heart, the staircase. The door of the antechamber was unfastened. I entered, totally regardless of disturbing the girl who slept within. The bed which she occupied was concealed by curtains. Whether she were there, I did not stop to examine. I cannot recollect that any tokens were given of wakefulness or alarm. It was not till I reached the door of her own apartment that my heart began to falter.

It was now that the momentousness of the question I was about to decide rushed with its genuine force upon my apprehension. Appalled and aghast, I had scarcely power to move the bolt. If the imagination of her death was not to be supported, how should I bear the spectacle of wounds and blood? Yet this was reserved for me. A few paces would set me in the midst of a scene of which I was the abhorred contriver. Was it right to proceed? There were still the remnants of doubt. My forebodings might possibly be groundless. All within might be safety and serenity. A respite might be gained from the execution of an irrevocable sentence. What could I do? Was not anything easy to endure in comparison with the agonies of suspense? If I could not obviate the evil I must bear it, but the torments of suspense were susceptible of remedy.

I drew back the bolt, and entered with the reluctance of fear, rather than the cautiousness of guilt. I could not lift my eyes from the ground. I advanced to the middle of the room. Not a sound like that of dying saluted my ear. At length, shaking off the fetters of hopelessness, I looked up.

I saw nothing calculated to confirm my fears. Everywhere there reigned quiet and order. My heart leaped with exultation. "Can it be," said I, "that I have been betrayed with shadows? But this is not sufficient."

Within an alcove was the bed that belonged to her. If her safety were inviolate, it was here that she reposed. What remained to convert tormenting doubt into ravishing certainty? I was insensible to the perils of my present situation. If she, indeed, were there, would not my intrusion awaken her? She would start and perceive me, at this hour, standing at her bedside. How should I account for an intrusion so unexampled and audacious? I could not communicate my fears. I could not tell her that the blood with which my hands were stained had flowed from the wounds of her brother.

My mind was inaccessible to such considerations. They did not even modify my predominant idea. Obstacles like these, had they existed, would have been trampled underfoot.

Leaving the lamp that I bore on the table, I approached the bed.

I slowly drew aside the curtain, and beheld her tranquilly slumbering. I listened, but so profound was her sleep that not even her breathings could be overheard. I dropped the curtain and retired.

How blissful and mild were the illuminations of my bosom at this discovery! A joy that surpassed all utterance succeeded the fierceness of desperation. I stood, for some moments, wrapped in delightful contemplation. Alas! it was a luminous but transient interval. The madness to whose black suggestions it bore so strong a contrast began now to make sensible approaches on my understanding.

"True," said I, "she lives. Her slumber is serene and happy. She is blind to her approaching destiny. Some hours will at least be rescued from anguish and death. When she wakes, the phantom that soothed her will vanish. The tidings cannot be withheld from her. The murderer of thy brother cannot hope to enjoy thy smiles. Those ravishing accents, with which thou hast used to greet me, will be changed. Scowling and reproaches, the invectives of thy anger and the maledictions of thy justice, will rest upon my head.

"What is the blessing which I made the theme of my boastful arrogance? This interval of being and repose is momentary. She will wake, but only to perish at the spectacle of my ingratitude. She will awake only to the consciousness of instantly-impending death. When she again sleeps she will wake no more. I, her son,— I, whom the law of my birth doomed to poverty and hardship, but whom her unsolicited beneficence snatched from those evils, and endowed with the highest good known to intelligent beings, the consolations of science and the blandishments of affluence,—to whom are faithfully preserved the lineaments of its angelic mother, she has not denied! What is the recompense that I have made? How have I discharged the measureless debt of gratitude to which she is entitled? Thus!. . .

"Cannot my guilt be extenuated? Is there not a good that I can do thee? Must I perpetrate unmingled evil? Is the province assigned me that of an infernal emissary, whose efforts are concentered in a single purpose, and that purpose a malignant one? I am the author of thy calamities. Whatever misery is reserved for thee, I am the source whence it flows. Can I not set bounds to the stream? Cannot I prevent thee from returning to a consciousness which till it ceases to exist, will not cease to be rent and mangled?

"Yes. It is in my power to screen thee from the coming storm; to accelerate thy journey to rest. I will do it."

The impulse was not to be resisted. I moved with the suddenness of lightning. Armed with a pointed implement that lay—it was a dagger. As I set down the lamp, I struck the edge. Yet I saw it not, or noticed it not till I needed its assistance. By what accident it came hither, to what deed of darkness it had already been subservient, I had no power to inquire. I stepped to the table and seized it.

The time which this action required was insufficient to save me. My doom was ratified by powers which no human energies can counterwork. Need I go further? Did you entertain any imagination of so frightful a catastrophe? I am overwhelmed by turns with dismay and with wonder. I am prompted by turns to tear my heart from my breast and deny faith to the verdict of my senses.

Was it I that hurried to the deed? No. It was the demon that possessed me. My limbs were guided to the bloody office by a power foreign and superior to mine. I had been defrauded, for a moment, of the empire of my muscles. A little moment for that sufficed.

If my destruction had not been decreed, why was the image of Clarice so long excluded? Yet why do I say long? The fatal resolution was conceived, and I hastened to the execution, in a period too brief for more than itself to be viewed by the intellect.

What then? Were my hands imbrued in this precious blood? Was it to this extremity of horror that my evil genius was determined to urge me? Too surely this was his purpose; too surely I was qualified to be its minister.

I lifted the weapon. Its point was aimed at the bosom of the sleeper. The impulse was given.

At the instant a piercing shriek was uttered behind me, and a stretched-out hand, grasping the blade, made it swerve widely from its aim. It descended, but without inflicting a wound. Its force was spent upon the bed.

Oh, for words to paint that stormy transition! I loosed my hold of the dagger. I started back, and fixed eyes of frantic curiosity on the author of my rescue. He that interposed to arrest my deed, that started into being and activity at a moment so pregnant with fate, without tokens of his purpose or his coming being previously imparted, could not, methought, be less than divinity.

The first glance that I darted on this being corroborated my conjecture. It was the figure and lineaments of Mrs. Lorimer. Negligently habited in flowing and brilliant white, with features bursting with terror and wonder, the likeness of that being who was stretched upon the bed now stood before me.

All that I am able to conceive of angel was comprised in the moral constitution of this woman. That her genius had overleaped all bounds, and interposed to save her, was no audacious imagination. In the state in which my mind then was, no other belief than this could occupy the first place.

My tongue was tied. I gazed by turns upon her who stood before me, and her who lay upon the bed, and who, awakened by the shriek that had been uttered, now opened her eyes. She started from her pillow, and, by assuming a new and more distinct attitude, permitted me to recognize *Clarice herself!*

Three days before, I had left her, beside the bed of a dying friend, at a solitary mansion in the mountains of Donegal. Here it had been her resolution to remain till her friend should breathe her last. Fraught with this persuasion, knowing this to be the place and hour of repose of my lady, hurried forward by the impetuosity of my own conceptions, deceived by the faint gleam which penetrated through the curtain and imperfectly-irradiated features which bore, at all times, a powerful resemblance to those of Mrs. Lorimer, I had rushed to the brink of this terrible precipice!

Why did I linger on the verge? Why, thus perilously situated, did I not throw myself headlong? The steel was yet in my hand. A single blow would have pierced my heart, and shut out from my remembrance and foresight the past and the future.

The moment of insanity had gone by, and I was once more myself. Instead of regarding the act which I had meditated as the dictate of compassion or of justice, it only added to the sum of my ingratitude, and gave wings to the whirlwind that was sent to bear me to perdition.

Perhaps I was influenced by a sentiment which I had not leisure to distribute into parts. My understanding was, no doubt, bewildered in the maze of consequences which would spring from my act. How should I explain my coming hither in this murderous guise, my arm lifted to destroy the idol of my soul and the darling child of my patroness? In what words should I unfold the tale of Wiatte, and enumerate the motives that terminated in the present scene? What penalty had not my infatuation and cruelty deserved? What could I less than turn the dagger's point against my own bosom?

A second time, the blow was thwarted and diverted. Once more this beneficent interposer held my arm from the perpetration of a new iniquity. Once more frustrated the instigations of that demon, of whose malice a mysterious destiny had consigned me to be the sport and the prey.

Every new moment added to the sum of my inexpiable guilt. Murder was succeeded, in an instant, by the more detestable enormity of suicide. She to whom my ingratitude was flagrant in proportion to the benefits of which she was the author, had now added to her former acts that of rescuing me from the last of mischiefs.

I threw the weapon on the floor. The zeal which prompted her to seize my arm, this action occasioned to subside, and to yield place to those emotions which this spectacle was calculated to excite. She watched me in silence, and with an air of ineffable solicitude. Clarice, governed by the instinct of modesty, wrapped her bosom and face in the bedclothes, and testified her horror by vehement but scarcely-articulate exclamations.

I moved forward, but my steps were random and tottering. My thoughts were fettered by reverie, and my gesticulations destitute of meaning. My tongue faltered with speaking, and I felt as if life and death were struggling within me for the mastery.

My will, indeed, was far from being neutral in this contest. To such as I, annihilation is the supreme good. To shake off the ills that fasten on us by shaking off existence, is a lot which the system of nature has denied to man. By escaping from life, I should be delivered from this scene, but should only rush into a world of retribution, and be immersed in new agonies.

I was yet to live. No instrument of my deliverance was within reach. I was powerless. To rush from the presence of these women, to hide me forever from their scrutiny and their upbraiding, to snatch from their minds all traces of the existence of Clithero, was the scope of unutterable longings.

Urged to flight by every motive of which my nature was susceptible, I was yet rooted to the spot. Had the pause been only to be interrupted by me, it would have lasted forever.

At length, the lady, clasping her hands and lifting them, exclaimed, in a tone melting into pity and grief,—

"Clithero! what is this? How came you hither, and why?

I struggled for utterance: "I came to murder you. Your brother has perished by my hands. Fresh from the commission of this deed, I have hastened hither to perpetrate the same crime upon you."

"My brother!" replied the lady, with new vehemence. "Oh, say not so! I have just heard of his return, from Sarsefield, and that he lives."

"He is dead," repeated I, with fierceness; "I know it. It was I that killed him."

"Dead!" she faintly articulated. "And by thee, Clithero? Oh! cursed chance that hindered thee from killing me also! Dead! Then is the omen fulfilled! Then am I undone! Lost forever!"

Her eyes now wandered from me, and her countenance sunk into a wild and rueful expression. Hope was utterly extinguished in her heart, and life forsook her at the same moment. She sunk upon the floor pallid and breathless.

How she came into possession of this knowledge I know not. It is possible that Scarsefield had repented of concealment, and, in the interval that passed between our separation and my encounter with Wiatte, had returned and informed her of the reappearance of this miscreant.

Thus, then, was my fate consummated. I was rescued from destroying her by a dagger, only to behold her perish by the tidings which I brought. Thus was every omen of mischief and misery fulfilled. Thus was the enmity of Wiatte rendered efficacious, and the instrument of his destruction changed into the executioner of his revenge.

Such is the tale of my crimes. It is not for me to hope that the curtain of oblivion will ever shut out the dismal spectacle. It will haunt me forever. The torments that grow out of it can terminate only with the thread of my existence, but that, I know full well, will never end. Death is but a shifting of the scene; and the endless progress of eternity, which to the good is merely the perfection of felicity, is to the wicked an accumulation of woe. The self-destroyer is his own enemy: this has ever been my opinion. Hitherto it has influenced my actions. Now, though the belief continues, its influence on my conduct is annihilated. I am no stranger to the depth of that abyss into which I shall plunge. No matter. Change is precious for its own sake.

Well, I was still to live. My abode must be somewhere fixed. My conduct was henceforth the result of a perverse and rebellious principle. I banished myself forever from my native soil. I vowed never more to behold the face of my Clarice, to abandon my friends, my books, all my wonted labors and accustomed recreations.

I was neither ashamed nor afraid. I considered not in what way the justice of the country would affect me. It merely made no part of my comtemplations. I was not embarrassed by the choice of expedients for trammelling up the visible consequences and for eluding suspicion. The idea of abjuring my country and flying forever from the hateful scene partook, to my apprehension, of the vast, the boundless, and strange; of plunging from the height of fortune to obscurity and indigence, corresponded with my present state of mind. It was of a piece with the tremendous and wonderful events that had just happened.

These were the images that haunted me, while I stood speechlessly gazing at the ruin before me. I heard a noise from without, or imagined that I heard it. My reverie was broken, and my muscular power restored. I descended into the street, through doors of which I possessed one set of keys, and hurried by the shortest way beyond the precincts of the city. I had laid no plan. My conceptions with regard to the future were shapeless and confused. Successive incidents supplied me with a clue, and suggested, as they rose, the next step to be taken.

I threw off the garb of affluence, and assumed a beggar's attire. That I had money about me for the accomplishment of my purposes was wholly accidental. I travelled along the coast, and, when I arrived at one town, knew not why I should go father; but my restlessness was unabated, and change was some relief. I at length arrived at Belfast. A vessel was preparing for America. I embraced eagerly the opportunity of passing into a new world. I arrived at Philadelphia. As soon as I landed I wandered hither, and was content to wear out my few remaining days in the service of Inglefield.

I have no friends. Why should I trust my story to another? I have no solicitude about concealment; but who is there who will derive pleasure or benefit from my rehearsal? And why should I expatiate on so hateful a theme? Yet now have I consented to this. I have confided in you the history of my disasters. I am not fearful of the use that you may be disposed to make of it. I shall quickly set myself myself beyond the reach of human tribunals. I shall relieve the ministers of law from the trouble of punishing. The recent events which induced you to summon me to this conference have likewise determined me to make this disclosure.

I was not aware, for some time, of my perturbed sleep. No wonder that sleep cannot soothe miseries like mine; that I am alike infested by memory in wakefulness and slumber. Yet I was anew distressed by the discovery that my thoughts found their way to my lips, without my being conscious of it, and that my steps wandered forth unknowingly and without the guidance of my will.

The story you have told is not incredible. The disaster to which you allude did not fail to excite my regret. I can still weep over the untimely fall of youth and worth. I can no otherwise account for my frequenting this shade than by the distant resemblance which the death of this man bore to that of which I was the perpetrator. This resemblance occurred to me at first. If time were able to weaken the impression which was produced by my crime, this stimilitude was adapted to revive and enforce them.

The wilderness, and the cave to which you followed me, were familiar to my Sunday rambles. Often have I indulged in audible griefs on the cliffs of that valley. Often have I brooded over my sorrows in the recesses of that cavern. This scene is adapted to my temper. Its mountainous asperities supply me with images of desolation and seclusion, and its headlong streams lull me into temporary forgetfulness of mankind.

I comprehend you. You suspect me of concern in the death of Waldegrave. You could not do otherwise. The conduct that you have witnessed was that of a murderer. I will not upbraid you for your suspicions, though I have bought exemption from them at a high price.

IX

There ended his narrative. He started from the spot where he stood, and, without affording me any opportunity of replying or commenting, disappeared amidst the thickest of the wood. I had no time to exert myself for his detention. I could have used no arguments for this end, to which it is probable he would have listened. The story I had heard was too extraordinary, too completely the reverse of all my expectations, to allow me to attend to the intimations of self-murder which he dropped.

The secret which I imagined was about to be disclosed was as inscrutable as ever. Not a circumstance, from the moment when Clithero's character became the subject of my meditations, till the conclusion of his tale, but served to confirm my suspicion. Was this error to be imputed to credulity? Would not anyone, from similar appearances, have drawn similar conclusions? Or is there a criterion by which truth can always be distinguished? Was it owing to my imperfect education that the inquietudes of this man were not traced to a deed performed at the distance of a thousand leagues, to the murder of his patroness and friend?

I had heard a tale which apparently related to scenes and persons far distant; but, though my suspicions have appeared to have been misplaced, what should hinder but that the death of my friend was, in like manner, an act of momentary insanity and originated in a like spirit of mistaken benevolence?

But I did not consider this tale merely in relation to myself. My life had been limited and uniform. I had communed with romancers and historians, but the impression made upon me by this incident was unexampled in my experience. My reading had furnished me with no instance in any degree parallel to this, and I found that to be a distant and second-hand spectator of events was widely different from witnessing them myself and partaking in their consequences. My judgment was, for a time, sunk into imbecility and confusion. My mind was full of the images unavoidably suggested by this tale, but they existed in a kind of chaos, and not otherwise than gradually was I able to reduce them to distinct particulars, and subject them to a deliberate and methodical inspection.

How was I to consider this act of Clithero? What a deplorable infatuation! Yet it was the necessary result of a series of ideas mutually linked and connected. His conduct was dictated by a motive allied to virtue. It was the fruit of an ardent and grateful spirit.

The death of Wiatte could not be censured. The life of Clithero was unspeakably more valuable than that of his antagonist. It was the instinct of self-preservation that swayed him. He knew not his adversary in time enough to govern himself by that knowledge. Had the assailant been an unknown ruffian, his death would have been followed by no remorse. The spectacle of his dying agonies would have dwelt upon the memory of his assassin like any other mournful sight, in the production of which he bore no part.

It must at least be said that his will was not concerned in this transaction. He acted in obedience to an impulse which he could not control nor resist. Shall we impute guilt where there is no design? Shall a man extract food for self-reproach from an action to which it is not enough to say that he was actuated by no culpable intention, but that he was swayed by no intention whatever? If consequences arise that cannot be foreseen, shall we find no refuge in the persuasion of our rectitude and of human frailty? Shall we deem ourselves criminal because we do not enjoy the attributes of Deity? Because our power and our knowledge are confined by impassable boundaries?

But whence arose the subsequent intention? It was the fruit of a dreadful mistake. His intents were noble and compassionate. But this is of no avail to free him from the imputation of guilt. No remembrance of past beneficence can compensate for this crime. The scale, loaded with the recriminations of his conscience, is immovable by any counterweight.

But what are the conclusions to be drawn by dispassionate observers? Is it possible to regard this person with disdain or with enmity? The crime originated in those limitations which nature has imposed upon human faculties. Proofs of a just intention are all that are requisite to exempt us from blame; he is thus in consequence of a double mistake. The light in which he views this event is erroneous. He judges wrong, and is therefore miserable.

How imperfect are the grounds of all our decisions! Was it of no use to superintend his childhood, to select his instructors and examples, to mark the operations of his principles, to see him emerging into youth, to follow him through various scenes and trying vicissitudes, and mark the uniformity of his integrity? Who would

have predicted his future conduct? Who would not have affirmed
the impossibility of an action like this?

How mysterious was the connection between the fate of Wiatte
and his sister! By such circuitous and yet infallible means were
the prediction of the lady and the vengeance of the brother accomplished! In how many cases may it be said, as in this, that the prediction was the cause of its own fulfillment! That the very act, which
considerate observers, and even himself, for a time, imagined to
have utterly precluded the execution of Wiatte's menaces, should
be that inevitably leading to it! That the execution should be assigned to him who, abounding in abhorrence, and in the act of self-
defense, was the slayer of the menacer!

As the obstructer of his designs, Wiatte waylaid and assaulted
Clithero. He perished in the attempt. Were his designs frustrated?
No. It was thus that he secured the gratification of his vengeance.
His sister was cut off in the bloom of life and prosperity. By a refine-
ment of good fortune, the voluntary minister of his malice had en-
'ailed upon himself exile without reprieve and misery without end.

But what chiefly excited my wonder was the connection of this tale
with the destiny of Sarsefield. This was he whom I have frequently
mentioned to you as my preceptor. About four years previous to
this era, he appeared in this district without fortune or friend. He
desired, one evening, to be accommodated at my uncle's house. The
conversation turning on the objects of his journey and his present
situation, he professed himself in search of lucrative employment.
My uncle proposed to him to become a teacher, there being a sufficient number of young people in this neighborhood to afford him
occupation and subsistence. He found it his interest to embrace this
proposal.

I, of course, became his pupil, and demeaned myself in such a
manner as speedily to grow into a favorite. He communicated to us
no part of his early history, but informed us sufficiently of his
adventures in Asia and Italy to make it plain that this was the same
person alluded to by Clithero. During his abode among us his conduct was irreproachable. When he left us, he manifested the most
poignant regret, but this originated chiefly in his regard to me. He
promised to maintain with me an epistolary intercourse. Since his
departure, however, I had heard nothing respecting him. It was
with unspeakable regret that I now heard of the disappointment of
his hopes, and was inquisitive respecting the measures which he
would adopt in his new situation. Perhaps he would once more re-

turn to America, and I should again be admitted to the enjoyment of his society. This event I anticipated with the highest satisfaction.

At present, the fate of the unhappy Clithero was the subject of abundant anxiety. On his suddenly leaving me, at the conclusion of his tale, I supposed that he had gone upon one of his usual rambles, and that it would terminate only with the day. Next morning a message was received from Inglefield, inquiring if anyone knew what had become of his servant. I could not listen to this message with tranquillity. I recollected the hints that he had given of some design upon his life, and admitted the most dreary forebodings. I speeded to Inglefield's. Clithero had not returned, they told me, the preceding evening. He had not apprised them of any intention to change his abode. His boxes, and all that composed his slender property, were found in their ordinary state. He had expressed no dissatisfaction with his present condition.

Several days passed, and no tidings could be procured of him. His absence was a topic of general speculation, but was a source of particular anxiety to no one but myself. My apprehensions were surely built upon sufficient grounds. From the moment that we parted, no one had seen or heard of him. What mode of suicide he had selected, he had disabled us from discovering, by the impenetrable secrecy in which he had involved it.

In the midst of my reflections upon this subject, the idea of the wilderness occurred. Could he have executed his design in the deepest of its recesses? These were unvisited by human footsteps, and his bones might lie for ages in this solitude without attracting observation. To seek them where they lay, to gather them together and provide for them a grave, was a duty which appeared incumbent on me, and of which the performance was connected with a thousand habitual sentiments and mixed pleasures.

Thou knowest my devotion to the spirit that breathes its inspiration in the gloom of forests and on the verge of streams. I love to immerse myself in shades and dells, and hold converse with the solemnities and secrecies of nature in the rude retreats of Norwalk. The disappearance of Clithero had furnished new incitements to ascend its cliffs and pervade its thickets, as I cherished the hope of meeting in my rambles with some traces of this man. But might he not still live? His words had imparted the belief that he intended to destroy himself. This catastrophe, however, was far from certain. Was it not in my power to avert it? Could I not restore a mind thus vigorous, to tranquil and wholesome existence? Could I not subdue his perverse disdain and immeasurable abhorrence of himself? His upbraiding and his scorn were unmerited and misplaced. Perhaps they argued frenzy rather than prejudice; but frenzy, like prejudice, was curable. Reason was no less an antidote to the illusions of insanity like his, than to the illusions of error.

I did not immediately recollect that to subsist in this desert was impossible. Nuts were the only fruits it produced, and these were inadequate to sustain human life. If it were haunted by Clithero, he must occasionally pass its limits and beg or purloin victuals. This deportment was too humiliating and flagitious to be imputed to him. There was reason to suppose him smitten with the charms of solitude, of a lonely abode in the midst of mountainous and rugged nature; but this could not be uninterruptedly enjoyed. Life could be supported only by occasionally visiting the haunts of men, in the guise of a thief or a mendicant. Hence, since Clithero was not known to have reappeared at any farmhouse in the neighborhood, I was compelled to conclude either that he had retired far from this district, or that he was dead.

Though I designed that my leisure should chiefly be consumed in the bosom of Norwalk, I almost dismissed the hope of meeting with the fugitive. There were indeed two sources of my hopelessness on this occasion. Not only was it probable that Clithero had fled far away, but, should he have concealed himself in some nook or cavern within these precincts, his concealment was not to be traced. This arose from the nature of that sterile region.

It would not be easy to describe the face of this district in a few words. Half of Solesbury, thou knowest, admits neither of plough nor spade. The cultivable space lies along the river, and the desert, lying on the north, has gained, by some means, the appellation of Norwalk. Canst thou imagine a space, somewhat circular, about six miles in diameter, and exhibiting a perpetual and intricate variety of craggy eminences and deep dells?

The hollows are single, and walled around by cliffs, ever varying in shape and height, and have seldom any perceptible communication with each other. These hollows are of all dimensions, from the narrowness and depth of a well, to the amplitude of one hundred yards. Winter's snow is frequently found in these cavities at midsummer. The streams that burst forth from every crevice are thrown, by the irregularities of the surface, into numberless cascades, often disappear in mists or in chasms and emerge from subterranean channels, and, finally, either subside into lakes or quietly meander through the lower and more level grounds.

Wherever nature left a flat it is made rugged and scarcely passable by enormous and fallen trunks, accumulated by the storms of ages, and forming, by their slow decay, a moss-covered soil, the haunt of rabbits and lizards. These spots are obscured by the melancholy umbrage of pines, whose eternal murmurs are in unison with vacancy and solitude, with the reverberations of the torrents and the whistling of the blasts. Hickory and poplar, which abound in the lowlands, find here no fostering elements.

A sort of continued vale, winding and abrupt, leads into the midst of this region and through it. This vale serves the purpose of a road. It is a tedious maze and perpetual declivity, and requires, from the passenger, a cautious and sure foot. Openings and ascents occasionally present themselves on each side, which seem to promise you access to the interior region, but always terminate, sooner or later, in insuperable difficulties, at the verge of a precipice or the bottom of a steep.

Perhaps no one was more acquainted with this wilderness than I, but my knowledge was extremely imperfect. I had traversed parts of it, at an early age, in pursuit of berries and nuts, or led by a roaming disposition. Afterwards the sphere of my rambles was enlarged and their purpose changed. When Sarsefield came among us, I became his favorite scholar and the companion of all his pedestrian excursions. He was fond of penetrating into these recesses, partly from the love of picturesque scenes, partly to investigate its botanical and mineral productions, and partly to carry on more effectually that species of instruction which he had adopted with regard to me, and which chiefly consisted in moralizing narratives or synthetical reasonings. These excursions had familiarized me with its outlines and most accessible parts; but there was much which, perhaps, could never be reached without wings, and much the only paths to which I might forever overlook.

Every new excursion, indeed, added somewhat to my knowledge. New tracks were pursued, new prospects detected, and new summits were gained. My rambles were productive of incessant novelty, though they always terminated in the prospect of limits that could not be overleaped. But none of these had led me wider from my customary paths than that which had taken

place when in pursuit of Clithero. I had a faint remembrance
of the valley into which I had descended after him; but till then
I had viewed it at a distance, and supposed it impossible to reach
the bottom but by leaping from a precipice some hundred feet
in height. The opposite steep seemed no less inaccessible, and
the cavern at the bottom was impervious to any views which my
former positions had enabled me to take of it.

My intention to re-examine this cave and ascertain whither
it led had, for a time, been suspended by different considerations. It was now revived with more energy than ever. I reflected
that this had formerly been haunted by Clithero, and might possibly have been the scene of the desperate act which he had meditated. It might at least conceal some token of his past existence.
It might lead into spaces hitherto unvisited, and to summits from
which wider landscapes might be seen.

One morning I set out to explore this scene. The road which
Clithero had taken was laboriously circuitous. On my return
from the first pursuit of him, I ascended the cliff in my former
footsteps, but soon lighted on the beaten tract which I have already described. This enabled me to shun a thousand obstacles
which had lately risen before me, and opened an easy passage
to the cavern.

I once more traversed this way. The brow of the hill was gained.
The ledges of which it consisted afforded sufficient footing, when
the attempt was made, though viewed at a distance they seemed
to be too narrow for that purpose. As I descended the rugged
stair, I could not but wonder at the termerity and precipitation
with which this descent had formerly been made. It seemed as if
noonday light and the tardiest circumspection would scarcely
enable me to accomplish it; yet then it had been done with headlong speed, and with no guidance but the moon's uncertain rays.

I reached the mouth of the cave. Till now I had forgotten that
a lamp or a torch might be necessary to direct my subterranean
footsteps. I was unwilling to defer the attempt. Light might possibly be requisite, if the cave had no other outlet. Somewhat
might present itself within to the eyes, which might forever elude
the hands, but I was more inclined to consider it merely as an
avenue terminating in an opening on the summit of the steep, or
on the opposite side of the ridge. Caution might supply the place
of light, or, having explored the cave as far as possible at present,
I might hereafter return, better furnished for the scrutiny.

X

With these determinations, I proceeded. The entrance was low, and compelled me to resort to hands as well as feet. At a few yards from the mouth the light disappeared, and I found myself immersed in the dunnest obscurity. Had I not been persuaded that another had gone before me, I should have relinquished the attempt. I proceeded with the utmost caution, always ascertaining, by outstretched arms, the height and breadth of the cavity before me. In a short time the dimensions expanded on all sides, and permitted me to resume my feet.

I walked upon a smooth and gentle declivity. Presently the wall on one side, and the ceiling, receded beyond my reach. I began to fear that I should be involved in a maze, and should be disabled from returning. To obviate this danger it was requisite to adhere to the nearest wall, and conform to the direction which it should take, without straying through the palpable obscurity. Whether the ceiling was lofty or low, whether the opposite wall of the passage was distant or near, this I deemed no proper opportunity to investigate.

In a short time, my progress was stopped by an abrupt descent. I set down the advancing foot with caution, being aware that I might at the next step encounter a bottomless pit. To the brink of such a one I seemed now to have arrived. I stooped, and stretched my hand forward and downward, but all was vacuity.

Here it was needful to pause. I had reached the brink of a cavity whose depth it was impossible to ascertain. It might be a few inches beyond my reach, or hundreds of feet. By leaping down I might incur no injury, or might plunge into a lake or dash myself to pieces on the points of rocks.

I now saw with new force the propriety of being furnished with a light. The first suggestion was to return upon my footsteps, and resume my undertaking on the morrow. Yet, having advanced thus far, I felt reluctance to recede without accomplishing my purposes. I reflected likewise that Clithero had boldly entered this recess, and had certainly come forth at a different avenue from that at which he entered.

107

At length it occurred to me that, though I could not go forward, yet I might proceed along the edge of this cavity. This edge would be as safe a guidance, and would serve as well for a clue by which I might return, as the wall which it was now necessary to forsake.

Intense dark is always the parent of fears. Impending injuries cannot in this state be descried, nor shunned, nor repelled. I began to feel some faltering of my courage, and seated myself, for a few minutes, on a stony mass which arose before me. My situation was new. The caverns I had hitherto met with in this desert were chiefly formed of low-browed rocks. They were chambers, more or less spacious, into which twilight was at least admitted; but here it seemed as if I were surrounded by barriers that would forever cut off my return to air and to light.

Presently I resumed my courage and proceeded. My road appeared now to ascend. On one side I seemed still upon the verge of a precipice, and on the other all was empty and waste. I had gone no inconsiderable distance, and persuaded myself that my career would speedily terminate. In a short time, the space on the left hand was again occupied, and I cautiously proceeded between the edge of the gulf and a rugged wall. As the space between them widened I adhered to the wall.

I was not insensible that my path became more intricate and more difficult to retread in proportion as I advanced. I endeavored to preserve a vivid conception of the way which I had already passed, and to keep the images of the left- and right-hand wall, and the gulf, in due succession in my memory.

The path, which had hitherto been considerably smooth, now became rugged and steep. Chilling damps, the secret trepidation which attended me, the length and difficulties of my way, enhanced by the ceaseless caution and the numerous expedients which the utter darkness obliged me to employ, began to overpower my strength. I was frequently compelled to stop and recruit myself by rest. These respites from toil were of use, but they could not enable me to prosecute an endless journey, and to return was scarcely a less arduous task than to proceed.

I looked anxiously forward, in the hope of being comforted by some dim ray, which might assure me that my labors were approaching an end. At last this propitious token appeared, and I issued forth into a kind of chamber, one side of which was open to the air and allowed me to catch a portion of the checkered sky. This spectacle never before excited such exquisite sensations in my bosom. The air, likewise, breathed into the cavern, was unspeakably delicious.

I now found myself on the projecture of a rock. Above and below, the hillside was nearly perpendicular. Opposite, and at the distance of fifteen or twenty yards, was a similar ascent. At the bottom was a glen, cold, narrow, and obscure. This projecture, which served as a kind of vestibule to the cave, was connected with a ledge, by which, though not without peril and toil, I was conducted to the summit.

This summit was higher than any of those which were interposed between itself and the river. A large part of this chaos of rocks and precipices was subjected, at one view, to the eye. The fertile lawns and vales which lay beyond this, the winding course of the river, and the slopes which rose on its farther side, were parts of this extensive scene. These objects were at any time fitted to inspire rapture. Now my delight was enhanced by the contrast which this lightsome and serene element bore to the glooms from which I had lately emerged. My station, also, was higher, and the limits of my view, consequently, more ample than any which I had hitherto enjoyed.

I advanced to the outer verge of the hill, which I found to overlook a steep no less inaccessible, and a glen equally profound. I changed frequently my station in order to diversify the scenery. At length it became necessary to inquire by what means I should return. I traversed the edge of the hill, but on every side it was equally steep and always too lofty to permit me to leap from it. As I kept along the verge, I perceived that it tended in a circular direction, and brought me back, at last, to the spot from which I had set out. From this inspection, it seemed as if return was impossible by any other way than that through the cavern.

I now turned my attention to the interior space. If you imagine a cylindrical mass, with a cavity dug in the center, whose edge conforms to the exterior edge; and if you place in this cavity another cylinder, higher than that which surrounds it, but so small as to leave between its sides and those of the cavity a hollow space, you will gain as distinct an image of this hill as words can convey. The summit of the inner rock was rugged and covered with trees of unequal growth. To reach this summit would not render my return easier; but its greater elevation would extend my view, and perhaps furnish a spot from which the whole horizon was conspicuous.

As I had traversed the outer, I now explored the inner edge of this hill. At length I reached a spot where the chasm, separating the two rocks, was narrower than at any other part. At first view, it seemed as if it were possible to leap over it, but a nearer examination showed me that the passage was impracticable. So far as my eye could estimate it, the breadth was thirty or forty feet. I could scarcely venture to look beneath. The height was dizzy, and the walls, which approached each other at top, receded at the bottom, so as to form the resemblance of an immense hall, lighted from a rift which some convulsion of nature had made in the roof. Where I stood there ascended a perpetual mist, occasioned by a torrent that dashed along the rugged pavement below.

From these objects I willingly turned my eye upon those before and above me, on the opposite ascent. A stream, rushing from above, fell into a cavity, which its own force seemed gradually to have made. The noise and the motion equally attracted my attention. There was a desolate and solitary grandeur in the scene, enhanced by the circumstances in which it was beheld, and by the perils through which I had recently passed, that had never before been witnessed by me.

A sort of sanctity and awe environed it, owing to the consciousness of absolute and utter loneliness. It was probable that human feet had never before gained this recess, that human eyes had never been fixed upon these gushing waters. The aboriginal inhabitants had no motives to lead them into caves like this and ponder on the verge of such a precipice. Their successors were still less likely to have wandered hither. Since the birth of this continent, I was probably the first who had deviated thus remotely from the customary paths of men.

While musing upon these ideas, my eye was fixed upon the foaming current. At length I looked upon the rocks which confined and embarrassed its course. I admired their fantastic shapes and endless irregularities. Passing from one to the other of these, my attention lighted, at length, as if by some magical transition, on—a human countenance!

My surprise was so abrupt, and my sensations so tumultuous, that I forgot for a moment the perilous nature of my situation. I loosened my hold of a pine-branch, which had been hitherto one of my supports, and almost started from my seat. Had my station been in a slight degree nearer the brink than it was, I should have fallen headlong into the abyss.

To meet a human creature, even on that side of the chasm which

I occupied, would have been wholly adverse to my expectation. My station was accessible by no other road than that through which I had passed, and no motives were imaginable by which others could be prompted to explore this road. But he whom I now beheld was seated where it seemed impossible for human efforts to have placed him.

But this affected me but little in comparison with other incidents. Not only the countenance was human, but, in spite of shaggy and tangled locks, and an air of melancholy wildness, I speedily recognized the features of the fugitive Clithero!

One glance was not sufficient to make me acquainted with this scene. I had come hither partly in pursuit of this man, but some casual appendage of his person, something which should indicate his past rather than his present existence, was all that I hoped to find. That he should be found alive in this desert, that he should have gained this summit, access to which was apparently impossible, were scarcely within the boundaries of belief.

His scanty and coarse garb had been nearly rent away by brambles and thorns; his arms, bosom, and cheeks were overgrown and half concealed by hair. There was somewhat in his attitude and looks denoting more than anarchy of thoughts and passions. His rueful, ghastly, and immovable eyes testified not only that his mind was ravaged by despair, but that he was pinched with famine.

These proofs of his misery thrilled to my inmost heart. Horror and shuddering invaded me as I stood gazing upon him, and, for a time, I was without the power of deliberating on the measures which it was my duty to adopt for his relief. The first suggestion was, by calling, to inform him of my presence. I knew not what counsel or comfort to offer. By what words to bespeak his attention, or by what topics to mollify his direful passions, I knew not. Though so near, the gulf by which we were separated was impassable. All that I could do was to speak.

My surprise and my horror were still strong enough to give a shrill and piercing tone to my voice. The chasm and the rocks loudened and reverberated my accents while I exclaimed,—"Man! Clithero!"

My summons was effectual. He shook off his trance in a moment. He had been stretched upon his back, with his eyes fixed upon the craggy projecture above, as if he were in momentary expectation of its fall and crushing him to atoms. Now he started on his feet. He was conscious of the voice, but not of the quarter from whence it came. He was looking anxiously around when I again spoke: "Look hither. It is I who called."

He looked. Astonishment was now mingled with every other dreadful meaning in his visage. He clasped his hands together and bent forward, as if to satisfy himself that his summoner was real. At the next moment he drew back, placed his hands upon his breast, and fixed his eyes on the ground.

This pause was not likely to be broken but by me. I was preparing again to speak. To be more distinctly heard, I advanced closer to the brink. During this action, my eye was necessarily withdrawn from him. Having gained a somewhat nearer station, I looked again, but—he was gone!

The seat which he so lately occupied was empty. I was not forewarned of his disappearance or directed to the course of his flight by any rustling among leaves. These, indeed, would have been overpowered by the noise of the cataract. The place where he sat was the bottom of a cavity, one side of which terminated in the verge of an abyss, but the other sides were perpendicular or overhanging. Surely he had not leaped into this gulf; and yet that he had so speedily scaled the steep was impossible.

I looked into the gulf, but the depth and the gloom allowed me to see nothing with distinctness. His cries or groans could not be overheard amidst the uproar of the waters. His fall must have instantly destroyed him, and that he had fallen was the only conclusion I could draw.

My sensations on this incident cannot be easily described. The image of this man's despair, and of the sudden catastrophe to which my inauspicious interference had led, filled me with compunction and terror. Some of my fears were relieved by the new conjecture, that, behind the rock on which he had lain, there might be some aperture or pit into which he had descended, or in which he might be concealed.

I derived consolation from this conjecture. Not only the evil which I dreaded might not have happened, but some alleviation of his misery was possible. Could I arrest his footsteps and win his attention, I might be able to insinuate the lessons of fortitude; but if words were impotent, and arguments were nugatory, yet to sit by him in silence, to moisten his hand with tears, to sigh in unison, to offer him the spectacle of sympathy, the solace of believing that his demerits were not estimated by so rigid a standard by others as by himself, that one at least among his fellow men regarded him with love and pity, could not fail to be of benign influence.

These thoughts inspired me with new zeal. To effect my purpose it was requisite to reach the opposite steep. I was now convinced that this was not an impracticable undertaking, since Clithero had already performed it. I once more made the circuit of the hill. Every side was steep and of enormous height, and the gulf was nowhere so narrow as at this spot. I therefore returned hither, and once more pondered on the means of passing this tremendous chasm in safety.

Casting my eyes upward, I noted the tree at the root of which I was standing. I compared the breadth of the gulf with the length of the trunk of this tree, and it appeared very suitable for a bridge. Happily it grew obliquely, and, if felled by an axe, would probably fall of itself, in such a manner as to be suspended across the chasm. The stock was thick enough to afford me footing, and would enable me to reach the opposite declivity without danger or delay.

A more careful examination of the spot, the site of the tree, its dimensions, and the direction of its growth, convinced me fully of the practicability of this expedient, and I determined to carry it into immediate execution. For this end I must hasten home, procure an axe, and return with all expedition hither. I took my former way, once more entered the subterranean avenue, and slowly re-emerged into day. Before I reached home, the evening was at hand, and my tired limbs and jaded spirits obliged me to defer my undertaking till the morrow.

Though my limbs were at rest, my thoughts were active through the night. I carefully reviewed the situation of this hill, and was unable to conjecture by what means Clithero could place himself upon it. Unless he occasionally returned to the habitable grounds, it was impossible for him to escape perishing by famine. He might intend to destroy himself by this means, and my first efforts were to be employed to overcome this fatal resolution. To persuade him to leave his desolate haunts might be a laborious and tedious task; meanwhile, all my benevolent intentions would be frustrated by his want of sustenance. It was proper, therefore, to carry bread with me, and to place it before him. The sight of food, the urgencies of hunger, and my vehement entreaties, might prevail on him to eat, though no expostulations might suffice to make him seek food at a distance.

XI

Next morning I stored a small bag with meat and bread, and, throwing an axe on my shoulder, set out, without informing anyone of my intentions, for the hill. My passage was rendered more difficult by these encumbrances, but my perseverance surmounted every impediment, and I gained, in a few hours, the foot of the tree whose trunk was to serve me for a bridge. In this journey I saw no traces of the fugitive.

A new survey of the tree confirmed my former conclusions, and I began my work with diligence. My strokes were repeated by a thousand echoes, and I paused at first, somewhat startled by reverberations which made it appear as if not one but a score of axes were employed at the same time on both sides of the gulf.

Quickly the tree fell, and exactly in the manner which I expected and desired. The wide-spread limbs occupied and choked up the channel of the torrent, and compelled it to seek a new outlet and multiplied its murmurs. I dared not trust myself to cross it in an upright posture, but clung, with hands and feet, to its rugged bark. Having reached the opposite cliff, I proceeded to examine the spot where Cithero had disappeared. My fondest hopes were realized, for a considerable cavity appeared, which, on a former day, had been concealed from my distant view by the rock.

It was obvious to conclude that this was his present habitation, or that an avenue, conducting hither and terminating in the unexplored sides of this pit, was that by which he had come hither, and by which he had retired. I could not hesitate long to slide into the pit. I found an entrance through which I fearlessly penetrated. I was prepared to encounter obstacles and perils similar to those which I have already described, but was rescued from them by ascending, in a few minutes, into a kind of passage, open above, but walled by a continued rock on both sides. The sides of this passage conformed with the utmost exactness to each other. Nature, at some former period, had occasioned the solid mass to dispart at this place, and had thus afforded access to the summit of the hill. Loose stones and ragged points formed the flooring of this passage, which rapidly and circuitously ascended.

114

I was now within a few yards of the surface of the rock. The passage opened into a kind of chamber or pit, the sides of which were not difficult to climb. I rejoiced at the prospect of this termination of my journey. Here I paused, and, throwing my weary limbs on the ground, began to examine the objects around me, and to meditate on the steps that were next to be taken.

My first glance lighted on the very being of whom I was in search. Stretched upon a bed of moss, at the distance of a few feet from my station, I beheld Clithero. He had not been roused by my approach, though my footsteps were perpetually stumbling and sliding. This reflection gave birth to the fear that he was dead. A nearer inspection dispelled my apprehensions, and showed me that he was merely buried in profound slumber. Those vigils must indeed have been long which were at last succeeded by a sleep so oblivious.

This meeting was, in the highest degree, propitious. It not only assured me of his existence, but proved that his miseries were capable of being suspended. His slumber enabled me to pause, to ruminate on the manner by which his understanding might be most successfully addressed; to collect and arrange the topics fitted to rectify his gloomy and disastrous perceptions.

Thou knowest that I am qualified for such tasks neither by my education nor my genius. The headlong and ferocious energies of this man could not be repelled or diverted into better paths by efforts so undisciplined as mine. A despair so stormy and impetuous would drown my feeble accents. How should I attempt to reason with him? How should I outroot prepossessions so inveterate,— the fruits of his earliest education, fostered and matured by the observation and experience of his whole life? How should I convince him that, since the death of Wiatte was not intended, the deed was without crime? that, if it had been deliberately concerted, it was still a virtue, since his own life could by no other means be preserved? that when he pointed a dagger at the bosom of his mistress he was actuated, not by avarice, or ambition, or revenge, or malice? He desired to confer on her the highest and the only benefit of which he believed her capable. He sought to rescue her from tormenting regrets and lingering agonies.

These positions were sufficiently just to my own view, but I was not called upon to reduce them to practice. I had not to struggle with the consciousness of having been rescued, by some miraculous contingency, from imbruing my hands in the blood of her whom I adored; of having drawn upon myself suspicions of ingratitude and murder too deep to be ever effaced; of having bereft myself of love, and honor, and friends, and spotless reputation; of having doomed myself to infamy and detestation, to hopeless exile, penury, and servile toil. These were the evils which his malignant destiny had made the unalterable portion of Clithero, and how should my imperfect eloquence annihilate these evils? Every man, not himself the victim of irretrievable disasters, perceives the folly of ruminating on the past, and of fostering a grief which cannot reverse or recall the decrees of an immutable necessity; but every man who suffers is unavoidably shackled by the errors which he censures in his neighbor, and his efforts to relieve himself are as fruitless as those with which he attempted the relief of others.

No topic, therefore, could be properly employed by me on the present occasion. All that I could do was to offer him food, and, by pathetic supplications, to prevail on him to eat. Famine, however obstinate, would scarcely refrain when bread was placed within sight and reach. When made to swerve from his resolution in one instance, it would be less difficult to conquer it a second time. The magic of sympathy, the perseverance of benevolence, though silent, might insensibly displace those desperate suggestions which now governed him.

Having revolved these ideas, I placed the food which I had brought at his right hand, and, seating myself at his feet, attentively surveyed his countenance. The emotions which were visible during wakefulness had vanished during this cessation of remembrance and remorse, or were faintly discernible. They served to dignify and solemnize his features, and to embellish those immutable lines which betokened the spirit of his better days. Lineaments were now observed which could never coexist with folly or associate with obdurate guilt.

I had no inclination to awaken him. This respite was too sweet to be needlessly abridged. I determined to await the operation of nature, and to prolong, by silence and by keeping interruption at a distance, this salutary period of forgetfulness. This interval permitted new ideas to succeed in my mind.

Clithero believed his solitude to be unapproachable. What new expedients to escape inquiry and intrusion might not my presence suggest! Might he not vanish, as he had done on the former day, and afford me no time to assail his constancy and tempt his hunger? If, however, I withdrew during his sleep, he would awake without disturbance, and be unconscious, for a time, that his secrecy had been violated. He would quickly perceive the victuals, and would need no foreign inducements to eat. A provision so unexpected and extraordinary might suggest new thoughts, and be construed into a kind of heavenly condemnation of his purpose. He would not readily suspect the motives or person of his visitant, would take no precaution against the repetition of my visit, and, at the same time, our interview would not be attended with so much surprise. The more I revolved these reflections, the greater force they acquired. At length, I determined to withdraw, and, leaving the food where it could scarcely fail of attracting his notice, I returned by the way that I had come. I had scarcely reached home, when a messenger from Inglefield arrived, requesting me to spend the succeeding night at his house, as some engagement had occurred to draw him to the city.

I readily complied with this request. It was not necessary, however, to be early in my visit. I deferred going till the evening was far advanced. My way led under the branches of the elm which recent events had rendered so memorable. Hence my reflections reverted to the circumstances which had lately occurred in connection with this tree.

I paused, for some time, under its shade. I marked the spot where Clithero had been discovered digging. It showed marks of being unsettled; but the sod which had formerly covered it, and which had lately been removed, was now carefully replaced. This had not been done by him on that occasion in which I was a witness of his behavior. The earth was then hastily removed, and as hastily thrown again into the hole from which it had been taken.

Some curiosity was naturally excited by this appearance. Either some other person, or Clithero, on a subsequent occasion, had been here. I was now likewise led to reflect on the possible motives that prompted the maniac to turn up this earth. There is always some significance in the actions of a sleeper. Somewhat was, perhaps, buried in this spot, connected with the history of Mrs. Lorimer or of Clarice. Was it not possible to ascertain the truth in this respect?

There was but one method. By carefully uncovering this hole, and digging as deep as Clithero had already dug, it would quickly appear whether anything was hidden. To do this publicly by daylight was evidently indiscreet. Besides, a moment's delay was superfluous. The night had now fallen, and before it was past this new undertaking might be finished. An interview was, if possible, to be gained with Clithero on the morrow, and for this interview the discoveries made on this spot might eminently qualify me. Influenced by these considerations, I resolved to dig. I was first, however, to converse an hour with the housekeeper, and then to withdraw to my chamber. When the family were all retired, and there was no fear of observation or interruption, I proposed to rise and hasten, with a proper implement, hither.

One chamber in Inglefield's house was usually reserved for visitants. In this chamber thy unfortunate brother died, and here it was that I was to sleep. The image of its last inhabitant could not fail of being called up, and of banishing repose; but the scheme which I had meditated was an additional incitement to watchfulness. Hither I repaired at the due season, having previously furnished myself with candles, since I knew not what might occur to make a light necessary.

I did not go to bed, but either sat musing by a table or walked across the room. The bed before me was that on which my friend breathed his last. To rest my head upon the same pillow, to lie on that pallet which sustained his cold and motionless limbs, were provocations to remembrance and grief that I desired to shun. I endeavored to fill my mind with more recent incidents, with the disasters of Clithero, my subterranean adventures, and the probable issue of the schemes which I now contemplated.

I recalled the conversation which had just ended with the housekeeper. Clithero had been our theme, but she had dealt chiefly in repetitions of what had formerly been related by her or by Inglefield. I inquired what this man had left behind, and found that it consisted of a square box, put together by himself with uncommon strength, but of rugged workmanship. She proceeded to mention that she had advised her brother, Mr. Inglefield, to break open this box and ascertain its contents; but this he did not think himself justified in doing. Clithero was guilty of no known crime, was responsible to no one for his actions, and might sometime return to claim his property. This box contained nothing with which others had a right to meddle. Somewhat might be found in it, throwing light upon his past or present situation; but curiosity was not to be gratified by these means. What Clithero thought proper to conceal, it was criminal for us to extort from him.

The housekeeper was by no means convinced by these arguments, and at length obtained her brother's permission to try whether any of her own keys would unlock this chest. The keys were produced, but no lock nor keyhole were discoverable. The lid was fast, but by what means it was fastened the most accurate inspection could not detect. Hence she was compelled to lay aside her project. This chest had always stood in the chamber which I now occupied.

These incidents were now remembered, and I felt disposed to profit by this opportunity of examining this box. It stood in a corner, and was easily distinguished by its form. I lifted it and found its weight by no means extraordinary. Its structure was remarkable. It consisted of six sides, square and of similar dimensions. These were joined, not by mortise and tennon, not by nails, not by hinges, but the junction was accurate. The means by which they were made to cohere were invisible.

Appearances on every side were uniform, nor were there any marks by which the lid was distinguishable from its other surfaces.

During his residence with Inglefield, many specimens of mechanical ingenuity were given by his servant. This was the workmanship of his own hands. I looked at it for some time, till the desire insensibly arose of opening it and examining its contents.

I had no more right to do this than the Inglefields: perhaps, indeed, this curiosity was more absurd, and the gratification more culpable, in me than in them. I was acquainted with the history of Clithero's past life, and with his present conditon. Respecting these, I had no new intelligence to gain, and no doubts to solve. What excuse could I make to the proprietor, should he ever reappear to claim his own, or to Inglefield for breaking open a receptacle which all the maxims of society combine to render sacred?

But could not my end be gained without violence? The means of opening might present themselves on a patient scrutiny. The lid might be raised and shut down again without any tokens of my act; its contents might be examined, and all things restored to their former condition, in a few minutes.

I intended not a theft. I intended to benefit myself without inflicting injury on others. Nay, might not the discoveries I should make throw light upon the conduct of this extraordinary man which his own narrative had withheld? Was there reason to confide implicitly on the tale which I had heard?

In spite of the testimony of my own feelings, the miseries of Clithero appeared in some degree fantastic and groundless. A thousand conceivable motives might induce him to pervert or conceal the truth. If he were thoroughly known, his character might assume a new appearance; and what is now so difficult to reconcile to common maxims might prove perfectly consistent with them. I desire to restore him to peace; but a thorough knowledge of his actions is necessary, both to show that he is worthy of compassion, and to suggest the best means of extirpating his errors. It was possible that this box contained the means of this knowledge.

There were likewise other motives, which, as they possessed some influence, however small, deserve to be mentioned. Thou knowest that I also am a mechanist. I had constructed a writing-desk and cabinet, in which I had endeavored to combine the properties of secrecy, security, and strength, in the highest possible degree. I looked upon this, therefore, with the eye of an artist, and was solicitous to know the principles on which it was formed. I determined to examine, and, if possible, to open it.

XII

I surveyed it with the utmost attention. All its parts appeared equally solid and smooth. It could not be doubted that one of its sides served the purpose of a lid, and was possible to be raised. Mere strength could not be applied to raise it, because there was no projecture which might be firmly held by the hand, and by which force could be exerted. Some spring, therefore, secretly existed, which might forever elude the senses, but on which the hand, by being moved over it in all directions, might accidentally light.

This process was effectual. A touch, casually applied at an angle, drove back a bolt, and a spring, at the same time, was set in action, by which the lid was raised above half an inch. No event could be supposed more fortuitous than this. A hundred hands might have sought in vain for this spring. The spot in which a certain degree of pressure was sufficient to produce this effect was, of all, the least likely to attract notice or awaken suspicion.

I opened the trunk with eagerness. The space within was divided into numerous compartments, none of which contained anything of moment. Tools of different and curious constructions, and remnants of minute machinery, were all that offered themselves to my notice.

My expectations being thus frustrated, I proceeded to restore things to their former state. I attempted to close the lid; but the spring which had raised it refused to bend. No measure that I could adopt enabled me to place the lid in the same situation in which I had found it. In my efforts to press down the lid, which were augmented in proportion to the resistance that I met with, the spring was broken. This obstacle being removed, the lid resumed its proper place; but no means, within the reach of my ingenuity to discover, enabled me to push forward the bolt, and thus to restore the fastening.

I now perceived that Clithero had provided not only against the opening of his cabinet, but likewise against the possibility of concealing that it had been opened. This discovery threw me into a some confusion. I had been tempted thus far by the belief that my action was without witnesses, and might be forever concealed. This opinion was now confuted. If Clithero should ever reclaim his property, he would not fail to detect the violence of which I had been guilty. Inglefield would disapprove in another what he had not permitted to himself, and the unauthorized and clandestine manner in which I had behaved would aggravate, in his eyes, the heinousness of my offense.

But now there was no remedy. All that remained was to hinder suspicion from lighting on the innocent, and to confess, to my friend, the offense which I had committed. Meanwhile my first project was resumed, and, the family being now wrapped in profound sleep, I left my chamber, and proceeded to the elm. The moon was extremely brilliant, but I hoped that this unfrequented road and unseasonable hour would hinder me from being observed. My chamber was above the kitchen, with which it communicated by a small staircase, and the building to which it belonged was connected with the dwelling by a gallery. I extinguished the light and left it in the kitchen, intending to relight it, by the embers that still glowed on the hearth, on my return.

I began to remove the sod and cast out the earth, with little confidence in the success of my project. The issue of my examination of the box humbled and disheartened me. For some time I found nothing that tended to invigorate my hopes. I determined, however, to descend, as long as the unsettled condition of the earth showed me that someone had preceded me. Small masses of stone were occasionally met with, which served only to perplex me with groundless expectations. At length my spade struck upon something which emitted a very different sound. I quickly drew it forth, and found it to be wood. Its regular form, and the crevices which were faintly discernible, persuaded me that it was human workmanship, and that there was a cavity within. The place in which it was found easily suggested some connection between this and the destiny of Clithero. Covering up the hole with speed, I hastened with my prize to the house. The door by which the kitchen was entered was not to be seen from the road. It opened on a field, the farther limit of which was a ledge of rocks, which formed, on this side, the boundary of Inglefield's estate and the westernmost barrier of Norwalk.

As I turned the angle of the house, and came in view of this door, methought I saw a figure issue from it. I was startled at this incident, and, stopping, crouched close to the wall, that I might not be discovered. As soon as the figure passed beyond the verge of the

shade, it was easily distinguished to be that of Clithero! He crossed
the field with a rapid pace, and quickly passed beyond the reach
of my eye.

This appearance was mysterious. For what end he should visit
this habitation could not be guessed. Was the contingency to be
lamented in consequence of which an interview had been avoided?
Would it have compelled me to explain the broken conditon of his
trunk? I knew not whether to rejoice at having avoided this interview, or to deplore it.

These thoughts did not divert me from examining the nature
of the prize which I had gained. I relighted my candle and hied
once more to the chamber. The first object which, on entering it,
attracted my attention was the cabinet broken into twenty fragments, on the hearth. I had left it on a low table, at a distant corner of the room.

No conclusion could be formed but that Clithero had been here,
had discovered the violence which had been committed on his property, and, in the first transport of his indignation, had shattered
it to pieces. I shuddered on reflecting how near I had been to being
detected by him in the very act, and by how small an interval I had
escaped that resentment which, in that case, would have probably been wreaked upon me.

My attention was withdrawn, at length, from this object, and
fixed upon the contents of the box which I had dug up. This was
equally inaccessible with the other. I had not the same motives
for caution and forbearance. I was somewhat desperate, as the consequences of my indiscretion could not be aggravated, and my curiosity was more impetuous with regard to the smaller than to the
larger cabinet. I placed it on the ground and crushed it to pieces
with my heel.

Something was within. I brought it to the light, and, after loosing
numerous folds, at length drew forth a volume. No object in the
circle of nature was more adapted than this to rouse up all my faculties. My feelings were anew excited on observing that it was a
manuscript. I bolted the door, and, drawing near the light, opened
and began to read.

A few pages were sufficient to explain the nature of the work.
Clithero had mentioned that his lady had composed a vindication
of her conduct towards her brother when her intercession in his
favor was solicited and refused. This performance had never been
published, but had been read by many, and was preserved by her

friends as a precious monument of her genius and her virtue. This manuscript was now before me.

That Clithero should preserve this manuscript, amidst the wreck of his hopes and fortunes, was apparently conformable to his temper. That, having formed the resolution to die, he should seek to hide this volume from the profane curiosity of survivors, was a natural proceeding. To bury it rather than to burn or disperse it into fragments, would be suggested by the wish to conceal, without committing what his heated fancy would regard as sacrilege. To bury it beneath the elm was dictated by no fortuitous or inexplicable caprice. This event could scarcely fail of exercising some influence on the perturbations of his sleep, and thus, in addition to other causes, might his hovering near this trunk, and throwing up this earth, in the intervals of slumber, be accounted for. Clithero, indeed, had not mentioned this proceeding in the course of his narrative; but that would have contravened the end for which he had provided a grave for this book.

I read this copious tale with unspeakable eagerness. It essentially agreed with that which had been told by Clithero. By drawing forth events into all their circumstances, more distinct impressions were produced on the mind, and proofs of fortitude and equanimity were here given to which I had hitherto known no parallel. No wonder that a soul like Clithero's, pervaded by these proofs of inimitable excellence, and thrillingly alive to the passion of virtuous fame and the value of that existence which he had destroyed, should be overborne by horror at the view of the past.

The instability of life and happiness was forcibly illustrated, as well as the perniciousness of error. Exempt as this lady was from almost every defect, she was indebted for her ruin to absurd opinions of the sacredness of consanguinity, to her anxiety for the preservation of a ruffian because that ruffian was her brother. The spirit of Clithero was enlightened and erect, but he weakly suffered the dictates of eternal justice to be swallowed up by gratitude. The dread of unjust upbraiding hurried him to murder and to suicide, and the imputation of imaginary guilt impelled him to the perpetration of genuine and enormous crimes.

The perusal of this volume ended not but with the night. Contrary to my hopes, the next day was stormy and wet. This did not deter me from visiting the mountain. Slippery paths and muddy torrents were no obstacles to the purposes which I had adopted.

I wrapped myself, and a bag of provisons, in a cloak of painted canvas, and speeded to the dwelling of Clithero.

I passed through the cave and reached the bridge which my own ingenuity had formed. At that moment, torrents of rain poured from above, and stronger blasts thundered amidst these desolate recesses and profound chasms. Instead of lamenting the prevalence of this tempest, I now began to regard it with pleasure. It conferred new forms of sublimity and grandeur on this scene.

As I crept with hands and feet along my imperfect bridge, a sudden gust had nearly whirled me into the frightful abyss below. To preserve myself, I was obliged to loose my hold of my burden, and it fell into the gulf. This incident disconcerted and distressed me. As soon as I had effected my dangerous passage, I screened myself behind a cliff and gave myself up to reflection.

The purpose of this arduous journey was defeated by the loss of the provisions I had brought. I despaired of winning the attention of the fugitive to supplications, or arguments tending to smother remorse or revive his fortitude. The scope of my efforts was to consist in vanquishing his aversion to food; but these efforts would now be useless, since I had no power to supply his cravings.

This deficiency, however, was easily supplied. I had only to return home and supply myself anew. No time was to be lost in doing this; but I was willing to remain under this shelter till the fury of the tempest had subsided. Besides, I was not certain that Clithero had again retreated hither. It was requisite to explore the summit of this hill, and ascertain whether it had any inhabitant. I might likewise discover what had been the success of my former experiment, and whether the food, which had been left here on the former day, was consumed or neglected.

While occupied with these reflections, my eyes were fixed upon the opposite steeps. The tops of the trees, waving to and fro in the wildest commotion, and their trunks, occasionally bending to the blast, which, in these lofty regions, blew with a violence unknown in the tracts below, exhibited an awful spectacle. At length, my attention was attracted by the trunk which lay across the gulf, and which I had converted into a bridge. I perceived that it had already somewhat swerved from its original position, that every blast broke or loosened some of the fibers by which its roots were connected with the opposite bank, and that, if the storm did not speedily abate, there was imminent danger of its being torn from the rock and precipitated into the chasm. Thus my retreat would be cut off, and the evils from which I was endeavoring to rescue another would be experienced by myself.

I did not just then reflect that Clithero had found access to this hill by other means, and that the avenue by which he came would be equally commodious to me. I believed my destiny to hang upon the expedition with which I should recross this gulf. The moments that were spent in these deliberations were critical, and I shuddered to observe that the trunk was held in its place by one or two fibers which were already stretched almost to breaking.

To pass along the trunk, rendered slippery by the wet and unsteadfast by the wind, was imminently dangerous. To maintain my hold, in passing, in defiance of the whirlwind, required the most vigorous exertions. For this end it was necessary to discommode myself of my cloak, and of the volume which I carried in the pocket of my cloak. I believed there was no reason to dread their being destroyed or purloined, if left, for a few hours or a day, in this recess. If left beside a stone, under shelter of this cliff, they would, no doubt, remain unmolested till the disappearance of the storm should permit me to revisit this spot in the afternoon or on the morrow.

Just as I had disposed of these encumbrances and had risen from my seat, my attention was again called to the opposite steep, by the most unwelcome object that, at this time, could possibly occur. Something was perceived moving among the bushes and rocks, which, for a time, I hoped was no more than a raccoon or opossum, but which presently appeared to be a panther. His gray coat, extended claws, fiery eyes, and a cry which he at that moment uttered, and which, by its resemblance to the human voice, is peculiarly terrific, denoted him to be the most ferocious and untamable of that detested race.*

The industry of our hunters has nearly banished animals of prey from these precincts. The fastnesses of Norwalk, however, could not but afford refuge to some of them. Of late I had met them so rarely, that my fears were seldom alive, and I trod, without caution, the ruggedest and most solitary haunts. Still, however, I had seldom been unfurnished in my rambles with the means of defense.

---

* The gray cougar. This animal has all the essential characteristics of a tiger. Though somewhat inferior in size and strength, these are such as to make him equally formidable to man. [C.B.B.]

My temper never delighted in carnage and blood. I found no pleasure in plunging into bogs, wading through rivulets, and penetrating thickets, for the sake of dispatching woodcocks and squirrels. To watch their gambols and flittings, and invite them to my hand, was my darling amusement when loitering among the woods and the rocks. It was much otherwise, however, with regard to rattlesnakes and panthers. These I thought it no breach of duty to exterminate wherever they could be found. These judicious and sanguinary spoilers were equally the enemies of man and of the harmless race that sported in the trees, and many of their skins are still preserved by me as trophies of my juvenile prowess.

As hunting was never my trade or sport, I never loaded myself with fowling-piece or rifle. Assiduous exercise had made me master of a weapon of much easier carriage, and, within a moderate distance, more destructive and unerring. This was the tomahawk. With this I have often severed an oak-branch, and cut the sinews of a catamount, at the distance of sixty feet.

The infrequency with which I had lately encountered this foe, and the encumbrance of provision, made me neglect, on this occasion, to bring with me my usual arms. The beast that was now before me, when stimulated by hunger, was accustomed to assail whatever could provide him with a banquet of blood. He would set upon the man and the deer with equal and irresistible ferocity. His sagacity was equal to his strength, and he seemed able to discover when his antagonist was armed and prepared for defense.

My past experience enabled me to estimate the full extent of my danger. He sat on the brow of the steep, eyeing the bridge, and apparently deliberating whether he should cross it. It was probable that he had scented my footsteps thus far, and, should he pass over, his vigilance could scarcely fail of detecting my asylum. The pit into which Clithero had sunk from my view was at some distance. To reach it was the first impulse of my fear, but this could not be done without exciting the observation and pursuit of this enemy. I deeply regretted the untoward chance that had led me, when I first came over, to a different shelter.

Should he retain his present station, my danger was scarcely lessened. To pass over in the face of a famished tiger was only to rush upon my fate. The falling of the trunk, which had lately been so anxiously deprecated, was now, with no less solicitude, desired. Every new gust, I hoped, would tear asunder its remaining bands, and, by cutting off all communication between the opposite steeps, place me in security.

My hopes, however, were destined to be frustrated. The fibers of the prostrate tree were obstinately tenacious of their hold, and presently the animal scrambled down the rock and proceeded to cross it.

Of all kinds of death, that which now menaced me was the most abhorred. To die by disease, or by the hand of a fellow-creature, was propitious and lenient in comparison with being rent to pieces by the fangs of this savage. To perish in this obscure retreat, by means so impervious to the anxious curiosity of my friends, to lose my portion of existence by so untoward and ignoble a destiny, was insupportable. I bitterly deplored my rashness in coming hither unprovided for an encounter like this.

The evil of my present circumstances consisted chiefly in suspense. My death was unavoidable, but my imagination had leisure to torment itself by anticipations. One foot of the savage was slowly and cautiously moved after the other. He struck his claws so deeply into the bark that they were with difficulty withdrawn. At length he leaped upon the ground. We were now separated by an interval of scarcely eight feet. To leave the spot where I crouched was impossible. Behind and beside me, the cliff rose perpendicularly, and before me was this grim and terrific visage. I shrunk still closer to the ground and closed my eyes.

From this pause of horror I was aroused by the noise occasioned by a second spring of the animal. He leaped into the pit, in which I had so deeply regretted that I had not taken refuge, and disappeared. My rescue was so sudden, and so much beyond my belief or my hope, that I doubted, for a moment, whether my senses did not deceive me. This opportunity of escape was not to be neglected. I left my place, and scrambled over the trunk with a precipitation which had liked to have proved fatal. The tree groaned and shook under me, the wind blew with unexampled violence, and I had scarcely reached the opposite steep when the roots were severed from the rock and the whole fell thundering to the bottom of the chasm.

My trepidations were not speedily quieted. I looked back with wonder on my hairbreadth escape, and on that singular concurrence of events which had placed me, in so short a period, in absolute security. Had the trunk fallen a moment earlier, I should have been imprisoned on the hill or thrown headlong. Had its fall been delayed another moment, I should have been pursued; for the beast now issued from his den, and testified his surprise and disappointment by tokens the sight of which made my blood run cold.

He saw me, and hastened to the verge of the chasm. He squatted on his hind-legs and assumed the attitude of one preparing to leap. My consternation was excited afresh by these appearances. It seemed at first as if the rift was too wide for any power of muscles to carry him in safety over; but I knew the unparalleled agility of this animal, and that his experience had made him a better judge of the practicability of this exploit than I was. Still there was hope that he would relinquish this design as desperate. This hope was quickly at an end. He sprung, and his fore-legs touched the verge of the rock on which I stood. In spite of vehement exertions, however, the surface was too smooth and too hard to allow him to make good his hold. He fell, and a piercing cry, uttered below, showed that nothing had obstructed his descent to the bottom.

Thus was I again rescued from death. Nothing but the pressure of famine could have prompted this savage to so audacious and hazardous an effort; but, by yielding to this impulse, he had made my future visits to this spot exempt from peril. Clithero was, likewise, relieved from a danger that was imminent and unforeseen. Prowling over these grounds, the panther could scarcely have failed to meet with this solitary fugitive.

Had the animal lived, my first duty would have been to have sought him out and assailed him with my tomahawk; but no undertaking would have been more hazardous. Lurking in the grass, or in the branches of a tree, his eye might have descried my approach, he might leap upon me unperceived, and my weapon would be useless.

With a heart beating with unwonted rapidity, I once more descended the cliff, entered the cavern, and arrived at Huntly farm, drenched with rain, and exhausted by fatigue.

By night the storm was dispelled; but my exhausted strength would not allow me to return to the mountain. At the customary hour I retired to my chamber. I incessantly ruminated on the adventures of the last day, and inquired into the conduct which I was next to pursue.

The bridge being destroyed, my customary access was cut off. There was no possibility of restoring this bridge. My strength would not suffice to drag a fallen tree from a distance, and there was none whose position would abridge or supersede that labor. Some other expedient must, therefore, be discovered to pass this chasm.

I reviewed the circumstances of my subterranean journey. The cavern was imperfectly explored. Its branches might be numerous. That which I had hitherto pursued terminated in an opening at a considerable distance from the bottom. Other branches might exist, some of which might lead to the foot of the precipice, and thence a communication might be found with the summit of the interior hill.

The danger of wandering into dark and untried paths, and the commodiousness of that road which had at first been taken, were sufficient reasons for having hitherto suspended my examination of the different branches of this labyrinth. Now my customary road was no longer practicable, and another was to be carefully explored. For this end, on my next journey to the mountain, I determined to take with me a lamp, and unravel this darksome maze: this project I resolved to execute the next day.

I now recollected what, if it had more seasonably occurred, would have taught me caution. Some months before this a farmer, living in the skirts of Norwalk, discovered two marauders in his field, whom he imagined to be a male and female panther. They had destroyed some sheep, and had been hunted by the farmer with long and fruitless diligence. Sheep had likewise been destroyed in different quarters; but the owners had fixed the imputation of the crime upon dogs, many of whom had atoned for their supposed offenses by death. He who had mentioned his discovery of panthers received little credit from his neighbors, because a long time had elapsed since these animals were supposed to have been exiled from this district, and because no other person had seen them. The truth of this seemed now to be confirmed by the testimony of my own senses; but, if the rumor were true, there still existed another of these animals, who might harbor in the obscurities of this desert, and against whom it was necessary to employ some precaution. Henceforth I resolved never to traverse the wilderness unfurnished with my tomahawk.

These images, mingled with those which the contemplation of futurity suggested, floated, for a time, in my brain, but at length gave place to sleep.

XIII

Since my return home, my mind had been fully occupied by schemes and reflections relative to Clithero. The project suggested by thee, and to which I had determined to devote my leisure, was forgotten, or remembered for a moment and at wide intervals. What, however, was nearly banished from my waking thoughts, occurred in an incongruous and half-seen form, to my dreams. During my sleep, the image of Waldegrave flitted before me. Methought the sentiment that impelled him to visit me was not affection or complacency, but inquietude and anger. Some service or duty remained to be performed by me, which I had culpably neglected: to inspirit my zeal, to awaken my remembrance, and incite me to the performance of this duty, did this glimmering messenger, this half-indignant apparition, come.

I commonly awake soon enough to mark the youngest dawn of the morning. Now, in consequence perhaps of my perturbed sleep, I opened my eyes before the stars had lost any of their lustre. This circumstance produced some surprise, until the images that lately hovered in my fancy were recalled, and furnished somewhat like a solution of the problem. Connected with the image of my dead friend was that of his sister. The discourse that took place at our last interview; the scheme of transcribing, for thy use, all the letters which, during his short but busy life, I received from him; the nature of this correspondence, and the opportunity which this employment would afford me of contemplating these ample and precious monuments of the intellectual existence and moral preeminence of my friend, occurred to my thoughts.

The resolution to prosecute the task was revived. The obligation of benevolence, with regard to Clithero, was not discharged. this neither duty nor curiosity would permit to be overlooked or delayed; but why should my whole attention and activity be devoted to this man? The hours which were spent at home and in my chamber could not be more usefully employed than in making my intended copy.

In a few hours after sunrise I purposed to resume my way to the mountain. Could this interval be appropriated to a better purpose than in counting over my friend's letters, setting them apart from my own, and preparing them for that transcription from which I expected so high and yet so mournful a gratification?

This purpose, by no violent union, was blended with the recollection of my dream. This recollection infused some degree of wavering and dejection into my mind. In transcribing these letters I should violate pathetic and solemn injunctions frequently repeated by the writer. Was there some connection between this purpose and the incidents of my vision? Was the latter sent to enforce the interdictions which had been formerly imposed?

Thou art not fully acquainted with the intellectual history of thy brother. Some information on that head will be necessary to explain the nature of that reluctance which I now feel to comply with thy request, and which had formerly so much excited thy surprise.

Waldegrave, like other men early devoted to meditation and books, had adopted, at different periods, different systems of opinion on topics connected with religion and morals. His earliest creeds tended to efface the impressions of his education; to deify necessity and universalize matter; to destroy the popular distinctions between soul and body, and to dissolve the supposed connection between the moral condition of man anterior and subsequent to death.

This creed he adopted with all the fullness of conviction, and propagated with the upmost zeal. Soon after our friendship commenced, fortune placed us at a distance from each other, and no intercourse was allowed but by the pen. Our letters, however, were punctual and copious. Those of Waldegrave were too frequently devoted to the defense of his favorite tenets.

Thou art acquainted with the revolution that afterwards took place in his mind. Placed within the sphere of religious influence, and listening daily to the reasonings and exhortations of Mr. S——, whose benign temper and blameless deportment was a visible and constant lesson, he insensibly resumed the faith which he had relinquished, and became the vehement opponent of all that he had formerly defended. The chief object of his labors, in this new state of his mind, was to counteract the effect of his former reasonings on my opinions.

At this time, other changes took place in his situation, in consequence of which we were once more permitted to reside under the same roof. The intercourse now ceased to be by letter, and the

subtle and laborious argumentations which he had formerly produced against religion, and which were contained in a permanent
form, were combated in transient conversation. He was not only
eager to subvert those opinions which he had contributed to instill
into me, but was anxious that the letters and manuscripts which
had been employed in their support should be destroyed. He
did not fear wholly or chiefly on my own account. He believed
that the influence of former reasonings on my faith would be
sufficiently eradicated by the new; but he dreaded lest these
manuscripts might fall into other hands, and thus produce mischiefs which it would not be in his power to repair. With regard
to me, the poison had been followed by its antidote; but with
respect to others, these letters would communicate the poison
when the antidote could not be administered.

I would not consent to this sacrifice. I did not entirely abjure the
creed which had, with great copiousness and eloquence, been defended in these letters. Besides, mixed up with abstract reasonings
were numberless passages which elucidated the character and history of my friend. These were too precious to be consigned to oblivion; and to take them out of their present connection and arrange-
ment would be to mutilate and deform them.

His entreaties and remonstrances were earnest and frequent, but
always ineffectual. He had too much purity of motives to be angry
at my stubbornness; but his sense of the mischievous tendency
of these letters was so great that my intractability cost him many
a pang.

He was now gone, and I had not only determined to preserve
these monuments, but had consented to copy them for the use
of another; for the use of one whose present and eternal welfare
had been the chief object of his cares and efforts. Thou, like
others of thy sex, art unaccustomed to metaphysical refinements.
Thy religion is the growth of sensibility and not of argument. Thou
art not fortified and prepossessed against the subleties with which
the being and attributes of the Deity have been assailed. Would
it be just to expose thee to pollution and depravity from this source?
To make thy brother the instrument of thy apostasy, the author
of thy fall? That brother whose latter days were so ardently devoted to cherishing the spirit of devotion in thy heart?

These ideas now occurred with more force than formerly. I had
promised, not without reluctance, to give thee the entire copy of
his letters; but I now receded from this promise. I resolved merely

to select for thy perusal such as were narrative or descriptive. This could not be done with too much expedition. It was still dark, but my sleep was at an end, and, by a common apparatus that lay beside my bed, I could instantly produce a light.

The light was produced, and I proceeded to the cabinet where all my papers and books are deposited. This was my own contrivance and workmanship, undertaken by the advice of Sarsefield, who took infinite pains to foster that mechanical genius which displayed itself so early and so forcibly in thy friend. The key belonging to this was, like the cabinet itself, of singular structure. For greater safety, it was constantly placed in a closet, which was likewise locked.

The key was found as usual, and the cabinet opened. The letters were bound together in a compact form, lodged in a parchment case, and placed in a secret drawer. This drawer would not have been detected by common eyes, and it opened by the motion of a spring, of whose existence none but the maker was conscious. This drawer I had opened before I went to sleep, and the letters were then safe.

Thou canst not imagine my confusion and astonishment, when, on opening the drawer, I perceived that the packet was gone. I looked with more attention, and put my hand within it; but the space was empty. Whither had it gone, and by whom was it purloined? I was not conscious of having taken it away, yet no hands but mine could have done it. On the last evening I had doubtless removed it to some other corner, but had forgotten it. I tasked my understanding and my memory. I could not conceive the possibility of any motives inducing me to alter my arrangements in this respect, and was unable to recollect that I had made this change.

What remained? This invaluable relic had disappeared. Every thought and every effort must be devoted to the single purpose of regaining it. As yet I did not despair. Until I had opened and ransacked every part of the cabinet in vain, I did not admit the belief that I had lost it. Even then this persuasion was tumultuous and fluctuating. It had vanished to my senses, but these senses were abused and depraved. To have passed, of its own accord, through the pores of this wood was impossible; but, if it were gone, thus did it escape.

I was lost in horror and amazement. I explored every nook a second and a third time, but still it eluded my eye and my touch. I opened my closets and cases. I pried everywhere, unfolded every article of clothing, turned and scrutinized every instrument and tool, but nothing availed.

My thoughts were not speedily collected or calmed. I threw myself on the bed and resigned myself to musing. That my loss was irretrievable was a supposition not to be endured. Yet ominous terrors haunted me—a whispering intimation that a relic which I valued more than life was torn forever away by some malignant and inscrutable destiny. The same power that had taken it from this receptacle was able to waft it over the ocean or the mountains, and condemn me to a fruitless and eternal search.

But what was he that committed the theft? Thou only, of the beings who live, wast acquainted with the existence of these manuscripts. Thou art many miles distant, and art utterly a stranger to the mode or place of their concealment. Not only access to the cabinet, but access to the room, without my knowledge and permission, was impossible. Both were locked during this night. Not five hours had elapsed since the cabinet and drawer had been opened, and since the letters had been seen and touched, being in their ordinary position. During this interval, the thief had entered, and despoiled me of my treasure.

This event, so inexplicable and so dreadful, threw my soul into a kind of stupor or distraction, from which I was suddenly roused by a footstep softly moving in the entry near my door. I started from my bed, as if I had gained a glimpse of the robber. Before I could run to the door, someone knocked. I did not think upon the propriety of answering the signal, but hastened with tremulous fingers and throbbing heart to open the door. My uncle, in his night-dress, and apparently just risen from his bed, stood before me!

He marked the eagerness and perturbation of my looks, and inquired into the cause. I did not answer his inquires. His appearance in my chamber and in this guise added to my surprise. My mind was full of the late discovery, and instantly conceived some connection between this unseasonable visit and my lost manuscript. I interrogated him in my turn as to the cause of his coming.

"Why," said he, "I came to ascertain whether it was you or not who amused himself so strangely at this time of night. What is the matter with you? Why are you up so early?"

I told him that I had been roused by my dreams, and, finding no inclination to court my slumber back again, I had risen, though earlier by some hours than the usual period of my rising.

"But why did you go upstairs? You might easily imagine that the sound of your steps would alarm those below, who would be puzzled to guess who it was that had thought proper to amuse himself in this manner."

"Upstairs? I have not left my room this night. It is not ten minutes since I awoke, and my door has not since been opened."

"Indeed! That is strange. Nay, it is impossible! It was your feet surely that I heard pacing so solemnly and indefatigably across the *long room* for near an hour. I could not for my life conjecture, for a time, who it was, but finally concluded that it was you. There was still, however, some doubt, and I came hither to satisfy myself."

These tidings were adapted to raise all my emotions to a still higher pitch. I questioned him with eagerness as to the circumstances he had noticed. He said he had been roused by a sound, whose power of disturbing him arose, not from its loudness, but from its uncommonness. He distinctly heard someone pacing to and fro with bare feet, in the long room. This sound continued, with little intermission, for an hour. He then noticed a cessation of the walking, and a sound as if someone were lifting the lid of the large cedar chest that stood in the corner of this room. The walking was not resumed, and all was silent. He listened for a quarter of an hour, and busied himself in conjecturing the cause of this disturbance. The most probable conclusion was, that the walker was his nephew, and his curiosity had led him to my chamber to ascertain the truth.

This dwelling has three stories. The two lower stories are divided into numerous apartments. The upper story constitutes a single room whose sides are the four walls of the house, and whose ceiling is the roof. This room is unoccupied, except by lumber, and imperfectly lighted by a small casement at one end. In this room were footsteps heard by my uncle.

The staircase leading to it terminated in a passage near my door. I snatched the candle, and, desiring him to follow me, added that I would ascertain the truth in a moment. He followed, but observed that the walking had ceased long enough for the person to escape.

I ascended to the room, and looked behind and among the tables, and chairs, and casks, which were confusedly scattered through it, but found nothing in the shape of man. The cedar chest, spoken of by Mr. Huntly, contained old books, and remnants of maps and charts, whose worthlessness unfitted them for accommodation elsewhere. The lid was without hinges or lock. I examined this repository, but there was nothing which attracted my attention.

The way between the kitchen door and the door of the long room had no impediments. Both were usually unfastened; but the motives by which any stranger to the dwelling, or indeed anyone within it, could be prompted to choose this place and hour for an employment of this kind, were wholly incomprehensible.

When the family rose, inquiries were made; but no satisfaction was obtained. The family consisted only of four persons: my uncle, my two sisters, and myself. I mentioned to them the loss I had sustained, but their conjectures were no less unsatisfactory on this than on the former incident.

There was no end to my restless meditations. Waldegrave was the only being, besides myself, acquainted with the secrets of my cabinet. During his life these manuscripts had been the objects of perpetual solicitude; to gain possession, to destroy or secrete them, was the strongest of his wishes. Had he retained his sensibility on the approach of death, no doubt he would have renewed, with irresistible solemnity, his injunctions to destroy them.

Now, however, they had vanished. There were no materials of conjecture; no probabilities to be weighed, or suspicions to revolve. Human artifice or power was unequal to this exploit. Means less than preternatural would not furnish a conveyance for this treasure.

It was otherwise with regard to this unseasonable walker. His inducements indeed were beyond my power to conceive; but to enter these doors and ascend these stairs demanded not the faculties of any being more than human.

This intrusion, and the pillage of my cabinet, were contemporary events. Was there no more connection between them than that which results from time? Was not the purloiner of my treasure and the wanderer the same person? I could not reconcile the former incident with the attributes of man; and yet a secret faith, not to be outrooted or suspended, swayed me, and compelled me to imagine that the detection of this visitant would unveil the thief.

These thoughts were pregnant with dejection and reverie. Clithero, during the day, was forgotten. On the succeeding night, my intentions, with regard to this man, returned. I derived some slender consolation from reflecting that time, in its long lapse and ceaseless revolutions, might dissipate the gloom that environed me. Meanwhile, I struggled to dismiss the images connected with my loss and to think only of Clithero.

My impatience was as strong as ever to obtain another interview with this man. I longed with vehemence for the return of day. I believed that every moment added to his sufferings, intellectual and physical, and confided in the efficacy of my presence to alleviate or suspend them. The provisions I had left would be speedily consumed, and the abstinence of three days was sufficient to undermine the vital energies. I sometimes hesitated whether I ought not instantly to depart. It was night indeed, but the late storm had purified the air, and the radiance of a full moon was universal and dazzling.

From this attempt I was deterred by reflecting that my own frame needed the repairs of sleep. Toil and watchfulness, if prolonged another day, would deeply injure a constitution by no means distinguished for its force. I must, therefore, compel, if it were possible, some hours of repose. I prepared to retire to bed, when a new incident occurred to divert my attention for a time from these designs.

XIV

While sitting alone by the parlor-fire, marking the effects of moonlight, I noted one on horseback coming towards the gate. At first sight, methought his shape and guise were not wholly new to me; but all that I could discern was merely a resemblance to someone whom I had before seen. Presently he stopped, and, looking towards the house, made inquiries of a passenger who chanced to be near. Being apparently satisfied with the answers he received, he rode with a quick pace into the court and alighted at the door. I started from my seat, and, going forth, waited with some impatience to hear his purpose explained.

He accosted me with the formality of a stranger, and asked if a young man, by name Edgar Huntly, resided here. Being answered in the affirmative, and being requested to come in, he entered, and seated himself, without hesitation, by the fire. Some doubt and anxiety were visible in his looks. He seemed desirous of information upon some topic, and yet betrayed terror lest the answers he might receive should subvert some hope or confirm some foreboding.

Meanwhile I scrutinized his features with much solicitude. A nearer and more deliberate view convinced me that the first impression was just; but still I was unable to call up his name or the circumstances of our former meeting. The pause was at length ended by his saying, in a faltering voice,—

"My name is Weymouth. I came hither to obtain information on a a subject in which my happiness is deeply concerned."

At the mention of his name, I started. It was a name too closely connected with the image of thy brother, not to call up affecting and vivid recollections. Weymouth, thou knowest, was thy brother's friend. It is three years since this man left America, during which time no tidings had been heard of him,—at least, by thy brother. He had now returned, and was probably unacquainted with the fate of his friend.

After an anxious pause, he continued: "Since my arrival I have heard of an event which has, on many accounts, given me the deepest sorrow. I loved Waldegrave, and know not any person in the

139

world whose life was dearer to me than his. There were considerations, however, which made it more precious to me than the life of one whose merits might be greater. With his life, my own existence and property were, I have reason to think, inseparably united.

"On my return to my country, after a long absence, I made immediate inquiries after him. I was informed of his untimely death. I had questions, of infinite moment to my happiness, to decide with regard to the state and disposition of his property. I sought out those of his friends who had maintained with him the most frequent and confidential intercourse, but they could not afford me any satisfaction. At length, I was informed that a young man of your name, and living in this district, had enjoyed more of his affection and society than any other, had regulated the property which he left behind, and was best qualified to afford the intelligence which I sought. You, it seems, are this person, and of you I must make inquiries to which I conjure you to return sincere and explicit answers."

"That," said I, "I shall find no difficulty in doing. Whatever questions you shall think proper to ask, I will answer with readiness and truth."

"What kind of property, and to what amount, was your friend possessed of at his death?"

"It was money, and consisted of deposits at the Bank of North America. The amount was little short of eight thousand dollars."

"On whom has this property devolved?"

"His sister was his only kindred, and she is now in possession of it."

"Did he leave any will by which he directed the disposition of his property?" While thus speaking, Weymouth fixed his eyes upon my countenance, and seemed anxious to pierce into my inmost soul. I was somewhat surprised at his questions, but much more at the manner in which they were put. I answered him, however, without delay: "He left no will, nor was any paper discovered by which we could guess at his intentions. No doubt, indeed, had he made a will, his sister would have been placed precisely in the same condition in which she now is. He was not only bound to her by the strongest ties of kindred, but by affection and gratitude."

Weymouth now withdrew his eyes from my face, and sunk into a mournful reverie. He sighed often and deeply. This deportment and the strain of his inquiries excited much surprise. His interest in the fate of Waldegrave ought to have made the information he had received a source of satisfaction rather than of regret. The property which Waldegrave left was much greater than his mode of life and his own professions had given us reason to expect, but it was no more than sufficient to insure to thee an adequate subsistence. It ascertained the happiness of those who were dearest to Waldegrave, and placed them forever beyond the reach of that poverty which had hitherto beset them. I made no attempt to interrupt the silence, but prepared to answer any new interrogatory. At length, Weymouth resumed:

"Waldegrave was a fortunate man to amass so considerable a sum in so short a time. I remember, when we parted, he was poor. He used to lament that his scrupulous integrity precluded him from all the common roads to wealth. He did not contemn riches, but he set the highest value upon competence, and imagined that he was doomed forever to poverty. His religious duty compelled him to seek his livelihood by teaching a school of blacks. The labor was disproportioned to his feeble constitution, and the profit was greatly disproportioned to the labor. It scarcely supplied the necessities of nature, and was reduced sometimes even below that standard by his frequent indisposition. I rejoice to find that his scruples had somewhat relaxed their force, and that he had betaken himself to some more profitable occupation. Pray, what was his new way of business?"

"Nay," said I, "his scruples continued as rigid, in this respect, as ever. He was teacher of the negro free-school when he died."

"Indeed! How, then, came he to amass so much money? Could he blend any more lucrative pursuit with his duty as a schoolmaster?"

"So it seems."

"What was his pursuit?"

"That question, I believe, none of his friends are qualified to answer. I thought myself acquainted with the most secret transactions of his life, but this had been carefully concealed from me. I was not only unapprised of any other employment of his time, but had not the slightest suspicion of his possessing any property besides his clothes and books. Ransacking his papers, with a different view, I lighted on his bank-book, in which was a regular receipt for seven thousand five hundred dollars. By what means he acquired this money, and even the acquisition of it, till his death put us in possession of his papers, was wholly unknown to us."

"Possibly he might have held it in trust for another. In this case some memorandums or letters would be found explaining this affair."

"True. This supposition could not fail to occur, in consequence of which the most diligent search was made among his papers, but no shred or scrap was to be found which countenanced our conjecture."

"You may reasonably be surprised, and perhaps offended," said Weymouth, "at these inquiries; but it is time to explain my motives for making them. Three years ago I was, like Waldegrave, indigent, and earned my bread by daily labor. During seven years' service in a public office, I saved, from the expenses of subsistence, a few hundred dollars. I determined to strike into a new path, and, with this sum, to lay the foundation of better fortune. I turned it into a bulky commodity, freighted and loaded a small vessel, and went with it to Barcelona in Spain. I was not unsuccessful in my projects, and, changing my abode to England, France, and Germany, according as my interest required, I became finally possessed of sufficient for the supply of all my wants. I then resolved to return to my native country, and, laying out my money in land, to spend the rest of my days in the luxury and quiet of an opulent farmer. For this end I invested the greatest part of my property in a cargo of wine from Madeira. The remainder I turned into a bill of exchange for seven thousand five hundred dollars. I had maintained a friendly correspondence with Waldegrave during my absence. There was no one with whom I had lived on terms of so much intimacy, and had boundless confidence in his integrity. To him therefore I determined to transmit this bill, requesting him to take the money into safekeeping until my return. In this manner I endeavored to provide against the accidents that might befall my person or my cargo in crossing the ocean.

"It was my fate to encounter the worst of these disasters. We were overtaken by a storm, my vessel was driven ashore on the coast of Portugal, my cargo was utterly lost, and the greater part of the crew and passengers were drowned. I was rescued from the same fate by some fishermen. In consequence of the hardships to which I had been exposed, having labored for several days at the pumps, and spent the greater part of a winter night hanging from the rigging of the ship and perpetually beaten by the waves, I contracted a severe disease, which bereaved me of the use of my limbs. The fishermen who rescued me carried me to their huts, and there I remained three weeks helpless and miserable.

"That part of the coast on which I was thrown was, in the highest degree, sterile and rude. Its few inhabitants subsisted precariously on the produce of the ocean. Their dwellings were of mud,—low, filthy, dark, and comfortless. Their fuel was the stalks of shrubs sparingly scattered over a sandy desert. Their poverty scarcely allowed them salt and black bread with their fish, which was obtained in unequal and sometimes insufficient quantities, and which they ate with all its impurities, and half-cooked.

"My former habits, as well as my present indisposition, required very different treatment from what the ignorance and penury of these people obliged them to bestow. I lay upon the moist earth, imperfectly sheltered from the sky, and with neither raiment nor fire to keep me warm. My hosts had little attention or compassion to spare to the wants of others. They could not remove me to a more hospitable district; and here, without doubt, I should have perished, had not a monk chanced to visit their hovels. He belonged to a convent of St. Jago, some leagues farther from the shore, which used to send one of its members annually to inspect the religious concerns of those outcasts. Happily, this was the period of their visitations.

"This monk was touched with compassion at my calamity, and speedily provided the means of my removal to his convent. Here I was charitably entertained, and the aid of a physician was procured for me. He was but poorly skilled in his profession, and rather confirmed than alleviated my disease. The Portuguese of his trade, especially in remoter districts, are little more than dealers in talismans and nostrums. For a long time I was unable to leave my pallet, and had no prospect before me but that of consuming my days in the gloom of this cloister.

"All the members of this convent but he who had been my first benefactor, and whose name was Chaledro, were bigoted and sordid. Their chief motive for treating me with kindness was the hope of obtaining a convert from heresy. They spared no pains to subdue my errors, and were willing to prolong my imprisonment, in the hope of finally gaining their end. Had my fate been governed by those, I should have been immured in this convent, and compelled either to adopt their fanatical creed or to put an end to my own life, in order to escape their well-meant persecutions. Chaledro, however, though no less sincere in his faith and urgent in his entreaties, yet finding me invincible, exerted his influence to obtain my liberty.

"After many delays, and strenuous exertions of my friend, they consented to remove me to Oporto. The journey was to be performed in an open cart, over a mountainous country, in the heats of summer. The monks endeavored to dissuade me from the enterprise, for my own sake, it being scarcely possible that one in my feeble state should survive a journey like this; but I despaired of improving my condition by other means. I preferred death to the imprisonment of a Portuguese monastery, and knew that I could hope for no alleviation of my disease but from the skill of Scottish or French physicians, whom I expected to meet with in that city. I adhered to my purpose with so much vehemence and obstinacy that they finally yielded to my wishes.

"My road lay through the wildest and most rugged districts. It did not exceed ninety miles, but seven days were consumed on the way. The motion of the vehicle racked me with the keenest pangs, and my attendants concluded that every stage would be my last. They had been selected without due regard to their characters. They were knavish and inhuman, and omitted nothing but actual violence to hasten my death. They purposely retarded the journey, and protracted to seven what might have been readily performed in four days. They neglected to execute the orders which they had received respecting my lodging and provisions; and from them, as well as from the peasants, who were sure to be informed that I was a heretic, I suffered every species of insult and injury. My constitution, as well as my frame, possessed a fund of strength of which I had no previous conception. In spite of hardship, and exposure, and abstinence, I at last arrived at Oporto.

"Instead of being carried, agreeably to Chaledro's directon, to a convent of St. Jago, I was left, late in the evening, in the porch of a common hospital. My attendants, having left me on the pavement and loaded me with imprecations, left me to obtain admission by my own efforts. I passed the livelong night in this spot, and in the morning was received into the house in a state which left it uncertain whether I was alive or dead.

"After recovering my sensibility, I made various efforts to procure a visit from some English merchant. This was no easy undertaking for one in my deplorable condition. I was too weak to articulate my words distinctly, and these words were rendered, by my foreign accents, scarcely intelligible. The likelihood of my speedy death made the people about me more indifferent to my wants and petitions.

"I will not dwell upon my repeated disappointments, but content myself with mentioning that I gained the attention of a French gentleman whose curiosity brought him to view the hospital. Through him I obtained a visit from an English merchant, and finally gained the notice of a person who formerly resided in America, and of whom I had imperfect knowledge. By their kindness I was removed from the hospital to a private house. A Scottish surgeon was summoned to my assistance, and in seven months I was restored to my present state of health.

"At Oporto, I embarked, in an American ship, for New York. I was destitute of all property, and relied, for the payment of the debts which I was obliged to contract, as well as for my future subsistence, on my remittance to Waldegrave. I hastened to Philadelphia, and was soon informed that my friend was dead. His death had taken place a long time since my remittance to him, hence this disaster was a subject of regret chiefly on his own account. I entertained no doubt but that my property had been secured, and that either some testamentary directions or some papers had been left behind respecting this affair.

"I sought out those who were formerly our mutual acquaintance. I found that they were wholly strangers to his affairs. They could merely relate some particulars of his singular death, and point out the lodgings which he formerly occupied. Hither I forthwith repaired, and discovered that he lived in this house with his sister, disconnected with its other inhabitants. They described his mode of life in terms that showed them to be very imperfectly acquainted with it. It was easy indeed to infer, from their aspect and manners, that little sympathy or union could have subsisted between them and their co-tenants; and this inference was confirmed by their insinuations, the growth of prejudice and envy. They told me that Waldegrave's sister had gone to live in the country, but whither, or for how long, she had not condescended to inform them, and they did not care to ask. She was a topping dame, whose notions were much too high for her station; who was more nice than wise, and yet was one who could stoop when it most became her to stand upright. It was no business of theirs; but they could not but mention their suspicions that she had good reasons for leaving the city and for concealing the place of her retreat. Some things were hard to be disguised. They spoke for themselves, and the only way to hinder disagreeable discoveries was to keep out of sight.

"I was wholly a stranger to Waldegrave's sister. I knew merely that he had such a relation. There was nothing, therefore, to out-balance this unfavorable report, but the apparent malignity and grossness of those who gave it. It was not, however, her character about which I was solicitous, but merely the place where she might be found and the suitable inquiries respecting her deceased brother be answered. On this head, these people professed utter ignor-ance, and were either unable or unwilling to direct me to any per-son in the city who knew more than themselves. After much dis-course, they, at length, let fall an intimation that, if anyone knew her place of retreat, it was probably a country lad, by name Huntly, who lived near the *Forks* of Delaware. After Waldegrave's death this lad had paid his sister a visit, and seemed to be admitted on a very confidential footing. She left the house, for the last time, in his company, and he, therefore, was most likely to know what had become of her.

"The name of Huntly was not totally unknown to me. I myself was born and brought up in the neighboring township of Chetasco. I had some knowledge of your family, and your name used often to be mentioned by Waldegrave as that of one who, at a maturer age, would prove himself useful to his country. I determined, there-fore, to apply to you for what information you could give. I de-signed to visit my father, who lives in Chetasco, and relieve him from that disquiet which his ignorance of my fate could not fail to have inspired, and both these ends could be thus, at the same time, accomplished.

"Before I left the city, I thought it proper to apply to the mer-chant on whom my bill had been drawn. If this bill had been pre-sented and paid, he had doubtless preserved some record of it, and hence a clue might be afforded, though every other expedient should fail. My usual ill fortune pursued me upon this occasion; for the merchant had lately become insolvent, and, to avoid the rage of his creditors, had fled, without leaving any vestige of this or similar transactions behind him. He had, some years since, been an adventurer from Holland, and was suspected to have returned thither.

XV

"I came hither with a heart desponding of success. Adversity had weakened my faith in the promises of the future, and I was prepared to receive just such tidings as you have communicated. Unacquainted with the secret motives of Waldegrave and his sister, it is impossible for me to weigh the probabilities of their rectitude. I have only my own assertion to produce in support of my claim. All other evidence, all vouchers and papers, which might attest my veracity or sanction my claim in a court of law, are buried in the ocean. The bill was transmitted just before my departure from Madeira, and the letters by which it was accompanied informed Waldegrave of my design to follow it immediately. Hence he did not, it is probable, acknowledge the receipt of my letters. The vessels in which they were sent arrived in due season. I was assured that all the letters were duly deposited in the post office, where, at present, mine are not to be found.

"You assure me that nothing has been found among his papers, hinting at any pecuniary transaction between him and me. Some correspondence passed between us previous to that event. Have no letters, with my signature, been found? Are you qualified, by your knowledge of his papers, to answer me explicitly? Is it not possible for some letters to have been mislaid?"

"I am qualified," said I, "to answer your inquiries beyond any other person in the world. Waldegrave maintained only general intercourse with the rest of mankind. With me his correspondence was copious, and his confidence, as I imagined, without bounds. His books and papers were contained in a single chest at his lodgings, the keys of which he had about him when he died. Those keys I carried to his sister, and was authorized by her to open and examine the contents of this chest. This was done with the utmost care. These papers are now in my possession. Among them no paper of the tenor you mention was found, and no letter with your signature. Neither Mary Waldegrave nor I are capable of disguising the truth or committing an injustice. The moment she receives conviction of your right, she will restore this money to you. The moment I imbibe his conviction, I will exert all my influence (and it is not small) to induce her to restore it. Permit me, however, to question you in your turn. Who was the merchant on whom your bill was drawn, what was the date of it, and when did the bill and it counterparts arrive?"

"I do not exactly remember the date of the bills. They were made out, however, six days before I myself embarked, which happened on the 10th of August, 1784. They were sent by three vessels, one of which was bound to Charleston and the others to New York. The last arrived within two days of each other, and about the middle of November in the same year. The name of the payer was Monteith."

After a pause of recollection, I answered, "I will not hesitate to apprise you of everything which may throw light upon this transaction, and whether favorable or otherwise to your claim. I have told you, among my friend's papers your name is not to be found. I must likewise repeat that the possession of this money by Waldegrave was wholly unknown to us till his death. We are likewise unacquainted with any means by which he could get possession of so large a sum in his own right. He spent no more than his scanty stipend as a teacher, though this stipend was insufficient to supply his wants. This bank-receipt is dated in December, 1784, a fortnight, perhaps, after the date that you have mentioned. You will perceive how much this coincidence, which could scarcely have taken place by chance, is favorable to your claim.

"Mary Waldegrave resides, at present, at Abingdon. She will rejoice, as I do, to see one who, as her brother's friend, is entitled to her affection. Doubt not but that she will listen with impartiality and candor to all that you can urge in defense of your title to this money. Her decision will not be precipitate, but it will be generous and just, and founded on such reasons that, even if it be adverse to your wishes, you will be compelled to approve it."

"I can entertain no doubt," he answered, "as to the equity of my claim. The coincidences you mention are sufficient to convince me that this sum was received upon my bill; but this conviction must necessarily be confined to myself. No one but I can be conscious to the truth of my own story. The evidence on which I build my faith, in this case, is that of my own memory and senses; but this evidence cannot make itself conspicuous to you. You have nothing but my bare assertion, in addition to some probabilities flowing from the conduct of Waldegrave. What facts may exist to corroborate my claim, which you have forgotten, or which you may think proper to conceal, I cannot judge. I know not what is passing in the secret of your hearts; I am unacquainted with the character of this lady and with yours. I have nothing on which to build surmises and suspicions of your integrity, and nothing to generate unusual confidence. The frailty of your virture and the strength of your temptations I know not. However she decides in this case, and whatever opinion I shall form as to the reasonableness of her decision, it will not become me either to upbraid her, or to nourish discontentment and repinings.

"I know that my claim has no legal support; that, if this money be resigned to me, it will be the impulse of spontaneous justice, and not the coercion of law, to which I am indebted for it. Since, therefore, the justice of my claim is to be measured not by law, but by simple equity, I will candidly acknowledge that, as yet, it is uncertain whether I ought to receive, even should Miss Waldegrave be willing to give it. I know my own necessities and schemes, and in what degree this money would be subservient to these; but I know not the views and wants of others, and cannot estimate the usefulness of this money to them. However I decide upon your conduct in withholding or retaining it, I shall make suitable allowance for my imperfect knowledge of your motives and wants, as well as for your unavoidable ignorance of mine.

"I have related my sufferings from shipwreck and poverty, not to bias your judgment or engage your pity, but merely because the impulse to relate them chanced to awake; because my heart is softened by the remembrance of Waldegrave, who has been my only friend, and by the sight of one whom he loved.

"I told you that my father lived in Chetasco. He is now aged, and I am his only child. I should have rejoiced in being able to relieve his gray hairs from labor to which his failing strength cannot be equal. This was one of my inducements in coming to America. Another was to prepare the way for a woman whom I married in Europe and who is now awaiting intelligence from me in London. Her poverty is not less than my own, and by marrying against the wishes of her kindred she has bereaved herself of all support but that of her husband. Whether I shall be able to rescue her from indigence, whether I shall alleviate the poverty of my father, or increase it by burdening his scanty funds by my own maintenance as well as his, the future alone can determine.

"I confess that my stock of patience and hope has never been large, and that my misfortunes have nearly exhausted it. The flower of my years has been consumed in struggling with adversity, and my constitution has received a shock, from sickness and mistreatment in Portugal, which I cannot expect long to survive. But I make you sad," he continued. "I have said all that I meant to say in this interview. I am impatient to see my father, and night has already come. I have some miles yet to ride to his cottage, and over a rough road. I will shortly visit you again, and talk to you at greater leisure on these and other topics. At present I leave you."

I was unwilling to part so abruptly with this guest, and entreated him to prolong his visit; but he would not be prevailed upon. Repeating his promise of shortly seeing me again, he mounted his horse and disappeared. I looked after him with affecting and complex emotions. I reviewed the incidents of this unexpected and extraordinary interview, as if it had existed in a dream. An hour had passed, and this stranger had alighted among us as from the clouds, to draw the veil from those obscurities which had bewildered us so long, to make visible a new train of disastrous consequences flowing from the untimely death of thy brother, and to blast that scheme of happiness on which thou and I had so fondly meditated.

But what wilt thou think of this new-born claim? The story, hadst thou observed the features and guise of the relater, would have won thy implicit credit. His countenance exhibited deep traces of the afflictions he had endured, and the fortitude which he had exercised. He was sallow and emaciated, but his countenance was full of seriousness and dignity. A sort of ruggedness of brow, the token of great mental exertion and varied experience, argued a premature old age.

What a mournful tale! Is such the lot of those who wander from their rustic homes in search of fortune? Our countrymen are prone to enterprise, and are scattered over every sea and every land in pursuit of that wealth which will not screen them from disease and infirmity, which is missed much oftener than found, and which, when gained, by no means compensates them for the hardships and vicissitudes endured in the pursuit.

But what if the truth of these pretensions be admitted? The money must be restored to its right owner. I know that, whatever inconveniences may follow the deed, thou wilt not hesitate to act justly. Affluence and dignity, however valuable, may be purchased too dear. Honesty will not take away its keenness from the winter blast, its ignominy and unwholesomeness from servile labor, or strip of its charms the life of elegance and leisure; but these, unaccompanied with self-reproach, are less deplorable than wealth and honor the possession of which is marred by our own disapprobation.

I know the bitterness of this sacrifice. I know the impatience with which your poverty has formerly been borne; how much your early education is at war with that degradation and obscurity to which your youth has been condemned; how earnestly your wishes panted after a state which might exempt you from dependence upon daily labor and on the caprices of others, and might secure to you leisure to cultivate and indulge your love of knowledge and your social and beneficent affections.

Your motive for desiring a change of fortune has been greatly enforced since we have become known to each other. Thou hast honored me with thy affection; but that union, on which we rely for happiness, could not take place while both of us were poor. My habits, indeed, have made labor and rustic obscurity less painful than they would prove to my friend, but my present condition is wholly inconsistent with marriage. As long as my exertions are insufficient to maintain us both, it would be unjustifiable to burden you with new cares and duties. Of this you are more thoroughly convinced than I am. The love of independence and ease, and impatience of drudgery, are woven into your constitution. Perhaps they are carried to an erroneous extreme, and derogate from that uncommon excellence by which your character is, in other respects, distinguished; but they cannot be removed.

This obstacle was unexpectedly removed by the death of your brother. However justly to be deplored was this catastrophe, yet, like every other event, some of its consequences were good. By giving you possession of the means of independence and leisure, by enabling us to complete a contract which poverty alone had thus long delayed, this event has been, at the same time, the most disastrous and propitious which could have happened.

Why thy brother should have concealed from us the possession of this money,—why, with such copious means of indulgence and leisure, he should still pursue his irksome trade, and live in so penurious a manner,—has been a topic of endless and unsatisfactory conjecture between us. It was not difficult to suppose that this money was held in trust for another; but in that case it was unavoidable that some document or memorandum, or at least some claimant, would appear. Much time has since elapsed, and you have thought yourself at length justified in appropriating this money to your own use.

Our flattering prospects are now shut in. You must return to your original poverty, and once more depend for precarious subsistence on your needle. You cannot restore the whole, for unavoidable expenses and the change of your mode of living have consumed some part of it. For so much you can consider yourself as Weymouth's debtor.

Repine not, my friend, at this unlooked-for reverse. Think upon the merits and misfortunes of your brother's friend; think upon his aged father, whom we shall enable him to rescue from poverty; think upon his desolate wife, whose merits are, probably, at least equal to your own, and whose helplessness is likely to be greater. I am not insensible to the evils which have returned upon us with augmented force, after having, for a moment, taken their flight. I know the precariousness of my condition and that of my sister; that our subsistence hangs upon the life of an old man. My uncle's death will transfer this property to his son, who is a stranger and an enemy to us, and the first act of whose authority will unquestionably be to turn us forth from these doors. Marriage with thee was anticipated with joyous emotions, not merely on my own account or on thine, but likewise for the sake of those beloved girls to whom that event would enable me to furnish an asylum.

But wedlock is now more distant than ever. My heart bleeds to think of the sufferings which my beloved Mary is again fated to endure; but regrets are only aggravations of calamity. They are pernicious, and it is our duty to shake them off.

I can entertain no doubt as to the equity of Weymouth's claim. So many coincidences could not have happened by chance. The non-appearance of any letters or papers connected with it is indeed a mysterious circumstance; but why should Waldegrave be studious of preserving these? They were useless paper, and might, without impropriety, be cast away or made to serve any temporary purpose. Perhaps, indeed, they still lurk in some unsuspected corner. To wish that time may explain this mystery in a different manner, and so as to permit our retention of this money, is, perhaps, the dictate of selfishness. The transfer to Weymouth will not be productive of less benefit to him and to his family than we should derive from the use of it.

These considerations, however, will be weighed when we meet. Meanwhile I will return to my narrative.

XVI

Here, my friend, thou must permit me to pause. The following incidents are of a kind to which the most ardent invention has never conceived a parallel. Fortune, in her most wayward mood, could scarcely be suspected of an influence like this. The scene was pregnant with astonishment and horror. I cannot, even now, recall it without reviving the dismay and confusion which I then experienced.

Possibly, the period will arrive when I shall look back without agony on the perils I have undergone. That period is still distant. Solitude and sleep are now no more than the signals to summon up a tribe of ugly phantoms. Famine, and blindness, and death, and savage enemies, never fail to be conjured up by the silence and darkness of the night. I cannot dissipate them by any efforts of reason. My cowardice requires the perpetual consolation of light. My heart droops when I mark the decline of the sun, and I never sleep but with candle burning at my pillow. If, by any chance, I should awake and find myself immersed in darkness, I know not what act of desperation I might be suddenly impelled to commit.

I have delayed this narrative longer than my duty to my friend enjoined. Now that I am able to hold a pen, I will hasten to terminate that uncertainty with regard to my fate in which my silence has involved thee. I will recall that series of unheard-of and disastrous vicissitudes which has constituted the latest portion of my life.

I am not certain, however, that I shall relate them in an intelligible manner. One image runs into another; sensations succeed in so rapid a train, that I fear I shall be unable to distribute and express them with sufficient perspicuity. As I look back, my heart is sore, and aches within my bosom. I am conscious to a kind of complex sentiment of distress and forlornness that cannot be perfectly portrayed by words; but I must do as well as I can. In the utmost vigor of my faculties, no eloquence that I possess would do justice to the tale. Now, in my languishing and feeble state, I shall furnish thee with little more than a glimpse of the truth. With these glimpses, transient and faint as they are, thou must be satisfied.

I have said that I slept. My memory assures me of this; it informs me of the previous circumstances of my laying aside my clothes, of placing the light upon a chair within reach of my pillow, of throwing myself upon the bed, and of gazing on the rays of the moon reflected on the wall and almost obscured by those of the candle. I remember my occasional relapses into fits of incoherent fancies, the harbingers of sleep. I remember, as it were, the instant when my thoughts ceased to flow and my senses were arrested by the leaden wand of forgetfulness.

My return to sensation and to consciousness took place in no such tranquil scene. I emerged from oblivion by degrees so slow and so faint, that their succession cannot be marked. When enabled at length to attend to the information which my senses afforded, I was conscious for a time of nothing but existence. It was unaccompanied with lassitude or pain, but I felt disinclined to stretch my limbs or raise my eyelids. My thoughts were wildering and mazy, and, though consciousness was present, it was disconnected with the locomotive or voluntary power.

From this state a transition was speedily effected. I perceived that my posture was supine, and that I lay upon my back. I attempted to open my eyes. The weight that oppressed them was too great for a slight exertion to remove. The exertion which I made cost me a pang more acute than any which I ever experienced. My eyes, however, were opened; but the darkness that environed me was as intense as before.

I attempted to rise, but my limbs were cold, and my joints had almost lost their flexibility. My efforts were repeated, and at length I attained a sitting posture. I was now sensible of pain in my shoulders and back. I was universally in that state to which the frame is reduced by blows of a club, mercilessly and endlessly repeated; my temples throbbed, and my face was covered with clammy and cold drops; but that which threw me into deepest consternation was my inability to see. I turned my head to different quarters; I stretched my eyelids, and exerted every visual energy, but in vain. I was wrapped in the murkiest and most impenetrable gloom.

The first effort of reflection was to suggest the belief that I was blind; that disease is known to assail us in a moment and without previous warning. This, surely, was the misfortune that had now befallen me. Some ray, however fleeting and uncertain, could not fail to be discerned, if the power of vision were not utterly extinguished. In what circumstances could I possibly be placed, from which every particle of light should, by other means, be excluded?

This led my thoughts into a new train. I endeavored to recall the past; but the past was too much in contradiction to the present, and my intellect was too much shattered by external violence, to allow me accurately to review it.

Since my sight availed nothing to the knowledge of my condition, I betook myself to other instruments. The element which I breathed was stagnant and cold. The spot where I lay was rugged and hard. I was neither naked nor clothed: a shirt and trousers composed my dress, and the shoes and stockings, which always accompanied these, were now wanting. What could I infer from this scanty garb, this chilling atmosphere, this stony bed?

I had awakened as from sleep. What was my condition when I fell asleep? Surely it was different from the present. Then I inhabited a lightsome chamber and was stretched upon a down bed; now I was supine upon a rugged surface and immersed in palpable obscurity. Then I was in perfect health; now my frame was covered with bruises and every joint was racked with pain. What dungeon or den had received me, and by whose command was I transported hither?

After various efforts I stood upon my feet. At first I tottered and staggered. I stretched out my hands on all sides, but met only with vacuity. I advanced forward. At the third step my foot moved something which lay upon the ground: I stooped and took it up, and found, on examination, that it was an Indian tomahawk. This incident afforded me no hint from which I might conjecture my state.

Proceeding irresolutely and slowly forward, my hands at length touched a wall. This, like the flooring, was of stone, and was rugged and impenetrable. I followed this wall. An advancing angle occurred at a short distance, which was followed by similar angles. I continued to explore this clue, till the suspicion occurred that I was merely going round the walls of a vast and irregular apartment.

The utter darkness disabled me from comparing directions and distances. This discovery, therefore, was not made on a sudden, and was still entangled with some doubt. My blood recovered some warmth, and my muscles some elasticity; but in proportion as my sensibility returned, my pains augmented. Overpowered by my fears and my agonies, I desisted from my fruitless search, and sat down, supporting my back against the wall.

My excruciating sensations for a time occupied my attention. These, in combination with other causes, gradually produced a species of delirium. I existed, as it were, in a wakeful dream. With nothing to correct my erroneous perceptions, the images of the past occurred in capricious combinations and vivid hues. Methought I was the victim of some tyrant who had thrust me into a dungeon of his fortress, and left me no power to determine whether he intended I should perish with famine, or linger out a long life in hopeless imprisonment. Whether the day was shut out by insuperable walls, or the darkness that surrounded me was owing to the night and to the smallness of those crannies through which daylight was to be admitted, I conjectured in vain.

Sometimes I imagined myself buried alive. Methought I had fallen into seeming death, and my friends had consigned me to the tomb, from which a resurrection was impossible. That, in such a case, my limbs would have been confined to a coffin, and my coffin to a grave, and that I should instantly have been suffocated, did not occur to destroy my supposition. Neither did this supposition overwhelm me with terror or prompt my efforts at deliverance. My state was full of tumult and confusion, and my attention was incessantly divided between my painful sensations and my feverish dreams.

There is no standard by which time can be measured but the succession of our thoughts and the changes that take place in the external world. From the latter I was totally excluded. The former made the lapse of some hours appear like the tediousness of weeks and months. At length, a new sensation recalled my rambling meditations, and gave substance to my fears. I now felt the cravings of hunger, and perceived that, unless my deliverance were speedily effected, I must suffer a tedious and lingering death.

I once more tasked my understanding and my senses to discover the nature of my present situation and the means of escape. I listened to catch some sound. I heard an unequal and varying echo, sometimes near and sometimes distant, sometimes dying away and sometimes swelling into loudness. It was unlike anything I had before heard, but it was evident that it arose from wind sweeping through spacious halls and winding passages. These tokens were incompatible with the result of the examinations I had made. If my hands were true, I was immured between walls through which there was no avenue.

I now exerted my voice, and cried as loud as my wasted strength

would admit. Its echoes were sent back to me in broken and confused sounds and from above. This effort was casual, but some part
of that uncertainty in which I was involved was instantly dispelled
by it. In passing through the cavern on the former day, I have mentioned the verge of the pit at which I arrived. To acquaint me as
far as was possible with the dimensions of the place, I had hallooed
with all my force, knowing that sound is reflected according to the
distance and relative positions of the substances from which it
is repelled.

The effect produced by my voice on this occasion resembled,
with remarkable exactness, the effect which was then produced.
Was I, then, shut up in the same cavern? Had I reached the brink
of the same precipice and been thrown headlong into that vacuity? Whence else could arise the bruises which I had received, but
from my fall? Yet all remembrance of my journey hither was lost.
I had determined to explore this cave on the ensuing day, but my
memory informed me not that this intention had been carried into
effect. Still, it was only possible to conclude that I had come hither
on my intended expedition, and had been thrown by another, or
had, by some ill chance, fallen, into the pit.

This opinion was conformable to what I had already observed.
The pavement and walls were rugged like those of the footing and
sides of the cave through which I had formerly passed.

But if this were true, what was the abhorred catastrophe to which
I was now reserved? The sides of this pit were inaccessible; human
footsteps would never wander into these recesses. My friends were
unapprised of my forlorn state. Here I should continue till wasted
by famine. In this grave should I linger out a few days in unspeakable agonies, and then perish forever.

The inroads of hunger were already experienced; and this knowledge of the desperateness of my calamity urged me to frenzy. I
had none but capricious and unseen fate to condemn. The author
of my distress, and the means he had taken to decoy me hither,
were incomprehensible. Surely my senses were fettered or depraved by some spell. I was still asleep, and this was merely a tormenting vision; or madness had seized me, and the darkness that
environed and the hunger that afflicted me existed only in my own
distempered imagination.

The consolation of these doubts could not last long. Every hour
added to the proof that my perceptions were real. My hunger
speedily became ferocious. I tore the linen of my shirt between

my teeth and swallowed the fragments. I felt a strong propensity to bite the flesh from my arm. My heart overflowed with cruelty, and I pondered on the delight I should experience in rending some living animal to pieces, and drinking its blood and grinding its quivering fibers between my teeth.

This agony had already passed beyond the limits of endurance. I saw that time, instead of bringing respite or relief, would only aggravate my wants, and that my only remaining hope was to die before I should be assaulted by the last extremes of famine. I now recollected that a tomahawk was at hand, and rejoiced in the possession of an instrument by which I could so effectually terminate my sufferings.

I took it in my hand, moved its edge over my fingers, and reflected on the force that was required to make it reach my heart. I investigated the spot where it should enter, and strove to fortify myself with resolution to repeat the stroke a second or third time, if the first should prove insufficient. I was sensible that I might fail to inflict a mortal wound, but delighted to consider that the blood which would be made to flow would finally release me, and that meanwhile my pains would be alleviated by swallowing this blood.

You will not wonder that I felt some reluctance to employ so fatal though indispensable a remedy. I once more ruminated on the possibility of rescuing myself by other means. I now reflected that the upper termination of the wall could not be an immeasurable distance from the pavement. I had fallen from a height; but if that height had been considerable, instead of being merely bruised, should I not have been dashed into pieces?

Gleams of hope burst anew upon my soul. Was it not possible, I asked, to reach the top of this pit? The sides were rugged and uneven. Would not their projectures and abruptnesses serve me as steps by which I might ascend in safety? This expedient was to be tried without delay. Shortly my strength would fail, and my doom would be irrevocably sealed.

I will not enumerate my laborious efforts, my alternations of despondency and confidence, the eager and unwearied scrutiny with which I examined the surface, the attempts which I made, and the failures which, for a time, succeeded each other. A hundred times, when I had ascended some feet from the bottom, I was compelled to relinquish my undertaking by the *untenable* smoothness of the spaces which remained to be gone over. A hundred times I threw myself, exhausted by fatigue and my pains, on the ground. The consciousness was gradually restored that, till I had attempted every part of the wall, it was absurd to despair, and I again drew my tottering limbs and aching joints to that part of the wall which had not been surveyed.

At length, as I stretched my hand upward, I found somewhat that seemed like a recession in the wall. It was possible that this was the top of the cavity, and this might be the avenue to liberty. My heart leaped with joy, and I proceeded to climb the wall. No undertaking could be conceived more arduous than this. The space between this verge and the floor was nearly smooth. The verge was higher from the bottom than my head. The only means of ascending that were offered me were by my hands, with which I could draw myself upward so as, at length, to maintain my hold with my feet.

My efforts were indefatigable, and at length I placed myself on the verge. When this was accomplished, my strength was nearly gone. Had I not found space enough beyond this brink to stretch myself at length, I should unavoidably have fallen backward into the pit, and all my pains had served no other end than to deepen my despair and hasten my destruction.

What impediments and perils remained to be encountered I could not judge. I was now inclined to forebode the worst. The interval of repose which was necessary to be taken, in order to recruit my strength, would accelerate the ravages of famine, and leave me without the power to proceed.

In this state, I once more consoled myself that an instrument of death was at hand. I had drawn up with me the tomahawk, being sensible that, should this impediment be overcome, others might remain that would prove insuperable. Before I employed it, however, I cast my eyes wildly and languidly around. The darkness was no less intense than in the pit below, and yet two objects were distinctly seen.

They resembled a fixed and obscure flame. They were motionless. Though lustrous themselves, they created no illumination around them. This circumstance, added to others, which reminded me of similar objects noted on former occasions, immediately explained the nature of what I beheld. These were the eyes of a panther.

Thus had I struggled to obtain a post where a savage was lurking and waited only till my efforts should place me within reach of his fangs. The first impulse was to arm myself against this enemy. The desperateness of my condition was, for a moment, forgotten. The weapon which was so lately lifted against my own bosom was now raised to defend my life against the assault of another.

There was no time for deliberation and delay. In a moment he might spring from his station and tear me to pieces. My utmost speed might not enable me to reach him where he sat, but merely to encounter his assault. I did not reflect how far my strength was adequate to save me. All the force that remained was mustered up and exerted in a throw.

No one knows the powers that are latent in his constitution. Called forth by imminent dangers, our efforts frequently exceed our most sanguine belief. Though tottering on the verge of dissolution, and apparently unable to crawl from this spot, a force was exerted in this throw probably greater than I had ever before exerted. It was resistless and unerring. I aimed at the middle space between those glowing orbs. It penetrated the skull, and the animal fell, struggling and shrieking, on the ground.

My ears quickly informed me when his pangs were at an end. His cries and his convulsions lasted for a moment and then ceased. The effect of his voice, in these subterranean abodes, was unspeakably rueful.

The abruptness of this incident, and the preternatural exertion of my strength, left me in a state of languor and sinking, from which slowly and with difficulty I recovered. The first suggestion that occurred was to feed upon the carcass of this animal. My hunger had arrived at that pitch where all fastidiousness and scruples are at an end. I crept to the spot. I will not shock you by relating the extremes to which dire necessity had driven me. I review this scene with loathing and horror. Now that it is past I look back upon it as on some hideous dream. The whole appears to be some freak of insanity. No alternative was offered, and hunger was capable of being appeased even by a banquet so detestable.

If this appetite has sometimes subdued the sentiments of nature, and compelled the mother to feed upon the flesh of her offspring, it will not excite amazement that I did not turn from the yet warm blood and reeking fibers of a brute.

One evil was now removed, only to give place to another. The first sensations of fullness had scarcely been felt when my stomach was seized by pangs, whose acuteness exceeded all that I ever before experienced. I bitterly lamented my inordinate avidity.

The excruciations of famine were better than the agonies which this abhorred meal had produced.

Death was now impending with no less proximity and certainty, though in a different form. Death was a sweet relief for my present miseries, and I vehemently longed for its arrival. I stretched myself on the ground. I threw myself into every posture that promised some alleviation of this evil. I rolled along the pavement of the cavern, wholly inattentive to the dangers that environed me. That I did not fall into the pit whence I had emerged must be ascribed to some miraculous chance.

How long my miseries endured, it is not possible to tell. I cannot even form a plausible conjecture. Judging by the lingering train of my sensations, I should conjecture that some days elapsed in this deplorable condition; but nature could not have so long sustained a conflict like this.

Gradually my pains subsided, and I fell into a deep sleep. I was visited by dreams of a thousand hues. They led me to flowing streams and plenteous banquets, which, though placed within my view, some power forbade me to approach. From this sleep I recovered to the fruition of solitude and darkness, but my frame was in a state less feeble than before. That which I had eaten had produced temporary distress, but on the whole had been of use. If this food had not been provided for me, I should scarcely have avoided death. I had reason, therefore, to congratulate myself on the danger that had lately occurred.

I had acted without foresight, and yet no wisdom could have prescribed more salutary measures. The panther was slain, not from a view to the relief of my hunger, but from the self-preserving and involuntary impulse. Had I foreknown the pangs to which my ravenous and bloody meal would give birth, I should have carefully abstained; and yet these pangs were a useful effort of nature to subdue and convert to nourishment the matter I had swallowed.

I was now assailed by the torments of thirst. My invention and my courage were anew bent to obviate this pressing evil. I reflected that there was some recess from this cavern, even from the spot where I now stood. Before, I was doubtful whether in this direction from this pit any avenue could be found; but, since the panther had come hither, there was reason to suppose the existence of some such avenue.

I now likewise attended to a sound, which, from its invariable tenor, denoted somewhat different from the whistling of a gale. It seemed like the murmur of a running stream. I now prepared to go forward and endeavor to move along in that direction in which this sound apparently came.

On either side, and above my head, there was nothing but vacuity. My steps were to be guided by the pavement, which, though unequal and rugged, appeared, on the whole, to ascend. My safety required that I should employ both hands and feet in exploring my way.

I went on thus for a considerable period. The murmur, instead of becoming more distinct, gradually died away. My progress was arrested by fatigue, and I began once more to despond. My exertions produced a perspiration, which, while it augmented my thirst, happily supplied me with imperfect means of appeasing it.

This expedient would, perhaps, have been accidentally suggested; but my ingenuity was assisted by remembering the history of certain English prisoners in Bengal, whom their merciless enemy imprisoned in a small room, and some of whom preserved themselves alive merely by swallowing the moisture that flowed from their bodies. This experiment I now performed with no less success.

This was slender and transitory consolation. I knew that, wandering at random, I might never reach the outlet of this cavern, or might be disabled, by hunger and fatigue, from going farther than the outlet. The cravings which had lately been satiated would speedily return, and my negligence had cut me off from the resource which had recently been furnished. I thought not till now that a second meal might be indispensable.

To return upon my footsteps to the spot where the dead animal lay was a heartless project. I might thus be placing myself at a hopeless distance from liberty. Besides, my track could not be retraced. I had frequently deviated from a straight direction for the sake of avoiding impediments. All of which I was sensible was that I was travelling up an irregular acclivity. I hoped some time to reach the summit, but had no reason for adhering to one line of ascent in preference to another.

To remain where I was was manifestly absurd. Whether I mounted or descended, a change of place was most likely to benefit me. I resolved to vary my direction, and, instead of ascending, keep along the side of what I accounted a hill. I had gone some hundred feet when the murmur, before described, once more saluted my ear.

This sound, being imagined to proceed from a running stream, could not but light up joy in the heart of one nearly perishing with thirst. I proceeded with new courage. The sound approached no nearer, nor became more distinct; but, as long as it died not away, I was satisfied to listen and to hope.

I was eagerly observant if any the least glimmering of light should visit this recess. At length, on the right hand, a gleam, infinitely faint, caught my attention. It was wavering and unequal. I directed my steps towards it. It became more vivid and permanent. It was of that kind, however, which proceeded from a fire, kindled with dry sticks, and not from the sun. I now heard the crackling of flames.

This sound made me pause, or, at least, to proceed with circumspection. At length the scene opened, and I found myself at the entrance of a cave. I quickly reached a station, when I saw a fire burning. At first no other object was noted, but it was easy to infer that the fire was kindled by men, and that they who kindled it could be at no great distance.

XVII

Thus was I delivered from my prison, and restored to the enjoyment of the air and the light. Perhaps the chance was almost miraculous that led me to this opening. In any other direction, I might have involved myself in an inextricable maze and rendered my destruction sure; but what now remained to place me in absolute security? Beyond the fire I could see nothing; but, since the smoke rolled rapidly away, it was plain that on the opposite side the cavern was open to the air.

I went forward, but my eyes were fixed upon the fire; presently, in consequence of changing my station, I perceived several feet, and the skirts of blankets. I was somewhat startled at these appearances. The legs were naked, and scored into uncouth figures. The *moccasins* which lay beside them, and which were adorned in a grotesque manner, in addition to other incidents, immediately suggested the suspicion that they were Indians. No spectacle was more adapted than this to excite wonder and alarm. Had some mysterious power snatched me from the earth, and cast me, in a moment, into the heart of the wilderness? Was I still in the vicinity of my parental habitation, or was I thousands of miles distant?

Were these the permanent inhabitants of this region, or were they wanderers and robbers? While in the heart of the mountain, I had entertained a vague belief that I was still within the precincts of Norwalk. This opinion was shaken for a moment by the objects which I now beheld, but it insensibly returned; yet how was this opinion to be reconciled to appearances so strange and uncouth, and what measure did a due regard to my safety enjoin me to take?

I now gained a view of four brawny and terrific figures, stretched upon the ground. They lay parallel to each other, on their left sides, in consequence of which their faces were turned from me. Between each was an interval where lay a musket. Their right hands seemed placed upon the stocks of their guns, as if to seize them on the first moment of alarm.

The aperture through which these objects were seen was at the back of the cave, and some feet from the ground. It was merely large enough to suffer a human body to pass. It was involved in profound darkness, and there was no danger of being suspected or discovered as long as I maintained silence and kept out of view.

It was easily imagined that these guests would make but a short sojourn in this spot. There was reason to suppose that it was now night, and that, after a short repose, they would start up and resume their journey. It was my first design to remain shrouded in this covert till their departure, and I prepared to endure imprisonment and thirst somewhat longer.

Meanwhile my thoughts were busy in accounting for this spectacle. I need not tell thee that Norwalk is the termination of a sterile and narrow tract which begins in the Indian country. It forms a sort of rugged and rocky vein, and continues upwards of fifty miles. It is crossed in a few places by narrow and intricate paths, by which a communication is maintained between the farms and settlements on the opposite sides of the ridge.

During former Indian wars, this rude surface was sometimes traversed by the red men, and they made, by means of it, frequent and destructive inroads into the heart of the English settlements. During the last war, notwithstanding the progress of population, and the multiplied perils of such an expedition, a band of them had once penetrated into Norwalk, and lingered long enough to pillage and murder some of the neighboring inhabitants.

I have reason to remember that event. My father's house was placed on the verge of this solitude. Eight of these assassins assailed it at the dead of night. My parents and an infant child were murdered in their beds; the house was pillaged, and then burnt to the ground. Happily, myself and my two sisters were abroad upon a visit. The preceding day had been fixed for our return to our father's house; but a storm occurred, which made it dangerous to cross the river, and, by obliging us to defer our journey, rescued us from captivity or death.

Most men are haunted by some species of terror or antipathy, which they are, for the most part, able to trace to some incident which befell them in their early years. You will not be surprised that the fate of my parents, and the sight of the body of one of this savage band, who, in the pursuit that was made after them, was overtaken and killed, should produce lasting and terrific images in my fancy. I never looked upon or called up the image of a savage without shuddering.

I knew that, at this time, some hostilities had been committed on the frontier; that a long course of injuries and encroachments had lately exasperated the Indian tribes; that an implacable and exterminating war was generally expected. We imagined ourselves at an inaccessible distance from the danger; but I could not but remember that this persuasion was formerly as strong as at present, and that an expedition which had once succeeded might possibly be attempted again. Here was every token of enmity and bloodshed. Each prostrate figure was furnished with a rifled musket, and a leathern bag tied round his waist, which was, probably, stored with powder and ball.

From these reflections, the sense of my own danger was revived and enforced; but I likewise ruminated on the evils which might impend over others. I should, no doubt, be safe by remaining in this nook; but might not some means be pursued to warn others of their danger? Should they leave this spot without notice of their approach being given to the fearless and pacific tenants of the neighboring district, they might commit, in a few hours, the most horrid and irreparable devastation.

The alarm could only be diffused in one way. Could I not escape unperceived, and without alarming the sleepers, from this cavern? The slumber of an Indian is broken by the slightest noise; but, if all noise be precluded, it is commonly profound. It was possible, I conceived, to leave my present post, to descend into the cave, and issue forth without the smallest signal. Sleep usually comes at their bidding, and if, perchance, they should be wakeful at an unseasonable moment, they always sit upon their haunches, and, leaning their elbows on their knees, consume the tedious hours in smoking. My peril would be great. Accidents which I could not foresee, and over which I had no command, might occur to awaken someone at the moment I was passing the fire. Should I pass in safety, I might issue forth into a wilderness, of which I had no knowledge, where I might wander till I perished with famine, or where my footsteps might be noted and pursued and overtaken by these implacable foes. These perils were enormous and imminent; but I likewise considered that I might be at no great distance from the habitations of men, and that my escape might rescue them from the most dreadful calamities. I determined to make this dangerous experiment without delay.

I came nearer to the aperture, and had, consequently, a larger view of this recess. To my unspeakable dismay, I now caught a glimpse of one seated at the fire. His back was turned towards me, so that I could distinctly survey his gigantic form and fantastic ornaments.

My project was frustrated. This one was probably commissioned to watch and to awaken his companions when a due portion of sleep had been taken. That he would not be unfaithful or remiss in the performance of the part assigned to him was easily predicted. To pass him without exciting his notice (and the entrance could not otherwise be reached) was impossible. Once more I shrunk back, and revolved with hopelessness and anguish the necessity to which I was reduced.

This interval of dreary foreboding did not last long. Some motion in him that was seated by the fire attracted my notice. I looked, and beheld him rise from his place and go forth from the cavern. This unexpected incident led my thoughts into a new channel. Could not some advantage be taken of his absence? Could not this opportunity be seized for making my escape? He had left his gun and hatchet on the ground. It was likely, therefore, that he had not gone far, and would speedily return. Might not these weapons be seized, and some provision be thus made against the danger of meeting him without, or of being pursued?

Before a resolution could be formed, a new sound saluted my ear. It was a deep groan, succeeded by sobs that seemed struggling for utterance but were vehemently counteracted by the sufferer. This low and bitter lamentation apparently proceeded from someone within the cave. It could not be from one of this swarthy band. It must, then, proceed from a captive, whom they had reserved for torment or servitude, and who had seized the opportunity afforded by the absence of him that watched to give vent to his despair.

I again thrust my head forward, and beheld, lying on the ground, apart from the rest and bound hand and foot, a young girl. Her dress was the coarse russet garb of the country, and bespoke her to be some farmer's daughter. Her features denoted the last degree of fear and anguish, and she moved her limbs in such a manner as showed that the ligatures by which she was confined produced, by their tightness, the utmost degree of pain.

My wishes were now bent not only to preserve myself and to frustrate the future attempts of these savages, but likewise to relieve this miserable victim. This could only be done by escaping from the cavern and returning with seasonable aid. The sobs of the girl were likely to rouse the sleepers. My appearance before her would prompt her to testify her surprise by some exclamation or shriek. What could hence be predicted but that the band would start on their feet and level their unerring pieces at my head?

I know not why I was insensible to these dangers. My thirst was rendered by these delays intolerable. It took from me, in some degree, the power of deliberation. The murmurs which had drawn me hither continued still to be heard. Some torrent or cascade could not be far distant from the entrance of the cavern, and it seemed as if one draught of clear water was a luxury cheaply purchased by death itself. This, in addition to considerations more disinterested, and which I have already mentioned, impelled me forward.

The girl's cheek rested on the hard rock, and her eyes were dim with tears. As they were turned towards me, however, I hoped that my movements would be noticed by her gradually and without abruptness. This expectation was fulfilled. I had not advanced many steps before she discovered me. This moment was critical beyond all others in the course of my existence. My life was suspended, as it were, by a spider's thread. All rested on the effect which this discovery should make upon this feeble victim.

I was watchful of the first movement of her eye which should indicate a consciousness of my presence. I labored, by gestures and looks, to deter her from betraying her emotion. My attention was, at the same time, fixed upon the sleepers, and an anxious glance was cast toward the quarter whence the watchful savage might appear.

I stooped and seized the musket and hatchet. The space beyond the fire was, as I expected, open to the air. I issued forth with trembling steps. The sensations inspired by the dangers which environed me, added to my recent horrors, and the influence of the moon, which had now gained the zenith, and whose lustre dazzled my long-benighted senses, cannot be adequately described.

For a minute, I was unable to distinguish objects. This confusion was speedily corrected, and I found myself on the verge of a steep. Craggy eminences arose on all sides. On the left hand was a space that offered some footing, and hither I turned. A torrent was below me, and this path appeared to lead to it. It quickly appeared in sight, and all foreign cares were, for a time, suspended.

This water fell from the upper regions of the hill, upon a flat projecture which was continued on either side, and on part of which I was now standing. The path was bounded on the left by an inaccessible wall, and on the right terminated, at the distance of two or three feet from the wall, in a precipice. The water was eight or ten paces distant, and no impediment seemed likely to rise between us. I rushed forward with speed.

My progress was quickly checked. Close to the falling water, seated on the edge, his back supported by the rock, and his legs hanging over the precipice, I now beheld the savage who left the cave before me. The noise of the cascade and the improbability of interruption, at least from this quarter, had made him inattentive to my motions.

I paused. Along this verge lay the only road by which I could reach the water, and by which I could escape. The passage was completely occupied by this antagonist. To advance toward him, or to remain where I was, would produce the same effect. I should, in either case, be detected. He was unarmed; but his outcries would instantly summon his companions to his aid. I could not hope to overpower him and pass him in defiance of his opposition. But, if this were effected, pursuit would be instantly commenced. I was unacquainted with the way. The way was unquestionably difficult. My strength was nearly annihilated; I should be overtaken in a moment, or their deficiency in speed would be supplied by the accuracy of their aim. Their bullets, at least, would reach me.

There was one method of removing this impediment. The piece which I held in my hand was cocked. There could be no doubt that it was loaded. A precaution of this kind would never be omitted by a warrior of this hue. At a greater distance than this, I should not fear to reach the mark. Should I not discharge it, and, at the same moment, rush forward to secure the road which my adversary's death would open to me?

Perhaps you will conceive a purpose like this to have argued a sanguinary and murderous disposition. Let it be remembered, however, that I entertained no doubts about the hostile designs of these men. This was sufficiently indicated by their arms, their guise, and the captive who attended them. Let the fate of my parents be, likewise, remembered. I was not certain but that these very men were the assassins of my family, and were those who had reduced me and my sisters to the condition of orphans and dependants. No words can describe the torments of my thirst. Relief to these torments, and safety to my life, were within view. How could I hesitate?

Yet I did hesitate. My aversion to bloodshed was not to be sub-

dued but by the direst necessity. I knew, indeed, that the discharge
of a musket would only alarm the enemies who remained behind;
but I had another and a better weapon in my grasp. I could rive
the head of my adversary, and cast him headlong, without any noise
which should be heard, into the cavern.

Still I was willing to withdraw, to re-enter the cave, and take
shelter in the darksome recesses from which I had emerged. Here
I might remain, unsuspected, till these detested guests should
depart. The hazards attending my re-entrance were to be boldly
encountered, and the torments of unsatisfied thirst were to be patiently endured, rather than imbrue my hands in the blood of my
fellowmen. But this expedient would be ineffectual if my retreat
should be observed by this savage. Of that I was bound to be incontestably assured. I retreated, therefore, but kept my eye fixed
at the same time upon the enemy.

Some ill fate decreed that I should not retreat unobserved.
Scarcely had I withdrawn three paces when he started from his
seat, and, turning towards me, walked with a quick pace. The shadow of the rock, and the improbability of meeting an enemy here,
concealed me for a moment from his observation. I stood still. The
slightest motion would have attracted his notice. At present, the
narrow space engaged all his vigilance. Cautious footsteps, and attention to the path, were indispensable to his safety. The respite
was momentary, and I employed it in my own defense.

How otherwise could I act? The danger that impended aimed
at nothing less than my life. To take the life of another was the only
method of averting it. The means were in my hand, and they were
used. In an extremity like this, my muscles would have acted almost in defiance of my will.

The stroke was quick as lightning, and the wound was mortal
and deep. He had not time to descry the author of his fate, but,
sinking on the path, expired without a groan. The hatchet buried
itself in his breast, and rolled with him to the bottom of the
precipice.

Never before had I taken the life of a human creature. On this
head I had, indeed, entertained somewhat of religious scruples.
These scruples did not forbid me to defend myself, but they made
me cautious and reluctant to decide. Though they could not withhold my hand when urged by a necessity like this, they were suf-

ficient to make me look back upon the deed with remorse and dismay.

I did not escape all compunction in the present instance, but the tumult of my feelings was quickly allayed. To quench my thirst was a consideration by which all others were supplanted. I approached the torrent, and not only drank copiously, but laved my head, neck, and arms in this delicious element.

XVIII

Never was any delight worthy of comparison with the raptures which I then experienced. Life, that was rapidly ebbing, appeared to return upon me with redoubled violence. My languors, my excruciating heat, vanished in a moment, and I felt prepared to undergo the labors of Hercules. Having fully supplied the demands of nature in this respect, I returned to reflection on the circumstances of my situation. The path winding round the hill was now free from all impediments. What remained but to precipitate my flight? I might speedily place myself beyond all danger. I might gain some hospitable shelter, where my fatigues might be repaired by repose, and my wounds be cured. I might likewise impart to my protectors seasonable information of the enemies who meditated their destruction.

I thought upon the condition of the hapless girl whom I had left in the power of the savages. Was it impossible to rescue her? Might I not relieve her from her bonds, and make her the companion of my flight? The exploit was perilous, but not impracticable. There was something dastardly and ignominious in withdrawing from the danger, and leaving a helpless being exposed to it. A single minute might suffice to snatch her from death or captivity. The parents might deserve that I should hazard or even sacrifice my life in the cause of their child.

After some fluctuation, I determined to return to the cavern and attempt the rescue of the girl. The success of this project depended on the continuance of their sleep. It was proper to approach with wariness, and to heed the smallest token which might bespeak their condition. I crept along the path, bending my ear forward to catch any sound that might arise. I heard nothing but the half-stifled sobs of the girl.

I entered with the slowest and most anxious circumspection. Everything was found in its pristine state. The girl noticed my entrance with a mixture of terror and joy. My gestures and looks enjoined upon her silence. I stooped down, and, taking another hatchet, cut asunder the deer-skin thongs by which her wrists and ankles were tied. I then made signs for her to rise and follow me. She willingly complied with my directions; but her benumbed joints and lacerated sinews refused to support her. There was no time to be lost; I therefore lifted her in my arms, and, feeble and tottering as I was, proceeded with this burden along the perilous steep and over a most rugged path.

I hoped that some exertion would enable her to retrieve the use of her limbs. I set her, therefore, on her feet, exhorting her to walk as well as she was able, and promising her my occasional assistance. The poor girl was not deficient in zeal, and presently moved along with light and quick steps. We speedily reached the bottom of the hill.

No fancy can conceive a scene more wild and desolate than that which now presented itself. The soil was nearly covered with sharp fragments of stone. Between these sprung brambles and creeping vines, whose twigs, crossing and intertwining with each other, added to the roughness below, made the passage infinitely toilsome. Scattered over this space were single cedars with their ragged spines and wreaths of moss, and copses of dwarf oaks, which were only new emblems of sterility.

I was wholly unacquainted with the scene before me. No marks of habitation or culture, no traces of the footsteps of men, were discernible. I scarcely knew in what region of the globe I was placed. I had come hither by means so inexplicable as to leave it equally in doubt whether I was separated from my paternal abode by a river or an ocean.

I made inquiries of my companion, but she was unable to talk coherently. She answered my questions with weeping, and sobs, and entreaties to fly from the scene of her distress. I collected from her, at length, that her father's house had been attacked on the preceding evening, and all the family but herself destroyed. Since this disaster she had walked very fast and a great way, but knew not how far or in what direction.

In a wilderness like this, my only hope was to light upon obscure paths, made by cattle. Meanwhile I endeavored to adhere to one line, and to burst through the vexatious obstacles which encumbered our way. The ground was concealed by the bushes, and we were perplexed and fatigued by a continual succession of hollows and prominences. At one moment we were nearly thrown headlong into a pit. At another we struck our feet against the angles of stones. The branches of the oak rebounded in our faces or entangled our legs, and the unseen thorns inflicted on us a thousand wounds.

I was obliged, in these arduous circumstances, to support not only myself, but my companion. Her strength was overpowered by her evening journey, and the terror of being overtaken incessantly harassed her.

Sometimes we lighted upon tracks which afforded us an easier footing and inspired us with courage to proceed. These, for a time, terminated at a brook or in a bog, and we were once more compelled to go forward at random. One of these tracks insensibly became more beaten, and, at length, exhibited the traces of wheels. To this I adhered, confident that it would finally conduct us to a dwelling.

On either side, the undergrowth of shrubs and brambles continued as before. Sometimes small spaces were observed, which had lately been cleared by fire. At length a vacant space, of larger dimensions than had hitherto occurred, presented itself to my view. It was a field of some acres, that had, apparently, been upturned by the hoe. At the corner of this field was a small house.

My heart leaped with joy at this sight. I hastened towards it, in the hope that my uncertainties, and toils, and dangers were now drawing to a close. This dwelling was suited to the poverty and desolation which surrounded it. It consisted of a few unhewn logs laid upon each other, to the height of eight or ten feet, including a quadrangular space of similar dimensions, and covered by a thatch. There was no window, light being sufficiently admitted into the crevices between the logs. These had formerly been loosely plastered with clay; but air and rain had crumbled and washed the greater part of this rude cement away. Somewhat like a chimney, built of half-burnt bricks, was perceived at one corner. The door was fastened by a leathern thong, tied to a peg.

All within was silence and darkness. I knocked at the door and called, but no one moved or answered. The tenant, whoever he was, was absent. His leave could not be obtained, and I, therefore, entered without it. The autumn had made some progress, and the air was frosty and sharp. My mind and muscles had been of late so strenuously occupied, that the cold had not been felt. The cessation of exercise, however, quickly restored my sensibility in this respect, but the unhappy girl complained of being half frozen.

Fire, therefore, was the first object of my search. Happily, some embers were found upon the hearth, together with potato-stalks and dry chips. Of these, with much difficulty, I kindled a fire, by which some warmth was imparted to our shivering limbs. The light enabled me, as I sat upon the ground, to survey the interior of this mansion.

Three saplings, stripped of their branches and bound together at their ends by twigs, formed a kind of bedstead, which was raised from the ground by four stones. Ropes stretched across these and, covered by a blanket, constituted the bed. A board, of which one end rested on the bedstead and the other was thrust between the logs that composed the wall, sustained the stale fragments of a rye-loaf, and a cedar bucket kept entire by withes instead of hoops. In the bucket was a little water, full of droppings from the roof, drowned insects, and sand. A basket or two neatly made, and a hoe, with a stake thrust into it by way of handle, made up all the furniture that was visible.

Next to cold, hunger was the most urgent necessity by which we were now pressed. This was no time to give ear to scruples. We, therefore, unceremoniously divided the bread and water between us. I had now leisure to bestow some regards upon the future.

These remnants of fire and food convinced me that this dwelling was usually inhabited, and that it had lately been deserted. Some engagement had probably carried the tenant abroad. His absence might be terminated in a few minutes, or might endure through the night. On his return, I questioned not my power to appease any indignation he might feel at the liberties which I had taken. I was willing to suppose him one who would readily afford us all the information and succor that we needed.

If he should not return till sunrise, I meant to resume my journey. By the comfortable meal we had made, and the repose of a few hours, we should be considerably invigorated and refreshed, and the road would lead us to some more hospitable tenement.

My thoughts were too tumultuous, and my situation too precarious, to allow me to sleep. The girl, on the contrary, soon sank into a sweet oblivion of all her cares. She laid herself, by my advice, upon the bed, and left me to ruminate without interruption.

I was not wholly free from the apprehension of danger. What influence this boisterous and solitary life might have upon the temper of the being who inhabited this hut, I could not predict. How soon the Indians might awake and what path they would pursue, I was equally unable to guess. It was by no means impossible that they might tread upon my footsteps, and knock, in a few minutes, at the door of this cottage. It behooved me to make all the preparations in my power against untoward incidents.

I had not parted with the gun which I had first seized in the cavern, nor with the hatchet which I had afterwards used to cut the bands of the girl. These were at once my trophies and my means of defense, which it had been rash and absurd to have relinquished. My present reliance was placed upon these.

I now, for the first time, examined the prize that I had made, Other considerations had prevented me, till now, from examining the structure of the piece; but I could not but observe that it had two barrels, and was lighter and smaller than an ordinary musket The light of the fire now enabled me to inspect it with accuracy.

Scarcely had I fixed my eyes upon the stock, when I perceived marks that were familiar to my apprehension. Shape, ornaments, and ciphers were evidently the same with those of a piece which I had frequently handled. The marks were of a kind which could not be mistaken. This piece was mine; and, when I left my uncle's house, it was deposited, as I believed, in the closet of my chamber.

Thou wilt easily conceive the inference which this circumstance suggested. My hairs rose and my teeth chattered with horror. My whole frame was petrified, and I paced to and fro, hurried from the chimney to the door, and from the door to the chimney, with the misguided fury of a maniac.

I needed no proof of my calamity more incontestable than this. My uncle and my sisters had been murdered; the dwelling had been pillaged, and this had been a part of the plunder. Defenseless and asleep, they were assailed by these inexorable enemies, and I, who ought to have been their protector and champion, was removed to an immeasurable distance, and was disabled, by some accursed chance, from affording them the succor which they needed.

For a time, I doubted whether I had not witnessed and shared this catastrophe. I had no memory of the circumstances that preceded my awaking in the pit. Had not the cause of my being cast into this abyss some connection with the ruin of my family? Had I not been dragged hither by these savages, and reduced, by their malice, to that breathless and insensible condition? Was I born to a malignant destiny never tired of persecuting? Thus had my parents and their infant offspring perished, and thus completed was the fate of all those to whom my affections cleaved, and whom the first disaster had spared.

Hitherto the death of the savage, whom I had dispatched with my hatchet, had not been remembered without some remorse. Now my emotions were totally changed. I was somewhat comforted in thinking that thus much of necessary vengeance had been executed. New and more vehement regrets were excited by reflecting on the forbearance I had practiced when so much was within my power. All the miscreants had been at my mercy, and a bloody retribution might, with safety and ease, have been inflicted on their prostrate bodies.

It was now too late. What of consolation or of hope remained to me? To return to my ancient dwelling, now polluted with blood, or, perhaps, nothing but a smoking ruin, was abhorred. Life, connected with the remembrance of my misfortunes, was detestable. I was no longer anxious for flight. No change of the scene but that which terminated all consciousness could I endure to think of.

Amidst these gloomy meditations the idea was suddenly suggested of returning, with the utmost expedition, to the cavern. It was possible that the assassins were still asleep. He who was appointed to watch, and to make, in due season, the signal for resuming their march, was forever silent. Without this signal it was not unlikely that they would sleep till dawn of day. But, if they should be roused, they might be overtaken or met, and, by choosing a proper station, two victims might at least fall. The ultimate event to myself would surely be fatal; but my own death was an object of desire rather than of dread. To die thus speedily, and after some atonement was made for those who had already been slain, was sweet.

The way to the mountain was difficult and tedious, but the ridge was distinctly seen from the door of the cottage, and I trusted that auspicious chance would lead me to that part of it where my prey was to be found. I snatched up the gun and tomahawk in a transport of eagerness. On examining the former, I found that both barrels were deeply loaded.

This piece was of extraordinary workmanship. It was the legacy of an English officer, who died in Bengal, to Sarsefield. It was constructed for the purposes not of sport but of war. The artist had made it a congeries of tubes and springs, by which every purpose of protection and offense was effectually served. A dagger's blade was attached to it, capable of being fixed at the end, and of answering the destructive purpose of a bayonet. On his departure from Solesbury, my friend left it, as a pledge of his affection, in my possession. Hitherto I had chiefly employed it in shooting at a mark, in order to improve my sight; now was I to profit by the gift in a different way.

Thus armed, I prepared to sally forth on my adventurous expedition. Sober views might have speedily succeeded to the present tempest of my passions. I might have gradually discovered the romantic and criminal temerity of my project, the folly of revenge, and the duty of preserving my life for the benefit of mankind. I might have suspected the propriety of my conclusion, and have admitted some doubts as to the catastrophe which I imagined to have befallen my uncle and sisters. I might, at least, have consented to ascertain their condition with my own eyes, and for this end have returned to the cottage, and have patiently waited till the morning light should permit me to resume my journey.

This conduct was precluded by a new incident. Before I opened the door I looked through a crevice of the wall, and perceived three human figures at the farther end of the field. They approached the house. Though indistinctly seen, something in their port persuaded me that these were the Indians from whom I had lately departed. I was startled but not dismayed. My thirst of vengeance was still powerful, and I believed that the moment of its gratification was hastening. In a short time they would arrive and enter the house. In what manner should they be received?

I studied not my own security. It was the scope of my wishes to kill the whole number of my foes; but, that being done, I was indifferent to the consequences. I desired not to live to relate or to exult in the deed.

To go forth was perilous and useless. All that remained was to sit upon the ground opposite the door, and fire at each as he entered. In the hasty survey I had taken of this apartment, one object had been overlooked, or imperfectly noticed. Close to the chimney was an aperture, formed by a cavity partly in the wall and in the ground. It was the entrance of an oven, which resembled, on the outside, a mound of earth, and which was filled with dry stalks of potatoes and other rubbish.

Into this it was possible to thrust my body. A sort of screen might be formed of the brushwood, and more deliberate and effectual execution be done upon the enemy. I weighed not the disadvantages of this scheme, but precipitately threw myself into this cavity. I discovered, in an instant, that it was totally unfit for my purpose; but it was too late to repair my miscarriage.

This wall of the hovel was placed near the verge of a sand-bank. The oven was erected on the very brink. This bank, being of a loose and mutable soil, could not sustain my weight. It sunk, and I sunk along with it. The height of the bank was three or four feet, so that, though disconcerted and embarrassed, I received no injury. I still grasped my gun, and resumed my feet in a moment.

What was now to be done? The bank screened me from the view of the savages. The thicket was hard by, and, if I were eager to escape, the way was obvious and sure. But, though single, though enfeebled by toil, by abstinence, and by disease, and though so much exceeded in number and strength by my foes, I was determined to await and provoke the contest.

In addition to the desperate impulse of passion, I was swayed by thoughts of the danger which beset the sleeping girl, and from which my flight would leave her without protection. How strange is the destiny that governs mankind! The consequence of shrouding myself in this cavity had not been foreseen. It was an expedient which courage and not cowardice suggested; and yet it was the only expedient by which flight had been rendered practicable. To have issued from the door would only have been to confront, and not to elude, the danger.

The first impulse prompted me to re-enter the cottage by this avenue, but this could not be done with certainty and expedition. What then remained? While I deliberated, the men approached, and, after a moment's hesitation, entered the house, the door being partly open.

The fire on the hearth enabled them to survey the room. One of them uttered a sudden exclamation of surprise. This was easily interpreted. They had noticed the girl who had lately been their captive lying asleep on the blanket. Their astonishment at finding her here, and in this condition, may be easily conceived.

I now reflected that I might place myself, without being observed, near the entrance, at an angle of the building, and shoot at each as he successively came forth. I perceived that the bank conformed to two sides of the house, and that I might gain a view of the front and of the entrance, without exposing myself to observation.

I lost no time in gaining this station. The bank was as high as my breast. It was easy, therefore, to crouch beneath it, to bring my eye close to the verge, and, laying my gun upon the top of it among the grass, with its muzzles pointed to the door, patiently to wait their forthcoming.

My eye and my ear were equally attentive to what was passing. A low and muttering conversation was maintained in the house. Presently I heard a heavy stroke descend. I shuddered, and my blood ran cold at the sound. I entertained no doubt but that it was the stroke of a hatchet on the head or breast of the helpless sleeper.

It was followed by a loud shriek. The continuance of these shrieks proved that the stroke had not been instantly fatal. I waited to hear it repeated, but the sounds that now arose were like those produced by dragging somewhat along the ground. The shrieks, meanwhile, were incessant and piteous. My heart faltered, and I saw that mighty efforts must be made to preserve my joints and my nerves steadfast. All depended on the strenuous exertions and the fortunate dexterity of a moment.

One now approached the door, and came forth, dragging the girl, whom he held by the hair, after him. What hindered me from shooting at his first appearance, I know not. This had been my previous resolution. My hand touched the trigger, and, as he moved, the piece was levelled at his right ear. Perhaps the momentous consequences of my failure made me wait till his ceasing to move might render my aim more sure.

Having dragged the girl, still piteously shrieking, to the distance of ten feet from the house, he threw her from him with violence. She fell upon the ground, and, observing him level his piece at her breast, renewed her supplications in a still more piercing tone. Little did the forlorn wretch think that her deliverance was certain and near. I rebuked myself for having thus long delayed. I fired, and my enemy sunk upon the ground without a struggle.

Thus far had success attended me in this unequal contest. The next shot would leave me nearly powerless. If that, however, proved as unerring as the first, the chances of defeat were lessened. The savages within, knowing the intentions of their associate with regard to the captive girl, would probably mistake the report which they heard for that of his piece. Their mistake, however, would speedily give place to doubts, and they would rush forth to ascertain the truth. It behooved me to provide a similar reception for him that next appeared.

It was as I expected. Scarcely was my eye again fixed upon the entrance, when a tawny and terrific visage was stretched fearfully forth. It was the signal of his fate. His glances, cast wildly and swiftly around, lighted upon me, and on the fatal instrument which was pointed at his forehead. His muscles were at once exerted to withdraw his head, and to vociferate a warning to his fellow; but his movement was too slow. The ball entered above his ear. He tumbled headlong to the ground, bereaved of sensation though not of life, and had power only to struggle and mutter.

XIX

Think not that I relate these things with exultation or tranquillity. All my education and the habits of my life tended to unfit me for a contest and a scene like this. But I was not governed by the soul which usually regulates my conduct. I had imbibed, from the unparalleled events which had lately happened, a spirit vengeful, unrelenting, and ferocious.

There was now an interval for flight. Throwing my weapons away, I might gain the thicket in a moment. I had no ammunition, nor would time be afforded me to reload my piece. My antagonist would render my poniard and my speed of no use to me. Should he miss me as I fled, the girl would remain to expiate, by her agonies and death, the fate of his companions.

These thoughts passed through my mind in a shorter time than is demanded to express them. They yielded to an expedient suggested by the sight of the gun that had been raised to destroy the girl, and which now lay upon the ground. I am not large of bone, but am not deficient in agility and strength. All that remained to me of these qualities was now exerted; and, dropping my own piece, I leaped upon the bank, and flew to seize my prize.

It was not till I snatched it from the ground, that the propriety of regaining my former post rushed upon my apprehension. He that was still posted in the hovel would mark me through the seams of the wall, and render my destruction sure. I once more ran towards the bank, with the intention to throw myself below it. All this was performed in an instant; but my vigilant foe was aware of his advantage, and fired through an opening between the logs. The bullet grazed my cheek, and produced a benumbing sensation that made me instantly fall to the earth. Though bereaved of strength, and fraught with the belief that I had received a mortal wound, my caution was not remitted. I loosened not my grasp on the gun, and the posture into which I accidentally fell enabled me to keep an eye upon the house and a hand upon the trigger. Perceiving my condition, the savage rushed from his covert in order to complete his work; but at three steps from the threshold he received my bullet in his breast. The uplifted tomahawk fell from his hand, and, uttering a loud shriek, he fell upon the body of his companion. His cries struck upon my heart, and I wished that his better fortune had cast this evil from him upon me.

Thus I have told thee a bloody and disastrous tale. When thou reflectest on the mildness of my habits, my antipathy to scenes of violence and bloodshed, my unacquaintance with the use of fire-arms and the motives of a soldier, thou wilt scarcely allow credit to my story. That one rushing into these dangers, unfurnished with stratagems or weapons, disheartened and enfeebled by hardships and pain, should subdue four antagonists trained from their infancy to the artifices and exertions of Indian warfare, will seem the vision of fancy, rather than the lesson of truth.

I lifted my head from the ground and pondered upon this scene. The magnitude of this exploit made me question its reality. By attending to my own sensations, I discovered that I had received no wound, or, at least, none of which there was reason to complain. The blood flowed plentifully from my cheek, but the injury was superficial. It was otherwise with my antagonists. The last that had fallen now ceased to groan. Their huge limbs, inured to combat and *war-worn*, were useless to their own defense, and to the injury of others.

The destruction that I witnessed was vast. Three beings, full of energy and heroism, endowed with minds strenuous and lofty, poured out their lives before me. I was the instrument of their destruction. This scene of carnage and blood was laid by me. To this havoc and horror was I led by such rapid footsteps!

My anguish was mingled with astonishment. In spite of the force and uniformity with which my senses were impressed by external objects, the transition I had undergone was so wild and inexplicable; all that I had performed, all that I had witnessed since my egress from the pit, were so contradictory to precedent events, that I still clung to the belief that my thoughts were confused by delirium. From these reveries I was at length recalled by the groans of the girl, who lay near me on the ground.

I went to her and endeavored to console her. I found that, while lying in the bed, she had received a blow upon the side, which was still productive of acute pain. She was unable to rise or to walk, and it was plain that one or more of her ribs had been fractured by the blow.

I knew not what means to devise for our mutual relief. It was possible that the nearest dwelling was many leagues distant. I knew not in what direction to go in order to find it, and my strength would not suffice to carry my wounded companion thither in my arms. There was no expedient but to remain in this field of blood till the morning.

I had scarcely formed this resolution before the report of a musket was heard at a small distance. At the same moment, I distinctly heard the whistling of a bullet near me. I now remembered that, of the five Indians whom I saw in the cavern, I was acquainted with the destiny only of four. The fifth might be still alive, and fortune might reserve for him the task of avenging his companions. His steps might now be tending hither in search of them.

The musket belonging to him who was shot upon the threshold was still charged. It was discreet to make all the provision in my power against danger. I possessed myself of this gun, and, seating myself on the ground, looked carefully on all sides, to descry the approach of the enemy. I listened with breathless eagerness.

Presently voices were heard. They ascended from that part of the thicket from which my view was intercepted by the cottage. These voices had something in them that bespoke them to belong to friends and countrymen. As yet I was unable to distinguish words.

Presently my eye was attracted to one quarter, by a sound as of feet trampling down bushes. Several heads were seen moving in succession, and at length the whole person was conspicuous. One after another leaped over a kind of mound which bordered the field, and made towards the spot where I sat. This band was composed of ten or twelve persons, with each a gun upon his shoulder. Their guise, the moment it was perceived, dissipated all my apprehensions.

They came within the distance of a few paces before they discovered me. One stopped, and, bespeaking the attention of his followers, called to know who was there. I answered that I was a friend, who entreated their assistance. I shall not paint their astonishment when, on coming nearer, they beheld me surrounded by the arms and dead bodies of my enemies.

I sat upon the ground, supporting my head with my left hand, and resting on my knee the stock of a heavy musket. My countenance was wan and haggard, my neck and bosom were dyed in blood, and my limbs, almost stripped by the brambles of their slender covering, were lacerated by a thousand wounds. Three savages, two of whom were steeped in gore, lay at a small distance, with the traces of recent life on their visages. Hard by was the girl, venting her anguish in the deepest groans, and entreating relief from the newcomers.

One of the company, on approaching the girl, betrayed the utmost perturbation. "Good God!" he cried, "is this a dream? Can it be you? Speak!"

"Ah, my father! my father!" answered she, "it is I indeed."

The company, attracted by this dialogue, crowded round the girl, whom her father, clasping in his arms, lifted from the ground, and pressed, in a transport of joy, to his breast. This delight was succeeded by solicitude respecting her condition. She could only answer his inquiries by complaining that her side was bruised to pieces. "How came you here?"—"Who hurt you?"—"Where did the Indians carry you?"—were questions to which she could make no reply but by sobs and plaints.

My own calamities were forgotten in contemplating the fondness and compassion of the man for his child. I derived new joy from reflecting that I had not abandoned her, and that she owed her preservation to my efforts. The inquiries which the girl was unable to answer were now put to me. Every one interrogated me who I was, whence I had come, and what had given rise to this bloody contest.

I was not willing to expatiate on my story. The spirit which had hitherto sustained me began now to subside. My strength ebbed away with my blood. Tremors, lassitude, and deadly cold invaded me, and I fainted on the ground.

Such is the capricious constitution of the human mind. While dangers were at hand, while my life was to be preserved only by zeal, and vigilance, and courage, I was not wanting to myself. Had my perils continued, or even multiplied, no doubt my energies would have kept equal pace with them; but the moment I was encompassed by protectors, and placed in security, I grew powerless and faint. My weakness was proportioned to the duration and intensity of my previous efforts, and the swoon into which I now sunk was, no doubt, mistaken by the spectators for death.

On recovering from this swoon, my sensations were not unlike those which I had experienced on awaking in the pit. For a moment a mistiness involved every object, and I was able to distinguish nothing. My sight, by rapid degrees, was restored, my painful dizziness was banished, and I surveyed the scene before me with anxiety and wonder.

I found myself stretched upon the ground. I perceived the cottage and the neighboring thicket, illuminated by a declining moon. My head rested upon something, which, on turning to examine, I found to be one of the slain Indians. The other two remained upon the earth, at a small distance, and in the attitudes in which they had fallen. Their arms, the wounded girl, and the troop who were near me when I fainted, were gone.

My head had reposed upon the breast of him whom I had shot in this part of his body. The blood had ceased to ooze from the wound, but my dishevelled locks were matted and steeped in that gore which had overflowed and choked up the orifice. I started from this detestable pillow, and regained my feet.

I did not suddenly recall what had lately passed, or comprehend the nature of my situation. At length, however, late events were recollected.

That I should be abandoned in this forlorn state by these men seemed to argue a degree of cowardice or cruelty of which I should have thought them incapable. Presently, however, I reflected that appearances might have easily misled them into a belief of my death. On this supposition, to have carried me away, or to have stayed beside me, would be useless. Other enemies might be abroad; or their families, now that their fears were somewhat tranquillized, might require their presence and protection.

I went into the cottage. The fire still burned, and afforded me a genial warmth. I sat before it, and began to ruminate on the state to which I was reduced, and on the measures I should next pursue. Daylight could not be very distant. Should I remain in this hovel till the morning, or immediately resume my journey? I was feeble, indeed; but, by remaining here, should I not increase my feebleness? The sooner I should gain some human habitation the better, whereas watchfulness and hunger would render me, at each minute, less able to proceed than on the former.

This spot might be visited on the next day; but this was involved in uncertainty. The visitants, should any come, would come merely to examine and bury the dead, and bring with them neither the clothing nor the food which my necessities demanded. The road was sufficiently discernible, and would, unavoidably, conduct me to some dwelling. I determined, therefore, to set out without delay. Even in this state I was not unmindful that my safety might require the precaution of being armed. Besides, the fusil which had been given me by Sarsefield, and which I had so unexpectedly recovered, had lost none of its value in my eyes. I hoped that it had escaped the search of the troop who had been here, and still lay below the bank in the spot where I had dropped it.

In this hope I was not deceived. It was found. I possessed myself of the powder and shot belonging to one of the savages, and loaded it. Thus equipped for defense, I regained the road, and proceeded, with alacrity, on my way. For the wound in my cheek nature had provided a styptic, but the soreness was extreme, and I thought of no remedy but water, with which I might wash away the blood. My thirst likewise incommoded me, and I looked with eagerness for the traces of a spring. In a soil like that of the wilderness around me, nothing was less to be expected than to light upon water. In this respect, however, my destiny was propitious. I quickly perceived water in the ruts. It trickled hither from the thicket on one side, and, pursuing it among the bushes, I reached the bubbling source. Though scanty and brackish, it afforded me unspeakable refreshment.

Thou wilt think, perhaps, that my perils were now at an end; that the blood I had already shed was sufficient for my safety. I fervently hoped that no new exigence would occur compelling me to use the arms that I bore in my own defense. I formed a sort of resolution to shun the contest with a new enemy, almost at the expense of my own life. I was satiated and gorged with slaughter, and thought upon a new act of destruction with abhorrence and loathing.

But, though I dreaded to encounter a new enemy, I was sensible that an enemy might possibly be at hand. I had moved forward with caution, and my sight and hearing were attentive to the slightest tokens. Other troops, besides that which I encountered, might be hovering near, and of that troop I remembered that one at least had survived.

The gratification which the spring had afforded me was so great, that I was in no haste to depart. I lay upon a rock, which chanced to be shaded by a tree behind me. From this post I could overlook the road to some distance, and, at the same time, be shaded from the observation of others.

My eye was now caught by movements which appeared like those of a beast. In different circumstances, I should have instantly supposed it to be a wolf, or panther, or bear. Now my suspicions were alive on a different account, and my startled fancy figured to itself nothing but a human adversary.

A thicket was on either side of the road. That opposite to my station was discontinued at a small distance by the cultivated field. The road continued along this field, bounded by the thicket on the one side and the open space on the other. To this space the being who was now described was cautiously approaching.

He moved upon all fours, and presently came near enough to be distinguished. His disfigured limbs, pendants from his ears and nose, and his shorn locks, were indubitable indications of a savage. Occasionally he reared himself above the bushes, and scanned, with suspicious vigilance, the cottage and the space surrounding it. Then he stooped, and crept along as before.

I was at no loss to interpret these appearances. This was my surviving enemy. He was unacquainted with the fate of his associates, and was now approaching the theater of carnage to ascertain their fate.

Once more was the advantage afforded me. From this spot might unerring aim be taken, and the last of this hostile troop be made to share the fate of the rest. Should I fire, or suffer him to pass in safety?

My abhorrence of bloodshed was not abated. But I had not foreseen this occurrence. My success hitherto had seemed to depend upon a combination of fortunate incidents, which could not be expected again to take place; but now was I invested with the same power. The mark was near; nothing obstructed or delayed; I incurred no danger, and the event was certain.

Why should he be suffered to live? He came hither to murder and despoil my friends; this work he has, no doubt, performed. Nay, has he not borne his part in the destruction of my uncle and my sisters? He will live only to pursue the same sanguinary trade: to drink the blood and exult in the laments of his unhappy foes and of my own brethren. Fate has reserved him for a bloody and violent death. For how long a time soever it may be deferred, it is thus that his career will inevitably terminate.

Should he be spared, he will still roam in the wilderness, and I may again be fated to encounter him. Then our mutual situation may be widely different, and the advantage I now possess may be his.

While hastily revolving these thoughts, I was thoroughly aware that one event might take place which would render all deliberation useless. Should he spy me where I lay, my fluctuations must end. My safety would indispensably require me to shoot. This persuasion made me keep a steadfast eye upon his motions, and be prepared to anticipate his assault.

It now most seasonably occurred to me that one essential duty remained to be performed. One operation, without which firearms are useless, had been unaccountably omitted. My piece was uncocked. I did not reflect that in moving the spring a sound would necessarily be produced sufficient to alarm him. But I knew that the chances of escaping his notice, should I be perfectly mute and still, were extremely slender, and that, in such a case, his movements would be quicker than the light; it behooved me, therefore, to repair my omission.

The sound struck him with alarm. He turned and darted at me an inquiring glance. I saw that forbearance was no longer in my power; but my heart sunk while I complied with what may surely be deemed an indispensable necessity. This faltering, perhaps, it was that made me swerve somewhat from the fatal line. He was disabled by the wound, but not killed.

He lost all power of resistance, and was, therefore, no longer to be dreaded. He rolled upon the ground, uttering doleful shrieks, and throwing his limbs into those contortions which bespeak the keenest agonies to which ill-fated man is subject. Horror, and compassion, and remorse, were mingled into one sentiment, and took possession of my heart. To shut out this spectacle, I withdrew from the spot, but I stopped before I had moved beyond hearing of his cries.

The impulse that drove me from the scene was pusillanimous and cowardly. The past, however deplorable, could not be recalled; but could not I afford some relief to this wretch? Could not I at least bring his pangs to a speedy close? Thus he might continue, writhing and calling upon death, for hours. Why should his miseries be uselessly prolonged?

There was but one way to end them. To kill him outright was the dictate of compassion and of duty. I hastily returned, and once more levelled my piece at his head. It was a loathsome obligation, and was performed with unconquerable reluctance. Thus to assault and to mangle the body of an enemy, already prostrate and powerless, was an act worthy of abhorrence; yet it was, in this case, prescribed by pity.

My faltering hand rendered this second bullet ineffectual. One expedient, still more detestable, remained. Having gone thus far, it would have been inhuman to stop short. His heart might easily be pierced by the bayonet, and his struggles would cease.

This task of cruel lenity was at length finished. I dropped the weapon and threw myself on the ground, overpowered by the horrors of this scene. Such are the deeds which perverse nature compels thousands of rational beings to perform and to witness! Such is the spectacle, endlessly prolonged and diversified, which is exhibited in every field of battle; of which habit and example, the temptations of gain, and the illusions of honor, will make us, not reluctant or indifferent, but zealous and delighted actors and beholders!

Thus, by a series of events impossible to be computed or foreseen, was the destruction of a band, selected from their fellows for an arduous enterprise, distinguished by prowess and skill, and equally armed against surprise and force, completed by the hand of a boy, uninured to hostility, unprovided with arms, precipitate and timorous! I have noted men who seemed born for no end but by their achievements to belie experience, and baffle foresight, and outstrip belief. Would to God that I had not deserved to be numbered among these! But what power was it that called me from the sleep of death just in time to escape the merciless knife of this enemy? Had my swoon continued till he had reached the spot, he would have effectuated my death by new wounds and torn away the skin from my brows. Such are the subtle threads on which hang the fate of man and of the universe!

While engaged in these reflections, I perceived that the moonlight had begun to fade before that of the sun. A dusky and reddish hue spread itself over the east. Cheered by this appearance, I once more resumed my feet and the road. I left the savage where he lay, but made prize of his tomahawk. I had left my own in the cavern; and this weapon added little to my burden. Prompted by some freak of fancy, I stuck his musket in the ground, and left it standing upright in the middle of the road.

XX

I moved forward with a quick a pace as my feeble limbs would permit. I did not allow myself to meditate. The great object of my wishes was a dwelling where food and repose might be procured. I looked earnestly forward, and on each side, in search of some token of human residence; but the spots of cultivation, the *well pole,* the *worm fence,* and the hayrick, were nowhere to be seen. I did not even meet with a wild hog or a bewildered cow. The path was narrow, and on either side was a trackless wilderness. On the right and left were the waving lines of mountainous ridges, which had no peculiarity enabling me to ascertain whether I had ever before seen them.

At length I noticed that the tracks of wheels had disappeared from the path that I was treading; that it became more narrow, and exhibited fewer marks of being frequented. These appearances were discouraging. I now suspected that I had taken a wrong direction, and, instead of approaching, was receding from the habitation of men.

I was wisest, however, to proceed. The road could not but have some origin as well as end. Some hours passed away in this uncertainty. The sun rose, and by noonday I seemed to be farther than ever from the end of my toils. The path was more obscure, and the wilderness more rugged. Thirst more incommoded me than hunger, but relief was seasonably afforded by the brooks that flowed across the path.

Coming to one of these, and having slaked my thirst, I sat down upon the bank, to reflect on my situation. The circuity of the path had frequently been noticed, and I began to suspect that, though I had travelled long, I had not moved far from the spot where I had commenced my pilgrimage.

Turning my eyes on all sides, I noticed a sort of pool, formed by the rivulet, at a few paces distant from the road. In approaching and inspecting it, I observed the footsteps of cattle, who had retired by a path that seemed much beaten; I likewise noticed a cedar bucket, broken and old, lying on the margin. These tokens revived my drooping spirits, and I betook myself to this new track. It was intricate, but, at length, led up a steep, the summit of which was of better soil than that of which the flats consisted. A clover-field, and sever apple trees,—sure attendants of man,—were now discovered. From this space I entered a cornfield, and at length, to my inexpressible joy, caught a glimpse of a house.

This dwelling was far different from that I had lately left. It was as small and as low, but its walls consisted of boards. A window of four panes admitted the light, and a chimney of brick, well burnt and neatly arranged, peeped over the roof. As I approached, I heard the voice of children and the hum of a spinning wheel.

I cannot make thee conceive the delight which was afforded me by all these tokens. I now found myself, indeed, among beings like myself, and from whom hospitable entertainment might be confidently expected. I compassed the house, and made my appearance at the door.

A good woman, busy at her wheel, with two children playing on the ground before her, were the objects that now presented themselves. The uncouthness of my garb, my wild and weatherworn appearance, my fusil and tomahawk, could not but startle them. The woman stopped her wheel, and gazed as if a specter had started into view.

I was somewhat aware of these consequences, and endeavored to elude them by assuming an air of supplication and humility. I told her that I was a traveller, who had unfortunately lost his way and had rambled in this wild till nearly famished for want. I entreated her to give me some food; anything, however scanty or coarse, would be acceptable.

After some pause she desired me, though not without some marks of fear, to walk in. She placed before me some brown bread and milk. She eyed me while I eagerly devoured this morsel. It was, indeed, more delicious than any I had ever tasted. At length she broke silence, and expressed her astonishment and commiseration at my seemingly forlorn state, adding that perhaps I was the man whom the men were looking after who had been there some hours before.

My curiosity was roused by this intimation. In answer to my interrogations, she said that three persons had lately stopped, to inquire if her husband had not met, within the last three days, a person of whom their description seemed pretty much to suit my person and dress. He was tall, slender, wore nothing but shirt and trousers, and was wounded on the cheek.

"What," I asked, "did they state the rank or condition of the person to be?"

He lived in Solesbury. He was supposed to have rambled in the mountains, and to have lost his way, or to have met with some mischance. It was three days since he had disappeared, but had been seen by someone, the last night, at Deb's hut.

What and where was Deb's hut?

It was a hut in the wilderness, occupied by an old Indian woman, known among her neighbors by the name of Old Deb. Some people called her Queen Mab. Her dwelling was eight *long* miles from this house.

A thousand questions were precluded and a thousand doubts solved by this information. *Queen Mab* were sounds familiar to my ears; for they originated with myself.

This woman originally belonged to the tribe of Delawares, or Lenni Lenape. All these districts were once comprised within the dominions of that nation. About thirty years ago, in consequence of perpetual encroachments of the English colonists, they abandoned their ancient seats and retired to the banks of the Wabash and Muskingum.

This emigration was concerted in a general council of the tribe, and obtained the concurrence of all but one female. Her birth, talents, and age gave her much consideration and authority among her countrymen; and all her zeal and eloquence were exerted to induce them to lay aside their scheme. In this, however, she could not succeed. Finding them refractory, she declared her resolution to remain behind and maintain possession of the land which her countrymen should impiously abandon.

The village inhabited by this clan was built upon ground which now constitutes my uncle's barnyard and orchard. On the departure of her countrymen, this female burnt the empty wigwams and retired into the fastnesses of Norwalk. She selected a spot suitable for an Indian dwelling and a small plantation of maize, and in which she was seldom liable to interruption and intrusion.

Her only companions were three dogs, of the Indian or wolf species. These animals differed in nothing from their kinsmen of the forest but in their attachment and obedience to their mistress. She governed them with absolute sway. They were her servants and protectors, and attended her person or guarded her threshold agreeably to her directions. She fed them with corn, and they supplied her and themselves with meat, by hunting squirrels, raccoons, and rabbits.

To the rest of mankind they were aliens or enemies. They never left the desert but in company with their mistress, and, when she entered a farmhouse, waited her return at a distance. They would suffer none to approach them, but attacked no one who did not imprudently crave their acquaintance, or who kept a respectful distance from their wigwam. That sacred asylum they would not suffer to be violated, and no stranger could enter it but at the imminent hazard of his life, unless accompanied and protected by their dame.

The chief employment of this woman, when at home, besides plucking the weeds from among her corn, bruising the grain between two stones, and setting her snares for rabbits and opossums, was to talk. Though in solitude, her tongue was never at rest but when she was asleep; but her conversation was merely addressed to her dogs. Her voice was sharp and shrill, and her gesticulations were vehement and grotesque. A hearer would naturally imagine that she was scolding; but, in truth, she was merely giving them directions. Having no other object of contemplation or subject of discourse, she always found, in their postures and looks, occasions for praise, or blame, or command. The readiness with which they understood, and the docility with which they obeyed, her movements and words were truly wonderful.

If a stranger chanced to wander near her hut and overhear her jargon, incessant as it was, and shrill, he might speculate in vain on the reason of these sounds. If he waited in expectation of hearing some reply, he waited in vain. The strain, always voluble and sharp, was never intermitted for a moment, and would continue for hours at a time.

She seldom left the hut but to visit the neighboring inhabitants and demand from them food and clothing, or whatever her necessities required. These were exacted as her due; to have her wants supplied was her prerogative, and to withhold what she claimed was rebellion. She conceived that by remaining behind her countrymen she succeeded to the government and retained the possession of all this region. The English were aliens and sojourners, who occupied the land merely by her connivance and permission, and whom she allowed to remain on no terms but those of supplying her wants.

Being a woman aged and harmless, her demands being limited to that of which she really stood in need, and which her own industry could not procure, her pretensions were a subject of mirth and good humor, and her injunctions obeyed with seeming deference and gravity. To me she early became an object of curiosity and speculation. I delighted to observe her habits and humor her prejudices. She frequently came to my uncle's house, and I sometimes visited her; insensibly she seemed to contract an affection for me, and regarded me with more complacency and condescension than any other received.

She always disdained to speak English, and custom had rendered her intelligible to most in her native language, with regard to a few simple questions. I had taken some pains to study her jargon, and could make out to discourse with her on the few ideas which she possessed. This circumstance, likewise, wonderfully prepossessed her in my favor.

The name by which she was formerly known was Deb; but her pretensions to royalty, the wildness of her aspect and garb, her shrivelled and diminutive form, a constitution that seemed to defy the ravages of time and the influence of the elements, her age (which some did not scruple to affirm exceeded a hundred years), her romantic solitude and mountainous haunts, suggested to my fancy the appellation of *Queen Mab*. There appeared to me some rude analogy between this personage and her whom the poets of old time have delighted to celebrate: thou perhaps wilt discover nothing but incongruities between them; but, be that as it may, Old Deb and Queen Mab soon came into indiscriminate and general use.

She dwelt in Norwalk upwards of twenty years. She was not forgotten by her countrymen, and generally received from her brothers and sons an autumnal visit; but no solicitations or entreaties could prevail on her to return with them. Two years ago, some suspicion or disgust induced her to forsake her ancient habitation and to seek a new one. Happily she found a more convenient habitation twenty miles to the westward, and in a spot abundantly sterile and rude.

This dwelling was of logs, and had been erected by a Scottish emigrant, who, not being rich enough to purchase land, and entertaining a passion for solitude and independence, cleared a field in the unappropriated wilderness and subsisted on its produce. After some time he disappeared. Various conjectures were formed as to the cause of his absence. None of them were satisfactory; but that which obtained most credit was, that he had been

murdered by the Indians, who, about the same period, paid their
annual visit to the *Queen*. This conjecture acquired some force
by observing that the old woman shortly after took possession of
his hut, his implements of tillage, and his cornfield.

She was not molested in her new abode, and her life passed in
the same quiet tenor as before. Her periodical rambles, her regal
claims, her guardian wolves, and her uncouth volubility, were
equally remarkable; but her circuits were new. Her distance
made her visits to Solesbury more rare, and had prevented me
from ever extending my pedestrian excursions to her present
abode.

These recollections were now suddenly called up by the information of my hostess. The hut where I had sought shelter and relief was, it seems, the residence of Queen Mab. Some fortunate
occurrence had called her away during my visit. Had she and her
dogs been at home, I should have been set upon by these ferocious sentinels, and, before their dame could have interfered,
have been, together with my helpless companion, mangled or
killed. These animals never barked; and I should have entered un-
aware of my danger, and my fate could scarcely have been averted
by my fusil.

Her absence at this unseasonable hour was mysterious. It was
now the time of year when her countrymen were accustomed to
renew their visit. Was there a league between her and the plun-
derers whom I had encountered?

But who were they by whom my footsteps were so industriously traced? Those whom I had seen at Deb's hut were strangers
to me, but the wound upon my face was known only to them. To
this circumstance was now added my place of residence and name.
I supposed them impressed with the belief that I was dead; but
this mistake must have speedily been rectified. Revisiting the
spot, finding me gone, and obtaining some intelligence of my former condition, they had instituted a search after me.

But what tidings were these? I was supposed to have been bewildered in the mountains, and three days were said to have
passed since my disappearance. Twelve hours had scarcely
elapsed since I emerged from the cavern. Had two days and a
half been consumed in my subterranean prison ?

These reflections were quickly supplanted by others. I now
gained a sufficient acquaintance with the region that was spread
around me. I was in the midst of a vale included between ridges

that gradually approached each other, and, when joined, were broken up into hollows and steeps, and, spreading themselves over a circular space, assumed the appellation of Norwalk. This vale gradually widened as it tended to the westward, and was, in this place, ten or twelve miles in breadth. My devious footsteps had brought me to the foot of the southern barrier. The outer basis of this was laved by the river; but, as it tended eastward, the mountain and river receded from each other, and one of the cultivable districts lying between them was Solesbury, my natal *township*. Hither it was now my duty to return with the utmost expedition.

There were two ways before me. One lay along the interior base of the hill, over a sterile and trackless space, and exposed to the encounter of savages, some of whom might possibly be lurking here. The other was the well-frequented road on the outside and along the river, and which was to be gained by passing over this hill. The practicability of the passage was to be ascertained by inquiries made to my hostess. She pointed out a path that led to the rocky summit and down to the river's brink. The path was not easy to be kept in view or to be trodden, but it was undoubtedly to be preferred to any other.

A route somewhat circuitous would terminate in the river road. Thenceforward the way to Solesbury was level and direct; but the whole space which I had to traverse was not less than thirty miles. In six hours it would be night, and to perform the journey in that time would demand the agile boundings of a leopard and the indefatigable sinews of an elk.

My frame was in a miserable plight. My strength had been assailed by anguish, and fear, and watchfulness, by toil, and abstinence, and wounds. Still, however, some remnant was left; would it not enable me to reach my home by nightfall? I had delighted, from my childhood, in feats of agility and perseverance. In roving though the maze of thickets and precipices, I had put my energies, both moral and physical, frequently to the test. Greater achievements than this had been performed, and I disdained to be outdone in perspicacity by the lynx, in his sure-footed instinct by the roe, or in patience under hardship, and contention with fatigue, by the Mohawk. I have ever aspired to transcend the rest of animals in all that is common to the rational and brute, as well as in all by which they are distinguished from each other.

XXI

I likewise burned with impatience to know the condition of my family, to dissipate at once their tormenting doubts and my own regard to our mutual safety. The evil that I feared had befallen them was too enormous to allow me to repose in suspense, and my restlessness and ominous forebodings would be more intolerable then any hardship or toils to which I could possibly be subjected during this journey.

I was much refreshed and invigorated by the food that I had taken, and by the rest of an hour. With this stock of recruited force I determined to scale the hill. After receiving minute directions, and, returning many thanks for my hospitable entertainment, I set out.

The path was indeed intricate, and deliberate attention was obliged to be exerted in order to preserve it. Hence my progress was slower than I wished. The first impulse was to fix my eye upon the summit, and to leap from crag to crag till I reached it; but this my experience had taught me was impracticable. It was only by winding through gullies, and coasting precipices and bestriding chasms, that I could hope finally to gain the top; and I was assured that by one way only was it possible to accomplish even this.

An hour was spent in struggling with impediments, and I seemed to have gained no way. Hence a doubt was suggested whether I had not missed the true road. In this doubt I was confirmed by the difficulties which now grew up before me. The brooks, the angles, and the hollows, which my hostess had described, were not to be seen. Instead of these, deeper dells, more headlong torrents, and wider-gaping rifts, were incessantly encountered.

To return was as hopeless as to proceed. I consoled myself with thinking that the survey which my informant had made of the hillside might prove inaccurate, and that, in spite of her predictions, the heights might be reached by other means than by those pointed out by her. I will not enumerate my toilsome expedients, my frequent disappointments, and my desperate exertions. Suffice it to say that I gained the upper space not till the sun had dipped beneath the horizon.

My satisfaction at accomplishing thus much was not small, and I hied, with renovated spirits, to the opposite brow. This proved to be a steep that could not be descended. The river flowed at its foot. The opposite bank was five hundred yards distant, and was equally towering and steep as that on which I stood. Appearances were adapted to persuade you that these rocks had formerly joined but by some mighty effort of nature had been severed, that the stream might find way through the chasm. The channel, however, was encumbered with asperities, over which the river fretted and foamed with thundering impetuosity.

I pondered for a while on these stupendous scenes. They ravished my attention from considerations that related to myself; but this interval was short, and I began to measure the descent, in order to ascertain the practicability of treading it. My survey terminated in bitter disappointment. I turned my eye successively eastward and westward. Solesbury lay in the former direction, and thither I desired to go. I kept along the verge in this direction till I reached an impassable rift. Beyond this I saw that the steep grew lower; but it was impossible to proceed farther. Higher up the descent might be practicable, and, though more distant from Solesbury, it was better to reach the road even at that distance than never to reach it.

Changing my course, therefore, I explored the space above. The night was rapidly advancing; the gray clouds gathered in the southeast, and a chilling blast, the usual attendant of a night in October, began to whistle among the pigmy cedars that scantily grew upon these heights. My progress would quickly be arrested by darkness, and it behooved me to provide some place of shelter and repose. No recess better than a hollow in the rock presented itself to my anxious scrutiny.

Meanwhile, I would not dismiss the hope of reaching the road, which I saw some hundred feet below, winding along the edge of the river, before daylight should utterly fail. Speedily these hopes derived new vigor from meeting a ledge that irregularly declined from the brow of the hill. It was wide enough to allow of cautious footing. On a similar stratum, or ledge, projecting still farther from the body of the hill, and close to the surface of the river, was the road. This stratum ascended from the level of the stream, while that on which I trod rapidly descended. I hoped that they would speedily be blended, or, at least, approach so near as to allow me to leap from one to the other without enormous hazard.

This fond expectation was frustrated. Presently I perceived that the ledge below began to descend, while that above began to tend upward and was quickly terminated by the uppermost surface of the cliff. Here it was needful to pause. I looked over the brink, and considered whether I might not leap from my present station without endangering my limbs. The road into which I should fall was a rocky pavement far from being smooth. The descent could not be less than forty or fifty feet. Such an attempt was, to to the last degree, hazardous; but was it not better to risk my life by leaping from this eminence than to remain and perish on the top of this inhospitable mountain? The toils which I had endured in reaching this height appeared, to my panic-struck fancy, less easy to be borne again than death.

I know not but that I should have finally resolved to leap, had not different views been suggested by observing that the outer edge of the road was, in like manner, the brow of a steep which terminated in the river. The surface of the road was twelve or fifteen feet above the level of the stream, which, in this spot, was still and smooth. Hence I inferred that the water was not of inconsiderable depth. To fall upon rocky points was, indeed, dangerous, but to plunge into water of sufficient depth, even from a height greater than that at which I now stood, especially to one to whom habit had rendered water almost as congenial an element as air, was scarcely attended with inconvenience. This expedient was easy and safe. Twenty yards from this spot, the channel was shallow, and to gain the road from the stream was no difficult exploit.

Some disadvantages, however, attended this scheme. The water was smooth; but this might arise from some other cause than its depth. My gun, likewise, must be left behind me; and that was a loss to which I felt invincible repugnance. To let it fall upon the road would put it in my power to retrieve the possession, but it was likely to be irreparably injured by the fall.

While musing upon this expedient, and weighing injuries with benefits, the night closed upon me. I now considered that, should I emerge in safety from the stream, I should have many miles to travel before I could reach a house. My clothes meanwhile would be loaded with wet. I should be heart-pierced by the icy blast that now blew, and my wounds and bruises would be chafed into insupportable pain.

I reasoned likewise on the folly of impatience and the necessity of repose. By thus long continuance in one posture, my sinews began to stiffen, and my reluctance to make new exertions to increase. My brows were heavy, and I felt an irresistible propensity to sleep. I concluded to seek some shelter, and resign myself, my painful recollections, and my mournful presages, to sweet forgetfulness. For this end, I once more ascended to the surface of the cliff. I dragged my weary feet forward, till I found somewhat that promised me the shelter that I sought.

A cluster of cedars appeared, whose branches overarched a space that might be called a bower. It was a slight cavity, whose flooring was composed of loose stones and a few faded leaves blown from a distance and finding a temporary lodgment here. On one side was a rock, forming a wall rugged and projecting above. At the bottom of the rock was a rift, somewhat resembling a coffin in shape, and not much larger in dimensions. This rift terminated, on the opposite side of the rock, in an opening that was too small for the body of a man to pass. The distance between each entrance was twice the length of a man.

This bower was open to the southeast, whence the gale now blew. It therefore imperfectly afforded the shelter of which I stood in need; but it was the best that the place and the time afforded. To stop the smaller entrance of the cavity with a stone, and to heap before the other branches lopped from the trees with my hatchet, might somewhat contribute to my comfort.

This was done, and, thrusting myself into this recess as far as I was able, I prepared for repose. It might have been reasonably suspected to be the den of rattlesnakes or panthers; but my late contention with superior dangers and more formidable enemies made me reckless of these. But another inconvenience remained. In spite of my precautions, my motionless posture and slender covering exposed me so much to the cold that I could not sleep.

The air appeared to have suddenly assumed the temperature of midwinter. In a short time, my extremities were benumbed, and my limbs shivered and ached as if I had been seized by an ague. My bed likewise was dank and uneven, and the posture I was obliged to assume, unnatural and painful. It was evident that my purpose could not be answered by remaining here.

I therefore crept forth, and began to reflect upon the possibility of continuing my journey. Motion was the only thing that could keep me from freezing, and my frame was in that state which allowed me to take no repose in the absence of warmth, since warmth was indispensable. It now occurred to me to ask whether it were not possible to kindle a fire.

Sticks and leaves were at hand. My hatchet and a pebble would enable me to extract a spark. From this, by suitable care and perseverance, I might finally procure sufficient fire to give me comfort and ease, and even enable me to sleep. This boon was delicious, and I felt as if I were unable to support a longer deprivation of it.

I proceeded to execute this scheme. I took the driest leaves, and endeavored to use them as tinder; but the driest leaves were moistened by the dews. They were only to be found in the hollows, in some of which were pools of water and others were dank. I was not speedily discouraged; but my repeated attempts failed, and I was finally compelled to relinquish this expedient.

All that now remained was to wander forth and keep myself in motion till the morning. The night was likely to prove tempestuous and long. The gale seemed freighted with ice, and acted upon my body like the points of a thousand needles. There was no remedy, and I mustered my patience to endure it.

I returned again to the brow of the hill. I ranged along it till I reached a place where the descent was perpendicular, and, in consequence of affording no substance to trees or bushes, was nearly smooth and bare. There was no road to be seen; and this circumstance, added to the sounds which the rippling current produced, afforded me some knowledge of my situation.

The ledge along which the road was conducted disappeared near this spot. The opposite sides of the chasm through which flowed the river approached nearer to each other, in the form of jutting promontories. I now stood upon the verge of that on the northern side. The water flowed at the foot, but, for the space of ten or twelve feet from the rock, was so shallow as to permit the traveller and his horse to wade through it, and thus to regain the road which the receding precipice had allowed to be continued on the farther side.

I knew the nature and dimensions of this ford. I knew that, at a few yards from the rock, the channel was of great depth. To leap into it, in this place, was a less dangerous exploit than at the spot where I had formerly been tempted to leap. There I was

unacquainted with the depth, but here I knew it to be considerable. Still, there was some ground of hesitation and fear. My present station was loftier, and how deeply I might sink into this
gulf, how far the fall and the concussion would bereave me of my
presence of mind, I could not determine. This hesitation vanished, and, placing my tomahawk and fusil upon the ground, I prepared to leap.

This purpose was suspended, in the moment of its execution,
by a faint sound, heard from the quarter whence I had come.
It was the warning of men, but had nothing in common with those
which I had been accustomed to hear. It was not the howling
of a wolf or the yelling of a panther. These had often been overheard by night during my last year's excursion to the lakes. My
fears whispered that this was the vociferation of a savage.

I was unacquainted with the number of the enemies who had
adventured into this district. Whether those whom I had encountered at *Deb's hut* were of that band whom I had met with in
the cavern, was merely a topic of conjecture. There might be a
half-score of troops, equally numerous, spread over the wilderness, and the signal I had just heard might betoken the approach
of one of these. Yet by what means they should gain this nook,
and what prey they expected to discover, were not easily conceived.

The sounds, somewhat diversified, nearer and rising from different quarters, were again heard. My doubts and apprehensions
were increased. What expedient to adopt for my own safety was
a subject of rapid meditation: whether to remain stretched upon
the ground or to rise and go forward. Was it likely the enemy
would coast along the edge of the steep? Would they ramble
hither to look upon the ample scene which spread on all sides
around the base of this rocky pinnacle? My arms were ready for
use. Could I not elude the necessity of shedding more blood?
Could I not anticipate their assault by casting myself without
delay into the stream?

The sense of danger demanded more attention to be paid to
external objects than to the motives by which my future conduct should be influenced. My post was on a circular projecture,
in some degree detached from the body of the hill, the brow of
which continued in a straight line, uninterrupted by this projecture, which was somewhat higher than the continued summit of
the ridge. This line ran at the distance of a few paces from my

post. Objects moving along this line could merely be perceived to move, in the present obscurity.

My scrutiny was entirely directed to this quarter. Presently the treading of many feet was heard, and several figures were discovered, following each other in that straight and regular succession which is peculiar to the Indians. They kept along the brow of the hill joining the promontory. I distinctly marked seven figures in succession.

My resolution was formed. Should any one cast his eye hither, suspect or discover an enemy, and rush towards me, I determined to start upon my feet, fire on my foe as he advanced, throw my piece on the ground, and then leap into the river.

Happily, they passed unobservant and in silence. I remained in the same posture for several minutes. At length, just as my alarms began to subside, the halloos, before heard, arose, and from the same quarter as before. This convinced me that my perils were not at an end. This now appeared to be merely the vanguard, and would speedily be followed by others, against whom the same caution was necessary to be taken.

My eye, anxiously bent the only way by which anyone could approach, now discerned a figure, which was indubitably that of a man armed. None other appeared in company; but doubtless others were near. He approached, stood still, and appeared to gaze steadfastly at the spot where I lay.

The optics of a *Lenni Lenape* I knew to be far keener than my own. A log or a couched fawn would never be mistaken for a man, nor a man for a couched fawn or a log. Not only a human being would be instantly detected, but a decision be unerringly made whether it were friend or foe. That my prostrate body was the object on which the attention of this vigilant and steadfast gazer was fixed could not be doubted. Yet, since he continued an inactive gazer, there was ground for a possibility to stand upon that I was not recognized. My fate therefore was still in suspense.

This interval was momentary. I marked a movement, which my fears instantly interpreted to be that of levelling a gun at my head. This action was sufficiently conformable to my prognostics. Supposing me to be detected, there was no need for him to change his post. Aim might be too fatally taken, and his prey be secured, from the distance at which he now stood.

These images glanced upon my thought, and put an end to my suspense. A single effort placed me on my feet. I fired with a precipitation that precluded the certainty of hitting my mark, dropped my piece upon the ground, and leaped from this tremendous height into the river. I reached the surface, and sunk in a moment to the bottom.

Plunging endlong into the water, the impetus created by my fall from such a height would be slowly resisted by this denser element. Had the depth been less, its resistance would not perhaps have hindered me from being mortally injured against the rocky bottom. Had the depth been greater, time enough would not have been allowed me to regain the surface. Had I fallen on my side, I should have been bereft of life or sensibility by the shock which my frame would have received. As it was, my fate was suspended on a thread. To have lost my presence of mind, to have forborne to counteract my sinking, for an instant, after I had reached the water, would have made all exertions to regain the air fruitless. To so fortunate a concurrence of events was thy friend indebted for his safety!

Yet I only emerged from the gulf to encounter new perils. Scarcely had I raised my head above the surface, and inhaled the vital breath, when twenty shots were aimed at me from the precipice above. A shower of bullets fell upon the water. Some of them did not fall farther than two inches from my head. I had not been aware of this new danger, and, now that it assailed me, continued gasping the air and floundering at random. The means of eluding it did not readily occur. My case seemed desperate, and all caution was dismissed.

This state of discomfiting surprise quickly disappeared. I made myself acquainted, at a glance, with the position of surrounding objects. I conceived that the opposite bank of the river would afford me most security, and thither I tended with all the expedition in my power.

Meanwhile, my safety depended on eluding the bullets that continued incessantly to strike the water at an arm's length from my body. For this end I plunged beneath the surface, and only rose to inhale fresh air. Presently the firing ceased, the flashes that lately illuminated the bank disappeared, and a certain bustle and murmur of confused voices gave place to solitude and silence.

XXII

I reached without difficulty the opposite bank, but the steep was inaccessible. I swam along the edge in hopes of meeting with some projection or recess where I might, at least, rest my weary limbs, and, if it were necessary to recross the river, to lay in a stock of recruited spirits and strength for that purpose. I trusted that the water would speedily become shoal, or that the steep would afford rest to my feet. In both these hopes I was disappointed.

There is no one to whom I would yield the superiority in swimming; but my strength, like that of other human beings, had its limits. My previous fatigues had been enormous, and my clothes, heavy with moisture, greatly encumbered and retarded my movements. I had proposed to free myself from this imprisonment; but I foresaw the inconveniences of wandering over this scene in absolute nakedness, and was willing therefore, at whatever hazard, to retain them. I continued to struggle with the current and to search for the means of scaling the steeps. My search was fruitless, and I began to meditate the recrossing of the river.

Surely my fate has never been paralleled! Where was this series of hardships and perils to end? No sooner was one calamity eluded, than I was beset by another. I had emerged from abhorred darkness in the heart of the earth, only to endure the extremities of famine and encounter the fangs of a wild beast. From these I was delivered only to be thrown into the midst of savages, to wage an endless and hopeless war with adepts in killing, with appetites that longed to feast upon my bowels and to quaff my heart's blood. From these likewise was I rescued, but merely to perish in the gulfs of the river, to welter on unvisited shores, or to be washed far away from curiosity or pity.

Formerly water was not only my field of sport but my sofa and my bed. I could float for hours on its surface, enjoying its delicious cool, almost without the expense of the slightest motion. It was an element as fitted for repose as for exercise; but now the buoyant spirit seemed to have flown. My muscles were shrunk, the air and water were equally congealed, and my most vehement exertions were requisite to sustain me on the surface.

At first I had moved along with my wonted celerity and ease, but quickly my forces were exhausted. My panting and efforts were augmented, and I saw that to cross the river again was impracticable. I must continue, therefore, to search out some accessible spot in the bank along which I was swimming.

Each moment diminished my stock of strength, and it behooved me to make good my footing before another minute should escape. I continued to swim, to survey the bank, and to make ineffectual attempts to grasp the rock. The shrubs which grew upon it would not uphold me, and the fragments which, for a moment, inspired me with hope, crumbled away as soon as they were touched.

At length I noticed a pine which was rooted in a crevice near the water. The trunk, or any part of the root, was beyond my reach; but I trusted that I could catch hold of the branch which hung lowest, and that, when caught, it would assist me in gaining the trunk, and thus deliver me from the death which could not be otherwise averted.

The attempt was arduous. Had it been made when I first reached the bank, no difficulty had attended it; but now to throw myself some feet above the surface could scarcely be expected from one whose utmost efforts seemed to be demanded to keep him from sinking. Yet this exploit, arduous as it was, was attempted and accomplished. Happily the twigs were strong enough to sustain my weight till I caught at other branches and finally placed myself upon the trunk.

This danger was now past; but I admitted the conviction that others, no less formidable, remained to be encountered, and that my ultimate destiny was death. I looked upward, New efforts might enable me to gain the summit of this steep, but perhaps I should thus be placed merely in the situation from which I had just been delivered. It was of little moment whether the scene of my imprisonment was a dungeon not to be broken, or a summit from which descent was impossible.

The river, indeed, severed me from a road which was level and safe, but my recent dangers were remembered only to make me shudder at the thought of incurring them a second time by attempting to cross it. I blush at the recollection of this cowardice. It was little akin to the spirit which I had recently displayed. It was, indeed, an alien to my bosom, and was quickly supplanted by intrepidity and perseverance.

I proceeded to mount the hill. From root to root, and from branch

to branch, lay my journey. It was finished, and I sat down upon the
highest brow to meditate on future trials. No road lay along this
side of the river. It was rugged and sterile, and farms were sparingly dispersed over it. To reach one of these was now the object
of my wishes. I had not lost the desire of reaching Solesbury before morning, but my wet clothes and the coldness of the night
seemed to have bereaved me of the power.

I traversed this summit, keeping the river on my right hand.
Happily, its declinations and ascents were by no means difficult,
and I was cheered, in the midst of my vexations, by observing that
every mile brought me nearer to my uncle's dwelling. Meanwhile
I anxiously looked for some tokens of a habitation. These at length
presented themselves. A wild heath, whistled over by October
blasts, meagerly adorned with the dry stalks of scented shrubs and
the bald heads of the sapless mullein, was succeeded by a fenced
field and a corn stack. The dwelling to which these belonged was
eagerly sought.

I was not surprised that all voices were still and all lights extinguished, for this was the hour of repose. Having reached a piazza
before the house, I paused. Whether, at this drowsy time, to knock
for admission, to alarm the peaceful tenants and take from them the
rest which their daily toils and their rural innocence had made so
sweet, or to retire to what shelter a haystack or barn could afford,
was the theme of my deliberations.

Meanwhile, I looked up at the house. It was the model of cleanli-
ness and comfort. It was built of wood; but the materials had undergone the plane, as well as the axe and the saw. It was painted white,
and the windows not only had sashes, but these sashes were supplied, contrary to custom, with glass. In most cases the aperture
where glass should be is stuffed with an old hat or a petticoat. The
door had not only all its parts entire, but was embellished with
moldings and a pediment. I gathered from these tokens that this
was the abode not only of rural competence and innocence, but
of some beings raised by education and fortune above the intellectual mediocrity of clowns.

Methought I could claim consanguity with such beings. Not to
share their charity and kindness would be inflicting as well as receiving injury. The trouble of affording shelter, and warmth, and
wholesome diet, to a wretch destitute as I was, would be eagerly
sought by them.

Still, I was unwilling to disturb them. I bethought myself that their kitchen might be entered, and all that my necessities required be obtained without interrupting their slumber. I needed nothing but the warmth which the kitchen-hearth would afford. Stretched upon the bricks, I might dry my clothes, and perhaps enjoy some unmolested sleep, in spite of presages of ill and the horrid remembrances of what I had performed and endured. I believed that nature would afford a short respite to my cares.

I went to the door of what appeared to be a kitchen. The door was wide open. This circumstance portended evil. Though it be not customary to lock or to bolt, it is still less usual to have entrances unclosed. I entered with suspicious steps, and saw enough to confirm my apprehensions. Several pieces of wood, half burned, lay in the midst of the floor. They appeared to have been removed hither from the chimney, doubtless with a view to set fire to the whole building.

The fire had made some progress on the floor, but had been seasonably extinguished by pailfuls of water thrown upon it. The floor was still deluged with wet; the pail, not emptied of all its contents, stood upon the hearth. The earthen vessels and plates, whose proper place was the dresser, were scattered in fragments in all parts of the room. I looked around me for someone to explain this scene, but no one appeared.

The last spark of fire was put out, so that, had my curiosity been idle, my purpose could not be accomplished. To retire from this scene, neither curiosity nor benevolence would permit. That some mortal injury had been intended was apparent. What greater mischief had befallen or whether greater might not, by my interposition, be averted, could only be ascertained by penetrating farther into the house. I opened a door on one side which led to the main body of the building and entered to a bed chamber. I stood at the entrance and knocked, but no one answered my signals.

The sky was not totally clouded, so that some light pervaded the room. I saw that a bed stood in the corner, but whether occupied or not its curtains hindered me from judging. I stood in suspense a few minutes, when a motion in the bed showed me that someone was there. I knocked again, but withdrew to the outside of the door. This roused the sleeper, who, half groaning, and puffing the air through his nostrils, grumbled out, in the hoarsest voice that I ever heard, and in a tone of surly impatience, "Who is there?"

I hesitated for an answer; but the voice instantly continued, in the manner of one half asleep and enraged at being disturbed, "Is't

you, Peg? Damn ye, stay away, now! I tell ye, stay away, or, by
God, I will cut your throat!—I will!" He continued to mutter and
swear, but without coherence or distinctness.

These were the accents of drunkenness, and denoted a wild and
ruffian life. They were little in unison with the external appearances of the mansion, and blasted all the hopes I had formed of
meeting under this roof with gentleness and hospitality. To talk
with this being, to attempt to reason him into humanity and sober-
ness, was useless. I was at a loss in what manner to address him,
or whether it was proper to maintain any parley. Meanwhile, my
silence was supplied by the suggestions of his own distempered
fancy. "Ay," said he; "ye will, will ye? Well, come on; let's see
who's the better at the oak stick. If I part with ye before I have
bared your bones!—I'll teach ye to be always dipping in my dish,
ye devil's dam ye."

So saying, he tumbled out of bed. At the first step, he struck his
head against the bedpost, but, setting himself upright, he staggered
towards the spot where I stood. Some new obstacle occurred. He
stumbled and fell at his length upon the floor.

To encounter or expostulate with a man in this state was plainly
absurd. I turned and issued forth, with an aching heart, into the
court before the house. The miseries which a debauched husband
or father inflicts upon all whom their evil destiny allies to him were
pictured by my fancy, and wrung from me tears of anguish. These
images, however, quickly yielded to reflections on my own state.
No expedient now remained but to seek the barn and find a covering and a bed of straw.

I had scarcely set foot within the barnyard when I heard a sound
as of the crying of an infant. It appeared to issue from the barn. I
approached softly and listened at the door. The cries of the babe
continued, but were accompanied by the entreaties of a nurse or a
mother to be quiet. These entreaties were mingled with heart-
breaking sobs, and exclamations of, "Ah, me, my babe! Canst thou
not sleep and afford thy unhappy mother some peace? Thou art
cold, and I have not sufficient warmth to cherish thee! What will
become of us? Thy deluded father cares not if we both perish."

A glimpse of the true nature of the scene seemed to be imparted
by these words. I now likewise recollected incidents that afforded
additional light. Somewhere on this bank of the river there formerly
resided one by name Selby. He was an aged person, who united
science and taste to the simple and laborious habits of a husband-

man. He had a son who resided several years in Europe, but on the death of his father returned home, accompanied by a wife. He had succeeded to the occupation of the farm, but rumor had whispered many tales to the disadvantage of his morals. His wife was affirmed to be of delicate and polished manners, and much unlike her companion.

It now occurred to me that this was the dwelling of the Selbys, and I seemed to have gained some insight into the discord and domestic miseries by which the unhappy lady suffered. This was no time to waste my sympathy on others. I could benefit her nothing. Selby had probably returned from a carousal, with all his malignant passions raised into frenzy by intoxication. He had driven his desolate wife from her bed and house, and, to shun outrage and violence, she had fled, with her helpless infant, to the barn. To appease his fury, to console her, to suggest a remedy for this distress, was not in my power. To have sought an interview would be merely to excite her terrors and alarm her delicacy, without contributing to alleviate her calamity. Here, then, was no asylum for me. A place of rest must be sought at some neighboring habitation. It was probable that one would be found at no great distance: the path that led from the spot where I stood, through a gate, into a meadow, might conduct me to the nearest dwelling; and this path I immediately resolved to explore.

I was anxious to open the gate without noise, but I could not succeed. Some creaking of its hinges was unavoidably produced, which I feared would be overheard by the lady and multiply her apprehensions and perplexities. This inconvenience was irremediable. I therefore closed the gate and pursued the footway before me with the utmost expedition. I had not gained the farther end of the meadow when I lighted on something which lay across the path, and which, on being closely inspected, appeared to be a human body. It was the corpse of a girl, mangled by a hatchet. Her head, gory and deprived of its locks, easily explained the kind of enemies by whom she had been assailed. Here was proof that this quiet and remote habitation had been visited, in their destructive progress, by the Indians. The girl had been slain by them, and her scalp, according to their savage custom, had been torn away to be preserved as a trophy.

The fire which had been kindled on the kitchen floor was now remembered, and corroborated the inferences which were drawn from this spectacle. And yet that the mischief had been thus lim-

ited, that the besotted wretch who lay helpless on his bed and careless of impending danger, and that the mother and her infant,
should escape, excited some degree of surprise. Could the savages have been interrupted in their work, and obliged to leave
their vengeance unfinished?

Their visit had been recent. Many hours had not elapsed since
they prowled about these grounds. Had they wholly disappeared,
and meant they not to return? To what new danger might I be exposed in remaining thus guideless and destitute of all defense?

In consequence of these reflections, I proceeded with more caution. I looked with suspicious glances before and on either side of
me. I now approached the fence which, on this side, bounded the
meadow. Something was discerned, or imagined, stretched close
to the fence, on the ground, and filling up the pathway. My apprehensions of a lurking enemy had been previously awakened, and
my fancy instantly figured to itself an armed man lying on the
ground and waiting to assail the unsuspecting passenger.

At first I was prompted to fly, but a second thought showed me
that I had already approached near enough to be endangered. Notwithstanding my pause, the form was motionless. The possibility
of being misled in my conjectures was easily supposed. What I saw
might be a log, or it might be another victim to savage ferocity.
This track was that which my safety required me to pursue. To
turn aside or go back would be merely to bewilder myself anew.

Urged by these motives, I went nearer, and at last was close
enough to perceive that the figure was human. He lay upon his face.
Near his right hand was a musket, unclenched. This circumstance,
his deathlike attitude, and the garb and ornaments of an Indian,
made me readily suspect the nature and cause of this catastrophe.
Here the invaders had been encountered and repulsed, and one
at least of their number had been left upon the field.

I was weary of contemplating these rueful objects. Custom, likewise, even in so short a period, had inured me to spectacles of horror. I was grown callous and immovable. I stayed not to ponder on
the scene, but, snatching the musket, which was now without an
owner, and which might be indispensable to my defense, I hastened
into the wood. On this side the meadow was skirted by a forest;
but a beaten road led into it, and might therefore be attempted
without danger.

XXIII

The road was intricate and long. It seemed designed to pervade the forest in every possible direction. I frequently noticed cut wood piled in heaps upon either side, and rejoiced in these tokens that the residence of man was near. At length I reached a second fence, which proved to be the boundary of a road still more frequented. I pursued this, and presently beheld before me the river and its opposite barriers.

This object afforded me some knowledge of my situation. There was a ford over which travellers used to pass, and in which the road that I was now pursuing terminated. The stream was rapid and tumultuous, but in this place did not rise higher than the shoulders. On the opposite side was a highway, passable by horses and men, though not by carriages, and which led into the midst of Solesbury. Should I not rush into the stream, and still aim at reaching my uncle's house before morning? Why should I delay?

Thirty hours of incessant watchfulness and toil, of enormous efforts and perils, preceded and accompanied by abstinence and wounds, were enough to annihilate the strength and courage of ordinary men. In the course of them, I had frequently believed myself to have reached the verge beyond which my force would not carry me; but experience as frequently demonstrated my error. Though many miles were yet to be traversed, though my clothes were once more to be drenched and loaded with moisture, though every hour seemed to add somewhat to the keenness of the blast, yet how should I know, but by trial, whether my stock of energy was not sufficient for this last exploit?

My resolution to proceed was nearly formed, when the figure of a man moving slowly across the road at some distance before me was observed. Hard by this ford lived a man by name Bisset, of whom I had slight knowledge. He tended his two hundred acres with a plodding and money-doting spirit, while his son overlooked a gristmill on the river. He was a creature of gain, coarse and harmless. The man whom I saw before me might be he, or someone belonging to his family. Being armed for defense, I less scrupled at meeting with anything in the shape of man. I therefore called. The figure stopped and answered me without surliness or anger. The voice was unlike that of Bisset, but this person's information I believed would be of some service.

Coming up to him, he proved to be a clown belonging to Bisset's habitation. His panic and surprise on seeing me made him aghast. In my present garb I should not have easily been recognized by my nearest kinsman, and much less easily by one who had seldom met me.

It may be easily conceived that my thoughts, when allowed to wander from the objects before me, were tormented with forebodings and inquietudes on account of the ills which I had so much reason to believe had befallen my family. I had no doubt that some evil had happened, but the full extent of it was still uncertain. I desired and dreaded to discover the truth, and was unable to interrogate this person in a direct manner. I could deal only in circuities and hints. I shuddered while I waited for an answer to my inquiries.

Had not Indians, I asked, been lately seen in this neighborhood? Were they not suspected of hostile designs? Had they not already committed some mischief? Some passenger, perhaps, had been attacked, or fire had been set to some house? On which side of the river had their steps been observed or any devastation been committed? Above the ford or below it? At what distance from the river?

When his attention could be withdrawn from my person and bestowed upon my questions, he answered that some alarm had indeed been spread about Indians, and that parties from Solesbury and Chetasco were out in pursuit of them, that many persons had been killed by them, and that one house in Solesbury had been rifled and burnt on the night before the last.

These tidings were a dreadful confirmation of my fears. There scarcely remained a doubt; but still my expiring hope prompted me to inquire, "To whom did the house belong?"

He answered that he had not heard the name of the owner. He was a stranger to the people on the other side of the river.

Were any of the inhabitants murdered?

Yes; all that were at home, except a girl whom they carried off. Some said that the girl had been retaken.

What was the name? Was it Huntly?

Huntly? Yes. No. He did not know. He had forgotten.

I fixed my eyes upon the ground. An interval of gloomy meditation succeeded. All was lost! All for whose sake I had desired to live had perished by the hands of these assassins! That dear home,

the scene of my sportive childhood, of my studies, labors, and recreations, was ravaged by fire and the sword,—was reduced to a
frightful ruin!

Not only all that embellished and endeared existence was destroyed, but the means of subsistence itself. Thou knowest that
my sisters and I were dependants on the bounty of our uncle. His
death would make way for the succession of his son, a man fraught
with envy and malignity, who always testified a mortal hatred to
us, merely because we enjoyed the protection of his father. The
ground which furnished me with bread was now become the property of one who, if he could have done it with security, would gladly have mingled poison with my food.

All that my imagination or my heart regarded as of value had likewise perished. Whatever my chamber, my closets, my cabinets
contained, my furniture, my books, the records of my own skill, the
monuments of their existence whom I loved, my very clothing,
were involved in indiscriminate and irretrievable destruction. Why
should I survive this calamity?

But did not he say that one had escaped? The only females in
the family were my sisters. One of these had been reserved for a
fate worse than death: to gratify the innate and insatiable cruelty
of savages, by suffering all the torments their invention can suggest, or to linger out years of weary bondage and unintermitted
hardship in the bosom of the wilderness. To restore her to liberty,
to cherish this last survivor of my unfortunate race, was a sufficient
motive to life and to activity.

But soft! Had not rumor whispered that the captive was retaken?
Oh! who was her angel of deliverance? Where did she now abide?
Weeping over the untimely fall of her protector and her friend?
Lamenting and upbraiding the absence of her brother? Why should
I not haste to find her?—to mingle my tears with hers, to assure
her of my safety, and expatiate the involuntary crime of my deser-
tion by devoting all futurity to the task of her consolation and
improvement?

The path was open and direct. My new motives would have trampled upon every impediment and made me reckless of all dangers and all toils. I broke from my reverie, and, without taking leave
or expressing gratitude to my informant, I ran with frantic expedition towards the river, and, plunging into it, gained the opposite
side in a moment.

I was sufficiently acquainted with the road. Some twelve or fifteen miles remained to be traversed. I did not fear that my own strength would fail in the performance of my journey. It was not my uncle's habitation to which I directed my steps. Inglefield was my friend. If my sister had existence, or was snatched from captivity, it was here that an asylum had been afforded to her, and here was I to seek the knowledge of my destiny. For this reason, having reached a spot where the road divided into two branches, one of which led to Inglefield's and the other to Huntly's, I struck into the former.

Scarcely had I passed the angle when I noticed a building on the right hand, at some distance from the road. In the present state of my thoughts, it would not have attracted my attention, had not a light gleamed from an upper window and told me that all within were not at rest.

I was acquainted with the owner of this mansion. He merited esteem and confidence, and could not fail to be acquainted with recent events. From him I should obtain all the information that I needed, and I should be delivered from some part of the agonies of my suspense. I should reach his door in a few minutes, and the window light was a proof that my entrance at this hour would not disturb the family, some of whom were stirring.

Through a gate I entered an avenue of tall oaks that led to the house. I could not but reflect on the effect which my appearance would produce upon the family. The sleek locks, neat apparel, pacific guise, sobriety and gentleness of aspect by which I was customarily distinguished, would in vain be sought in the apparition which would now present itself before them. My legs, neck, and bosom were bare, and their native hue was exchanged for the livid marks of bruises and scarifications. A horrid scar upon my cheek, and my uncombed locks; hollow eyes, made ghastly by abstinence and cold, and the ruthless passions of which my mind had been the theater, added to the musket which I carried in my hand, would prepossess them with the notion of a maniac or ruffian.

Some inconveniences might hence arise, which, however, could not be avoided. I must trust to the speed with which my voice and my words should disclose my true character and rectify their mistake.

I now reached the principal door of the house. It was open, and I unceremoniously entered. In the midst of the room stood a German stove, well heated. To thaw my half-frozen limbs was my first care. Meanwhile I gazed around me, and marked the appearances of things.

Two lighted candles stood upon the table. Beside them were cider bottles and pipes of tobacco. The furniture and room was in that state which denoted it to have been lately filled with drinkers and smokers; yet neither voice, nor visage, nor motion, were anywhere observable. I listened; but neither above nor below, within nor without, could any tokens of a human being be perceived.

This vacancy and silence must have been lately preceded by noise, and concourse, and bustle. The contrast was mysterious and ambiguous. No adequate cause of so quick and absolute a transition occurred to me. Having gained some warmth and lingered some ten or twenty minutes in this uncertainty, I determined to explore the other apartments of the building. I knew not what might betide in my absence, or what I might encounter in search to justify precaution, and, therefore, kept the gun in my hand. I snatched a candle from the table and proceeded into two other apartments on the first floor and the kitchen. Neither was inhabited, though chairs and tables were arranged in their usual order, and no traces of violence or hurry were apparent.

Having gained the foot of the staircase, I knocked, but my knocking was wholly disregarded. A light had appeared in an upper chamber. It was not, indeed, in one of those apartments which, according to rural custom, was reserved for guests; but it indubitably betokened the presence of some being by whom my doubts might be solved. These doubts were too tormenting to allow of scruples and delay. I mounted the stairs.

At each chamber door I knocked, but I knocked in vain. I tried to open, but found them to be locked. I at length reached the entrance of that in which a light had been discovered. Here it was certain that someone would be found; but here, as well as elsewhere, my knocking was unnoticed.

To enter this chamber was audacious, but no other expedient was afforded me to determine whether the house had any inhabitants. I therefore entered, though with caution and reluctance. No one was within, but there were sufficient traces of some person who had lately been here. On the table stood a travelling escritoire, open, with pens and inkstand. A chair was placed before it, and a candle on the right hand. This apparatus was rarely seen in this country. Some traveller, it seemed, occupied this room, though the rest of the mansion was deserted. The pilgrim, as these appearances testified, was of no vulgar order, and belonged not to the class of periodical and everyday guests.

It now occurred to me that the occupant of this apartment could not be far off, and that some danger and embarrassment could not fail to accrue from being found, thus accoutred and garbed, in a place sacred to the study and repose of another. It was proper, therefore, to withdraw, and either to resume my journey, or wait for the stranger's return, whom perhaps some temporary engagement had called away, in the lower and public room. The former now appeared to be the best expedient, as the return of this unknown person was uncertain, as well as his power to communicate the information which I wanted.

Had paper, as well as the implements of writing, lain upon the desk, perhaps my lawless curiosity would not have scrupled to have pried into it. On the first glance nothing of that kind appeared; but now, as I turned towards the door, somewhat, lying beside the desk, on the side opposite the candle, caught my attention. The impulse was instantaneous and mechanical that made me leap to the spot and lay my hand upon it. Till I felt it between my fingers, till I brought it near my eyes and read frequently the inscriptions that appeared upon it, I was doubtful whether my senses had deceived me.

Few, perhaps, among mankind, have undergone vicissitudes of peril and wonder equal to mine. The miracles of poetry, the transitions of enchantment, are beggarly and mean compared with those which I had experienced. Passage into new forms, overleaping the bars of time and space, reversal of the laws of inanimate and intelligent existence, had been mine to perform and to witness.

No event had been more fertile of sorrow and perplexity than the loss of thy brother's letters. They went by means invisible, and disappeared at a moment when foresight would have least predicted their disappearance. They now placed themselves before me, in a manner equally abrupt, in a place and by means no less contrary to expectation. The papers which I now seized were those letters. The parchment cover, the string that tied and the wax that sealed them, appeared not to have been opened or violated.

The power that removed them from my cabinet, and dropped them in this house,—a house which I rarely visited, which I had not entered during the last year, with whose in inhabitants I maintained no cordial intercourse, and to whom my occupations and amusements, my joys and my sorrows, were unknown,—was no object even of conjecture. But they were not possessed by any of the family. Some stranger was here, by whom they had been stolen, or into whose possession they had, by some incomprehensible chance, fallen.

That stranger was near. He had left this apartment for a moment. He would speedily return. To go hence might possibly occasion me to miss him. Here, then, I would wait, till he should grant me an interview. The papers were mine, and were recovered. I would never part with them. But to know by whose force or by whose stratagems I had been bereaved of them thus long, was now the supreme passion of my soul. I seated myself near a table and anxiously waited for an interview, on which I was irresistibly persuaded to believe that much of my happiness depended.

Meanwhile, I could not but connect this incident with the destruction of my family. The loss of these papers had excited transports of grief; and yet to have lost them thus was perhaps the sole expedient by which their final preservation could be rendered possible. Had they remained in my cabinet, they could not have escaped the destiny which overtook the house and its furniture. Savages are not accustomed to leave their exterminating work unfinished. The house which they have plundered they are careful to level with the ground. This not only their revenge, but their caution, prescribes. Fire may originate by accident as well as by design, and the traces of pillage and murder are totally obliterated by the flames.

These thoughts were interrupted by the shutting of a door below, and by footsteps ascending the stairs. My heart throbbed at the sound. My seat became uneasy and I started on my feet. I even advanced halfway to the entrance of the room. My eyes were intensely fixed upon the door. My impatience would have made me guess at the person of this visitant by measuring his shadow, if his shadow were first seen; but this was precluded by the position of the light. It was only when the figure entered, and the whole person was seen, that my curiosity was gratified. He who stood before me was the parent and fosterer of my mind, the companion and instructor of my youth, from whom I had been parted for years, from whom I believed myself to be forever separated,—*Sarsefield* himself!

XXIV

My deportment, at an interview so much desired and so wholly unforeseen, was that of a maniac. The petrifying influence of surprise yielded to the impetuosities of passion. I held him in my arms; I wept upon his bosom; I sobbed with emotion which, had it not found passage at my eyes, would have burst my heartstrings. Thus I, who had escaped the deaths that had previously assailed me in so many forms, should have been reserved to solemnize a scene like this by—*dying for joy!*

The sterner passions and habitual austerities of my companion exempted him from pouring out this testimony of his feelings. His feelings were, indeed, more allied to astonishment and incredulity than mine had been. My person was not instantly recognized. He shrunk from my embrace as if I were an apparition or impostor. He quickly disengaged himself from my arms, and, withdrawing a few paces, gazed upon me as on one whom he had never before seen.

These repulses were ascribed to the loss of his affection. I was not mindful of the hideous guise in which I stood before him, and by which he might justly be misled to imagine me a ruffian or a lunatic. My tears flowed now on a new account, and I articulated, in a broken and faint voice, "My master! my friend! Have you forgotten, have you ceased to love me?"

The sound of my voice made him start and exclaim, "Am I alive? am I awake? Speak again, I beseech you, and convince me that I am not dreaming or delirious."

"Can you need any proof," I answered, "that it is Edgar Huntly, your pupil, your child, that speaks to you?"

He now withdrew his eyes from me and fixed them on the floor. After a pause he resumed, in emphatic accents: "Well, I have lived to this age in unbelief. To credit or trust in miraculous agency was foreign to my nature, but now I am no longer skeptical. Call me to any bar, and exact from me an oath that you have twice been dead and twice recalled to life; that you move about invisibly, and change your place by the force, not of muscles, but of thought, and I will give it.

"How came you hither? Did you penetrate the wall? Did you rise through the floor?

"Yet surely 'tis an error. You could not be he whom twenty witnesses affirmed to have beheld a lifeless and mangled corpse upon the ground, whom my own eyes saw in that condition.

"In seeking the spot once more to provide you a grave, you had vanished. Again I met you. You plunged into a rapid stream, from a height from which it was impossible to fall and to live; yet, as if to set the limits of nature at defiance, to sport with human penetration, you rose upon the surface; you floated; you swam; thirty bullets were aimed at your head, by marksmen celebrated for the exactness of their sight. I myself was of the number, and I never missed what I desired to hit.

"My predictions were confirmed by the event. You ceased to struggle; you sunk to rise no more; and yet, after these accumulated deaths, you light upon this floor, so far distant from the scene of your catastrophe, over spaces only to be passed, in so short a time as has since elapsed, by those who have wings.

"My eyes, my ears, bear testimony to your existence now, as they formerly convinced me of your death. What am I to think? what proofs am I to credit?" There he stopped.

Every accent of this speech added to the confusion of my thoughts. The allusions that my friend had made were not unintelligible. I gained a glimpse of the complicated errors by which we had been mutually deceived. I had fainted on the area before Deb's hut. I was found by Sarsefield in this conditon, and imagined to be dead.

The man whom I had seen upon the promontory was not an Indian. He belonged to a numerous band of pursuers, whom my hostile and precipitate deportment caused to suspect me for an enemy. They that fired from the steep were friends. The interposition that screened me from so many bullets was indeed miraculous. No wonder that my voluntary sinking, in order to elude their shots, was mistaken for death, and that, having accomplished the destruction of this foe, they resumed their pursuit of others. But how was Sarsefield apprised that it was I who plunged into the river? No subsequent event was possible to impart to him the incredible truth.

A pause of mutual silence ensued. At length Sarsefield renewed his expressions of amazement at this interview, and besought me to explain why I had disappeared by night from my uncle's house, and by what series of unheard-of events this interview was brought about. Was it indeed Huntly whom he examined and mourned over at the threshold of Deb's hut. Whom he had sought in every thicket and cave in the ample circuit of Norwalk and Chetasco? Whom he had seen perish in the current of the Delaware?

Instead of noticing his questions, my soul was harrowed with anxiety respecting the fate of my uncle and sisters. Sarsefield could communicate the tidings which would decide on my future lot and set my portion in happiness or misery. Yet I had not breath to speak my inquiries. Hope tottered, and I felt as if a single word would be sufficient for its utter subversion. At length I articulated the name of my uncle.

The single word sufficiently imparted my fears, and these fears needed no verbal confirmation. At that dear name my companion's features were overspread by sorrow.

"You uncle," said he, "is dead."

"Dead? Merciful Heaven! Any my sisters too! Both?"

"Your sisters are alive and well."

"Nay," resumed I, in faltering accents, "jest not with my feelings. Be not cruel in your pity. Tell me the truth."

"I have said the truth. They are well, at Mr. Inglefield's."

My wishes were eager to assent to the truth of these tidings. The better part of me was, then, safe; but how did they escape the fate that overtook my uncle? How did they evade the destroying hatchet and the midnight conflagration? These doubts were imparted in a tumultuous and obscure manner to my friend. He no sooner fully comprehended them, than he looked at me with some inquietude and surprise.

"Huntly," said he, "are you mad? What has filled you with these hideous prepossessions? Much havoc has indeed been committed in Chetasco and the wilderness, and a log hut has been burnt, by design or by accident, in Solesbury; but that is all. Your house has not been assailed by either firebrand or tomahawk. Everything is safe and in its ancient order. The master indeed is gone, but the old man fell a victim to his own temerity and hardihood. It is thirty years since he retired with three wounds from the field of Braddock; but time in no degree abated his adventurous and military spirit. On the first alarm, he summoned his neighbors, and led them in pursuit of the invaders. Alas! he was the first to attack them, and the only one who fell in the contest."

These words were uttered in a manner that left me no room to doubt of their truth. My uncle had already been lamented, and the discovery of the nature of his death, so contrary to my forebodings, and of the safety of my girls, made the state of my mind partake more of exultation and joy than of grief or regret.

But how was I deceived? Had not my fusil been found in the hands of an enemy? Whence could he have plundered it but from my own chamber? It hung against the wall of a closet, from which no stranger could have taken it except by violence. My perplexities and doubts were not at an end, but those which constituted my chief torment were removed. I listened to my friend's entreaties to tell him the cause of my elopement, and the incidents that terminated in the present interview.

I began with relating my return to consciousness in the bottom of the pit; my efforts to free myself from this abhorred prison; the acts of horror to which I was impelled by famine, and their excruciating consequences; my gaining the outlet of the cavern, the desperate expedient by which I removed the impediment to my escape, and the deliverance of the captive girl; the contest I maintained before Deb's hut; my subsequent wanderings; the banquet which hospitality afforded me; my journey to the river bank; my meditations on the means of reaching the road; my motives for hazarding my life by plunging into the stream; and my subsequent perils and fears till I reached the threshold of this habitation.

"Thus," continued I, "I have complied with your request. I have told all that I myself know. What were the incidents between my sinking to rest at my uncle's and my awaking in the chambers of the hill; by what means and by whose contrivance, preternatural or human, this transition was effected, I am unable to explain; I cannot even guess.

"What has eluded my sagacity may not be beyond the reach of another. Your own reflections on my tale, or some facts that have fallen under your notice, may enable you to furnish a solution. But, meanwhile, how am I to account for your appearance on this spot? This meeting was unexpected and abrupt to you, but it has not been less so to me. Of all mankind, Sarsefield was the furthest from my thoughts when I saw these tokens of a traveller and a stranger.

"You were imperfectly acquainted with my wanderings. You saw me on the ground before Deb's hut. You saw me plunge into the river. You endeavored to destroy me while swimming; and you knew, before my narrative was heard, that Huntly was the object of your enmity. What was the motive of your search in the desert,

and how were you apprised of my condition? These things are not
less wonderful than any of those which I have already related."

During my tale the features of Sarsefield betokened the deepest
attention. His eye strayed not a moment from my face. All my perils
and forebodings were fresh in my remembrance: they had scarcely
gone by; their skirts, so to speak, were still visible. No wonder that
my eloquence was vivid and pathetic; that I portrayed the past as
if it were the present scene; and that not my tongue only, but every
muscle and limb, spoke.

When I had finished my relation, Sarsefield sank into thought-
fulness. From this, after a time, he recovered, and said, "Your tale,
Huntly, is true; yet, did I not see you before me, were I not acquainted with the artlessness and rectitude of your character, and,
above all, had not my own experience, during the last three days,
confirmed every incident, I should question its truth. You have
amply gratified my curiosity, and deserve that your own should
be gratified as fully. Listen to me.

"Much has happened since we parted, which shall not be now
mentioned. I promised to inform you of my welfare by letter, and
did not fail to write; but whether my letters were received, or any
were written by you in return, or if written were ever transmitted,
I cannot tell: none were ever received.

"Some days since, I arrived, in company with a lady who is my
wife, in America. You have never been forgotten by me. I knew
your situation to be little in agreement with your wishes, and one
of the benefits which fortune has lately conferred upon me is the
power of snatching you from a life of labor and obscurity, whose
goods, scanty as they are, were transient and precarious, and affording you the suitable leisure and means of intellectual gratification and improvement.

"Your silence made me entertain some doubts concerning your
welfare, and even your existence. To solve these doubts, I hastened
to Solesbury. Some delays upon the road hindered me from accomplishing my journey by daylight. It was night before I entered
the Norwalk path; but my ancient rambles with you made me
familiar with it, and I was not afraid of being obstructed or bewildered.

"Just as I gained the southern outlet, I spied a passenger on foot,
coming towards me with a quick pace. The incident was of no moment; and yet the time of night, the seeming expedition of the
walker, recollection of the mazes and obstacles which he was going

to encounter, and a vague conjecture that perhaps he was unacquainted with the difficulties that awaited him, made me eye him with attention as he passed.

"He came near, and I thought I recognized a friend in this traveller. The form, the gesture, the stature, bore a powerful resemblance to those of Edgar Huntly. This resemblance was so strong that I stopped, and, after he had gone by, called him by your name. That no notice was taken of my call proved that the person was mistaken; but, even though it were another, that he should not even hesitate or turn at a summons which he could not but perceive to be addressed, though erroneously, to him, was the source of some surprise. I did not repeat my call, but proceeded on my way.

"All had retired to repose in your uncle's dwelling. I did not scruple to rouse them, and was received with affectionate and joyous greetings. That you allowed your uncle to rise before you was a new topic of reflection. To my inquiries concerning you, answers were made that accorded with my wishes. I was told that you were in good health and were then in bed. That you had not heard and risen at my knocking was mentioned with surprise; but your uncle accounted for your indolence by saying that during the last week you had fatigued yourself by rambling, night and day, in search of some maniac or visionary who was supposed to have retreated into Norwalk.

"I insisted upon awakening you myself. I anticipated the effect of this sudden and unlooked-for meeting with some emotions of pride as well as of pleasure. To find, in opening your eyes, your old preceptor standing by your bedside and gazing in your face, would place you, I conceived, in an affecting situation.

"Your chamber door was open, but your bed was empty. Your uncle and sister were made acquainted with this circumstance. Their surprise gave way to conjectures that your restless and romantic spirit had tempted you from your repose, that you had rambled abroad on some fantastic errand, and would probably return before the dawn. I willingly acquiesced in this opinion, and, my feelings being too thoroughly aroused to allow me to sleep, I took possession of your chamber and patiently awaited your return.

"The morning returned, but Huntly made not his appearance. Your uncle became somewhat uneasy at this unseasonable absence. Much speculation and inquiry as to the possible reasons of your flight was made. In my survey of your chamber, I noted that only a part of your clothing remained beside your bed. Coat, hat, stockings and shoes lay upon the spot where they had probably been thrown when you had disrobed yourself; but the pantaloons, which, according to Mr. Huntly's report, completed your dress, were nowhere to be found. That you should go forth on so cold a night so slenderly apparelled was almost incredible. Your reason or your senses had deserted you, before so rash an action could be meditated.

"I now remembered the person I had met in Norwalk. His resemblance to your figure, his garb, which wanted hat, coat, stockings and shoes, and your absence from your bed at that hour, were remarkable coincidences; but why did you disregard my call? Your name, uttered by a voice that could not be unknown, was surely sufficient to arrest your steps.

"Each hour added to the impatience of your friends. To their recollections and conjectures I listened with a view to extract from them some solution of this mystery. At length a story was alluded to of someone who, on the preceding night, had been heard walking in the long room; to this was added the tale of your anxieties and wonders occasioned by the loss of certain manuscripts.

"While ruminating upon these incidents, and endeavoring to extract from this intelligence a clue explanatory of your present situation, a single word, casually dropped by your uncle, instantly illuminated my darkness and dispelled my doubts. 'After all,' said the old man, 'ten to one but Edgar himself was the man whom we heard walking, but the lad was asleep, and knew not what he was about.'

" 'Surely,' said I, 'this inference is just. His manuscripts could not be removed by any hands but his own, since the rest of mankind were unacquainted not only with the place of their concealment, but with their existence. None but a man insane or asleep would wander forth so slightly dressed, and none but a sleeper would have disregarded my calls.' This conclusion was generally adopted; but it gave birth in my mind to infinite inquietudes. You had roved into Norwalk, a scene of inequalities, of prominences and pits, among which, thus destitute of the guidance of your senses, you could scarcely fail to be destroyed, or, at least, irretrievably bewildered. I painted to myself the dangers to which you were subjected. Your careless feet would bear you into some whirlpool or to the edge of some precipice; some internal revolution or outward shock would recall you to consciousness at some perilous moment. Surprise and fear would disable you from taking seasonable or suitable precautions, and your destruction be made sure.

"The lapse of every new hour, without bringing tidings of your state, enhanced these fears. At length the propriety of searching for you occurred; Mr. Huntly and I determined to set out upon this pursuit, as well as to commission others. A plan was laid by which every accessible part of Norwalk, the wilderness beyond the flats of Solesbury, and the valley of Chetasco, should be traversed and explored.

"Scarcely had we equipped ourselves for this expedition, when a messenger arrived, who brought the disastrous news of Indians being seen within these precincts, and on the last night a farmer was shot in his fields, a dwelling in Chetasco was burnt to the ground, and its inhabitants murdered or made captives. Rumor and inquiry had been busy, and a plausible conjecture had been formed as to the course and number of the enemies. They were said to be divided into bands, and to amount in the whole to thirty or forty warriors. This messenger had come to warn us of the danger which might impend, and to summon us to join in the pursuit and extirpation of these detestable foes.

"Your uncle, whose alacrity and vigor age had not abated, eagerly engaged in this scheme. I was not averse to contribute my efforts to an end like this. The road which we had previously designed to take, in search of my fugitive pupil, was the same by which we must trace or intercept the retreat of the savages. Thus two purposes, equally momentous, would be answered by the same means.

"Mr. Huntly armed himself with your fusil; Inglefield supplied me with a gun. During our absence the dwelling was closed and locked, and your sisters placed under the protection of Inglefield, whose age and pacific sentiments unfitted him for arduous and sanguinary enterprises. A troop of rustics was collected, half of whom remained to traverse Solesbury, and the other, whom Mr. Huntly and I accompanied, hastened to Chetasco.

XXV

"It was noonday before we reached the theater of action. Fear and revenge combined to make the people of Chetasco diligent and zealous in their own defense. The havoc already committed had been mournful. To prevent a repetition of the same calamities, they resolved to hunt out the hostile footsteps and exact a merciless retribution.

"It was likely that the enemy, on the approach of day, had withdrawn from the valley and concealed themselves in the thickets between the parallel ridges of the mountain. This space, which, according to the object with which it is compared, is either a vale or the top of a hill, was obscure and desolate. It was undoubtedly the avenue by which the robbers had issued forth, and by which they would escape to the Ohio. Here they might still remain, intending to emerge from their concealment on the next night and perpetrate new horrors.

"A certain distribution was made of our number, so as to move in all directions at the same time. I will not dwell upon particulars. It will suffice to say that keen eyes and indefatigable feet brought us at last to the presence of the largest number of these marauders. Seven of them were slain by the edge of a brook, where they sat wholly unconscious of the danger which hung over them. Five escaped, and one of these secured his retreat by wrestling your fusil from your uncle and shooting him dead. Before our companion could be rescued or revenged, the assassin, with the remnant of the troop, disappeared, and bore away with him the fusil as a trophy of his victory.

"This disaster was deplored, not only on account of that life which had thus been sacrificed, but because a sagacious guide and intrepid leader was lost. His acquaintance with the habits of the Indians, and his experience in their wars, made him trace their footsteps with more certainty than any of his associates.

"The pursuit was still continued, and parties were so stationed that the escape of the enemy was difficult, if not impossible. Our search was unremitted, but, during twelve or fourteen hours, unsuccessful. Queen Mab did not elude all suspicion. Her hut was visited by different parties, but the old woman and her dogs had disappeared.

"Meanwhile your situation was not forgotten. Everyone was charged to explore your footsteps as well as those of the savages; but this search was no less unsuccessful than the former. None had heard of you or seen you.

"This continued till midnight. Three of us made a pause at a brook, and intended to repair our fatigues by a respite of a few hours; but scarcely had we stretched ourselves on the ground when we were alarmed by a shot which seemed to have been fired at a short distance. We started on our feet and consulted with each other on the measures to be taken. A second, a third, and a fourth shot, from the same quarter, excited our attention anew. Mab's hut was known to stand at the distance and in the direction of this sound, and thither we resolved to repair.

"This was done with speed, but with the utmost circumspection. We shortly gained the road that leads near this hut, and at length gained a view of the building. Many persons were discovered, in a sort of bustling inactivity, before the hut. They were easily distinguished to be friends, and were therefore approached without scruple.

"The objects that presented themselves to a nearer view were five bodies stretched upon the ground. Three of them were savages. The fourth was a girl, who, though alive, seemed to have received a mortal wound. The fifth, breathless and mangled, and his features almost concealed by the blood that overspread his face, was Edgar,—the fugitive for whom I had made such anxious search.

"About the same hour on the last night I had met you hastening into Norwalk. Now were you lying in the midst of savages, at the distance of thirty miles from your home, and in a spot which it was impossible for you to have reached unless by an immense circuit over rocks and thickets. That you had found a rift at the basis of a hill, and thus penetrated its solidities, and thus precluded so tedious and circuitous a journey as must otherwise have been made, was not to be imagined.

"But whence arose this scene? It was obvious to conclude that my associates had surprised their enemies in this house, and exacted from them the forfeit of their crimes; but how you should have been confounded with their foes, or whence came the wounded girl, was a subject of astonishment.

"You will judge how much this surprise was augmented when I was informed that the party whom we found had been attracted hither by the same signals by which we had been alarmed; that on reaching this spot you had been discovered, alive, seated on the ground, and still sustaining the gun with which you had apparently completed the destruction of so many adversaries. In a moment after their arrival you sunk down and expired.

"This scene was attended with inexplicable circumstances. The musket which lay beside you appeared to have belonged to one of the savages. The wound by which each had died was single. Of the four shots we had distinguished at a distance, three of them were therefore fatal to the Indians, and the fourth was doubtless that by which you had fallen; yet three muskets only were discoverable.

"The arms were collected, and the girl carried to the nearest house in the arms of her father. Her situation was deemed capable of remedy, and the sorrow and wonder which I felt at your untimely and extraordinary fate did not hinder me from endeavoring to restore the health of this unfortunate victim. I reflected, likewise, that some light might be thrown upon transactions so mysterious by the information which might be collected from her story. Numberless questions and hints were necessary to extract from her a consistent or intelligible tale. She had been dragged, it seems, for miles, at the heels of her conquerors, who at length stopped in a cavern for the sake of some repose. All slept but one, who sat and watched. Something called him away, and, at the same moment, you appeared at the bottom of the cave, half naked and without arms. You instantly supplied the last deficiency by seizing the gun and tomahawk of him who had gone forth, and who had negligently left his weapons behind. Then, stepping over the bodies of the sleepers, you rushed out of the cavern.

"She then mentioned your unexpected return, her deliverance and flight, and arrival at Deb's hut. You watched upon the hearth, and she fell asleep upon the blanket. From this sleep she was roused by violent and cruel blows. She looked up: you were gone, and the bed on which she lay was surrounded by the men from whom she had so lately escaped. One dragged her out of the hut and levelled his gun at her breast. At the moment when he touched the trigger, a shot came from an unknown quarter, and he fell at her feet. Of subsequent events she had an incoherent recollection. The Indians were successively slain, and you came to her, and interrogated and consoled her.

"In your journey to the hut you were armed. This in some degree accounted for appearances; but where were your arms? Three muskets only were discovered, and these undoubtedly belonged to your enemies.

"I now had leisure to reflect upon your destiny. I had arrived soon enough on this shore merely to witness the catastrophe of two beings whom I most loved. Both were overtaken by the same fate, nearly at the same hour. The same hand had possibly accomplished the destruction of uncle and nephew.

"Now, however, I began to entertain a hope that your state might not be irretrievable. You had walked and spoken after the firing had ceased and your enemies had ceased to contend with you. A wound had, no doubt, been previously received. I had hastily inferred that the wound was mortal, and that life could not be recalled. Occupied with attention to the wailings of the girl, and full of sorrow and perplexity, I had admitted an opinion which would never have been adopted in different circumstances. My acquaintance with wounds would have taught me to regard sunken muscles, lividness, and cessation of the pulse, as mere indications of a swoon, and not as tokens of death.

"Perhaps my error was not irreparable. By hastening to the hut, I might ascertain your condition, and at least transport your remains to some dwelling and finally secure to you the decencies of burial.

"Of twelve savages discovered on the preceding day, ten were now killed. Two at least remained, after whom the pursuit was still zealously maintained. Attention to the wounded girl had withdrawn me from the party, and I had now leisure to return to the scene of these disasters. The sun had risen, and, accompanied by two others, I repaired thither.

"A sharp turn in the road, at the entrance of a field, set before us a startling spectacle. An Indian, mangled by repeated wounds of bayonet and bullet, was discovered. His musket was stuck in the ground, by way of beacon attracting our attention to the spot. Over this space I had gone a few hours before, and nothing like this was then seen. The parties abroad had hied away to a distant quarter. Some invisible power seemed to be enlisted in our defense and to preclude the necessity of our arms.

"We proceeded to the hut. The savages were there, but Edgar had risen and flown! Nothing now seemed to be incredible. You had slain three foes, and the weapon with which the victory had been achieved had vanished. You had risen from the dead, had assailed one of the surviving enemies, had employed bullet and dagger in his destruction, with both of which you could only be supplied by supernatural means, and had disappeared. If any inhabitant of Chetasco had done this, we should have heard of it.

"But what remained? You were still alive. Your strength was sufficient to bear you from this spot. Why were you still invisible? and to what dangers might you not be exposed before you could disinvolve yourself from the mazes of this wilderness?

"Once more I procured indefatigable search to be made after you. It was continued till the approach of evening, and was fruitless. Inquiries were twice made at the house where you were supplied with food and intelligence. On the second call I was astonished and delighted by the tidings received from the good woman. Your person, and demeanor, and arms, were described, and mention made of your resolution to cross the southern ridge and traverse the Solesbury Road with the utmost expedition.

"The greater part of my inquietudes were now removed. You were able to eat and to travel, and there was little doubt that a meeting would take place between us on the next morning. Meanwhile, I determined to concur with those who pursued the remainder of the enemy. I followed you, in the path that you were said to have taken, and quickly joined a numerous party who were searching for those who, on the last night, had attacked a plantation that lies near this, and destroyed the inhabitants.

"I need not dwell upon our doublings and circuities. The enemy was traced to the house of Selby. They had entered, they had put fire on the floor, but were compelled to relinquish their prey. Of what number they consisted could not be ascertained; but one, lingering behind his fellows, was shot, at the entrance of the wood, and on the spot where you chanced to light upon him.

"Selby's house was empty, and before the fire had made any progress we extinguished it. The drunken wretch whom you encountered had probably returned from his nocturnal debauch after we had left the spot.

"The flying enemy was pursued with fresh diligence. They were found, by various tokens, to have crossed the river, and to have ascended the mountain. We trod closely on their heels. When we arrived at the promontory described by you, the fatigues of the night and day rendered me unqualified to proceed. I determined that this should be the bound of my excursions. I was anxious to obtain an interview with you, and, unless I paused here, should not be able to gain Inglefield's as early in the morning as I wished. Two others concurred with me in this resolution, and prepared to return to this house, which had been deserted by its tenants till the danger was past, and which had been selected as the place of rendezvous.

"At this moment, dejected and weary, I approached the ledge which severed the headland from the mountain. I marked the appearance of someone stretched upon the ground where you lay. No domestic animal would wander hither and place himself upon this spot. There was something likewise in the appearance of the object that bespoke it to be man; but, if it were man, it was incontrovertibly a savage and a foe. I determined, therefore, to rouse you by a bullet.

"My decision was perhaps absurd. I ought to have gained more certainty before I hazarded your destruction. Be that as it will, a moment's lingering on your part would have probably been fatal. You started on your feet, and fired. See the hole which your random shot made through my sleeve! This surely was a day destined to be signalized by hairbreadth escapes.

"Your action seemed incontestably to confirm my prognostics. Everyone hurried to the spot and was eager to destroy an enemy. No one hesitated to believe that some of the shots aimed at you had reached their mark, and that you had sunk to rise no more.

"The gun which was fired and thrown down was taken and examined. It had been my companion in many a toilsome expedition. It had rescued me and my friends from a thousand deaths. In order to recognize it, I needed only to touch and handle it. I instantly discovered that I held in my hand the fusil which I had left with you on parting, with which your uncle had equipped himself, and which had been ravished from him by a savage. What was I hence to infer respecting the person of the last possessor?

"My inquiries respecting you, of the woman whose milk and bread you had eaten, were minute. You entered, she said, with a hatchet and gun in your hand. While you ate, the gun was laid upon the table. She sat near, and the piece became the object of inquisitive attention. The stock and barrels were described by her in such terms as left no doubt that this was the *fusil*.

"A comparison of incidents enabled me to trace the manner in which you came into possession of this instrument. One of those whom you found in the cavern was the assassin of your uncle. Ac-

cording to the girl's report, on issuing from your hiding place you
seized a gun that was unoccupied, and this gun chanced to be
your own.

"Its two barrels were probably the cause of your success in that
unequal contest at Mab's hut. On recovering from *deliquium,* you
found it where it had been dropped by you, out of sight and unsuspected by the party that had afterwards arrived. In your passage
to the river, had it once more fallen into hostile hands? or had you
missed the way, wandered to this promontory, and mistaken a
troop of friends for a band of Indian marauders?

"Either supposition was dreadful. The latter was the most plausible. No motives were conceivable by which one of the fugitives
could be induced to post himself here, in this conspicuous station;
whereas, the road which led you to the summit of the hill, to that
spot where descent to the river road was practicable, could not
be found but by those who were accustomed to traverse it. The
directions which you had exacted from your hostess proved your
previous unacquaintance with these tracts.

"I acquiesced in this opinion with a heavy and desponding heart.
Fate had led us into a maze which could only terminate in the destruction of one or the other. By the breadth of a hair had I escaped
death from your hand. The same fortune had not befriended you.
After my tedious search, I had lighted on you, forlorn, bewildered,
perishing with cold and hunger. Instead of recognizing and affording you relief, I compelled you to leap into the river, from a perilous height, and had desisted from my persecution only when I had
bereaved you of life and plunged you to the bottom of the gulf.

"My motives in coming to America were numerous and mixed.
Among these was the parental affection with which you had inspired
me. I came with fortune, and a better gift than fortune, in my hand.
I intended to bestow both upon you, not only to give you competence, but one who would endear to you that competence, who
would enhance, by participating, every gratification.

"My schemes were now at an end. You were gone, beyond the
reach of my benevolence and justice. I had robbed your two sisters of a friend and guardian. It was some consolation to think that
it was in my power to stand, with regard to them, in your place;
that I could snatch them from the poverty, dependence, and
humiliation to which your death and that of your uncle had reduced them.

"I was now doubly weary of the enterprise in which I was engaged, and returned with speed to this rendezvous. My companions have gone to know the state of the family who resided under this roof, and left me to beguile the tedious moments in whatever manner I pleased.

"I have omitted mentioning one incident that happened between the detection of your flight and our expedition to Chetasco. Having formed a plausible conjecture as to him who walked in the long room, it was obvious to conclude that he who purloined your manuscript, and the walker, was the same personage. It was likewise easily inferred that the letters were secreted in the cedar chest or in some other part of the room. Instances similar to this have heretofore occurred. Men have employed anxious months in search of that which, in a freak of noctambulation, was hidden by their own hands.

"A search was immediately commenced, and your letters were found, carefully concealed between the rafters and shingles of the roof, in a spot where, if suspicion had not been previously excited, they would have remained till the vernal rains and the summer heats had insensibly destroyed them. This packet I carried with me, knowing the value which you set upon it, and there being no receptacle equally safe but your own cabinet, which was locked.

"Having, as I said, reached this house, and being left alone, I bethought me of the treasure I possessed. I was unacquainted with the reasons for which these papers were so precious. They probably had some momentous and intimate connection with your own history. As such, they could not be of little value to me, and this moment of inoccupation and regrets was as suitable as any other to the task of perusing them. I drew them forth, therefore, and laid them on the table in this chamber.

"The rest is known to you. During a momentary absence you entered. Surely no interview of ancient friends ever took place in so unexpected and abrupt a manner. You were dead. I mourned for you, as one whom I loved, and whom fate had snatched forever from my sight. Now, in a blissful hour, you had risen, and my happiness in thus embracing you is tenfold greater than would have been experienced if no uncertainties and perils had protracted our meeting."

XXVI

Here ended the tale of Sarsefield. Humiliation and joy were mingled in my heart. The events that preceded my awakening in the cave were now luminous and plain. What explication was more obvious? What but this solution ought to have been suggested by the conduct I had witnessed in Clithero?

Clithero? Was not this the man whom Clithero had robbed of his friend? Was not this the lover of Mrs. Lorimer, the object of the persecutions of Wiatte? Was it not now given me to investigate the truth of that stupendous tale? To dissipate the doubts which obstinately clung to my imagination respecting it?

But soft! Had not Sarsefield said that he was married? Was Mrs. Lorimer so speedily forgotten by him, or was the narrative of Clithero the web of imposture or the raving of insanity?

These new ideas banished all personal considerations from my mind. I looked eagerly into the face of my friend, and exclaimed, in a dubious accent, "How say you? Married? When? To whom?"

"Yes, Huntly, I am wedded to the most excellent of women. To her am I indebted for happiness, and wealth, and dignity, and honor. To her do I owe the power of being the benefactor and protector of you and your sisters. She longs to embrace you as a son. To become truly her son will depend upon your own choice, and that of one who was the companion of our voyage."

"Heavens!" cried I, in a transport of exultation and astonishment. "Of whom do you speak? Of the mother of Clarice? The sister of Wiatte? The sister of the ruffian who laid snares for her life? Who pursued you and the unhappy Clithero with the bitterest animosity?"

My friend started at these sounds as if the earth had yawned at his feet. His countenance was equally significant of terror and rage. As soon as he regained the power of utterance, he spoke: "Clithero! Curses light upon thy lips for having uttered that detested name! Thousands of miles have I flown to shun the hearing of it. Is the madman here? Have you set eyes upon him? Does he yet crawl upon the face of the earth? Unhappy? Unparalleled, unheard-of, thankless miscreant! Has he told his execrable falsehoods here?

Has he dared to utter names so sacred as those of Euphemia Lorimer and Clarice?"

"He has; he has told a tale that had all the appearances of truth—"

"Out upon the villain! The truth! Truth would prove him to be unnatural, devilish; a thing for which no language has yet provided a name! He has called himself unhappy? No doubt, a victim to injustice! Overtaken by unmerited calamity. Say! Has he fooled thee with such tales?"

"No. His tale was a catalogue of crimes and miseries of which he was the author and sufferer. You know not his motives, his horrors—"

"His deeds were monstrous and infernal. His motives were sordid and flagitious. To display all their ugliness and infamy was not his province. No; he did not tell you that he stole at midnight to the chamber of his mistress, a woman who astonished the world by her loftiness and magnanimity, by indefatigable beneficence and unswerving equity; who had lavished on this wretch, whom she snatched from the dirt, all the goods of fortune, all the benefits of education, all the treasures of love, every provocation to gratitude, every stimulant to justice.

"He did not tell you that, in recompense for every benefit, he stole upon her sleep and aimed a dagger at her breast. There was no room for flight, or ambiguity, or prevarication. She whom he meant to murder stood near, saw the lifted weapon, and heard him confess and glory in his purposes.

"No wonder that the shock bereft her, for a time, of life. The interval was seized by the ruffian to effect his escape. The rebukes of justice were shunned by a wretch conscious of his inexpiable guilt. These things he has hidden from you, and has supplied their place by a tale specious as false."

"No. Among the number of his crimes, hypocrisy is not to be numbered. These things are already known to me: he spared himself too little in the narrative. The excellencies of his lady, her claims to gratitude and veneration, were urged beyond their true bounds. His attempts upon her life were related. It is true that he desired and endeavored to destroy her."

"How? Has he told you this?"

"He has told me all. Alas! the criminal intention has been amply expiated."

"What mean you? Whence and how came he hither? Where is he now? I will not occupy the same land, the same world, with him.

Have this woman and her daughter lighted on the shore haunted by
this infernal and implacable enemy?"

"Alas! It is doubtful whether he exists. If he lives, he is no longer
to be feared; but he lives not. Famine and remorse have utterly
consumed him."

"Famine? Remorse? You talk in riddles."

"He has immured himself in the desert. He has abjured the intercourse of mankind. He has shut himself in caverns where famine
must inevitably expedite that death for which he longs as the only
solace of his woes. To no imagination are his offenses blacker and
more odious than to his own. I had hopes of rescuing him from
this fate, but my own infirmities and errors have afforded me sufficient occupation."

Sarsefield renewed his imprecations on the memory of that unfortunate man, and his inquiries as to the circumstances that led him
into this remote district. His inquiries were not to be answered by
one in my present condition. My languors and fatigues had now
gained a pitch that was insupportable. The wound in my face had
been chafed and inflamed by the cold water and the bleak air; and
the pain attending it would no longer suffer my attention to stray.
I sunk upon the floor, and entreated him to afford me the respite of
a few hours' repose.

He was sensible of the deplorableness of my condition, and chid
himself for the negligence of which he had already been guilty.
He lifted me to the bed, and deliberated on the mode he should
pursue for my relief. Some mollifying application to my wound was
immediately necessary; but, in our present lonely condition, it
was not at hand. It could only be procured from a distance. It was
proper therefore to hasten to the nearest inhabited dwelling, which
belonged to one by name Walton, and supply himself with such
medicines as could be found.

Meanwhile, there was no danger of molestation and intrusion.
There was reason to expect the speedy return of those who had gone
in pursuit of the savages. This was their place of rendezvous, and
hither they appointed to reassemble before the morrow's dawn.
The distance of the neighboring farm was small, and Sarsefield
promised to be expeditious. He left me to myself and my own
ruminations.

Harrassed by fatigue and pain, I had yet power to ruminate on
that series of unparalleled events that had lately happened. I wept,

but my tears flowed from a double source: from sorrow, on account of the untimely fate of my uncle, and from joy, that my sisters were preserved, that Sarsefield had returned and was not unhappy.

I reflected on the untoward destiny of Clithero. Part of his calamity consisted in the consciousness of having killed his patroness; but it now appeared, though by some infatuation I had not previously suspected, that the first impulse of sorrow in the lady had been weakened by reflection and by time; that the prejudice persuading her that her life and that of her brother were to endure and to terminate together was conquered by experience or by argument. She had come, in company with Sarsefield and Clarice, to America. What influence might these events have upon the gloomy meditations of Clithero? Was it possible to bring them together; to win the maniac from his solitude, wrest from him his fatal purposes, and restore him to communion with the beings whose imagined indignation is the torment of his life?

These musings were interrupted by a sound from below, which was easily interpreted into tokens of the return of those with whom Sarsefield had parted at the promontory. Voices were confused and busy, but not turbulent. They entered the lower room and the motion of chairs and tables showed that they were preparing to rest themselves after their toils.

Few of them were unacquainted with me, since they probably were residents in this district. No inconvenience, therefore, would follow from an interview, though, on their part, wholly unexpected. Besides, Sarsefield would speedily return, and none of the present visitants would be likely to withdraw to this apartment.

Meanwhile, I lay upon the bed, with my face turned towards the door, and languidly gazing at the ceiling and walls. Just then a musket was discharged in the room below. The shock affected me mechanically, and the first impulse of surprise made me almost start upon my feet.

The sound was followed by confusion and bustle. Some rushed forth and called on each other to run different ways, and the words, "That is he,"—"Stop him!" were spoken in a tone of eagerness and rage. My weakness and pain were for a moment forgotten, and my whole attention was bent to discover the meaning of this hubbub. The musket which I had brought with me to this chamber lay across the bed. Unknowing of the consequences of this affray with regard to myself, I was prompted, by a kind of self-preserving instinct, to lay hold of the gun and prepare to repel any attack that might be made upon me.

A few moments elapsed, when I thought I heard light footsteps in the entry leading to this room. I had no time to construe these signals, but, watching fearfully the entrance, I grasped my weapon with new force, and raised it so as to be ready at the moment of my danger. I did not watch long. A figure cautiously thrust itself forward. The first glance was sufficient to inform me that this intruder was an Indian, and, of consequence, an enemy. He was unarmed. Looking eagerly on all sides, he at last spied me as I lay. My appearance threw him into consternation, and, after the fluctuation of an instant, he darted to the window, threw up the sash, and leaped out upon the ground.

His flight might have been easily arrested by my shot, but surprise, added to my habitual antipathy to bloodshed unless in cases of absolute necessity, made me hesitate. He was gone, and I was left to mark the progress of the drama. The silence was presently broken by firing at a distance. Three shots, in quick succession, were followed by the deepest pause.

That the party, recently arrived, had brought with them one or more captives, and that by some sudden effort the prisoners had attempted to escape, was the only supposition that I could form. By what motives either of them could be induced to seek concealment in my chamber could not be imagined.

I now heard a single step on the threshold below. Someone entered the common room. He traversed the floor during a few minutes, and then, ascending the staircase, he entered my chamber. It was Sarsefield. Trouble and dismay were strongly written on his countenance. He seemed totally unconscious of my presence; his eyes were fixed upon the floor, and, as he continued to move across the room, he heaved forth deep sighs.

This deportment was mournful and mysterious. It was little in unison with those appearances which he wore at our parting, and must have been suggested by some event that had since happened. My curiosity impelled me to recall him from his reverie. I rose, and, seizing him by the arm, looked at him with an air of inquisitive anxiety. It was needless to speak.

He noticed my movement, and, turning towards me, spoke in a tone of some resentment: "Why did you deceive me? Did you not say Clithero was dead?"

"I said so because it was my belief. Know you anything to the contrary? Heaven grant that he is still alive, and that our mutual efforts may restore him to peace!"

'Heaven grant," replied my friend, with a vehemence that bordered upon fury,—"Heaven grant that he may live thousands of years, and know not, in their long course, a moment's respite from remorse and from anguish! But this prayer is fruitless. He is not dead, but death hovers over him. Should he live, he will live only to defy justice and perpetrate new horrors. My skill might perhaps save him, but a finger shall not be moved to avert his fate.

"Little did I think that the wretch whom my friends rescued from the power of the savages, and brough wounded and expiring hither, was Clithero. They sent for me in haste to afford him surgical assistance. I found him stretched upon the floor below, deserted, helpless, and bleeding. The moment I beheld him, he was recognized. The last of evils was to look upon the face of his assassin; but that evil is past, and shall never be endured again.

"Rise, and come with me. Accommodation is prepared for you at Walton's. Let us leave this house, and, the moment you are able to perform a journey, abandon forever this district."

I could not readily consent to this proposal. Clithero had been delivered from captivity, but was dying for want of that aid which Sarsefield was able to afford. Was it not inhuman to desert him in this extremity? What offense had he committed that deserved such implacable vengeance? Nothing I had heard from Sarsefield was in contradiction to his own story. His deed, imperfectly observed, would appear to be atrocious and detestable; but the view of all its antecedent and accompanying events and motives would surely place it in the list, not of crimes, but of misfortunes.

But what is that guilt which no penitence can expiate? Had not Clithero's remorse been more than adequate to crimes far more deadly and enormous than this? This, however, was no time to argue with the passions of Sarsefield. Nothing but a repetition of Clithero's tale could vanquish his prepossessions and mollify his rage; but this repetition was impossible to be given by me, till a moment of safety and composure.

These thoughts made me linger, but hindered me from attempting to change the determination of my friend. He renewed his importunities for me to fly with him. He dragged me by the arm, and, wavering and reluctant, I followed where he chose to lead. He crossed the common room with hurried steps, and eyes averted from a figure which instantly fastened my attention.

It was indeed Clithero whom I now beheld, supine, polluted with blood, his eyes closed, and apparently insensible. This object was gazed at with emotions that rooted me to the spot. Sarsefield, perceiving me determined to remain where I was, rushed out of the house, and disappeared.

XXVII

I hung over the unhappy wretch, whose emaciated form and rueful features sufficiently bespoke that savage hands had only completed that destruction which his miseries had begun. He was mangled by the tomahawk in a shocking manner, and there was little hope that human skill could save his life.

I was sensible of nothing but compassion. I acted without design, when, seating myself on the floor, I raised his head and placed it on my knees. This movement awakened his attention, and, opening his eyes, he fixed them on my countenance. They testified neither insensibility, nor horror, nor distraction. A faint emotion of surprise gave way to an appearance of tranquillity. Having perceived these tokens of a state less hopeless than I at first imagined, I spoke to him: "My friend, how do you feel? Can anything be done for you?"

He answered me in a tone more firm and with more coherence of ideas than previous appearances had taught me to expect. "No," said he; "thy kindness, good youth, can avail me nothing. The end of my existence here is at hand. May my guilt be expiated by the miseries that I have suffered, and my good deeds only attend me to the presence of my divine Judge!

"I am waiting, not with trembling or dismay, for this close of my sorrows. I breathed but one prayer, and that prayer has been answered. I asked for an interview with thee, young man; but, feeling as I now feel, this interview, so much desired, was beyond my hope. Now thou art come, in due season, to hear the last words that I shall need to utter.

"I wanted to assure thee that thy efforts for my benefit were not useless. They have saved me from murdering myself, a guilt more inexpiable than any which it was in my power to commit.

"I retired to the innermost recess of Norwalk, and gained the summit of a hill, by subterranean paths. This hill I knew to be on all sides inaccessible to human footsteps, and the subterranean passages were closed up by stones. Here I believed my solitude exempt from interruption, and my death, in consequence of famine, sure.

"This persuasion was not taken away by your appearance on the opposite steep. The chasm which severed us I knew to be impassable. I withdrew from your sight.

"Some time after, awakening from a long sleep, I found victuals beside me. He that brought it was invisible. For a time, I doubted whether some messenger of heaven had not interposed for my salvation. How other than by supernatural means my retreat should be explored, I was unable to conceive. The summit was encompassed by dizzy and profound gulfs, and the subterranean passages were still closed.

"This opinion, though corrected by subsequent reflection, tended to change the course of my desperate thoughts. My hunger, thus importunately urged, would not abstain, and I ate of the food that was provided. Henceforth I determined to live, to resume the path of obscurity and labor which I had relinquished, and wait till my God should summon me to retribution. To anticipate his call is only to redouble our guilt.

"I designed not to return to Inglefield's service, but to choose some other and remoter district. Meanwhile, I had left in his possession a treasure, which my determination to die had rendered of no value, but which my change of resolution restored. Enclosed in a box at Inglefield's were the memoirs of Euphemia Lorimer, by which, in all my vicissitudes, I had been hitherto accompanied, and from which I consented to part only because I had refused to live. My existence was now to be prolonged, and this manuscript was once more to constitute the torment and the solace of my being.

"I hastened to Inglefield's by night. There was no need to warn him of my purpose. I desired that my fate should be an eternal secret to my ancient master and his neighbors. The apartment containing my box was well known, and easily accessible.

"The box was found, but broken and rifled of its treasure. My transports of astonishment, and indignation, and grief, yielded to the resumption of my fatal purpose. I hastened back to the hill, and determined anew to perish.

"This mood continued to the evening of the ensuing day. Wandering over rocks and pits, I discovered the manuscript lying under a jutting precipice. The chance that brought it hither was not less propitious and miraculous than that by which I had been supplied with food. It produced a similar effect upon my feelings, and, while in possession of this manuscript, I was reconciled to the means of life. I left the mountain, and, traversing the wilderness, stopped in Chetasco. That kind of employment which I sought was instantly procured; but my new vocation was scarcely assumed when a band of savages invaded our security.

"Rambling in the desert by moonlight, I encountered these foes. They rushed upon me, and, after numerous wounds, which for the present neither killed nor disabled me, they compelled me to keep pace with them in their retreat. Some hours have passed since the troop was overtaken and my liberty redeemed. Hardships, and repeated wounds, inflicted at the moment when the invaders were surprised and slain, have brought me to my present condition. I rejoice that my course is about to terminate."

Here the speaker was interrupted by the tumultuous entrance of the party by whom he had been brought hither. Their astonishment at seeing me sustaining the head of the dying man may be easily conceived. Their surprise was more strongly excited by the disappearance of the captive whom they had left in this apartment, bound hand and foot. It now appeared that, of the savage troop who had adventured thus far in search of pillage and blood, all had been destroyed but two, who had been led hither as prisoners. On their entrance into this house, one of the party had been sent to Walton's to summon Sarsefield to the aid of the wounded man, while others had gone in search of cords to secure the arms and legs of the captives, who had hitherto been manacled imperfectly.

The cords were brought and one of them was bound; but the other, before the same operation was begun upon him, broke, by a sudden effort, the feeble ligatures by which he was at present constrained, and, seizing a musket that lay near him, fired on his enemies, and then rushed out of doors. All eagerly engaged in the pursuit. The savage was fleet as a deer, and finally eluded his pursuers.

While their attention was thus engaged abroad, he that remained found means to extricate his wrists and ankles from his bonds, and, betaking himself to the stairs, escaped, as I before described, through the window of the room which I had occupied. They pestered me with their curiosity and wonder, for I was known to all of them; but, waiving the discussion of my own concerns, I entreated their assistance to carry Clithero to the chamber and the bed which I had just deserted.

I now, in spite of pain, fatigue, and watchfulness, set out to go to Walton's. Sarsefield was ready to receive me at the door, and the kindness and compassion of the family were active in my behalf. I was conducted to a chamber and provided with suitable attendance and remedies.

I was not unmindful of the more deplorable condition of Clithero. I incessantly meditated on the means for his relief. His case stood in need of all the vigilance and skill of a physician, and Sarsefield was the only one of that profession whose aid could be seasonably administered. Sarsefield, therefore, must be persuaded to bestow this aid.

There was but one mode of conquering his abhorrence of this man: to prepossess my friend with the belief of the innocence of Clithero, or to soothe him into pity by a picture of remorse and suffering. This could be done, and in the manner most conformable to truth, by a simple recital of the incidents that had befallen, and by repeating the confession which had been extorted from Clithero.

I requested all but my friend to leave my chamber, and then, soliciting a patient hearing, began the narrative of Waldegrave's death; of the detection of Clithero beneath the shade of the elm; of the suspicions which were thence produced; and of the forest interview to which these suspicions gave birth. I then repeated, without variation or addition, the tale which was then told. I likewise mentioned my subsequent transactions in Norwalk, so far as they illustrated the destiny of Clithero.

During this recital, I fixed my eyes upon the countenance of Sarsefield, and watched every emotion as it arose or declined. With the progress of my tale, his indignation and his fury grew less, and at length gave place to horror and compassion.

His seat became uneasy; his pulse throbbed with new vehemence. When I came to the motives which prompted the unhappy man to visit the chamber of his mistress, he started from his seat, and sometimes strode across the floor in a troubled mood, and sometimes stood before me, with his breath almost suspended in the eagerness of his attention. When I mentioned the lifted dagger, the shriek from behind, and the apparition that interposed, he shuddered and drew back, as if a dagger had been aimed at his breast.

When the tale was done, some time elapsed in mutual and profound silence. My friend's thoughts were involved in a mournful and indefinable reverie. From this he at length recovered and spoke:

"It is true. A tale like this could never be the fruit of invention, or be invented to deceive. He has done himself injustice. His character was spotless and fair. All his moral properties seemed to have resolved themselves into gratitude, fidelity, and honor.

"We parted at the door, late in the evening, as he mentioned, and he guessed truly that subsequent reflection had induced me to return and to disclose the truth to Mrs. Lorimer. Clarice, relieved by the sudden death of her friend, and unexpectedly by all, arrived at the same hour.

"These tidings astonished, afflicted, and delighted the lady. Her brother's death had been long believed by all but herself. To find her doubts verified, and his existence ascertained, was the dearest consolation that he ever could bestow. She was afflicted at the proofs that had been noted of the continuance of his depravity, but she dreaded no danger to herself from his malignity or vengeance.

"The ignorance and prepossessions of this woman were remarkable. On this subject only she was perverse, headstrong, obstinate. Her anxiety to benefit this arch-ruffian occupied her whole thoughts, and allowed her no time to reflect upon the remonstrances of others. She could not be prevailed on to deny herself to his visits, and I parted from her in the utmost perplexity.

"A messenger came to me at midnight, entreating my immediate presence. Some disaster had happened, but of what kind the messenger was unable to tell. My fears easily conjured up the image of Wiatte. Terror scarcely allowed me to breathe. When I entered the house of Mrs. Lorimer, I was conducted to her chamber. She lay upon the bed in a state of stupefaction, that arose from some mental cause. Clarice sat by her, wringing her hands, and pouring forth her tears without intermission. Neither could explain to me the nature of the scene. I made inquiries of the servants and attendants. They merely said that the family as usual had retired to rest, but their lady's bell rung with great violence, and called them in haste to her chamber, where they found her in a swoon upon the floor, and the young lady in the utmost affright and perturbation.

"Suitable means being used, Mrs. Lorimer had, at length, recovered, but was still nearly insensible. I went to Clithero's apartments; but he was not to be found, and the domestics informed me that, since he had gone with me, he had not returned. The doors between this chamber and the court were open; hence, that some dreadful interview had taken place, perhaps with Wiatte, was an unavoidable conjecture. He had withdrawn, however, without committing any personal injury.

"I need not mention my reflections upon this scene. All was tormenting doubt and suspense, till the morning arrived, and tidings were received that Wiatte had been killed in the streets. This event was antecedent to that which had occasioned Mrs. Lorimer's distress and alarm. I now remembered that fatal prepossession by which the lady was governed, and her frantic belief that her death and that of her brother were to fall out at the same time. Could some witness of his death have brought her tidings of it? Had he penetrated, unexpected and unlicensed, to her chamber? and were these the effects produced by the intelligence?

"Presently I knew that not only Wiatte was dead, but that Clithero had killed him. Clithero had not been known to return, and was nowhere to be found. He, then, was the bearer of these tidings, for none but he could have found access or egress without disturbing the servants.

"These doubts were at length at an end. In a broken and confused manner, and after the lapse of some days, the monstrous and portentous truth was disclosed. After our interview, the lady and her daughter had retired to the same chamber; the former had withdrawn to her closet, and the latter to bed. Someone's entrance alarmed the lady, and, coming forth after a moment's pause, the spectacle which Clithero has too faithfully described presented itself.

"What could I think? A life of uniform hypocrisy, or a sudden loss of reason, were the only suppositions to be formed. Clithero was the parent of fury and abhorrence in my heart. In either case I started at the name. I shuddered at the image of the apostate or the maniac.

"What? Kill the brother whose existence was interwoven with that of his benefactress and his friend? Then hasten to her chamber, and attempt her life? Lift a dagger to destroy her who had been the author of his being and his happiness?

"He that could meditate a deed like this was no longer a man. An agent from hell had mastered his faculties. He was become the engine of infernal malice, against whom it was the duty of all mankind to rise up in arms and never to desist till, by shattering it to atoms, its power to injure was taken away.

"All inquiries to discover the place of his retreat were vain. No wonder, methought, that he wrapped himself in the folds of impenetrable secrecy. Curbed, checked, baffled in the midst of his career, no wonder that he shrunk into obscurity, that he fled from justice and revenge, that he dared not meet the rebukes of that eye which, dissolving in tenderness or flashing with disdain, had ever been irresistible.

"But how shall I describe the lady's condition? Clithero she had cherished from his infancy. He was the stay, the consolation, the pride of her life. His projected alliance with her daughter made him still more dear. Her eloquence was never tired of expatiating on his purity and rectitude. No wonder that she delighted in this theme, for he was her own work. His virtues were the creatures of her bounty.

"How hard to be endured was this sad reverse! She can be tranquil, but never more will she be happy. To promote her forgetfulness of him, I persuaded her to leave her country, which contained a thousand memorials of past calamity, and which was lapsing fast into civil broils. Clarice has accompanied us, and time may effect the happiness of others by her means, though she can never remove the melancholy of her mother.

"I have listened to your tale, not without compassion. What would you have me to do? To prolong his life would be merely to protract his misery.

"He can never be regarded with complacency by my wife. He can never be thought of without shuddering by Clarice. Common ills are not without a cure less than death, but here all remedies are vain. Consciousness itself is the malady, the pest, of which he only is cured who ceases to think."

I could not but assent to this mournful conclusion; yet, though death was better to Clithero than life, could not some of his mistakes be rectified? Euphemia Lorimer, contrary to his belief, was still alive. He dreamed that she was dead, and a thousand evils were imagined to flow from that death. This death, and its progeny of ills, haunted his fancy, and added keenness to his remorse. Was it not our duty to rectify this error?

Sarsefield reluctantly assented to the truth of my arguments on this head. He consented to return, and afford the dying man the consolation of knowing that the being whom he adored as a benefactor and parent had not been deprived of existence, though bereft of peace by his act.

During Sarsefield's absence my mind was busy in revolving the incidents that had just occurred. I ruminated on the last words of Clithero. There was somewhat in his narrative that was obscure and contradictory. He had left the manuscript, which he so much and so justly prized, in his cabinet. He entered the chamber in my absence, and found the cabinet unfastened and the manuscript gone. It was I by whom the cabinet was opened; but the manuscript supposed to be contained in it was buried in the earth beneath the elm. How should Clithero be unacquainted with its situation, since none but Clithero could have dug for it this grave?

This mystery vanished when I reflected on the history of my own manuscript. Clithero had buried his treasure with his own hands, as mine had been secreted my myself; but both acts had been performed during sleep. The deed was neither prompted by the will nor noticed by the senses of him by whom it was done. Disastrous and humiliating is the state of man! By his own hands is constructed the mass of misery and error in which his steps are forever involved.

Thus it was with thy friend. Hurried on by phantoms too indistinct to be now recalled, I wandered from my chamber to the desert. I plunged into some unvisited cavern, and easily proceeded till I reached the edge of a pit. There my step was deceived, and I tumbled headlong from the precipice. The fall bereaved me of sense, and I continued breathless and motionless during the remainder of the night and the ensuing day.

How little cognizance have men over the actions and motives of each other! How total is our blindness with regard to our own performances! Who would have sought me in the bowels of this mountain? Ages might have passed away, before my bones would be discovered in this tomb by some traveller whom curiosity had prompted to explore it.

I was roused from these reflections by Sarsefield's return. Inquiring into Clithero's condition, he answered that the unhappy man was insensible, but that, notwithstanding numerous and dreadful gashes in different parts of his body, it was possible that, by submitting to the necessary treatment, he might recover.

Encouraged by this information, I endeavored to awaken the zeal and compassion of my friend in Clithero's behalf. He recoiled with involuntary shuddering from any task which would confine him to the presence of this man. Time and reflection, he said, might introduce different sentiments and feelings, but at present he could not but regard this person as a maniac, whose disease was irremediable, and whose existence could not be protracted but to his own misery and the misery of others.

Finding him irreconcilably averse to any scheme connected with the welfare of Clithero, I began to think that his assistance as a surgeon was by no means necessary. He had declared that the sufferer needed nothing more than common treatment; and to this the skill of a score of aged women in this district, furnished with simples culled from the forest, and pointed out, of old time, by Indian *leeches*, was no less adequate than that of Sarsefield. These women were ready and officious in their charity, and none of them were prepossessed against the sufferer by a knowledge of his genuine story.

Sarsefield, meanwhile, was impatient for my removal to Inglefield's habitation, and that venerable friend was no less impatient to receive me. My hurts were superficial, and my strength sufficiently repaired by a night's repose. Next day I went thither, leaving Clithero to the care of his immediate neighbors.

Sarsefield's engagements compelled him to prosecute his journey into Virginia, from which he had somewhat deviated in order to visit Solesbury. He proposed to return in less than a month, and then to take me in his company to New York. He has treated me with paternal tenderness, and insists upon the privilege of consulting for my interests as if he were my real father. Meanwhile these views have been disclosed to Inglefield, and it is with him that I am to remain, with my sisters, until his return.

My reflections have been various and tumultuous. They have been busy in relation to you, to Weymouth, and especially to Clithero. The latter, polluted with gore and weakened by abstinence, fatigue, and the loss of blood, appeared in my eyes to be in a much more dangerous condition than the event proved him to be. I was punctually informed of the progress of his cure, and proposed in a few days to visit him. The duty of explaining the truth, respecting the present condition of Mrs. Lorimer, had devolved upon me. By imparting this intelligence, I hoped to work the most auspicious revolutions in his feelings, and prepared, therefore, with alacrity, for an interview.

In this hope I was destined to be disappointed. On the morning on which I intended to visit him, a messenger arrived from the house in which he was entertained, and informed us that the family, on entering the sick man's apartment, had found it deserted. It appeared that Clithero had, during the night, risen from his bed and gone secretly forth. No traces of his flight have since been discovered.

But, oh, my friend, the death of Waldegrave, thy brother, is at length divested of uncertainty and mystery. Hitherto, I had been able to form no conjecture respecting it; but the solution was found shortly after this time.

Queen Mab, three days after my adventure, was seized in her hut on suspicion of having aided and counselled her countrymen in their late depredations. She was not to be awed or intimidated by the treatment she received, but readily confessed and gloried in the mischief she had done, and accounted for it by enumerating the injuries which she had received from her neighbors.

These injuries consisted in contemptuous or neglectful treatment, and in the rejection of groundless and absurd claims. The people of Chetasco were less obsequious to her humors than those of Solesbury, her ancient neighborhood, and her imagination brooded for a long time over nothing but schemes of revenge. She became sullen, irascible, and spent more of her time in solitude than ever.

A troop of her countrymen at length visited her hut. Their intentions being hostile, they concealed from the inhabitants their presence in this quarter of the country. Some motives induced them to withdraw and postpone, for the present, the violence which they meditated. One of them, however, more sanguinary and audacious than the rest, would not depart without some gratification of his vengeance. He left his associates and penetrated by night into Solesbury, resolving to attack the first human being whom he should meet. It was the fate of thy unhappy brother to encounter this ruffian, whose sagacity made him forbear to tear away the usual trophy from the dead, lest he should afford grounds for suspicion as to the authors of the evil.

Satisfied with this exploit, he rejoined his companions, and, after an interval of three weeks, returned with a more numerous party, to execute a more extensive project of destruction. They were counselled and guided, in all their movements, by Queen Mab, who now explained these particulars and boldly defied her oppressors. Her usual obstinacy and infatuation induced her to remain in her ancient dwelling and prepare to meet the consequences.

This disclosure awakened anew all the regrets and anguish which flowed from that disaster. It has been productive, however, of some benefit. Suspicions and doubts, by which my soul was harassed, and which were injurious to the innocent, are now at an end. It is likewise some imperfect consolation to reflect that the assassin has himself been killed, and probably by my own hand. The shedder of blood no longer lives to pursue his vocation, and justice is satisfied.

Thus have I fulfilled my promise to compose a minute relation of my sufferings. I remembered my duty to thee, and, as soon as I was able to hold a pen, employed it to inform thee of my welfare. I could not at that time enter into particulars, but reserved a more copious narrative till a period of more health and leisure.

On looking back, I am surprised at the length to which my story has run. I thought that a few days would suffice to complete it; but one page has insensibly been added to another, till I have consumed weeks and filled volumes. Here I will draw to a close; I will send you what I have written, and discuss with you in conversation my other immediate concerns, and my schemes for the future. As soon as I have seen Sarsefield, I will visit you. FAREWELL.   E. H.

SOLESBURY, November 10.

LETTER I.

To Mr. Sarsefield.

PHILADELPHIA.

I came hither but ten minutes ago, and write this letter in the bar of the stage house. I wish not to lose a moment in informing you of what has happened. I cannot do justice to my own feelings when I reflect upon the rashness of which I have been guilty.

I will give you the particulars tomorrow. At present, I shall only say that Clithero is alive, is apprised of your wife's arrival and abode in New York, and has set out with mysterious intentions to visit her.

May Heaven avert the consequences of such a design! May you be enabled, by some means to prevent their meeting! If you cannot prevent it—but I must not reason on such an event, nor lengthen out this letter.

E. H.

LETTER II.

To the Same.

I will now relate the particulars which I yesterday promised to send you. You heard through your niece of my arrival at Inglefield's, in Solesbury; my inquiries, you may readily suppose, would turn upon the fate of my friend's servant Clithero, whose last disappearance was so strange and abrupt, and of whom, since that time, I had heard nothing. You are indifferent to his fate, and are anxious only that his existence and misfortunes may be speedily forgotten. I confess that it is somewhat otherwise with me. I pity him; I wish to relieve him, and cannot admit the belief that his misery is without a cure. I want to find him out. I want to know his condition, and, if possible, to afford him comfort and inspire him with courage and hope.

Inglefield replied to my questions: "Oh yes! He has appeared. The strange being is again upon the stage. Shortly after he left his sickbed, I heard from Philip Beddington, of Chetasco, that Deb's hut had found a new tenant. At first I imagined that the Scotsman who built it had returned; but, making closer inquiries, I found that the new tenant was my servant. I had no inclination to visit him myself, but frequently inquired respecting him of those who lived or passed that way, and find that he still lives there."

"But how!" said I: "what is his mode of subsistence? The winter has been no time for cultivation; and he found, I presume, nothing in the ground."

"Deb's hut," replied my friend, "is his lodging and his place of retirement, but food and clothing he procures by laboring on a neighboring farm. This farm is next to that of Beddington, who consequently knows something of his present situation. I find little or no difference in his present deportment and those appearances which he assumed while living with me, except that he retires every night to his hut, and holds as little intercourse as possible with the rest of mankind. He dines at his employer's table; but his supper, which is nothing but rye-bread, he carries home with him, and, at all those times when disengaged from employment, he secludes himself in his hut, or wanders nobody knows whither."

This was the substance of Inglefield's intelligence. I gleaned from it some satisfaction. It proved the condition of Clithero to be less deplorable and desperate than I had previously imagined. His fatal and gloomy thoughts seemed to have somewhat yielded to tranquillity.

In the course of my reflections, however, I could not but perceive that his condition, though negligible when compared with what it once was, was likewise disastrous and humiliating, compared with his youthful hopes and his actual merits. For such a one to mope away his life in this unsocial and savage state was deeply to be deplored. It was my duty, if possible, to prevail on him to relinquish his scheme. And what would be requisite, for that end, but to inform him of the truth?

The source of his dejection was the groundless belief that he had occasioned the death of his benefactress. It was this alone that could justly produce remorse or grief. It was a distempered imagination both in him and in me that had given birth to this opinion, since the terms of his narrative, impartially considered, were far from implying that catastrophe. To him, however, the existence which he possessed was incontestable. No deductions from probability could overthrow his belief. This could only be effected by similar and counter evidence. To apprise him that she was now alive, in possession of some degree of happiness, the wife of Sarsefield, and an actual resident on this shore, would dissipate the sanguinary apparition that haunted him, cure his diseased intellect, and restore him to those vocations for which his talents, and that rank in society for which his education, had qualified him. Influenced by these thoughts, I determined to visit his retreat. Being obliged to leave Solesbury the next day, I resolved to set out the same afternoon, and, stopping in Chetasco for the night, seek his habitation at the hour when he had probably retired to it.

This was done. I arrived at Beddington's at nightfall. My inquiries respecting Clithero obtained for me the same intelligence from him which I had received from Inglefield. Deb's hut was three miles from this habitation, and thither, when the evening had somewhat advanced, I repaired. This was the spot which had witnessed so many perils during the last year; and my emotions, on approaching it, were awful. With palpitating heart and quick steps I traversed the road, skirted on each side by thickets, and the area before the house. The dwelling was by no means in so ruinous a state as when I last visited it. The crannies between the logs had been filled up, and the light within was perceivable only at a crevice in the door.

Looking through this crevice, I perceived a fire in the chimney, but the object of my visit was nowhere to be seen. I knocked and requested admission, but no answer was made. At length I lifted the latch and entered. Nobody was there.

It was obvious to suppose that Clithero had gone abroad for a short time, and would speedily return; or perhaps some engagement had detained him at his labor later than usual. I therefore seated myself on some straw near the fire, which, with a woolen rug, appeared to constitute his only bed. The rude bedstead which I formerly met was gone. The slender furniture, likewise, which had then engaged my attention, had disappeared. There was nothing capable of human use but a heap of fagots in the corner, which seemed intended for fuel. How slender is the accommodation which nature has provided for man, and how scanty is the portion which our physical necessities require!

While ruminating upon this scene, and comparing past events with the objects before me, the dull whistling of the gale without gave place to the sound of footsteps. Presently the door opened, and Clithero entered the apartment. His aspect and guise were not essentially different from those which he wore when an inhabitant of Solesbury.

To find his hearth occupied by another appeared to create the deepest surprise. He looked at me without any tokens of remembrance. His features assumed a more austere expression, and, after scowling on my person for a moment, he withdrew his eyes, and, placing in a corner a bundle which he bore in his hand, he turned and seemed preparing to withdraw.

I was anxiously attentive to his demeanor, and, as soon as I perceived his purpose to depart, leaped on my feet to prevent it. I took his hand, and, affectionately pressing it, said, "Do you not know me? Have you so soon forgotten me, who is truly your friend?"

He looked at me with some attention, but again withdrew his eyes, and placed himself in silence on the seat which I had left. I seated myself near him, and a pause of mutual silence ensued.

My mind was full of the purpose that brought me hither, but I knew not in what manner to communicate my purpose. Several times I opened my lips to speak, but my perplexity continued, and suitable words refused to suggest themselves. At length I said, in a confused tone,—

"I came hither with a view to benefit a man with whose misfortunes his own lips have made me acquainted, and who has awakened in my breast the deepest sympathy. I know the cause and extent of his dejection. I know the event which has given birth to horror and remorse in his heart. He believes that, by his means, his patroness and benefactress has found an untimely death."

These words produced a visible shock in my companion, which evinced that I had at least engaged his attention. I proceeded:—

"This unhappy lady was cursed with a wicked and unnatural brother. She conceived a disproportionate affection for this brother, and erroneously imagined that her fate was blended with his, that their lives would necessarily terminate at the same period, and that, therefore, whoever was the contriver of his death was likewise, by a fatal and invincible necessity, the author of her own.

"Clithero was her servant, but was raised by her bounty to the station of her son and the rank of her friend. Clithero, in self-defense, took away the life of that unnatural brother, and, in that deed, falsely but cogently believed that he had perpetrated the destruction of his benefactress.

"To ascertain the truth, he sought her presence. She was found, the tidings of her brother's death were communicated, and she sank breathless at his feet."

At these words Clithero started from the ground, and cast upon me looks of furious indignation. "And come you hither," he muttered, "for this end?—to recount my offenses and drive me again to despair?"

"No," answered I, with quickness; "I come to outroot a fatal but powerful illusion. I come to assure you that the woman with whose destruction you charge yourself is *not dead*."

These words, uttered with the most emphatical solemnity, merely produced looks in which contempt was mingled with anger. He continued silent.

"I perceive," resumed I, "that my words are disregarded. Would to Heaven I were able to conquer your incredulity, could show you not only the truth but the probability of my tale! Can you not confide in me? that Euphemia Lorimer is now alive, is happy, is the wife of Sarsefield? that her brother is forgotten and his murderer regarded without enmity or vengeance?"

He looked at me with a strange expression of contempt. "Come," said he, at length; "make out thy assertion to be true. Fall on thy knees, and invoke the thunder of Heaven to light on thy head if thy words be false. Swear that Euphemia Lorimer is alive; happy, forgetful of Wiatte, and compassionate of me. Swear that thou hast seen her; talked with her; received from her own lips the confession of her pity for him who aimed a dagger at her bosom. Swear that she is Sarsefield's wife."

I put my hands together, and, lifting my eyes to heaven, exclaimed, "I comply with your conditions. I call the omniscient God to witness that Euphemia Lorimer is alive; that I have seen her with these eyes; have talked with her; have inhabited the same house for months."

These asseverations were listened to with shuddering. He laid not aside, however, an air of incredulity and contempt. "Perhaps," said he, "thou canst point out the place of her abode?—canst guide me to the city, the street, the very door of her habitation?"

"I can. She resides at this moment in the city of New York; in Broadway; in a house contiguous to the—."

" 'Tis well!" exclaimed my companion, in a tone loud, abrupt, and in the utmost degree vehement. " 'Tis well! Rash and infatuated youth, thou hast ratified, beyond appeal or forgiveness, thy own doom. Thou hast once more let loose my steps, and sent me on a fearful journey. Thou has furnished the means of detecting thy imposture. I will fly to the spot which thou describest. I will ascertain thy falsehood with my own eyes. If she be alive, then am I reserved for the performance of a new crime. My evil destiny will have it so. If she be dead, I shall make *thee* expiate."

So saying, he darted through the door, and was gone in a moment beyond my sight and my reach. I ran to the road, looked on every side, and called; but my calls were repeated in vain. He had fled with the swiftness of a deer.

My own embarrassment, confusion, and terror were inexpressible. His last words were incoherent. They denoted the tumult and vehemence of frenzy. They intimated his resolution to seek the presence of your wife. I had furnished a clue which could not fail to conduct him to her presence. What might not be dreaded from the interview? Clithero is a maniac. This truth cannot be concealed. Your wife can with difficulty preserve her tranquillity when his image occurs to her remembrance. What must it be when he starts up before her in his neglected and ferocious guise, and armed with purposes perhaps as terrible as those which had formerly led him to her secret chamber and her bedside?

His meaning was obscurely conveyed. He talked of a deed for the performance of which his malignant fate had reserved him, which was to ensue their meeting, and which was to afford disastrous testimony of the infatuation which had led me hither.

Heaven grant that some means may suggest themselves to you of intercepting his approach! Yet I know not what means can be conceived. Some miraculous chance may befriend you; yet this is scarcely to be hoped. It is a visionary and fantastic base on which to rest our security.

I cannot forget that my unfortunate temerity has created this evil. Yet who could foresee this consequence of my intelligence? I imagined that Clithero was merely a victim of erroneous gratitude, a slave of the errors of his education and the prejudices of his rank; that his understanding was deluded by phantoms in the mask of virtue and duty, and not, as you have strenuously maintained, utterly subverted.

I shall not escape your censure, but I shall, likewise, gain your compassion. I have erred, not through sinister or malignant intentions, but from the impulse of misguided, indeed, but powerful, benevolence.

LETTER III.

To Edgar Huntly.

NEW YORK.

EDGAR:

After the fatigues of the day, I returned home. As I entered, my wife was breaking the seal of a letter; but, on seeing me, she forbore, and presented the letter to me.

"I saw," said she, "by the superscription of this letter, who the writer was. So, agreeably to your wishes, I proceeded to open it; but you have come just time enough to save me the trouble."

This letter was from you. It contained information relative to Clithero. See how imminent a chance it was that saved my wife from a knowledge of its contents! It required all my efforts to hide my perturbation from her and excuse myself from showing her the letter.

I know better than you the character of Clithero, and the consequences of a meeting between him and my wife. You may be sure that I would exert myself to prevent a meeting. The method for me to pursue was extremely obvious. Clithero is a madman, whose liberty is dangerous, and who requires to be fettered and imprisoned as the most atrocious criminal.

I hastened to the chief magistrate, who is my friend, and, by proper representations, obtained from him authority to seize Clithero wherever I should meet with him, and effectually debar him from the perpetration of new mischiefs.

New York does not afford a place of confinement for lunatics as suitable to his case as Pennsylvania. I was desirous of placing him as far as possible from the place of my wife's residence. Fortunately there was a packet for Philadelphia on the point of setting out on her voyage. This vessel I engaged to wait a day or two, for the purpose of conveying him to Pennsylvania Hospital. Meanwhile, proper persons were stationed at Powles Hook, and at the quays where the various stage boats from Jersey arrive.

These precautions were effectual. Not many hours after the receipt of your intelligence, this unfortunate man applied for a passage at Elizabethtown, was seized the moment he set his foot on shore, and was forthwith conveyed to the packet, which immediately set sail.

I designed that all these proceedings should be concealed from the women, but unfortunately neglected to take suitable measures for hindering the letter, which you gave me reason to expect on the ensuing day, from coming into their hands. It was delivered to my wife in my absence, and opened immediately by her.

You know what is, at present, her personal condition. You know what strong reasons I had to prevent any danger or alarm from approaching her. Terror could not assume a shape more ghastly than this. The effects have been what might have been easily predicted. Her own life has been imminently endangered, and an untimely birth has blasted my fondest hope. Her infant, with whose future existence so many pleasures were entwined, *is dead*.

I assure you, Edgar, my philosophy has not found itself lightsome and active under this burden. I find it hard to forbear commenting on your rashness in no very mild terms. You acted in direct opposition to my counsel and to the plainest dictates of propriety. Be more circumspect and more obsequious for the future.

You knew the liberty that would be taken of opening my letters; you knew of my absence from home during the greatest part of the day, and the likelihood, therefore, that your letters would fall into my wife's hands before they came into mine. These considerations should have prompted you to send them under cover to Whitworth or Harvey, with directions to give them immediately to *me*.

Some of these events happened in my absence; for I determined to accompany the packet myself, and see the madman safely delivered to the care of the hospital.

I will not torture your sensibility by recounting the incidents of his arrest and detention. You will imagine that his strong but perverted reason exclaimed loudly against the injustice of his treatment. It was easy for him to out-reason his antagonist, and nothing but force could subdue his opposition. On me devolved the province of his jailer and his tyrant,—a province which required a heart more steeled by spectacles of suffering and the exercise of cruelty than mine had been.

Scarcely had we passed the Narrows, when the lunatic, being suffered to walk the deck (as no apprehensions were entertained of his escape in such circumstances), threw himself overboard, with a seeming intention to gain the shore. The boat was immediately manned; the fugitive was pursued; but, at the moment when his flight was overtaken, he forced himself beneath the surface, and was seen no more.

With the life of this wretch, let our regrets and our forebodings terminate. He saved himself from evils for which no time would have provided a remedy, from lingering for years in the noisome dungeon of a hospital. Having no reason to continue my voyage, I put myself on board a coasting sloop, and regained this city in a few hours. I persuade myself that my wife's indisposition will be temporary. It was impossible to hide from her the death of Clithero, and its circumstances. May this be the last arrow in the quiver of adversity! Farewell.

THE END.